a fine time to leave me

A NOVEL BY TERRY PRINGLE

a fine time

to leave me

ALGONQUIN BOOKS OF CHAPEL HILL

1989

Published by
Algonquin Books of Chapel Hill
Post Office Box 2225
Chapel Hill, North Carolina 27515-2225
a division of
Workman Publishing Company, Inc.
708 Broadway
New York, New York 10003

Design by Molly Renda.

Library of Congress Cataloging-in-Publication Data

Pringle, Terry, 1947–
A fine time to leave me.

I. Title.
PS3566.R576F5   1989   813'.54   88-7670
ISBN 0-945575-16-5

FIRST EDITION

To my wife, who wishes to remain anonymous

a fine time to leave me

part one

1

He remembered seeing it later, as though he were watching a movie, reviewing the event in slow motion. The girl, a blonde, wearing a wrinkled sort of colorless jumpsuit, reached and lifted a quart soft drink bottle from the shelf, gripping it by the top, and then dropped it before she realized what had happened.

An explosion, the release of violent force as a result of pressure within. An extreme upheaval. An event that changes things.

Then too the bottle broke when it hit the floor.

Usually when a customer dropped something, the sound that followed was a parental scream or reprimand, occasionally a laugh, but when the blonde dropped the bottle, she stood as still as a bronze statue, looking at her foot. Blood pulsed out of a gash on the top of her foot, streaming over her shoe and into the quart puddle of cola she seemed to have arisen from.

Another customer, a woman with a box of saltines in her hand, supplied the scream, fist at her mouth: "Aaiiiii!"

Christopher Gray, working at the store to supplement his GI Bill payments while he attended Baylor University, was on his knees twenty feet away from the wounded blonde, stocking the shelves with canned Cokes, and had been thinking about Saul on the road to Damascus. Instead of a light from heaven, he'd been struck by the sight of a blonde, and an explosion had occurred in his heart. Unlike Saul, this change was going to last more than three days and he probably wouldn't change his name.

He briefly considered calling an ambulance before he sent another employee to get a box of gauze while he tried to stanch the flow of blood with his handkerchief. Then, while the second employee held the wad of gauze on the wound, Chris carried to

3

his car the girl who smelled more of springtime than disaster. He set her in the front seat and asked if she could hold the impromptu dressing on her foot.

She nodded, a careful sort of answer that made him think she was willing to engage only part of her faculties. If her full brain had geared up, windows all over Waco would have shattered from the scream.

He drove like a maniac to the hospital, hazard flashers blinking, horn blowing, running red lights and stop signs, not because of the severity of the laceration but because he wanted the girl to know that he understood the importance of the mission.

Cute didn't really convey the appeal of her looks, and he watched her closely when she came out of the treatment room with four stitches in her foot. She had wide-open eyes that made her look truly gullible (a clue to her personality that was partly accurate and therefore misleading), short blonde hair, and a face that should have been smiling from the side of a cereal box, not one that contained 100 percent bran or promised complete nutrition, but one that hinted at food value while supplying abundant sugar and hallucinogens.

Now in the wheelchair with her pants leg rolled up, she seemed truly injured, her leg so small and thin that the tragedy was compounded. He wanted to wheel her to his car and take her home to his apartment and nurse her back to health. He wanted to kill her pain and restore her sense of security.

He accepted her floral checkbook and wrote out a check for her signature, supplementing the information he had gleaned during the admission process. Lori Lynn Conner was from Abilene and used the First State Bank. He also noticed, when handing back her combination checkbook-wallet, that her student ID picture was just about the first good one he'd ever seen.

Driving back to the store, he looked more at her than at the road, and she didn't notice because she was shocked that such a thing could ever have happened to her. Her face revealed the

4

bewilderment of the victim: all she'd done was walk into the store to get a bottle of Coke.

"Do you have blood on your clothes?" she asked.

He nodded, looking at dried stains on the wrist of his shirt and several places on his Levi's.

"My father'll pay for your clothes. I'll give you his address so you can write him."

There was something wrong with her attitude, but he couldn't initially determine what it was. Girls as cute as that did no wrong, did they? Every act was true and correct according to their existence. He almost thanked her for bleeding on him, and wondered if he should scrape the dried blood from his clothes. Probably he was prohibited from keeping it by the Precious Commodities Act. But from deep within him, he heard a shout from the Jeffersonian Democrat who lived there. "Hey, this girl's acting like the daughter of King George. Don't let her get away with it." Then quickly another voice, which represented the viewpoint of a love-starved twenty-one-year-old male, countered with, "If you're lucky, luckier than you've been the past few years, which isn't likely, but after all, this is America, you might get a date with this girl."

The Democrat won because it always won in East Texas. He had been reared there believing there were only two obligations in life —respect the individual and vote straight Democratic no matter what.

"Would he be the one to thank me?"

She gave him a puzzled look, then realized that he'd insulted her. She started to turn away, but the movement caused a pain in her foot and a wince in her face. She sighed. "I've lost a lot of blood and I'll probably have a scar on my foot forever. And I'm really not myself. But thank you."

"You're welcome. And don't worry about my clothes. The last time I checked, cold water would get blood out."

"I guess you're right."

He didn't realize until he had returned to the store, which was

5

closed, that Lori Lynn Conner had parked in one of the two parking spots reserved for the handicapped.

He read her personalized license plates. "'Lori L.' You brought this on yourself, you know."

"How?" she asked, indignant.

"Parking in the handicapped spot."

She gave him a sigh of disgust and he had to admit he was mishandling an opportunity, something he had always done. In the navy, when he'd been on the Island of Capri near a swimming pool high on a hill overlooking the Mediterranean, he'd come across a beautiful lady tying on the top of her bikini. She had looked directly at him and smiled and said hello. Since he was wearing navy-issue swimwear and sporting a military haircut, he had known she wasn't talking to him, and he had looked around, trying to find the person she had *really* been talking to. There was no one there, and then she wasn't there.

Lori offered her hand, a symbolic gesture of gratitude, and he took it, her thin cool fingers suggesting the wonder of her presence.

"You really are welcome," he said, even though she hadn't actually thanked him again. "Really. You are."

"I don't even know your name."

Chris Gray, he told her, wishing it were Elvis Presley Waylon Jennings Robert Redford.

"I hope you don't take something somebody said in pain and shock and everything else and form an opinion. I'm really a very nice person." She gave him a winning smile, which was a total turnabout from the shock and insult she'd just been demonstrating, and he was so surprised his jaw dropped.

He left the car and opened her door for her. She stepped out, gingerly testing her foot. When she let her weight bear on it, her body gave.

"I'll get you," he said.

For the second time that evening he picked her up, one arm beneath her legs, the other under her torso. Their cheeks were

6

within inches of meeting, and again he inhaled the springtime scent. Why hadn't he parked all the way across the lot? He wanted to carry her for miles. When he turned, she put her arm around his neck and smiled.

"You're pretty strong," she said.

"Well, you're not very big."

After he had crossed the fifteen feet of pavement to her car, he stopped and said, "How do we open your door?"

She giggled. "I'll do it."

"Shoot. I was hoping we couldn't find a way."

Squatting slightly, he lowered her until she could reach the door handle, then backed so she could pull the door open.

"Just put me down. I'll hop in."

She maneuvered into the car on one foot, ready to leave. And as she got in the car and shifted around behind the steering wheel, he thought, This is the exact moment I should ask her for a date. Instead he got lost in an interior dialogue on whether he should ask out a socialite. He didn't know where River Oaks Drive in Abilene was, but the name carried an imposing sound. Big bucks, out of his league. Personalized license plates and a father who would pay for clothes by mail.

"Well, if it wasn't for the scar I'll probably have forever, this would've been kinda like an adventure." She smiled again, sending a tremor through his heart, and started the car.

No way, he thought. He'd seen too many of these rich girls at school, and the ultimate in rejection would have been a haughty, "Oh, no, I don't think so." So he merely backed up and closed the door, waving as she drove off.

He couldn't stop thinking about her. She was the first thought that popped into his mind when he awoke, and his last thought before he went to sleep at night was a devout wish that he'd dream about her. Over the next few days, under the pretext of checking on her health, he made several attempts to look up Lori L. at the

7

dorm, but she was at the center of so much oohing and ahhing as she valiantly attempted to walk that he backed off. Lori L. seemed almost crippled, barely capable of ambulation.

She walked better than that the other night, he thought.

Once, as she was helped down the front stairs of the dorm by two preppies, she looked at him. For several long seconds, her eyes fixed on him and she delivered a conspiratorial smile. You ought to try cutting your foot too, she seemed to say. Now her entire foot was wrapped.

He walked off feeling magnified, glorified.

For a while, he tried to quit thinking of her. The son of a farmer had no business with Miss Photogenic. But the school conspired against him. He saw her everywhere. Lori Lynn Conner, senior elementary education major from Abilene. Miss this and Miss that; occupant of every office. She moved in a sea of smiling young ladies who radiated happiness and beauty and contentment.

She was quoted in the school paper in a man-on-the-street poll, in which students were asked what they believed were the major issues facing the world in the 1980s. There were the usual answers —whether the world would acknowledge and follow the Lord Jesus Christ, would the superpowers realize the folly of nuclear weapons and disarm. Lori Lynn Conner, senior from Abilene, was quoted as saying, "There are mainly two things on my mind—world peace and whether the cleaners will ever find my coat."

Chris liked that answer.

The next time he saw her was again at the store. One day when the last cold front of the year was interrupting spring and he was hurrying to work, his face turned down in his jacket to avoid the wind, he saw the red Cutlass parked, naturally enough, in front of the blue-and-white handicapped parking sign. The car was un-occupied but idling—its exhaust vapor practically inviting some delinquent to rip it off—just so the driver could return to a warm car.

He stood for a moment behind the car, looking at the magical name o.. the license plates, wondering what was more irresponsible than a rich girl. He didn't know. He didn't care. He didn't want to mishandle another opportunity.

If she was ever in the company of a male, he was usually some preppie jerk with his sleeves pushed up, sunglasses riding atop his head, whose first name should have been a last name. And since Chris couldn't compete on that level, he had to get her attention in some other manner. Without cutting her foot.

So he stole her car.

Driving it behind the store, he parked it by the dumpster. And when he returned to the empty parking space out front, he found the senior from Abilene looking around in utter befuddlement. He could almost hear her thoughts: she had cut her foot, the cleaners had lost her coat, and now, now her car had disappeared. She was wearing designer jeans and a quilted jacket with a bright blue scarf around her neck, and the wind and cold had turned her cheeks red.

"Hey," he said loudly, scaring her. "The cleaners ever find your coat?"

Her eyes narrowed, the culprit in view. "You. What'd you do with my car?"

"You know, I thought that was your car. About a minute ago, I saw this ten-year-old black kid drive it off. I said to myself, 'I bet his name's not Lori L.'"

"Where is it?"

"Sometimes I do locate cars, but I've got to tell you, I don't do things like that for free. I take girls with nearly amputated feet to the hospital for free, but I don't help them find their cars. Not for free. I just want you to know in advance."

She was trying not to smile, was trying instead to convey a look that threatened severe retaliation. She took the few steps that separated them and grabbed his right forefinger, giving it a twist.

"Where is it?"

"We'll have to discuss my fee first."

"This sounds like blackmail," she said. She stopped twisting and simply held his finger. "Okay. Let's hear your fee."

"It's high. You have to accompany me to a local restaurant and let me buy your dinner."

Why did he feel she possessed the power of life and death over him, this polished apple of a girl? And why was she continuing to grasp his finger?

"That sounds pretty outrageous, a freshman boy blackmailing a senior girl."

How'd she know he was a freshman? Her satisfied smile told him to forego any inquiries on the subject. Like a journalist, she'd never divulge her methods or sources. But she had been interested enough to find out!

And still she held his finger.

"I know the chief waitress at George's Surf and Sirloin. She'll hold a table for me, but I've got to let her know. In the next thirty minutes."

"If I say yes, you'll think I'm easy. Whenever you want a date, you'll steal my car." She shrugged and released his finger. "Okay. Now. Where's my car?"

He led her to the rear of the building, handing her the key as they walked.

The day had acquired a significance he hadn't expected to see for a long time. The day he'd walked out the gate of the Naval Amphibious Base in Little Creek, Virginia, had been significant. He'd been set free. At the age of twenty-one, his life stretched into a blue sky, covering any and all options. The world had awaited. He could do anything, everything. And finding the right girl had been very high on his list. He hadn't, however, expected to find her this fast.

When they got to the car, he turned serious, almost reverent, over this unexpected stroke of good fortune. As he held the car door open, she got in and he said, "My mother used to list important dates in this big family Bible she kept on the coffee table. If she was still alive, I'd call her and tell her to write this one down."

Lori, looking through the windshield of the car, didn't respond immediately. So he stood leaning on the door and waited, the wind and cold forgotten.

"Is that why you took Home Economics in high school? Because you didn't have a mother?"

The question caught him totally by surprise and he stood up straight, looking at the apartments behind the store. Not only had Lori L. done her research, but she didn't mind letting him know she had. And if he had possessed even a tiny doubt that he had found the right girl, that small doubt vanished.

"No, I took Home Economics because the teacher was pretty."

She looked at him and smiled. "That figures. Did you learn anything?"

"How to cook an omelet. And I made an apron. It was real pretty, red-and-white-checked."

He wanted to look at his watch to see how late he was but didn't. Talking to Lori was worth more than a job. More than any job. But Lori, without looking at her watch, displayed a practical side in addition to her other, a combination of mystery and directness.

"If you were supposed to be at work by three, you're late."

"I was," he said, wondering when she'd glanced at her watch.

"Then you need to go."

"Yeah, I know. Tonight?"

She nodded, giving him a pleasant look that a spoiled rich girl wouldn't have been capable of. It was a look that sent him walking to the front of the store with an exceedingly warm sensation. It had been a look he'd have expected to see a wife give a husband, a very comfortable look.

Still, he couldn't believe his luck. As they ate at George's Surf and Sirloin, he lied. Carefully. Since he wasn't sure what she had learned about him, he stuck to lies about the navy, which she couldn't verify. Instead of telling her he'd served illustriously as a radioman aboard an amphibious ship, he said he'd just finished four years of arduous duty with Underwater Demolition Team Twenty-Two at Little Creek, Virginia. He explained his duties as one of the navy's murderous frogmen as though he'd been living on the set of a James Bond movie. Big knives, plastic explosives, hand-to-hand combat in the violent bubbles of the sea a hundred feet down.

"I don't believe that," she said.

He took from his wallet a pink Naval Reserve ID card, the one he'd been issued upon his release from active duty. Lori inspected it as though she could detect forgeries.

"What's RM2 mean?"

It meant radioman second class, but he said, "Registered Madman, second degree. Everybody in the UDT was crazy. You had to be."

"No doubt."

What was he doing, trying to sell her on his brother, the war hero? His brother, Carl, the marine with the Silver Star. Chris had joined the navy with the intention of proving he was tougher than his brother. Since there were no wars to fight at the time, he'd decided on UDT, which required a degree of dedication and toughness that would cancel out Vietnam War decorations. But once he was away from home, from his brother and father, he'd seen another, more appealing option—having a good time. So he'd foregone volunteering for UDT even though he'd still ended up in the amphibious force. And the promise of good times had proven to be illusory. More than a few times he wished he'd stuck to his plans.

"I'm lying," he said. "RM2 means radioman second class."

She'd been holding a french fry speared on her fork for several minutes and she still hadn't eaten it. "Can I say something?"

"Sure."

"You seem to be trying to impress me. You don't have to. Really."

"You might not like the real me."

"Take a chance."

"Okay. My father's a farmer, and my brother has driven me crazy since the day I was born. My mother brought me home and set me in a bassinet and within five minutes, he'd knocked it over and rolled me against the wall. His best season in football, he gained over fourteen hundred yards. I barely broke a thousand. He joined the marines and got a Silver Star for valor in the Tet Offensive. I joined the navy and got drunk and peed in a potted palm in Valetta, Malta. He's a lawyer, I'm a student." He paused for a drink of iced tea. "How about you? Brothers or sisters?"

"Not a one."

"An only child? Really?"

"Really."

"I wouldn't have thought it."

"Why?"

Without divulging a large number of preconceived notions about people with money, he didn't know what to tell her. He certainly didn't want to insult her. And the behavior she'd exhibited, and which he considered the rich incapable of, well, maybe he had only imagined it. But she'd asked for honesty, so that's what he'd deliver.

"Your family has money, right?"

"Not all of it."

"Well, I don't know exactly how to say this, but you don't seem like a little rich girl. In a way, maybe, like that business about world peace and wondering if the cleaners would find your coat. Incidentally, I loved that. It was great. But there seems to be much more to you than that." He paused. "I'm not sure I can explain it. An only child from a rich family could really be a bitch, if you'll pardon the expression, and I don't think that applies to you."

She finally ate the french fry and then pushed a fried scallop around her plate. Chris had finished eating twenty minutes ago, his fast eating a characteristic left over from the military. The restaurant, on Friday night, was crowded, and he ignored the hostile looks from those waiting to be seated.

Lori leaned toward him and with a mock look of confusion asked, "Did you compliment me?"

He laughed. "I don't know." And he didn't. He was too interested in watching her to think about much else. Wearing a pale green dress with a darker green jacket, she would occasionally offer such a direct look that he felt related to her, as though she were a cousin he'd known very well as a child and was now seeing again. How could he feel they shared a history when he'd met her less than a month ago?

"What about you?" he asked.

Her father was in the oil business, had a drilling company, a production company, and sold oil field supplies. He had done very well; he also had worked exceedingly hard. "So hard I barely saw him." Her mother did a lot of volunteer work, for the rehab center, the arts festival, restoration projects, those kinds of things. She and Lori had always been close. "But you know one thing I learned from her? Speaking of money? That you can worry about it too much. She says, 'I've been poor and I've been rich, and I like rich a lot better.' I think *maybe* she puts too much emphasis on money."

"Well, this is truly amazing. I've never been rich and you've never been poor. We can educate each other. You know the people who have personalized license plates; I know the people who *make* them. I'll cook you red beans and rice and you can fix me broasted rack of prime lamb, or whatever it is rich people eat. No, we're both lucky to have met each other whether you realized it or not."

Changing the subject without so much as a blink, she asked, "Do you ever relax?"

"Relax? Well, I don't know. I never thought about it. Should I?"

"I don't know. You just don't seem like a person who relaxes very much."

Mimicking her earlier mock confusion, he leaned over his empty plate and asked, "Did you compliment me?"

She laughed, holding a napkin in front of her mouth. "I don't know."

"We don't know much about compliments, do we?"

"It doesn't seem that way."

Chris doubted his own statement. If anyone gathered compliments, Lori did. She had to. She not only had the physical attributes to draw them, but she'd been taught well. Everything she did—with the exception of shopping for Cokes—was correct, graceful. He'd be afraid to take her home. Well, maybe not so much anymore, since only the old man resided there, but she'd have been appalled by the meals when both kids had lived at home. When they had fried fish, french fries, and coleslaw, the table had been left with a million crumbs, liberal dollops of tartar sauce, streaks of mayonnaise, and rings from sweating iced tea glasses.

"Do you think we should leave?" he asked. "Look at those people over there. That one lady keeps elbowing her husband and telling him we're through and dilly-dallying around."

"Don't you want to learn how to be rich? Well, now we ask about dessert, tell the waitress we're not quite ready, and ask for coffee. And we ignore all the peasants. Or. We could ask for the check so those people can sit down. The poor man's probably got sore ribs from his wife's pointed elbow."

Chris asked for the check and they left. Since he hadn't wished to embarrass Lori by wheeling her around in a 1972 Chevelle, they had come in her car, and he fished her keys from his pocket. The ring had a tag that warned, "Spoiled Rotten." And now he couldn't decide if she was or not.

In the car, she sat in the middle, within easy touching distance of him, causing the veins in his neck to throb. The darkness, her proximity. In the cool evening, he shivered.

"Why'd you go in the navy?" she asked.

"Oh, I don't know that it was any one reason. It was several. The main one was that I didn't want to farm. My father wanted me to, and I didn't want to spend the summer avoiding him. We didn't talk much, and he'd never ask me if I was staying, and I never wanted to tell him I wasn't. So the day after graduation, I told him I was going to Great Lakes."

"What'd he say?"

"He didn't say anything, not immediately. Later he said, 'I hope you write more than Carl did.' Carl's my older brother."

"The competition," she said.

"Yeah, the competition. I don't know why I've spent so much of my life trying to outdo him. It's all pretty stupid."

"Maybe it's just normal."

Her hand rested palm down on her leg, and he covered it with his when they stopped at a light. Turning hers over, she grasped his. And just like that, they were holding hands.

The past seemed to fall into oblivion. Nothing that had ever happened to him seemed important except the fact that he had met Lori. The cotton fields of his youth were from a previous century. He could barely remember standing under the summer sun in a field so far from trees that he couldn't even hear the cicadas, in a spot so quiet that his ears had supplied a buzzing, when he'd been so hot that his skin had felt numbed and the day had seemed white, waiting on a wisp of a breeze to turn his sweaty clothes cool.

That had been someone else maybe, just as it had been someone else in the navy, drunk and urinating in a potted palm tree on the Island of Valetta. It had been someone else the shore patrol had picked up for fighting with marines in Palermo, someone else waking up in the bed of a pregnant woman in Norfolk, staring at the blue veins in her swollen breasts. Each time he'd done something disgusting, he'd thought, am I having fun? Is this the fun I intended to have?

After four years of such fun, he had decided the answer to his problems was simple, simple but unattainable in the Norfolk area, where normal girls avoided all contact with sailors. For good reasons. What he needed was someone to love, to love him in return.

And now he was holding a warm slim hand. And he was as close to realizing a dream as he had ever been. Or hoped to be.

The first time he ever walked up behind Lori and put his arms around her, she stretched, hands over her head, and invited him to

16

stroke. He did. Her body was as smooth and firm as a young sapling stripped of its bark. Once they started kissing, they didn't seem able to stop, and they sat for what seemed hours with their mouths locked, squirming and moaning and touching. He was hesitant to invite her to his apartment, but he longed for privacy, and he finally suggested they go.

It was in a white frame house that had been converted to apartments, cheap housing stocked with dust, barren carpet, and ragged furniture. The only lock it had was on a hasp over the screen door, and as he inserted the key into the padlock, he kept looking at Lori, searching for contempt, the desire for flight. But all he saw was curiosity.

"This could be a quaint old home," she said.

Once inside, he gave her the four-second tour. Look right at the kitchen, and as your head swings left, you'll see the bathroom. At the end of your pivot, you'll see the bedroom. Lori gazed with the same curious look—so *this* is how poor people live.

She gave him a compensatory kiss.

They sat, they kissed, they got carried away.

He really hadn't intended to undress her, but he did. Partly. She was dressed for a cool spring day in green shorts that fell almost to her knees and thick green socks that rose almost to her knees, and a green sweater. The sweater went first, leaving her sitting beside him on the ragged couch in a silky blouse. Which he unbuttoned. She wore the most wonderful wisp of a lacy bra he'd ever seen. It unhooked between the cups.

Her breasts were virgin hills, wonderfully smooth humps that had never actually developed into breasts. They were large enough, just not separate enough from her chest. Somehow, in a world that lusted after voluptuous women, he was thrilled with the way she looked. She had the body of a boy almost, and it looked new and unused and undiscovered. There was almost something perverted about his response.

"Lori Lynn Conner, you are absolutely perfect."

17

She expressed her gratitude with a kiss.

The longer she sat without her blouse on, the more nervous Chris became. He felt as though he'd found a million dollars in cash that had been stashed in his apartment and any minute some officer of the law was going to come confiscate it. Although he hadn't stolen the money, he certainly wasn't allowed to keep it.

He kissed her powdered breasts, rubbed them with his nose, wondered how he could swallow her whole.

He wondered too why she wasn't stopping him, ordering him to cease. Finally, he stopped on his own and laid his head in her lap, feeling as though he'd been through a near-death experience, had glimpsed the other side, peeked into heaven.

"You're dangerous," she said, lifting his head to kiss him.

"What?"

"You're dangerous. I quit thinking when you're around."

He wasn't sure how to respond, so he sat up and kissed her breasts again. They were as smooth as air, pure air.

"You have to think for us," she said.

He shook his head, latched onto a nipple, letting his tongue stroke, all while he pulled her into a standing position so he could remove her shorts. He'd never do this again, if only he were allowed to, but he had to see all of her. He had to see her standing naked in his apartment. God could kill him afterward, should kill him, but first he wanted to see all of her.

Pretty soon they were both naked and kissing.

"We've got to stop," he said.

"I know."

"Let's put our clothes back on."

"Okay."

Instead he led her into the bedroom and laid her on his old iron bed with the mushy mattress. He looked, loving what he saw, then lay down beside her.

"I can't believe you," he said. "You're more than beautiful."

"Umm," she said, licking his ear.

"I want to make love to you."

"No," she said. "Anything but that."

He didn't think she was serious. He thought she meant no theo-retically, as they had meant when they'd agreed to put their clothes back on. But when he moved to enter her, she made a small noise and sat up.

"Time out," she said, taking a deep breath as if to reorient herself to a nonsexual world. She got off the bed and walked to his closet. Uh oh, he thought, watching, this is where she leaves, where she discovers I have only two pairs of pants and four shirts. But she got a blue chambray shirt, part of his navy dungaree uniform, with its ghostly black second-class chevrons and eagle on the sleeve. He watched and prayed.

Please, God, let this all be real. And if it's not, don't let me wake up. If she'll stay, I won't touch her anywhere I shouldn't. I won't touch her pussy. Please, God, forgive me for saying pussy. Just let her stay. With the shirt unbuttoned.

They returned to the living room. Lori sat on the couch and smiled at him, a great and generous smile. He was encouraged enough to reach between her legs and lose his hand in her soaked secrets. He just couldn't help it. His eyes played games with the tails of the shirt. The more the hidden region appeared and disappeared, the more obsessed he became.

Finally he knelt in front of her, between her legs. He wanted to catch honey on his tongue. He kissed her soft blonde hair.

"That?" he asked.

"Um hmm," she said, barely.

His life had changed. He was a light year away from the person he'd been in the navy. He quit drinking. Someone else using his body had done all those things in Toulon and Naples and Barce-lona. And although he hadn't gone to church in years, he bought a suit, a nice one, and went with Lori, holding the hymnal with her and singing as though he could. He was a foxhole Baptist, his

19

prayers reflexive, coming only when he saw the prospect of wonder or disaster on the horizon. He had the same amount of confidence in prayer that he'd had in the special request chits in the navy. When the request got to the end of the line for final approval or disapproval, logic and reason no longer applied. Whims and winds did. But with Lori at his side, he began to think he could become a real Baptist, one who wanted prayer back in the public schools.

At night he wrote her letters. "Remember the night you cut your foot? I wanted to take you home with me and nurse you back to health. I wanted to spoonfeed you soup. I'd blow on it until it was cool and then put the spoon in your mouth. I'd give you little bites of cracker. I'd carry you everywhere you needed to go, even to the bathroom, and would quit school so you'd never be alone."

He'd hand her the letter the next day as they sat on a bench between classes and wait for her reaction, closing his eyes and holding his breath.

"Registered madman," she'd say and kiss him.

He'd exhale relief.

It was an idyllic spring, the best time of his life, and the more he tried not to think about her graduation and departure, for a job teaching third grade in Abilene, the more his life seemed to have acquired a point of termination.

He grew sick with worry.

"Is there a guy waiting on you out there?"

She nodded, very serious. "My father."

"You know what I mean."

"I think he's the only one waiting on me."

He wanted a pledge from her, some sign of his permanence in her life, but he couldn't get one. If he told her that he loved her, her answer was invariably the same—a grateful and enthusiastic kiss. If he told her he was going to miss her and be miserable, she said, "Poor baby. Don't be sad."

He discovered a new side of her, one that refused to be serious. Or one that refused serious consideration of important matters. He could never work up sufficient nerve to tell her she was frustrating him. The closest he came was asking, "What have we been doing the past two months? Just passing time?"

She gave him an open-mouthed looked of faked offense. "You mean you don't know what we've been doing?"

She reminded him more than once that Abilene was barely a three-hour drive. She wasn't, after all, moving to Alaska.

A few days before graduation, her father appeared to help her move home. Chris had been expecting Slim Pickens in a hardhat, but Milton Conner was a nice-looking man dressed in a suit. His car, a dark blue Lincoln, was covered with mud, as though he had driven all the way to Waco on oil-lease roads, but Mr. Conner looked at home in his suit. His face was well defined, sharply etched. An outdoors face.

As Chris helped them move Lori's belongings to the car, Mr. Conner asked what Chris was studying.

"Business."

"I was hoping you were a geologist with a nose for oil."

Chris shook his head. "I've never smelled it outside a can. I've never *seen* it outside a can. Unless it was on the driveway."

Mr. Conner laughed.

"I guess things are good in Abilene now."

Mr. Conner leaned up against the car and looked up at the windows of the dorm. "They're great. Forty-dollar oil's got everybody in the oil business. Restaurant owners are buying pulling units and football coaches are in the drilling business. They all think it's going to last forever, but it won't. And it's a long hard drop from boom to bust. These young guys have never felt the floor fall out from under them."

After a few more trips with boxes and suitcases and dresses still on the hangers, Milton Conner pulled Chris's shirt and held him at the car while Lori returned to the dorm. They silently watched her walk through the door.

When she was out of sight, Mr. Conner asked, "You serious about Lori Lynn?"

Chris nodded, wondering exactly what he should say. But before

21

he had the chance to say anything, Mr. Conner began smiling. It was almost an evil smile, a smile formed at the expense of another person, say, a buffoon attempting to gain an audience with the queen.

"Why're you smiling like that?"

"You pretty tough?"

"Well, as tough as the next guy, I guess. What's wrong?"

Now he laughed. "Put your old clothes on, son. You got your work cut out for you."

Mr. Conner started up the walk toward the dorm.

"Wait," Chris said. "What're you talking about? You mean I'm gonna have trouble? With Lori?"

"No, not directly. Hell, son, women don't work that way anyway." He shook his head, as if he'd just learned Chris was dying. "You'll never pass muster with her mother."

"Why?"

"Because you're a boy," he said, laughing, as though Chris were ignoring the first fact of logic.

He silently transported the remaining belongings to Lori's car, his happiness over apparently being accepted by Lori's father cancelled out by his depression over being a boy. And he couldn't help but notice the disparity in emotions between him and Lori. He was dying, very slowly, and she was shooting out the birth canal.

"I love you," he said.

She gave him an explosive smile and said, "Three hours is just like that," and snapped her fingers.

You bet. Just like that, he thought.

2

Lori turned into the driveway, following her father's car, and parked in front of the garage (which had an apartment on top where Lori had played house as a child, the envy of her friends) and saw her mother in the backyard, standing on the patio, frowning. When her mother stood in that spot and frowned, she was pondering the curse of nut grass.

Mrs. Conner saw Lori and smiled, and the two of them met in the driveway and engaged in their ritualistic greeting—lots of fake Hollywood kisses—which always caused them both to laugh so much that Mr. Conner would shake his head. Then they hugged for real. No one ever wondered whether Lori and Mrs. Conner were related, since they looked like older and younger variations of the same model, a fact which pleased both of them. Sometimes people did wonder if Mr. Conner belonged with them. If one of the women got hiccups in a restaurant, a condition which automatically ignited the giggles in both mother and daughter, Mr. Conner would look away as though he wished he were sitting in another restaurant. Far away. In Guatemala, maybe.

Lori knew before entering the house what was on the menu for dinner—stuffed shoulder of lamb, her favorite meal. They always had that the first night Lori was home, just as they would have tuna melt sandwiches for lunch tomorrow.

Lori loved their house. It was built on a double lot among pecan trees on River Oaks Drive. The house had a very simple floorplan—a seventy-five foot hall off of which were constructed some very large rooms. Lori's bedroom was bigger than her parents', and one friend from college had squinted as if she couldn't see all the way across to the opposite wall and asked, "Does the weather ever change in here? Do you get rain or snow?" The room contained her two most important possessions—her brass bed and a collection of Madame Alexander dolls.

She did however feel a twinge of discomfort upon returning home, not because she didn't want to be there but because people were asking her, "Well, Lori, what're you going to do?" And when she said she was going to teach third grade in Abilene, they always said, "Oh," and then paused before adding, as if to comfort her, "That's real nice." She'd never liked the words "real nice." Yards could be real nice, and so could wire wheel covers. She didn't want to do something people considered *real nice.* Maybe she should have gone to graduate school in California or to New Orleans for a good job. Or maybe people should just quit asking her, "Well, Lori, what're you going to do?"

Mrs. Conner helped her unpack and return her clothes to the drawers and shelves and closets.

"I'm so glad you're back," Mrs. Conner said.

"I'm glad to be back."

"Stan called this morning. Wanting to know when you'd be in."

Lori, suddenly trying to remember where she had put the stack of letters Chris had written her, didn't respond.

"Do you want me to invite him over?"

"No, not today."

Her mother liked Stan. Lori thought he was real nice. Kind of like teaching in Abilene. His father was an oil producer and their house sat atop the tax appraisal rolls with the highest evaluation in town. Someone had written into "Action Line" wanting to know the highest appraised residential property in Abilene, and Mrs. Conner had clipped the article showing the house of Stan's family with the prize.

"I guess you're too tired," Mrs. Conner said, refolding slips.

"I am a little tired."

"Why don't we have a welcome-home party?"

"That'd be nice," Lori said.

Mrs. Conner frowned. She didn't like anything that was nice, either. "Well, we don't have to decide now."

Her mother advised her on the boys who had been inquiring into her return, making Lori remember a fantasy she'd had before. She would hear the news that a guy who looked like Robert Redford's son, driving a white Mercedes 380SL with California plates, had been cruising the neighborhood, trying to find her house. He'd be a mysterious stranger, wearing sunglasses, and he wouldn't say why he was looking for Lori. What happened after he found Lori had usually depended on her emotional state at the time.

And now she hadn't thought about the mysterious stranger for a few months, not since Chris had appeared.

Eventually she was going to have to tell her mother about Chris. And her mother was going to hit the ceiling because she hadn't yet even heard his name mentioned. Lori had failed to mention him by design; she couldn't say his name without having an emotional reaction, and Mrs. Conner's senses were acute in that regard. Overly acute. Besides, she had never liked any boy who was serious about her daughter. Mrs. Conner's favorite among all of Lori's boyfriends had been a guy who had thought Lori was wonderful but not as wonderful as hunting rattlesnakes or playing football. He had called once every three weeks. Lori and her mother had conversed several times on the subject of boyfriends.

"You want me to marry some guy who doesn't even love me?"

"What do you mean? I want you to marry a boy who thinks the sun rises and sets behind your beautiful face."

"And that's why you hate every boy who seems to love me that much?"

"The right boy hasn't come along."

"The right boy has to suit you and not me?"

"No, of course not. He has to suit you. I don't have anything to do with it."

"No, not much, you don't."

25

"Well, maybe just a little."

Chris wasn't going to be the right boy in her mother's eyes. Even her father had seen that. Lori wasn't sure what her father had told Chris, but he'd bordered on a nervous breakdown trying to figure out what Mr. Conner had meant. He had asked over and over what Lori had told her mother about him, thinking Mrs. Conner's resistance would be personal.

Well, Chris would have his work cut out for him. But he hadn't been the kind of boy Lori had seen in her future, and he had certainly convinced her. If he could convince her, then surely he could win her mother over.

Lori had thought she'd been in love before, and Chris had shown her she hadn't. Lord, he made her toes curl. When he appeared, she smiled and wanted to kiss his eyes. He was only twenty-two but the sun-burnt summers of his youth made him look older. His grin would turn his face soft and winning as though he were some sort of loving and friendly cowboy. She'd never wanted to be so close to another person, had never experienced such sexual urges.

Lori should have mentioned him. While talking, Mrs. Conner had been absently opening boxes to see what went where, and there beneath a little pile of panties was the stack of letters and notes Chris had written.

Mrs. Conner read the top note and said, "Oh, my."

"Mother."

She was slow in releasing the note, which covered a sheet of paper torn from a spiral notebook. "This is the boy who took you to the hospital when you cut your foot? He's a—bag boy?"

Mrs. Conner had almost read the entire page before Lori jerked it unceremoniously from her hand. It was a tame letter compared to some he wrote. Lori refolded it and tried to decide where she could now hide the messages to protect them from a prying mother. Mrs. Conner wouldn't be pleased to read Chris's description of how the powder on her daughter's breasts tasted.

Mrs. Conner asked, "He *really* wanted to spoonfeed you soup?"

"Well, he said he did." Where on earth was Lori going to hide these things?

"And the reason you haven't told me about him is . . ." She waited for Lori to fill in the blank.

"The reason I haven't told you . . ." Where would the letters be safe? Maybe her father would install a safe in one of her closets. "His name is Chris Gray—"

"And he works in a grocery store."

"If you want to know why I didn't tell you, this is it."

Mrs. Conner sat on the bed in what Lori would call a defensive posture, legs crossed, hands folded very properly in her lap. A mother awaiting her wayward daughter's explanation.

"He doesn't have credentials, Mother. You'll just have to meet him."

"Where's the unknown boyfriend from?"

"East Texas." Why did "east Texas" sound like "a Bulgarian ghetto"? "He's twenty-two and this is his first year in school. He was in the navy."

"Was he an officer?"

"No, he wasn't an officer. He was eighteen years old when he joined. Officers aren't eighteen years old."

"Are you going to hold those letters the rest of your life?"

"I may. I may because they're personal and the first time I leave the house, you'll be in here reading them."

"He writes things I shouldn't read?"

Lori wanted to go sit and rest her head on her mother's shoulder and tell her that her daughter was in love. But Mrs. Conner would only resist Chris that much more when he appeared. Why couldn't their families have known each other for years? But they wouldn't have. Farmers were held in low esteem around the Conner household. They were always trying to keep her father's drilling company from making locations or they presented outrageous demands for property damage. They filed for injunctions and restraining orders, and every time Mr. Conner saw a news story about farmers going

27

bankrupt, he said, "Well, if they'd stick to farming and stay out of the courthouse, maybe they could make a living."

There was no way to make Chris's entry into their lives smoother. She hoped he had more charm than her mother had resistance.

"Mother, would you just try to withhold judgment until you meet him?"

"That's twice you've told me I'm going to meet him. I thought he lived all the way across the state."

"He does, but he's probably going to come for a visit sometime this summer."

"What do you know about his family?"

What about his family? she wondered. Didn't the fact that Mr. Gray grew cotton put him in the textile business? He shipped his cotton to the gin, so he was partly in the shipping business. Lord, she was glad Chris wasn't witness to the conversation. She was ashamed of the position her mother was putting her in; or she was ashamed of herself for not just telling her mother the facts. But she was trying to walk a very tricky line.

"Mother, I'm tired and I'm getting a headache. Can we please talk about this later?"

Mrs. Conner left the room in something of a huff because Lori was still trying to think of a good hiding place for the letters.

That night during dinner, the phone rang. Mrs. Conner had shown her displeasure over the unknown boyfriend by setting the kitchen table in a normal everyday manner rather than the dining room table with silver and candles. And to answer the phone, she only had to reach a foot or two to the wall.

She uttered her always-friendly hello. But within a matter of seconds, a look of shock infused her face and her jaw dropped. She slammed the receiver back onto its base on the wall and, obviously flustered, wanted to resume eating the stuffed shoulder of lamb but couldn't focus on the task.

Mr. Conner, at the other end of the table, hadn't looked up from his magazine, confident with the knowledge that he'd be paged if the call was for him.

Lori asked, "Who was it?"

Mrs. Conner put her fork down and fixed the napkin on her lap several times. "It was an obscene call," she said quietly, as though newspaper reporters lurked beneath the table, anxious to print such news in the morning edition.

Lori giggled. "What'd he say?"

"He said—" She shook her head, unable to repeat the words.

"Oh, come on. What'd he say?"

Mrs. Conner stretched toward Lori and said, "He said he wanted to—he said he wanted to—*love my whole body*."

Lori laughed, genuinely amused by both the call and her mother's reaction. She laughed until she went suddenly silent, open-eyed. "I want to love your whole body" was Chris's favorite line. Oh, no. Oh, please no. He had called and mistaken Mrs. Conner's voice for Lori's, an error almost every caller made. No one, even her father, could distinguish between their voices over the phone. Before Lori could recover, Mrs. Conner, who knew far too much about her daughter, had already correctly read Lori's face.

"The bag boy," she said.

Lori didn't answer.

"It's the bag boy and he thought I was you." She looked at the still-reading Mr. Conner. "I've got wonderful news. A bag boy wants to love your daughter's entire body."

"Hmm," Mr. Conner said.

"Mother, it's a figure of speech."

"Yes, and he's speaking about your figure."

Lori left the table and went to her father's den, knowing Chris would call back. He probably thought Lori had failed to recognize his voice. She sat at the big wooden desk, wishing she still had her own phone and number. In an uncharacteristic fit of economy, she'd suggested to her father that the phone be removed when she'd left for Baylor.

29

She was sitting, chin propped by the heel of her hand, when her father walked in and pitched the *Drilling Contractor* magazine onto a built-in shelf. "I've got to go check on Rig Three. You want to ride along?"

"No, I'm waiting on the bag boy to call."

Mr. Conner laughed and sat in a leather chair to change shoes, removing shiny loafers and putting on old boots covered with drilling mud.

"Those boots don't match your blue suit," she said.

"Just like your face doesn't match the enthusiasm of your boyfriend. If he saw you right now, he'd think somebody died."

He sat across the room smiling at her, trying to cheer her up, just as he had over the years. But his efforts had always been on the sly, out of Mrs. Conner's vision. Lori had often wondered why he didn't stand up to his wife and had one day asked. "Because," he'd said, "I don't have time. There's only twenty-four hours in a day."

Now he walked across the room and leaned on the desk, bringing his face slightly lower. "Don't worry. She'll come around."

"Why does she do this to me?"

"Because she thinks you're the finest thing God ever set on this earth and nobody's good enough for you. She's like a tool pusher looking for the perfect roughneck. Strong as an ox, don't need sleep, man who'll double over every other day. Without ever drinking. Of course, there's no such thing. A roughneck's drunk when he's not working, and he throws money every which way. Don't pay his rent and can't keep a wife. But don't worry. She'll come around. I think she'll like Chris when she meets him. She won't at first, but she will. She will."

The phone rang and Lori, after recovering from the initial fright from the sound, jerked the receiver up. She waved to her father as he left, then said hello.

"Can I speak to Lori?"

"You should have been speaking to her a while ago."

"Oh, God. Who was it? Your mother?"

"Yes, it was my mother."

"Dang, I would've *sworn* it was you."

"Don't be danging. You're in enough trouble as it is."

They were all in trouble, Lori soon learned. Chris was in Abilene, already registered in a motel, having come for a visit on the same day she had told him good-bye. He'd almost beat her home. Lori sat at the desk with her eyes closed, wanting to cry, until she decided maybe the hand of Providence was behind this early visit. Maybe the sooner Chris met her mother, the better for everyone.

Wrong again.

He appeared at her front door in Levi's and a T-shirt. On the T-shirt was a fierce-looking alligator holding guns in his front hands/feet/paws, bandoliers crossing his chest, walking down the ramp of a navy boat that had just landed on the beach. Beneath the terroristic alligator were the words, "Gator Navy."

Chris, noticing Lori's attention focused on his shirt, said, "I just got it in the mail today. From a guy still in the navy. You like it?"

As Lori left the house, she shouted back at her mother, "I'll be back in a little bit," before she quickly slammed the front door.

"Where're we going?" he asked.

"I have a lot to tell you. Let's go."

She directed Chris back to his car, overcoming his reluctance and confusion by helping him start the car, her hand placed over his. "Trust me on this. Let's go."

He put the gearshift lever in reverse but didn't back out of the driveway. "Why don't I just go apologize?"

Lori shook her head. The poor boy didn't understand. "Mother would see you and think about boys on motorcycles. Maybe counting bugs on their stomachs. She'd think of bored-looking girls with tattoos on their shoulders. Please, we need to go dress you in something else. Did you bring some nice clothes?"

"Yeah, I brought that shirt you gave me. In case we went out to eat or something."

Lori smiled. She'd bought him a pink and aqua Izod that looked

31

good on him. Since he hated to be thought of as a farmer's son, she didn't understand why his wardrobe was right out of the cotton field. He had a pleasing build, one Lori wanted to clothe herself. He was a wiry sort and looked strong enough to pull nails out of a post with his fingers.

When they returned to the house, Chris looked like the perfect candidate for son-in-law. Even Lori's own mother seemed nervous. She had not only cleaned the kitchen, but she'd changed clothes also. Dressed in flowing pink leisure wear, she looked as beautiful as Lori could imagine. But when Lori introduced her to Chris, she offered to shake hands, something she would have done with a policeman who had come to investigate her complaint of a possible prowler.

Worse, Chris seemed even more offended than Lori did by the gesture. And he fell into some kind of good-old-boy role Lori had never seen.

"How you doing, Miz Conner," he said, pumping her hand with vigor. "Good to see you."

"Hello, Chris. I'm glad to meet you."

"Never been out to this part of the country before. Hell, to tell the truth, I didn't even know it was here. I always thought the state line was just this side of Mineral Wells. What do you people do out here?"

Lori sat at the kitchen table and closed her eyes, wondering what she had done to deserve such pressures. Who were these people?

"We find most of the oil that provides gas for your car, Chris."

"You don't say. So y'all work for Exxon or Texaco or one of those big oil companies?"

"We do some drilling for the majors. Mostly we drill for independent producers."

"You drill for the army?" Chris asked, smiling, unable to let Mrs. Conner fall for the joke. "You said the majors. I thought you were talking about the army."

32

Lori stood and said, "Come on, Chris." To her mother, she said, "We're going to a movie. I'll be back after a while."

She grabbed Chris by the arm and jerked his hand while simultaneously squeezing, trying to dig her nails into his bones. She wasn't sure which of these morons she hated the most at the moment, but she couldn't physically punish her mother, so Chris would have to take the brunt of her frustration.

On his way out, Chris said, "Nice to meet you, Miz Conner. Keep those tanks and jeeps running. Eternal vigilance is the price of liberty."

Lori was so upset by the time they got outside that she stopped on the porch, closed her eyes, made fists, and thought about screaming as loud as she could. The temptation was great. Instead she found herself crying. She placed her head against one of the white posts along the front of the porch and watched a tear drop onto the cement.

"Lori," Chris said. "There's one thing I just can't take. I just can't take a limp fish handshake, I don't care who offers it. It means, 'Here, peasant, you may kiss my cheek,' and you know what cheek they're talking about. It isn't a facial cheek. I just can't take it."

Lori had nothing to say.

"I can't help it. I hate it when I'm around people who think they're better than me. Actually, you should be glad I didn't do any more than I did. Usually when I'm around people who think I'm a crumb, I show them I'm a whole lot worse than they think."

Lori walked the length of the porch, dabbing at her eye with her finger. She hadn't even picked up so much as a Kleenex on her way out of the house. Maybe she'd just keep walking, off the porch, across the driveway, through the yard, just keep walking until she stopped somewhere else. In someone else's life.

Why did God hate her?

"Lori. Lori, stop. I'm sorry. I didn't mean to make you cry."

He caught her and pulled her to a stop, turning her around. With the end of his thumb, he wiped the tears from her eyes, then kissed the damp spots. "I'm sorry. I'll go back in and apologize. If that's all right with you." When she didn't answer, he asked, "Is it all right with you?"

Lori shrugged. Unless he beat her up, he couldn't make things worse. She sat on a white wrought-iron chair.

"Okay, I'll go apologize."

Lori exhaled a sigh.

"Tell me what you want me to do."

"It's not all your fault. I don't know what I want you to do. I just want my mother to like the boy I love."

She had never said she loved him, and she hadn't intended to say it now. But she had. She had decided never to tell a boy she loved him until she had first decided that she wanted to marry him. And she couldn't remember ever making that decision. She rubbed her right eye. She didn't know anything.

Chris sat down and hugged her, a move which only made her cry again.

He kissed her hair and said, "Just stay here. I'll be back in a few minutes."

3

Chris spent a long night in the motel. Someone kept calling his room looking for Mindy, and his denials of Mindy's presence only made the caller suspicious.

"You put her on the line *right now.*"

As soon as Chris hung up, the phone rang again. Finally he removed the receiver and listened to the dial tone.

A pickup truck drove back and forth through the parking lot, the clattering diesel engine just above idling speed.

He couldn't have slept anyway.

He had indeed overreacted at Lori's house, and the reason eluded him for some time, until he admitted that his own disappointment was at the root of his reaction. He had envisioned himself as the perfect son-in-law, the Conners' pride and joy. After all, if he had found the perfect girl, then the family situation would be perfect as well, wouldn't it? He'd sit down and visit with them and tell them how much he loved their daughter. He'd change the oil in their cars and repair the roof on the house.

And he'd have a mother again. What could have been better than an older Lori as mother? Nothing.

And then he'd met the Ice Queen face to face and been offered that goddamn limp hand. What made the offering even more galling was that Mrs. Conner was even better-looking than Lori, if that was possible. She was Lori with class and maturity, a blonde woman whose pictures belonged in magazines, in ads for champagne. Had she smiled, he would have gladly kissed whatever cheek she'd offered. Instead, she'd slipped him the dead fish.

His apology had changed nothing. Sitting at the kitchen table, she'd cooly received his regrets, the expression of which had been the most difficult lines of his life. What he really wanted to do was backhand her across the room. But he said, "I was really uncomfortable coming here, and I just blew it, that's all. I hope you'll forgive me."

Her nod had been given without the benefit of an accompanying smile. Chris hadn't seen her smile yet.

He finally turned on the TV and watched a spaghetti Western in which Lee Van Cleef played a priest and Richard Boone was cast as a cowardly sheriff with a high squeaky voice. It was a movie which seemed to demonstrate the entire world was indeed a stage and a person changed along with his role. Lee Van Cleef as a priest was only slightly more absurd than Richard Boone as a eunuch.

He kept seeing surprising changes in character, and one of them was Lori as daughter. Lori in Waco and Lori in Abilene were not the same person.

His hope that the transformation of Lori from spontaneous girlfriend to dour daughter was only temporary (four hours at the most) was dashed when he arrived at the Conner house the next morning, yawning from his sleepless night. She was dressed in a pale green dress that fit her perfectly and showed her slim limbs to great advantage. But she appeared to have mentally prepared herself for the Lord's Supper. All she lacked was a Bible in her hand. Her manner said, "I have resumed my position as junior ice chip." She now gave the same impression as her mother: mess with her, and, poof, she'd freeze your blood.

"You'll have to excuse my yawning," he said. "Somebody was determined to find Mindy in my room last night."

"She wasn't there, was she?"

"No," he said, yawning.

In a way he understood the transformation of Lori. The Conner house was imposing, not quite like Frankenstein's castle but at least like the White House. Step inside and you acquired the desire to judge people by the cut of their clothes. Did they scream K-Mart? The carpets in the house were so thick he could hardly tell if his feet were working.

He steered Lori toward her father's study. "Is your mother here?"

"No."

"Good. I'd hate for her to see me wearing the same shirt two days in a row."

He'd attempted a joke, something to put a smile on her face, but she hadn't seen the humor. They sat on a leather couch in the comfortable room, facing a silent TV. The room was obviously Mr. Conner's. The built-in shelves were messy and there was even an unused calendar (still showing January) with a scantily clad lady of the month.

Lori sat with her legs crossed and rubbed the material of the dress between thumb and forefinger as if testing it for house standards. Her distant manner suddenly worried him. What if Lori the daughter had no use for him?

Within an instant he felt as uncertain as he had the night he'd rushed her to the hospital. Chris Gray, outside looking in. Was this the girl who had last night said she loved him?

"Lori, I'm sorry about last night."

For a moment she seemed on the verge of tears. "Maybe we shouldn't talk about last night."

"I'd feel better if only you smiled."

She gave him a weak smile, then let her eyes drop. She seemed to him preoccupied, her mind elsewhere.

"I'm going to look around," he said, standing.

"Don't look in my room. I didn't make the bed."

Great, he thought. Let's see some signs of anarchy, a little rebellion.

He left the den and wandered down the hall, silently sinking in carpet. The hall of history. One side was a pictorial guide to the life of Lori Lynn Conner, from baby who knew at the age of three months that the sudden appearance of a camera was an invitation to smile and charm, to high school homecoming queen and Baylor Beauty. He stood looking at the pictures believing that he was guilty of desecrating the concept of beauty. Here he was, Christopher Gray, a nothing from nowhere, wanting to believe he was worthy of such blonde hair, sculptured cheekbones, the implicit promise of a wondrous life. No wonder Lori had been appalled by his T-shirt. Her mother, had she seen her in his company, would have grabbed her by the arm and rushed her to this hallway. "Look. Here. This is who you are. This is Lori Lynn Conner."

He'd be more thoughtful. He promised.

From the hall he entered Lori's bedroom. It was huge, big enough for midgets to play basketball in. Right in the middle of her unmade bed was a pink pile—her nightgown. He picked it up and sniffed. It smelled both of powder and Lori. He was encouraged. A human lived here. With the material pressed to his nose, he looked around. One end of the bedroom was bedroom, the other a combination sitting room–study. Against one wall stood two glass cases of dolls. A display. All of the furniture was white with the exception of the brass bed, which had white ceramic ornamentation. Lori had several different paintings and posters of rainbows on the walls, and in the corner lay a pile of stuffed animals, fuzzy legs and arms entangled. They had been evicted from the bed apparently.

At the far end of the room was a bathroom, and he silently walked into it. The counter of the sink was as long as a sidewalk, and it was littered with bottles and jars of makeup and cleansers. Next to the sink were three tubes of opened lipstick. She'd obviously had trouble making a decision on the color of her lips. Overall, the room was a mess. Wet towel in the tub, blowdryer still plugged in, a brush sprouting blonde hair.

"I can't believe you're snooping in my bathroom," she said from behind him. Grabbing the back of his shirt, she pulled him back into the bedroom and then closed the bathroom door.

"You made a mess," he said.

She was shocked either by his belief that she'd made a mess or by the fact that he'd openly comment on it. "Pretend you didn't see it."

"You didn't even hang up your towel."

She grew embarrassed and gave him a little-girl look, head tilted, bottom lip stuck out. She played with the buttons at the neck of his shirt. Then suddenly, as though the embarrassment were over-whelming, she buried her face in his chest, pulling his shirt against her as though it were a rag she could hide in. He tried to move her away but she had hooked her finger into his shirt.

"Lori," he said, looking at her blonde hair, smelling shampoo, cleanliness with a wonderful scent.

No response.

They stood in that same position for a few minutes until he noticed in the mirror of her dresser that she had turned her head enough so she could watch their images in the mirror.

Out of the blue, she asked, "Are you a sailor with a line?"

Something in his brain clicked. He could hear the conversation she'd had with her mother upon his departure last night. "Well, Lori Lynn, what on earth are you doing bringing home a sailor with a line?" He didn't mind the tag because it conferred on him an aura he didn't possess. Such a description was no more insulting than "wild bull rider." Or "pirate."

"Do you think I'm a sailor with a line?"

"No." She watched him in the mirror. "Are you?"

The strangest thing. Her hip bone was giving him a massage. The more erect he got, the more expert her hip bone became, exerting just the right amount of pressure and movement. She reached with her hand to measure the results of her efforts.

He turned her face upward and gave her a long kiss, and it turned into a kiss that was suddenly beyond the control of both of them, one of those that affected his system like the bite of a poisonous snake. Suddenly they were both writhing, out of control, trying to consume each other.

They ended up on the bed with Lori on top. She seemed as far gone as he did, straddling him, holding his face, sitting on her knees. Her dress was up around her waist, and his hands fit naturally on the rather thin straps of panties that failed to cover her cheeks. Her teeth pressed into his lips.

Then she kissed his ear, filling it with her tongue, and said, "I want to make love."

He thought he'd misunderstood. The girl who had conditioned him to "Not that" and "Time out" had erred in her speech. But that same girl had moved to his side and was unbuttoning his pants.

He had to clear his throat before he could speak. "Where's your mother?"

"We have at least two hours," she said, having given him direction with his pants and now removing her own clothes.

He was suddenly as nervous as he was anxious, wondering if, after these months of wanting and waiting, he was capable. And now Lori, faster than he, sat beside him on her legs, naked, looking like a figurine. Youth in bloom. Not at all self-conscious. And then he was naked as well, unable to match her beauty but exceeding her in appreciation.

And then he wasn't in such a hurry. Well, part of him was, stretched and eager, but that part would have to wait while Chris enjoyed looking at Lori, this time knowing he could do what he had wanted to do so intensely before. He laid her on her back and put her arms over her head, then, starting at her hands and following the inner sides of her arms, he touched her everywhere.

And then he was as close as he'd wanted to be. The feelings of elation combined with the exquisite sensations radiating into and out of his loins caused him to reach the mountaintop much sooner —at least four or five hours sooner—than he had desired.

Lori held his face and kissed his eyes. "I love you."

"That doesn't even begin to cover it," he said.

Later, both of them dressed and lying still on her bed, she started crying.

"What's wrong?" he asked, fearing the worst, that the first time had also been the last.

"I don't want my mother to treat you like a Mexican."

"Lori, it doesn't matter. I'd like for her to think I'm the finest thing since cruise control, but if she doesn't she doesn't. Basically, it just doesn't matter; it doesn't have anything to do with the way I feel about you. If she thinks I'm a sailor with a line, then she thinks I'm a sailor with a line."

"I didn't say she said that."

"But she did, didn't she?"

"Yes."

"It's no big deal."

Instead of answering him, she wrapped her arm around his neck and burrowed her head into his shoulder as if she planned on entering there.

After a few minutes, she said, "This isn't the way it's supposed to be."

He started to answer, able to think of a hundred clichés to fit the occasion, but he didn't. Instead, with his right hand—Lori was lying on his left—he reached to make sure her dress was down where it belonged.

He thought he'd just stare at the ceiling, but he fell asleep instead.

He awoke looking at Mrs. Conner as she stood in the doorway of Lori's bedroom. She wore a summer dress of mixed pastels with a matching broad-brimmed hat, and his first thought was that she was the only person he had ever known who could get away with wearing such a hat. In fact, she looked classy wearing it.

His second thought wasn't so rational. He lay in this postcoital stupor as if on exhibit, right in the middle of an unmade bed with this lady's daughter wrapped around him. He wanted more than anything else to check his fly but he didn't dare. He thought, I need to get the hell out of here.

But the daughter was sleeping soundly, her even breathing almost part of his shoulder, and he couldn't move without startling her. So he didn't.

He didn't for another reason. Mrs. Conner's face seemed caught in an expression that said more than she could have spoken. It was one of sad realization. A girl didn't lie in the position Lori had assumed without possessing a strong feeling for the boy whose neck she hugged. Maybe Mrs. Conner had been able to believe her daughter was suffering a minor infatuation, an emotional aberration that would clear up under motherly guidance, neither of which would explain what she saw before her.

Mrs. Conner's eyes shifted to Chris.

He gave her a small shake of the head and a sympathetic look acknowledging her sadness.

She turned and walked off.

†

Loving Lori ruined his life. He kept thinking that once a person had been introduced to life as it could be, then life as it usually is, sucks. He hated driving back to Waco after a weekend visit in Abilene more than he'd hated returning to the navy after a two-week leave. Why did he have to sit around his apartment in Waco watching the dust dance in the sunbeams when he wanted to be with Lori? He got up in the morning and read the cereal box as he ate breakfast and then checked the length of the noodles in the canned spaghetti at night.

What extremes. Abilene to Waco, A to W, almost A to Z. He began avoiding his apartment, instead working overtime at the store or studying in the library. He was so overwhelmed with a desire for Lori that he was despondent. How could he be in love but so unhappy? Where was his euphoria?

There was only one thing to do—get married. He starting writing her a letter because he couldn't wait until the next weekend to ask. He'd write and have the letter delivered by Federal Express. (If successful, they could be in a commercial. "When Chris Gray wanted to get married . . .") Then he'd call Lori for her answer. He wrote letter after letter and threw them all away, crushing the paper and trying to exorcise the loneliness and despair the letters contained. They sounded like the Salvation Army's Sponsor-a-Student program. He was lonely all right but he didn't want to sound like it.

He could call. But since he didn't have a phone, he'd have to use a booth and there in a public place he'd be a dollar eighty-five away from a death sentence if she said no. If she did, he could see himself spiraling downward, just as he had in the navy, in a truly useless existence. Somehow he had pinned all his hopes on Lori Lynn Conner and nothing else mattered.

He gave serious consideration to becoming a good Baptist so he could rely on God to deliver unto him Lori and all her glory, but the consequence of that good fortune gave him pause—probably God would also see fit to punish him for past sins.

The more he thought about calling and getting an immediate answer, the more he rehearsed the conversation. He rehearsed until he got diarrhea.

By the time he got to the phone booth, his hands were shaking. It took him several tries and two queries on his health from the operator to get the coins into the phone, and he discovered his voice was quivering.

He couldn't stand the tension. As soon as Lori answered, he blurted out the truth: "I want to marry you."

"You're, let's see, twenty-six years too late."

He closed his eyes, cursing his stupidity, his inability to distinguish the voices of mother and daughter, and gave serious consideration to decapitating himself. If he hit the wall of the glass booth with his head, at the right angle, with enough force. . . .

Off the line, he heard Mrs. Conner say, "He can't decide which one of us he wants to marry."

"What?"

"Chris. He wants to marry *me*. He said so."

Back on the line, Mrs. Conner said, "I don't think it's legal, Chris, so you'll have to ask Lori. She's going to the other phone."

He eyed the Safeway where he worked, just down the street, trying to remember if they sold rat poison. Had God been just, he would have endowed Chris with patience. Instead, God had given him a double portion of wretched obsession.

Then Lori was on the line laughing. "I never dated a boy who asked my mother to marry him. She didn't say yes, did she?"

Slowly, he said, "I'm going to hang up and call some other time."

"Oh, don't be so serious. It's funny. You just can't see it. And it's sweet, too. Thank you for liking my mother enough to ask."

"It may be funny in seven or eight thousand years. Please don't make jokes. Please."

"Okay. No jokes."

He debated on making the call again later, when his sense of humiliation wasn't so great, but then he'd be stuck replaying the conversation over and over, and he'd drive himself nuts. And probably end up eating rat poison. So he stayed on the line.

After a long pause, Lori said, "Were you going to ask me something?"

There was a change in her voice, a forbidding tone that let him know one thing—she wasn't going to say yes, and the best he could hope for was not no. She didn't want him to ask for reasons he didn't want to guess at.

"Lori, I feel like one-hundred-percent dogshit right now, and I don't think I'm up to the conversation. So please, let me just call you back. And forget this call."

"No one's ever asked me before. If you don't do it now, you may not be the first."

Her tone was conciliatory. Maybe she knew he'd go price rat poison if they didn't discuss marriage now.

"I've never thought about living in Waco," she said.

Chris had rehearsed all possible statements on every option, but not once had he spoken that line for her. Why was she so practical?

"I'm not asking you to marry the city of Waco."

"Well, if you want to get technical, you haven't asked anyone but Mother to marry you."

"God, I'll never, *ever* live this down."

She laughed. "I know. You made a mistake. You seem almost human."

For a few minutes, they discussed practicalities, the amount of her salary plus his GI bill payments. Rent. She didn't like the word. Appliances. That was a word he hated although he didn't tell her that. The price of groceries, which he knew and she didn't. His remaining three years of school. He couldn't foresee surviving three more years without her. They talked until they had eliminated all the questions, in his mind, until one remained—did Lori want to marry him. And he didn't ask it. As long as she didn't say no, then he could believe she'd eventually say yes.

He left the phone booth in spirits better than he deserved. By God, she hadn't said no. And she'd agreed to think about it so they could talk about it over the weekend.

He looked at the sky and smiled. One of these days he and Lori would be together as much as they wanted to be.

He knew that before Saturday arrived, he'd be crazy with anxiety, so on Thursday night, unable to tolerate the thought of vegetating in the apartment, he decided to visit his father. The ninety miles to Ashworth, his hometown, would give him the opportunity for speed and motion, and he needed to visit anyway.

Since he'd been old enough to comprehend his father's hopes— that one of his sons would take over the family tradition of farming —their relationship had been strained. The old man had farmed, as had his father, the good black land in the river bottom that Chris's grandfather had acquired during the depression. Mr. Gray had discovered early that his older son, Carl, eight years older than Chris, would never be a farmer. At the age of ten, Carl discovered that kids in the neighborhood would pay good money for things they didn't need. So on trips to the county seat, about twelve miles away, to buy groceries, Carl began accompanying his mother. Upon his return, he sold hunting arrows to kids who didn't own bows, .22 cartridges to kids who had no rifles, and shining ball bearings to children unacquainted with machinery. When sales of an item slowed, Carl ran a sale. Get two ball bearings with any purchase of an arrow.

Chris was never sure whether his father wanted him to farm because it was an honorable and useful occupation or because he thought Chris's being there would protect the land when he died. Chris was sure his father could see his children pissing the place away, cashing it in on riotous living, throwing a party instead of a funeral. But Chris didn't want to farm. He didn't want a job where the most exciting thing he did most days was turn the tractor at the end of a row and start back in the other direction. He hadn't liked such a life at the age of fourteen; he wouldn't like it a bit now.

He sat that evening in the living room of their house with his father. Cleburne Gray was a big man, and he wore two kinds of outfits—dark suits to church every Sunday and overalls with khaki shirts every other day. An overly zealous adherent to the work ethic, he welded when he wasn't farming, and he had his own shop in town.

Chris wanted just one time to have some insight into the man's thoughts. Every evening he came home and ate the food that Mattie, his black cook, had earlier prepared and left in the oven. He then sat in the same chair in the corner of the living room and read the Dallas *Morning News* that had been delivered that morning. On the table beside his chair sat a pack of Camels, a Zippo lighter, and an ashtray. How can you do this every night, Dad? he wanted to ask. Every night of your life.

Chris never knew what his father thought. He had gone to every football game he'd played in, and later they would always trade comments, but his father had never once commented on Chris's performance. He had heard from others that his father was proud of him and frequently got excited, but he got this news from people other than his father. "Lordy mercy, Chris," a lady had told him once. "When you scored that touchdown, your daddy came unglued. He was jumping up and down like he'd heard the trumpet of the Lord."

Now, in a living room barely illuminated by one lamp, they sat on furniture that hadn't been moved in at least fifteen years.

"Well, we gonna have a football team next year?" Chris asked.

"Maybe. They only graduated six. Get a little beef on the line and they might do all right."

The Ashworth Eagles had won district for seventeen of the last twenty years, ever since a little wiry coach named Mallory had come along with his marine haircut and cheekful of Beechnut. If

46

Chris had been asked whether his father or Coach Mallory had been more of an influence on his life, he wouldn't have known the answer.

"I may be getting married," Chris said.

"Nice girl?"

"Real nice. You'll like her."

"Well, good. Bring her over sometime."

The marriage plans of his children didn't excite him. Carl had been married and divorced twice. He probably thought both his boys were abnormally attracted to divorce and married only because it was a prerequisite.

"She lives out in Abilene. Her father's in the oil business."

"Hmm. Money, huh?"

"Yeah, they've got a house you wouldn't believe. Right now oil's going for forty dollars a barrel, but Mr. Conner, her father, says it won't last."

"I'm sure he's right. Cotton can be sixty-five cents when you plant and twenty-nine when you sell."

"I meant to bring a picture of her but I forgot."

"You can bring it next time."

They sat in silence, looking at a dead TV. Mr. Gray watched only the news, nothing else, not even football. He filled in the time between his supper and the ten o'clock news by reading the paper. If he ate a late supper and had only five minutes between eating and the news, then he finished off the paper in five minutes. If he finished supper at nine, reading the paper took an hour.

Lori had asked Chris if he was bothered by grief when he went home, and he'd said no. He wasn't. He couldn't clearly remember a family with two parents. The feeling of grief remained and could settle on him at odd times—when he saw a boy smiling at his mother, when he saw a mother lift a crying child to comfort him—but the strange attacks of sadness were never related to the house or his father.

"Still working at that store over there?" Mr. Gray asked.

Chris nodded, standing because it was ten o'clock. Time for the news.

He turned on the television and looked at his father.

"Well, I'll see you next time."

"Okay. Bring your girlfriend."

Chris left, realizing he hadn't even told his father that his girlfriend's name was Lori. Oh, well. The old man wouldn't bother learning her name until she'd been around for a few years.

4

Lori was passing the summer months as she always had—by sleeping until noon and yawning through her first meal. The menu of breakfast/lunch depended upon the activities of her mother. If Mrs. Conner was home, Lori ate lunch, usually some soup and salad or a fruit plate. If she was on her own, she drank a glass of orange juice for breakfast.

The afternoon she spent at the country club, swimming or, more rarely, playing tennis. Although she didn't especially like tennis, she had taken lessons out of self-defense. There was always some macho woman athlete prowling around trying to find a game and an opponent whose Adam's apple she could smash with a three-hundred-mile-per-hour ball. Lori preferred a slow game where no one got livid if the ball was hit over the fence into the parking lot. Mostly she lay by the pool and collected vitamin D.

Into the middle of these lazy days came Chris's unexpected call about marriage. She was perfectly happy with the progress of their relationship and wished he was as well, although she did wish they were much closer than a three-hour drive. And she did know that she'd have to make her decision on marriage while she was in Abilene and he was in Waco. There really hadn't been any question in her mind; they would marry. The only question was when, and she had to decide before the weekend. If Chris appeared and she wasn't prepared, he'd probably talk her into a quick trip to the justice of the peace. Only God knew the power Chris wielded over her emotions, and if there was any justice in the world, only God would ever know. She could resist his wackier suggestions on the phone; when he was with her all he had to do was smile and he could have her eating concrete for a snack.

Still, with marriage being such a serious matter, she had to do one thing. She needed someone standing beside Chris in her imagination so she'd have the proper perspective. And when Hal asked her if she wanted to accompany him to a picnic on Thursday afternoon, she said yes.

Hal was theoretically perfect, a petroleum engineering student at the University of Texas. His face was that of a male model, cleanly lined with shining cheeks, and it would easily fall into place beside her in a wedding picture.

He provided her with immediate assistance by arriving at her house and foregoing the long and tiresome walk to her front door, instead parking in the driveway and honking the horn.

When Lori climbed unassisted into the car, he said, "The Rangers have a man on third." He was listening to a baseball game on the radio.

"And hello to you," she said.

He drove them to a friend's ranch with one ear cocked at the speaker, his eyes fixed on the road at an angle. Hal. Yes, she remembered him now. He was the one who had begged her to come watch him play in a Little League all-star game and then he'd never even checked the bleachers to see if she was there. How many snowcones had she eaten, wondering why he never looked?

The picnic was a catered barbecue affair to celebrate the end of school. Seventy or eighty young people had gathered at the foot of a mesa amid cedar and mesquite trees near beer kegs and the caterer's trailer, a great tank of a smoker on wheels. Two games had been organized—a beer-chugging contest and a frisbee football game for those not yet drunk and still capable of movement. When Lori and Hal arrived, several of the frisbee tossers invited Hal to join the game, and he looked at Lori as though he expected her to object. Object? Her? Ha. This was the boy who'd been unable to tear himself away from the radio so he could ring her doorbell but who could now leave a game that was tied 2-2 in the eighth inning.

When Lori offered no objection, he patted her on the bottom, said, "Wish me luck," and trotted off as though he were General Patton about to win the war.

Lori wandered around, visiting with friends. The day was one of those peaceful ones of early summer, beneath a long blue sky, without wind or real heat. They all kept waiting for someone—no one knew exactly whom—to come sailing off the cliff several hundred feet above them, a hang glider.

Hal was still Hal. As Lori went to sit in a lawn chair that Hal was resting his hand on, he jerked the chair up and handed it to another person. Lori plopped onto the ground. Her tailbone hit the concretelike earth and she could hardly get up, her legs numb with pain. Everyone was too busy laughing to help her.

Dignity and tailbone severely wounded, she limped toward the caterer's trailer, intending to sneak behind it and cry, but three boys, already drunk, had beat her to the property and were using it for a piss-for-distance contest. Had she not been hurting, she might have stayed to watch because one of the drunks had an incredibly long liquid arc, at least twenty feet. Through the cloud of pain she wondered how on earth he could manage such a feat.

By the time she got to Hal's car, she didn't need to cry. What she wanted was Chris to comfort her. She wanted to sit in his lap and be held; she wanted to smell his neck and hear him say, "You poor baby."

Hal did come looking for her. He leaned, arms on the car door, and asked, "What's wrong, babe?"

"You almost maimed me. I don't have any feeling in my legs."

"How'd you get over here?"

"I drug myself with my elbows."

He tousled her hair and said, "Gotta play with pain. Hey, let's go get a cold one, what do you say?"

Lori judged the afternoon a success because Hal had told her definitely that what she felt for Chris wasn't merely an emotion any boy could conjure up from her heart. Before going to bed she smiled at his picture and apologized for the afternoon's experiment.

God spoke to her the next morning. As she ate lunch, she watched an old movie on TV with Jimmy Stewart as the spokesman for your normal male population. He was married to June Allyson and he knew exactly what June wanted him to do—get out of the air force and return to baseball. And what did Jimmy "Hal" Stewart do? He remained in the air force so he could fly nuclear bombs over the North Pole and be gone all the time, all the while knowing *exactly* how unhappy he was making his wife. Obviously Lori watched the movie for a reason, and it was for more than learning to dislike Jimmy Stewart. God wanted her to know how fortunate she was, serving as Chris's reason for being.

While Lori waited for Chris to arrive in the afternoon—he had to work Saturday morning—she sat with her mother on the patio as Mrs. Conner listed potential donors for a local restoration project.

Lori said, "Well, you heard the conversation with Chris the other night but you've never asked what I told him."

Mrs. Conner, sitting in the shade of the house but sunning her legs, gave her a sad look. "I don't want to know."

"Why?"

"Because I don't want to lose my little girl."

"Especially to Chris?"

Mrs. Conner set her tablet and pen on the patio. "I wouldn't have chosen Chris, but listen, I remember the fit *my* mother had when I told her I was marrying your father. She threatened to have me committed."

Lori smiled. She'd never heard any such story.

"He was oil field trash. And he was almost ten years older than I was. And my mother's favorite line was, 'You remember what I told you when he comes home drunk and beats you.' He had a pickup that was older than that car Chris drives, and you could hear him coming from a mile away."

"But you were in love."

Somehow in the telling, Mrs. Conner seemed to lose ten years at least. Her smile was bigger, her eyes brighter. She leaned toward Lori as if telling a secret and said, "I used to sneak out of the house when he worked till midnight. He not only worked on a drilling rig, but he was also a pumper. And there was a lease up near Albany at the top of a hill, and we'd drive out there and sit in that old pickup and talk. Sometimes all night. I was always home before Mother got up, but a few times I almost met her on the way to the kitchen."

"So you and Daddy used to talk."

Mrs. Conner gave her a look of moderate disgust. "We still talk. You don't know what we do."

"I can't believe you used to sneak out of the house. I can't picture you doing that."

"It wasn't something I wanted you picturing."

Lori enjoyed the image of her parents as kids in love, sitting on one of the rugged hills near Albany in a battered pickup talking. But at the same time she was distressed over her inability to ever remember seeing her parents as the adult versions of those two loving kids. They acted, had always acted, like two people committed to a marriage for any number of reasons, none of them involving love. Her father made the money and her mother spent it. That's the way things had always been, as far as Lori could remember, and the arrangement had seemed agreeable.

But that wasn't the kind of marriage Lori wanted.

When Chris arrived, Lori had already decided when he brought up the topic of marriage, she was going to say yes but was going to resist setting a date in the immediate future. She'd beg him, if necessary, to finish school first.

They rode to the small lake near the zoo and sat beneath a warm summer sky, listening to the sounds of softball games behind them. Ducks paddled lazily across the water between the car and the zoo. The world seemed a relaxed place.

Dressed in the same clothes he had worn to work—Levi's and a pale blue short-sleeved shirt—he leaned against the door of the car and smiled at her.

"Well, are we getting married?"

"Who would we marry?"

"Does this mean we're not going to have a serious conversation?"

"No, this means you've never asked me. You don't even have a suit on, so you can't very well get down on one knee and beg for my hand properly."

"This means we're not going to have a serious conversation."

"I'm going to have to tell my kids some day that my husband asked my mother to marry him, she was already married, so I got him?"

He took her hand in both of his, held it to his mouth, and asked, "Lori Lynn, will you marry me? Say yes or I'll break all your fingers."

"Somehow this isn't as romantic as it's supposed to be."

He put the index finger of her right hand in his mouth and sucked. Closing her eyes, she shook her head. She wanted both to laugh at the part-babyish, part-sexual sucking and to cry over the imminent lack of romance in her life.

"I can't be serious," he said. "I'm afraid you'll say no."

She opened her eyes and reclaimed her finger. "Okay. I'll be serious if you'll be serious."

"Then come over here."

Turned in the seat and facing her, he pulled her against him. She wore white shorts and a T-shirt with a teddy bear appliquéd on the front. He put one arm around her shoulders, the other hand on her bare leg, and the romantic feeling she wanted floated in on the soft breeze. His warm hand on her thigh created a current that ran throughout her body, stirring up pleasurable sensations.

"Since you'd probably already have said no if you were going to, I'll tell you seriously what I want to tell you. I want to marry you. I want to be with you all day, every day. I can't tell you how miserable I am when I'm not with you, and how happy I am when you're sitting this close to me. I love you and I want to marry you, so I'm asking, will you marry me?"

Lori felt like purring. The clouds had turned deep blue and were laced with little ribbons of orange from the setting sun. A soft warm breeze floated in through the window. And Chris's hand had slipped into her shorts, his finger making her eyes close.

Suddenly he jerked his hand from her pants, all but ripping out the seams, and sat straight up. His eyes were fixed on the passenger's side door. Lori turned to see a black child, possibly ten years old, dressed in a white T-shirt that was too large for him. He reached into the car with one hand and offered a grass-stained softball.

"Sell you this for a dollah," he said.

Chris cleared his throat, looking through the windshield for a moment, and said, "I don't need a softball."

"Man, it's just a *dollah*."

"I don't care how much it is, I don't want it."

"I got a skateboard in layaway," the child said in way of explanation, checking to his left to see if anyone had yet sounded the alarm on a missing softball on the field behind them.

Lori looked at the skinny black arm, thinking it was terribly dry and in need of moisturizing lotion.

"Take the ball back to the field," Chris said. "You can get ten years for trying to sell a stolen softball."

The kid looked the ball over as if to examine the laces, then looked directly at Chris. "I seen what you was doing to her."

"Give him a dollar," Lori said. "Here, I'll give him a dollar just to take the ball back."

She reached for her purse but Chris already was starting the car, preparing to back up and leave. "Don't be encouraging blackmail."

"Hey," the child said, protesting. "She said she'd give me a dollah."

Before Chris could back the car up, she gave the boy a dollar bill, wanting to suggest he go buy some lotion for his dry skin. The kid, still half in the car, accepted the money, then backed out.

"You take that ball back," Lori said as they left.

But the child was headed to the next car, parked thirty feet away, stuffing the money in his pocket, ball in hand.

She sat back and sighed as they drove out of the park. "Did I answer your question? I was going to say yes, but now I can't remember if I told you."

"No, you didn't," he said, returning his hand to her thigh. "And thank you. That makes me happier than I can tell you."

"It makes me happy that you asked."

After several succeeding weekends with Chris, Mrs. Conner quit asking if Chris was coming this weekend and started asking instead when Lori was going to accompany her to Dallas to pick out a fall wardrobe. Over the years, Lori and her mother had made the annual clothes-hunting trip to Dallas, and each year they stayed in a different hotel. They'd been fun trips, filled with good food and good times and large expenditures. This year, however, Mrs. Conner's local obligations prevented her from leaving before Friday afternoon—or so she said—and Lori didn't think she could ask Chris to skip a weekend because reasons for being weren't permitted that leeway.

"If we don't go soon," Mrs. Conner said, "we're going to end up buying next summer's clothes."

"What am I supposed to tell Chris?"

"Oh, I don't know. Tell him something really crazy, like you're going to Dallas to shop."

Just about the time Lori really started feeling the pressure from both sides, Chris's uncle died.

He called and said he was going to have to miss the coming weekend because of the funeral. Lori felt such a burden lifted that she was being overly sympathetic until Chris said, "Maybe you could drive over here and go to the funeral with me."

"Driving at night makes me so nervous."

"You don't have to drive at night. Come Friday afternoon and you can go home Sunday."

Lori closed her eyes and begged, don't say please. Don't, don't, don't say please.

"Please?" he said.

Lori didn't know what to say. Trying to act like the perfect daughter and simultaneously serving as a reason for being was like walking a tightrope.

He said, "I've come out there every weekend for almost two months. Can't you make one trip over here?"

She wanted to ask him if the very warm feeling in his heart, the certain knowledge that she loved him, couldn't carry him over one missed weekend. She didn't want to say no, but on the other hand, she had the trip to Dallas and she also had a bad case of nerves. She'd never driven on the highway unless she'd been accompanied by some other person, usually her father, who knew what he was doing.

Then, too, Chris sounded as though he were trying to establish a ratio. For every seven or eight trips he made to Abilene, she was supposed to make one trip to Waco. If she agreed, then he'd reduce the ratio. Four to one, then two to one. So she told him the truth.

"Chris, I need this weekend for Mother anyway. She's been pressuring me all summer to go visit a sick aunt in Dallas. She's always been my favorite of all my aunts, and I haven't seen her since Christmas. So why don't you go to the funeral, I'll go visit my aunt, and then we'll enjoy seeing each other that much more the next weekend." Since Chris didn't understand the importance of clothes, she didn't mention that in addition to having lunch with Aunt Celia, whose allergies were always acting up and making her sick, she and her mother would also shop for clothes.

And when Chris didn't respond immediately to her alternative plan, she said, "Let's do that, okay? Sometime I'll come to Waco, but not this weekend. Okay?"

"You'll come to Waco?" Suddenly he sounded as happy as a child.

"Sure."

"When?"

"Well, I don't know. You're not giving me time to think."

My God, she thought. What demon had possessed her to say she'd drive to Waco? What would she do, park in front of Chris's apartment and carry in her luggage? Then climb in his bed at night? And she'd never stayed in a motel by herself, didn't have a clue on how to make a reservation or check in. She wasn't even sure she was old enough to stay in a motel. And if she stayed with one of her girlfriends, someone, probably Chris, would get upset over the diversion of her time between friends.

She felt certain she was going to get a headache over this deal. It reminded her of the time she'd had to register for a history course that met at 8:00 A.M. She'd always hated history, and she especially hated it at 8:00 A.M. in the morning. Her life had been a living hell for three and a half months.

"I know," she said. "One of these days I'll come over there and we can go visit your father. I haven't met him yet."

"Yeah, that'd be a good idea."

Lori could tell, he'd almost asked, "When?" but hadn't. The operator saved her by asking him to deposit a dollar eighty-five for another three minutes, and while Lori heard the chimes caused by the dropping coins, she remembered the story her mother had told her about being in love and sitting on the hill in the old pickup. Lori's version lasted exactly three minutes. Then she told him that she did truly love him, because she did, and they hung up.

The only time he ever seemed perturbed with her was when she got (he said in a fatherly voice) *silly*. She didn't understand why he'd want her serious all the time, and of course, he didn't. If she crossed her eyes in church, he thought she was hilarious. If she crossed them when they were in a motel, which was apparently a sacred place, he accused her of being silly. At times, he reminded her of her own father.

Going to the motel was risky, but not as risky as getting carried away in public, and besides, anyone seeing them going into a motel at midnight was engaged in similar mischief anyway. Lori refused to go before midnight. At that time every Saturday night, the Midnight Express, as she had dubbed Chris's car, ran.

The night Chris wanted a decision on a wedding date, they were at the motel, and Chris was naked on the bed before she had even removed her shoes.

"Can we please decide right now when we're going to get married? I'm going crazy thinking about it."

Lori started giggling because he seemed so nervous but he was also naked. And you could tell, from his leaning tower, that he wasn't all that concerned with a wedding date.

"That looks like a jack handle," she said, grabbing it and pumping.

He yelled and sat up, covering her hands with his and bringing them to a stop.

"It works. See that?" she said. "I just jacked you up."

"That *hurts!*"

He had brought a towel to the bed, and she sat beside him, putting the towel over her face like a veil, thinking one of them should exhibit some modesty. Chris watched and gave her his fatherly look. Well, I can see you're going to act like a child. She noticed that with every inhalation, the towel was sucked into her mouth; it released on exhalation. In, out, in, out. She laughed.

"Don't start that. Please," he said.

"Don't breathe?"

Chris looked at the ceiling and said, "Please, let her be serious for two minutes. All I need is two minutes."

"The effective, fervent prayer of a naked man availeth nothing."

He turned onto his side, propping his head up on his elbow, and looked at her, sucking his lips in, trying not to laugh.

Lori decided to be serious, and she placed the towel over her shoulders as though it were a shawl. She took several deep breaths and then sat reverently with her hands prayerfully held before her chest. "Okay, I'm ready. Time me, big boy. I know I can be serious for two minutes."

"When are we getting married?"

"Can you guess who I am?"

"Lori, please."

"No, really, guess who I am. This'll be fun." Sitting somberly on the bed, she drew, with her finger, the letter A across her chest. "Did you get that? Here, I'll do it again." When Chris's expression remained blank, uninterested, she repeated the motion. "I'll give you a hint even though you probably don't need one. That was an A. The letter A." She resumed her position of reverence, complete with shawl and properly placed hands.

"Lori, could we please discuss the fact that we're supposed to be getting married and have never set a date? I tell people I'm getting married and they always ask when. And I don't even know. I sound like a sixth grader planning to marry a girl I've known all day long. So can we please talk about it?"

"I'll give you a hint."

"Great."

"I'm a character in a book."

"Lori!" he shouted, then rolled onto his stomach, primarily to hide the fact that he was laughing. She could tell he was laughing because his stomach was shaking like Santa's bowlful of jelly. He started to speak, twice, but both times he looked at her sitting stone-faced beside him, and he was overcome with the giggles. Finally he said, "Okay, you're King Arthur."

"If I am a man, then where is my jack handle?"

"Annabel Lee. Anna Karenina. Anne Boleyn."

"My name does not start with an A."

Shaking his head, still laughing, he turned back onto his side and lifted her dress up. They'd gone to a movie and she was wearing an orange and white dress, and he lifted it as though it were a circus tent and he was a child looking for the animals.

"What do I get if I guess right?" he asked.

59

"A feeling of accomplishment."

"If I'm right, will you marry me next June?"

"Characters in books can't marry."

"Characters in books don't wear little nothing panties like this either," he said, touching her with his finger. It slid over the fabric without friction almost, here and there, teasing, avoiding the spot where the swirls began.

"Will you marry me in June if I'm right?"

I'll marry you right now, she thought, suddenly conscious of the fact that she was holding her breath.

"You're Hester Prynne."

"Who?"

"Hester Prynne. The lady with the scarlet letter."

"Was that her name?"

"You mean you didn't know?"

"I just figured out what the A was for. I always thought it was a grade."

5

The word "wedding" acquired new connotations for Chris, just as "Incoming!" did for the green soldiers and "Uh, oh," did for patients not feeling well. He couldn't believe what he'd started by asking Lori to marry him in June. (No, let him rethink that: he couldn't believe what Lori had started by agreeing to marry him in June.) He'd never seen such serious plans. Every time he saw her, she was consumed with ideas, overburdened with books and magazines. And if he expressed any opinion on any segment of the coming affair, Mrs. Conner gave Lori a look that said, "I didn't invite him in here. Did you?" And Lori's expression responded, "Mother, I don't even know him." And Madame Giggles, who had never found any matter beyond her silliness, became ramrod stiff. She and her mother seemed to discuss beads more than anything.

At times it seemed they'd planned to bead everything, maybe even the punch.

When he saw her, he'd say, "The bride is wearing empirical A-line shorts of stunning peau de soie, topped by a whipped cream shirt that faintly reveals her nuptials."

The process wasn't without irony. Mrs. Conner had to acknowledge him as someone with a future in her family, Gator Navy T-shirt and all. Her attitude toward him hadn't seemed to change —although he wasn't certain what it was because Lori would never say anything other than, "Oh, Chris, Mother loves you"—but her treatment of him before others had. She acted as though she and Lori had been waiting a good twenty years for him to make an appearance.

"And this young man is Chris Gray," she'd say. "His family helped establish the Republic of Texas."

He was generally amused by the introduction since his family tree was clouded and Mrs. Conner's statement was based on one tall tale Chris had spun in her kitchen one night, and he got angry only if someone expressed skepticism.

Amidst all the talk about invitations and china and silver patterns and floral arrangements and caterers, while thousands of dollars were being committed or spent, Chris was going broke. The trips back and forth from Waco and staying in a motel in Abilene had sapped his savings from the navy and his wallet was growing fat with credit card receipts. He told Lori he envisioned a halt to his weekend visits because of his finances.

"I'll give you money, if that's all you need," she said.

He disliked the idea of accepting money from her, but he disliked even more the idea of sitting in Waco on weekends. Still, once she made the offer of a loan, she never mentioned it again. He dropped hints. "I'm developing a list to port from sitting on this wallet. It's got so many credit card receipts in it, I can hardly get it in my pocket anymore." He figured his budget aloud, he moaned over deficits, but she was too busy thinking about lace and beads.

Finally he asked, "Did you say once you'd loan me some money?"

"How much do you need?"

He wandered around her living room trying to determine the amount that would transform him from needy boyfriend to moocher. "Fifty bucks?"

He felt peculiar, somewhere between a charity case and a con man, but he took her check. The next time he asked, she deliberated over the amount in what she thought was a comical manner. "Let's see, you were rude to Aunt Elizabeth, and you told Grandmother that your great uncle invented football cleats, which was a lie, of course, so I figure this check can't be more than three dollars."

He was unable to joke about the matter, was afraid to even look at the amount for fear she had actually written the check for three dollars when he'd been hoping for an increase to a hundred.

She handed him the check and said, "Do you want to see my driver's license?" He shook his head, sneaking a peek at the numbers before he folded the check and stuck it in his shirt pocket. Fifty. He should have started out with a hundred. Lori said, "Thanks a lot now and I'll be sure and recommend you to *all* my friends."

One weekend in the fall, Lori finally agreed to drive to Waco so they could visit Chris's father. She left Abilene at sunrise so she'd have at least twelve hours of daylight to make the three-hour trip. Chris thought she envisioned the 180 miles as an obstacle course through the badlands, and she arrived in Waco with a sense of relief he had observed only in his father once when they got all the cotton stripped before a tropical storm dropped ten inches of rain on the farm.

They drove Lori's car to Ashworth, and he gave her the five-minute tour, starting at the football field. The stop was more for him than her because football had been such a large part of his life in high school. They left the car and walked onto the field; it was hardly worth looking at. How had those wooden bleachers held the screaming thousands he remembered? And cows grazed beyond the north goal posts, just across a fence. The field didn't even bear the scars of the previous night's game, Ashworth versus somebody; there was no sign of the hopes and fears that had been realized twenty hours ago.

Lori, standing on the forty-yard line, asked, "Is this where you learned to commit personal fouls?"

He laughed. "It's where I learned almost everything I know about myself, and I realize it as I go along. This is where what-you-think-you-are meets what-you-really-are." He turned and looked back at the small brick field house where they dressed and showered and got chewed out by Coach Mallory. "And if you've got a good coach, you can learn a lot. I always wanted to coach. I don't know why I'm majoring in business."

"You're majoring in business because teachers get paid peanuts. If you don't believe me, I'll show you my next check."

Chris pointed at the white door of the field house. "You come out that door dressed in shorts the first day with this fantasy in your head about how tough you are, how much stamina you've got, and then in the first hour of the first two-a-day, you've discovered the truth." He shook his head. "The truth is hell."

He took her hand and led her off the empty field, taking her to the other spot where he'd made a number of decisions—the farm. They drove into the river bottom where four hundred acres of black land lay barren. The remnants of the summer's cotton crop remained, all those dead stalks that had been turned under, leaving some sticking up like brown needles.

This time they didn't leave the car but simply sat on the dirt road that bordered the farm on one side.

"When'd you decide you didn't want to be a farmer?" she asked.

"The first time my father ever handed me a hoe and said, 'Here, go chop those weeds.' You get your hoe and you start here, and you go right down that row chopping the weeds out of the cotton. And when you get down to that far end where the trees are, you turn around and you come back, chopping all the way. It's the worst,

63

hottest, most boring job in the world. I told my father one time that I'd rather be unemployed than farm and I got an hour-long lecture on what's wrong with the world today. That's his favorite subject, what's wrong with the world today."

"Well, our fathers should get along then," Lori said. "That's *my* father's favorite subject."

Their last stop was Mr. Gray's welding shop, a big sheet metal building that Chris had helped erect, thereby learning the second job he didn't want. Mr. Gray was out front working on the hitch of a horse trailer. They didn't interrupt his work—he would have ignored them anyway—and instead browsed through the metal building that was filled with washtubs full of scrap, piles of angle iron, stacks of rusted oil field pipe that were used in fence construction. Lori looked around in awe as though she'd never seen the *actual place* where work was done.

Their arrival at the shop roughly coincided with Mr. Gray's supper hour, and when he was ready, they took him to the one and only café downtown, where he ate all his weekend meals. Chris had been rather nervous about this meeting, fearing his father would show the same lack of interest in Lori as he had with Carl's two wives. Mr. Gray made quick judgments on character, which he seemed unable to overcome later in the face of evidence which contradicted his opinion. But he warmed to Lori immediately.

"I'm glad to finally meet you, Lori," he said as they drove downtown. He sat in the back seat of Lori's car and she turned in the seat so she could talk to him. "You're just about all Chris talks about anymore. And you're even prettier than your pictures."

"Thank you."

Chris watched him in the rearview mirror, and he looked at Chris, then Lori, several times as though he were having trouble putting them together. Chris wondered what his father had expected him to arrive with—a sixty-year-old washwoman?

"You're really going to marry him?" Mr. Gray asked Lori. He tried to avoid laughing and failed.

The son would have enjoyed seeing the father laugh, had the humor not been at his expense.

They sat at a table in the small café with several other older people, all of whom Chris knew, and he listened to Lori ask questions about her unlikely intended and his father give unvarnished answers.

"He was always his mother's favorite," Mr. Gray said.

Chris had never heard that opinion expressed but he had no reason to question the old man's honesty because he spoke about his son in the same way he would have a coon dog which was widely believed to be the best but which he knew for a fact would chase every rabbit in the woods. To balance Mrs. Gray's faulty selection of a favorite, Mr. Gray then gave Lori example after example of his son's foolishness, everything from the time he was frying bacon and dropped his fork into the pan, which he then retrieved with fingers that had been previously unburnt, to the time he had attempted to replace a light bulb in a lamp without removing the shade.

"He stuck his finger in the socket and looked like he'd caught a lightning bolt."

"Too bad Carl's not here," Chris said. "He could tell you even more about how stupid I am."

Mr. Gray waved him off, accepting a menu from the only waitress in the café, the lady who owned it. The dissection of Chris's personality was halted briefly while Mr. Gray introduced Lori to the waitress. Chris looked at the menu, which he had probably seen several times before in the past twenty years. The only changes were on the prices. The printed prices had been marked out with a ballpoint pen; the penned-in prices had been whited out; the blue ink corrections had been corrected by red ink.

"You go to the game last night?" the waitress asked Chris.

"No, we just got here a little while ago."

"Well, we coulda used you. We almost lost it in the fourth quarter."

Chris turned toward Lori, wanting to make sure she'd heard the compliment, only to hear the waitress say, "Better yet, we coulda used Carl. Where is he nowadays?"

Chris let his father answer, comforted only slightly by the uninterested manner in which Mr. Gray answered the question. Other parents thought their children were perfect—witness Mrs. Conner —but Chris had been born into a family fathered by a man who believed children should be given chances daily to correct their faults. The more they were enumerated, the more motivated the children would be to shape up.

After the waitress had taken their orders, Mr. Gray continued the examination of his son, speaking to Lori as if only the two of them were present. "Chris was what I called selectively lazy. Put a hoe in his hand and he almost quit moving. You woulda needed one of those things doctors wear around their necks to make sure his heart was still beating. But when it came to football, he wasn't lazy a bit. He'd lift weights and run and do whatever that coach wanted him to do."

The discussion continued through the meal and on the way back to Mr. Gray's shop, where they dropped him off so he could drive his pickup home. And Lori seemed to be enjoying the jaundiced view of her husband-to-be so much that once they arrived at the house, he took her into his old bedroom, hoping his father would go read his newspaper.

The bedroom, like the house, looked just as it had when Chris had walked out of it five and a half years ago, on his way to Great Lakes. The exterior had been repainted with the same pale-yellow-and-white color scheme, and the same brown bedspreads remained on the twin beds that he and Carl had slept on. The room had been cleared of most of the personal belongings that had once cluttered it, with the exception of a stack of high school yearbooks on the chest of drawers.

Lori picked one up and then sat on a bed to look at it.

"You were the president of your sophomore class?" she asked.

"Yeah, and freshman and junior and senior."

"You don't sound like you were very happy about it."

He sighed and didn't answer, remembering instead all that campaigning he had engaged in, hoping no one would notice he was campaigning as he did so. The class presidency hadn't been a significant position, but Carl had been president and Chris hadn't been able to ignore the opportunity to match his accomplishment.

"*What* is this?" she asked, pointing at an inscription.

Chris stood beside her, looking at, "Dear Chris, I'm going to miss you because you were the best piece of ass I ever had. Love, Robert."

"A friend's idea of creativity."

Lori didn't believe him and sat with a look of pain on her face, as though she had severe indigestion. "Did you have a girlfriend?" she asked, probably hoping he'd say yes and give her a name other than Robert.

"Yeah," he said, suddenly growing tired, so tired that he lay on the other bed, covering his eyes with his arms. "Carl's first wife. Look at the cheerleaders. Her name was Lisa Patterson. She wrote me while I was in the navy and said she was marrying Carl."

"I've got to see Carl," Lori said, standing and replacing the yearbook, picking up an older one.

Why did he feel so insecure suddenly? Because Carl had either stolen or placed his mark on every girl Chris had ever liked, and he could see the same thing happening with Lori. Carl had been like a child who wanted every cookie in sight. Even if he hadn't been hungry, he'd lick an Oreo to keep other kids away from it. Chris's first post-puberty girlfriend had refused to let him kiss her. And then he walked into the church kitchen one night, turned on the light, and found the girl madly making out with Carl.

"He's nice-looking," Lori said. "But since he's your brother, I expected him to be. I also expected him to look like a jerk, but he doesn't. Actually, he looks like a nice guy."

Wonderful, Chris thought.

"Why'd he marry your girlfriend?"

"Because she was my girlfriend. Hell, they were only married a year, just long enough to make sure she'd never be interested in me again."

"Why were you—so competitive?"

"I don't know," Chris said, and he didn't. "I used to have to hide money if I had any."

"He'd steal it?"

"No, he'd talk me out of it. He was always promising me something but he never delivered. Not once. And I was always stupid enough to believe him."

"You were trusting."

"No. I was stupid."

Mr. Gray appeared in the doorway and asked if they wanted popcorn. Popcorn? Chris was twenty-two years old and had never seen his father eat popcorn. But he had a hot-air popper in the kitchen that had appeared out of a cabinet, and he made popcorn and poured all three of them Cokes. Everything was prepared just as "Love Boat" came on, and his father announced that every Saturday night he ate popcorn and watched "Love Boat." Chris could hardly eat the popcorn because his mouth was open. He couldn't have been more surprised had his father said he'd never again read the Dallas *Morning News*.

"You watch this *every* Saturday night?" he asked.

"Oh, Chris, everybody watches it."

"I don't."

"That's because you have a date with me every Saturday night."

Chris spent the hour-long "Love Boat" program trying to figure out, unsuccessfully, why his father would speak freely to Lori about his son but wouldn't do the same directly to the son. The remark about Chris's dedication to football was as close to a compliment as his father had ever come in his presence. And he had never heard the favorite-son theory before. If he had ever asked his father directly what his mother had thought of him, the old man would have given him a serious look and said, "She thought you were her son."

Lori offered further proof that he knew very little about his father by asking how long Mr. Gray had been suffering heart trouble.

"He doesn't have heart trouble."

"Then why does he have nitroglycerin tablets on the counter?"

"He must be making dynamite," Chris said more lightly than he felt.

He asked while they cleaned up the kitchen and Mr. Gray waved the question into insignificance. He had a little angina pain now and again and the doctor had told him to take the pills. Sometimes he did and sometimes he didn't. Nothing to get concerned about. When the good Lord was ready for him, he'd be going, pills or no pills. Chris started to probe further but his father announced his intention of going to bed and leaving the young people to themselves.

Chris watched him go, drying the last plastic bowl, and as soon as Mr. Gray had disappeared into the hall, he leaned over and kissed Lori, who was watching the soapy water go down the drain. She looked wonderfully sensual in designer jeans and a beige silk blouse, the epitome of softness and femininity. Her breasts seemed caught and held by small hands beneath the blouse, as though they were being offered to him.

"That's all," she said.

"One kiss?"

"Yes," she said definitely, wringing out the dishcloth and then draping it over the faucet. "I'm not going to get caught doing anything in your father's house."

"To paraphrase Jesus, in my father's house, there are many passions. I go to prepare some for you."

"No," she said, drawing out the "O."

"I can't believe this," he said, moving behind her and covering her breasts with his hands, finding they were as soft as they

69

looked beneath the beige blouse. "If I'd known we were going to be celibate, I would've planned to stay at a motel."

She removed his hands and turned to face him, keeping her grasp on his wayward hands secure. "I don't stay in motels for more than an hour, and I don't do things in your father's house. And that's all there is to it."

Although she held his hands, his fingertips reached her crotch, and he ran them over the rough material of her jeans. It was more a gesture of defiance than sexuality since the material felt like sandpaper. "When my father finds out you're the kind of girl who wastes birth control pills, he won't let me marry you."

"No," she said again with the same definite meaning.

He couldn't believe it. Sex with her had always been good, but it had passed into the realm of indescribable. Lori grew more enthusiastic each time, and she seemed to lose herself and her inhibitions, transformed into a purely sexual being whose own excitement increased his beyond his immediate comprehension. They didn't seem to be engaged in a sexual experience, even though he was aware of the intense physical sensations flooding his body. They didn't even seem engaged in an earthly experience. It was a spiritual joint venture. He wasn't doing something; *they* were. He wasn't even conscious of himself, only of them.

He didn't know how to explain what she was denying him. "I think I'll just cut it off if I can't use it."

"You want scissors? Or a knife?"

"You're serious, aren't you?"

She nodded. And continued to hold his hands.

"Okay, get the scissors."

Later, he did watch from his bedroom door as she walked in a short robe from the bathroom to the third bedroom and felt only that much more dissatisfied. This weekend-only routine was depressing. He wanted to be married; he didn't know how he could wait until June.

†

Lori made several more trips to Waco before the wedding so they could find a house. There were certain phrases that gave her trouble, such as "rent house," and the search didn't help. They found houses in which the previous tenants had put their fists through the sheetrock, and they once stepped on a tile floor only to find water squishing up through the cracks. They found cabinets that had served as home to untold generations of roaches.

Another phrase she had difficulty comprehending was "all we can afford." These words were from Latin or some other dead language. And Chris learned, after looking at enough trashed houses, that he didn't care much for the words either.

It was only through coincidence and a stroke of luck that they found a decent house. One of Chris's teachers overheard his lament over his housing situation; the man had a clean and decent place in a quiet and established neighborhood. The only thing wrong with it was the lack of appliances.

Appliance was a word Chris hated. It connoted much more than he wanted to consider. He kept thinking about all the times he had wanted to return to Europe, without obligations or schedules, and bum around. He had frequently envisioned doing so; he would just store his clothes at home and take off. And going with Lori would have been even better. Except Lori didn't bum. She wouldn't care to see the beach at Cannes if she had to hitchhike to get there. And she wouldn't understand a guy who didn't want a refrigerator, particularly if he felt a refrigerator was going to immobilize him. Nor would she want a junk store refrigerator that could be left in a rent house when they suddenly decided to up and leave, bound for Rome.

Worse, they could afford a new one. She had saved all her teaching salary, and various relatives had kicked in several thousand dollars in wedding present cash.

71

Every time he called her, she asked the same question: "Have you looked at appliances?"

Not only did they need a refrigerator, but the house lacked a stove as well.

"I haven't found anything that seems just right," he said.

"You know what I think?"

"What?"

"I don't think you've even looked."

She was right. He hadn't. Did a person voluntarily go out and buy burdens?

"You're moving in in two weeks, and you won't be able to cook anything or keep food."

"I'll barbecue."

"Chris."

He wanted to say, "I'll buy a stove and refrigerator when I find a pair that'll fit in the trunk of my car." Not only was a leisurely trek across Europe out, but now he wasn't even going to be able to set off for the journey around Texas he'd always planned, stopping at a bar here, a small café there, for a chat with cowboys or a group of nuns.

"Chris."

"Yes, ma'am?"

"Do you think you can get a stove and refrigerator this week?"

"Maybe. I'll try."

"What am I going to do with you?"

"Can I make some suggestions?"

Lori solved the problem before the weekend arrived. One night as Chris came home from work, he found Mrs. Conner's blue Cadillac parked at the curb in front of his apartment, with both Conner women inside. Lori met him on the sidewalk, gave him an enthusiastic kiss, and told him they had a surprise waiting; get in the car.

The surprise was at the house. One of the flatbed trucks from Mr. Conner's oil field supply business was sitting in the driveway,

72

and two of his employees were wheeling the refrigerator into the house.

Lori squeezed Chris's hand and said, "It even makes ice cream."

But would it run away from home when Chris was ready to set off on his odyssey?

"Mother's wedding present," Lori said. "Or should I say, presents."

Presents. Inside the house was the largest collection of almond-colored appliances one person could amass. Along with the refrigerator and stove were a washer and dryer, a microwave oven, and a portable dishwasher. He was speechless. Mrs. Conner assumed his silence derived from unspeakable gratitude.

He could manage only a one-word eulogy: "Europe."

"No, no," Mrs. Conner said. "You know us better than that. We only buy made-in-America."

He almost felt a tear in his eye. He remembered talking to a guy sitting on a bench near the beach in Cannes, a guy who had recently got out of the navy and who had returned for his year of bumming. They'd watched a woman on the beach remove her bikini top and then lie down on a towel, so brown and beautiful she would have melted in one's mouth. And now she did, leaving the slightly metallic residue of almond-colored enamel.

The wedding was, with one exception, the splendid affair Lori and her mother had hoped for. Even Chris was impressed.

He had asked his brother, Carl, to perform as best man in hopes the lawyer would then forego sabotaging the proceedings. In a sense, the ploy worked; in another, it failed. Carl appeared in his three-piece suit and shining black beard looking slick and exuding an air of evil—just enough to promise excitement—and upstaged his younger brother all the way around.

At the rehearsal, he timed the proceedings for Mrs. Conner, pointing out whenever possible any inappropriate comments Chris made, apologizing as well as though he were the father and had worked years and years trying to make Chris into a socially acceptable creature. He spoke with Mr. Conner knowledgeably about the oil business and told Lori more than once she was so pretty the wedding merited TV coverage. He kept the bridesmaids tittering, took one home, and met another for breakfast the next day.

He made Chris overly aware of his presence until the wedding itself. The church had been transformed into a candlelit garden, the illusion so perfect that Chris looked up once to see the moon. Lori looked stunning in her gown, and for the first time, he saw it as he was supposed to and not as an expenditure that could have supported them for two years. In fact, she looked so wonderful, he was certain that as she was escorted down the aisle by her father, she'd stop and say, "No, no, I can't do it. I can't marry a sailor with a line. But I can marry his brother."

But when she arrived at the altar, to the oohs and ahs of the crowd, when she took his offered arm and smiled at him from beneath the veil, he wanted to tell her, "Now I know what it means when you hear 'lived happily ever after.'"

She had spoken to him on several occasions on how meaningful and blessed the vows were, about how they should both pay particular attention, about how they needed to recite them periodically after they were married, but Chris waltzed through them because he was thinking of something else—an entire week that he would have her totally to himself in a condo on Mustang Island. He pictured her running down the beach, splashing in the surf, in the black bikini he had picked out for her.

His greatest fear was that he was merely dreaming, that he'd wake up in his old dusty apartment in Waco, still a freshman at Baylor, just out of the navy, in a life without Lori. There was, he decided, a fate worse than death.

At the direction of the minister, they recited the vows, and Chris decided that this was it, the best thing that could possibly happen to him, and he was so happy he wanted to shout.

The minister offered a short prayer, asking a blessing on their married life, and then gave a short sermon on rings and circles of unending love. He then directed Chris to place the ring on Lori's finger.

When he turned to get the ring from Carl, he knew from the look on his brother's face that the time for sabotage had arrived. The clue was in his smile. It was the same smile Carl had given him upon marrying his girlfriend, just after Carl had been told, "You may kiss the bride." Carl had in fact kissed her, all but sent her into a swoon, and then smiled at Chris over her shoulder.

Chris gave him the most threatening look he could muster, checking the small case to make sure there was a ring inside and not a pop-top from a beer can.

The ring was there, sparkling.

Maybe I'm wrong, Chris thought.

He placed the ring on Lori's finger.

The minister said, for Chris's recitation, "With this ring, I thee wed."

Just as Chris started to speak, Carl, behind him, offered an alternative line. Quietly he said, "Put this ring, in your nose."

When Chris opened his mouth to speak, he knew he couldn't. If he tried, he'd laugh. Right in the middle of Lori's perfectly beautiful wedding ceremony. He chewed on his lip for a moment, waiting for the urge to pass.

It didn't.

Behind him Carl prompted with more authority, "Put this ring, in your nose."

"I'm going to get you both," Lori whispered, glaring from beneath the veil.

Chris, wanting to plead his innocence, still couldn't chance opening his mouth.

The minister, not a bit distressed, turned as though Chris had recited perfectly, and indicated it was Lori's turn. He presented his finger and she put the ring on and kept right on pushing as though it was supposed to be embedded in a metacarpal bone.

And then it was all over and he and Lori were skipping down the aisle to joyous organ music. Lori, smiling for the audience, said, "I will never *ever* forgive you."

6

Lori thought that marriage was much like playing house had been when she was a child except now all the pantries and appliances and walls were hers to do with as she pleased. She had an entire house to fix up, and instead of the pretend husband she'd loved dearly at the age of ten and the empty Quaker Oats barrel, she had the real things. She wasn't at all sure what Quaker Oats were for, but she hadn't been able to pass them up in the store.

The house needed a lot of work. It was sided with asbestos shingles that had been chipped by baseball-playing children, and the only green part of the yard was a huge patch of weeds. The bedrooms had hardwood floors that not only needed refinishing but manufactured dustballs. She was on dustball patrol so often her back began to ache from all the bending. But she discovered if she stomped her foot and created a little wind, she could blow the offending dustball under some nearby piece of furniture.

She bought all the magazines at the checkout stand in the grocery store and spent hours clipping recipes, all of which she carefully filed away and saved for the future when she learned to cook. Their immediate neighbor, an elderly widow named Analene, was concerned about Lori's progress as a cook and often appeared as though by magic, sent from heaven, wearing an apron just before dinnertime to see if she could help. Analene would ask what she had planned.

"Stuffed peppers."

"Is there anything I can do to help?"

"What do I do first?"

Analene would show Lori how to cut and clean the peppers and how to start the ground beef. And then she'd suggest Lori go sit down at the kitchen table and talk to her and that way Lori wouldn't get any tomato sauce or grease on her clothes. And before you knew it, Analene would have the entire meal prepared about the time Chris came in from school.

He'd invite Analene to eat with them and she'd murmur some quiet objections before sitting down with them to eat. It was, as far as Lori was concerned, a perfect arrangement. Chris got a good meal, Lori didn't have to cook, and Analene didn't have to eat alone.

The only real problem Lori had experienced in the first two months of marriage had been about money. Lori's money. She had saved most of her salary the previous year and Chris had saved credit card receipts. So she didn't understand why when she went shopping one day for a few items to brighten their home Chris got upset. They needed a rug for their bare bedroom floor, some drapes and curtains to replace the sunburnt rags that presently hung over the windows, some pretty placemats for the kitchen table, and some other odds and ends.

When Chris came in, he yelled, "Jesus Christ, what is all this?"

Lori was so shocked by his reaction that she started crying. Besides, she hated hearing the Lord's name taken in vain, especially when Jesus would want her to have every item she'd just purchased.

He went about the room like an auditor, checking price tags. "Lori, you spent over six hundred dollars. *Six hundred dollars.*"

Since all the items were there in the open, their existence and need obvious, Lori didn't see the point in enumerating the reasons she'd bought them. All one had to do was look around the house to see the items that needed replacing.

And rather than appear selfish by pointing out that all the money they had almost was Lori's and that Chris was no longer even working, and that it was probably illegal to shout at a person for spending her own money, she just got up and walked out of the house.

77

A few blocks away she found a Little League baseball game in progress and decided to disappear into the small crowd in the bleachers. There she would sit until Chris grew frantic with worry over her whereabouts and hired a private detective with a bloodhound to find her. Or until her bottom got tired from sitting on the board seat. Whichever came first.

Something else. One morning in church Chris had been looking through her wallet and found, stuck between some pictures, the cancelled checks she'd written him before they'd married, back when he'd been flat broke and needed money to come visit her. He'd written a nasty little note (Lori could tell it was nasty because he had scribbled it so rapidly) that asked, "Are you going to carry these until I pay you back?" Lori had felt bad because she had considered the money a gift and had simply forgotten the cancelled checks were even in her wallet. She'd put them there only so her mother wouldn't find them. Lori had torn up the checks right in church to demonstrate the money had been an outright gift, like God's love. But now, now she wished she had them back. She'd turn them over to a collection agency so a little man with slits for eyes, wearing bright yellow pants, could go harass Chris.

Lori sighed, deciding she couldn't hold out for more than another minute. Her bottom was numb. She watched the smallest boy on either team approach the plate, dragging his bat through the dirt and looking at his mother, who happened to be sitting next to Lori.

The mother smiled and crossed her fingers. "Oh, I hope he gets a hit."

The child stood at the plate and pushed his too-big batting helmet up from his nose, standing with his head tilted back so he could see the pitcher. The batter was a tiny ten-year-old, and the pitcher was a whopping twelve-year-old left-hander.

"He gets so nervous," the child's mother said. "He thinks if he doesn't get a hit, his father'll be mad."

"Here's hoping," Lori said, crossing her fingers too, thinking that when the batter was on base, she'd go find the rude person yelling, "Easy out, easy out!" and tell him off.

Just as the pitcher began winding up, two hands came up through the wooden bleachers and grabbed both of Lori's ankles.

She jumped and screamed. A banshee wail. She hadn't yet recovered from the emotional scene at the house and was still edgy.

Her scream caused the little baseball player at the plate to drop his bat and start crying.

Chris was under the bleachers, smiling up at Lori, his hands still on her ankles.

Lori patted the hand of the batter's mother and said, "I'm so sorry. Really, I am so sorry."

She ran from the bleachers, head ducked, thinking that such horrible moments had never entered her life before Chris had. There had been the black child in Abilene, watching Chris explore inside her shorts; the wedding, with the put-this-ring-in-your-nose line; now this. She felt as though she had to dodge bullets.

Chris caught her and took her hand but she didn't stop running until she was well away from the stunned Little Leaguers.

"Lori, I'm sorry I yelled. It's a bad habit from my childhood. I'll try to do better."

She didn't answer. He was going to have to work on more than volume control.

As the summer wore down, Lori began to feel a great dread, as though the plague were spreading quickly toward Waco and she'd be the first to get it. But the plague wasn't coming; she wished it were so simple. It was school.

She loved the kids but there was always going to be at least one parent who saw his or her (usually her) mission in life as harassing the teacher. This parent always believed her child was exceptional and you could see her coming, smiling without a bit of warmth. They kept these smiles refrigerated until needed. And they said things like, "Well, we're having Jimmy tested next Monday. The doctor doesn't know whether he's hyperactive or a genius."

And these parents gave her killing headaches. In fact, Lori hadn't left Abilene until she'd made certain she had a prescription for

Darvon. She could have left all her shoes in Abilene, but not that prescription.

Right in the middle of her anxiety about the resumption of school, Chris gave her something else to think about. Lately he kept mentioning Sandy. Sandy this, Sandy that, Sandy just about everything. Lori had never even seen the girl and felt as though they should have been sisters. And Lori couldn't understand when Chris was supposed to be studying at the library all afternoon, how he was spending so much time in conversation with this girl.

"*Who* is Sandy?"

Chris looked shocked. "God, I've known her since I started school. She was in my freshman English class."

"Why is it you've suddenly started talking about her all the time?"

"I don't know. I guess because I didn't see her much last year."

"Where do you see her now?"

"At lunch sometimes."

"And what does Sandy look like?"

"She's fat."

Right, Lori thought. About as fat as that nurse at the doctor's office. Lori had thought she'd broken her back trying to lift a window, and the doctor's nurse had a wide, but not fat, body, very healthy legs, and women like that could swing their hips to beat everything. Chris had drooled all over himself watching her walk up and down the hall of the office. Poor Lori couldn't swing her hips; she couldn't swing what she didn't have.

"Well, if you enjoy this girl's company so much, why don't you bring her over so I can meet her?"

"I don't think you'd have much in common."

"When a man has something in common with a woman and another woman doesn't, that means there's only one thing they could have in common."

"Oh, Lori, come on. You have as much reason to worry about Sandy as I have to worry about you and—I don't know, Sandy's ex-husband."

"Wonderful. You're spending every day with a divorced woman.

80

That's just the most lovely thing I've ever heard."

Being a wife was nothing like being a daughter. Daughters never got dumped. Your parents had you and always loved you regardless. But husbands weren't parents, and they dumped their wives all the time. As the wonderful Sandy had found out. Unless of course she had jettisoned her own husband because she saw a man she liked much better. Say, Chris. Lori felt a tremor of insecurity.

"Well, invite this fat girl over for supper Saturday night. If she's your friend, I want to meet her."

"I can't Saturday night. Carl's going to be here. I forgot to tell you. He's in Dallas this week at some kind of seminar and he's going home Saturday. He's stopping by here and I invited him to eat with us."

"Carl is going to eat with us Saturday night?"

"Yeah. He called. I forgot to tell you."

"*This* Saturday night?"

"Yeah."

"Oh, *shit.*"

"Lori! When'd you start talking like that?"

Cooking, especially cooking for Carl, was one of those activities that Lori viewed with suspicion, something like auto mechanics. Some people could cook, some couldn't. The last time Carl had eaten with them, Lori had made spaghetti, something relatively simple that seemed like a complete meal, and all was going according to plan until she used an entire teaspoon, instead of one-eighth teaspoon, of curry powder. And then she had to listen to comments about the meal all night long. It tasted like floor tile. Were the noodles nonskid? Had she used Mop & Glo? From there the Bawdy Brothers got on the salad, which had been perfect. The tomatoes were rubber. The carrot slices looked almost real but you could tell they were made by Fisher-Price. And on and on and on.

There should have been some family edict that prevented the brothers from getting together, but there wasn't, and Lori had to live through Saturday night. And since the brothers were going to rag her anyway, she'd just make spaghetti again, and this time since she was already warned about the curry powder, the meal would go according to plan.

She wasn't at all sure what she thought of Carl. And Chris seemed to hate him almost as much as he loved him. He couldn't talk to you without getting right in your face, and when he told a joke, he didn't laugh because it was funny; he laughed to make you laugh. And if he had to, he'd jerk on your arm or push your shoulder until you did.

Then too, she felt guilty around him because she wished, in one or two very limited ways, that Chris was more like him. Carl was probably better-looking, in a commercial kind of way, and much more social, but the biggest difference seemed to be in their attitudes toward money. Carl didn't really care how he obtained it; he simply wanted as much as he could get. Chris was, as his father had said, selectively lazy and wanted to acquire it only in particular ways. Somewhere between the two brothers was the right attitude.

On Saturday, Chris seemed especially cheery, and he put on his Gator Navy T-shirt, which was showing some real signs of wear.

"Why're you wearing that?" she asked.

"Because Carl doesn't have one."

"He doesn't have a beanie with a propeller on it either."

"What?"

"Nothing."

She was too concerned with spaghetti to converse at length about clothes. This meal was looming over her like the final exam had in her 8:00 A.M. history class. Besides, she was going to have to fry ground beef, and every time she saw hot grease, she thought about the little boy at church years ago who had been horribly disfigured by boiling water. If water could do that, what could evil spitting hot grease do? She didn't like thinking about it.

Right before Carl arrived, Chris left to go to the store and returned with a case of Coors, carrying it on his shoulder as though he were a roofer carrying a bundle of shingles. And she'd thought he had quit drinking. Not only had he not quit, but now she was going to have to put up with drunk Bawdy Brothers. They were bad enough sober.

Carl arrived looking like a male model for sportswear out of a men's fashion magazine, wearing white pants and a yellow shirt, his beard gone and now appearing even younger than Chris. In fact, he made his younger brother, who hadn't shaved that morning and may as well have not bothered dressing, look downright grubby.

Carl looked him over and said, "Hey, you didn't have to dress up for me."

"I didn't."

He kissed Lori on the cheek as she stood at the sink shredding lettuce for salads and said, "Salads by Fisher-Price?"

She sighed. "Whatever you say."

He looked at the stove and opened his mouth. "God, I didn't realize I was going to be so lucky. Floor tile too."

The brothers went out back to oil their spirits with Coors while Lori cooked. Everything was proceeding perfectly—she had properly set the table, the ground beef had received only one-eighth teaspoon of curry powder, she had remembered the parsley flakes for the garlic bread. Except the brothers returned to the house, probably just to confuse her, and sat in the dining room as though she were running behind. She couldn't be behind though because she had never given them a specific time to eat.

Okay, now, she told herself. Ignore them and watch the bread. But she listened to them anyway because she never knew exactly what she might learn. The Grays were one weird family.

"You tell her about the trial?" Carl asked.

"Are you kidding? You think I'm crazy?"

"Well, she's going to find out anyway. You think she'll watch the six o'clock news next week and think, well, there are two brothers named Chris and Carl, and they look just like my husband and his brother, but I know that's not them."

"I'll just disconnect the TV next week and take all the newspapers to school."

Lori, watching the bread under the broiler in the oven with one eye, walked to the kitchen doorway and looked into the dining room where the brothers sat. The table looked nice with her china and silver and linen napkins in silver rings. "What trial are you talking about?"

Chris looked at Carl and shook his head. "You've got a big mouth."

Carl shrugged.

"What trial?"

The brothers looked at each other as though silently trying to decide who'd answer her. Finally Chris said, "We've got a cousin named Robert Lewis who's going on trial next week for molesting a child."

This was news to Lori, both about the cousin and the trial. Robert Lewis, he had said. Fortunately for them, the man's name wasn't Gray. "What's that got to do with you?"

"He subpoenaed both of us," Chris said.

Lori began to feel sick, understanding now the reference to the TV and newspaper. Her husband was going to testify in some pervert's trial? What was she going to tell people at church who happened to see Chris on the news? That it wasn't Chris but his twin brother Chris? See, one's named Christopher and the other is named . . . what? Christobal? "Why did he subpoena you?"

Carl picked up a knife from the table and looked at his reflection in the blade. "It's a complicated legal strategy, what we call the victimization defense. He's going to blame all his problems on us."

Forgetting about the bread, she walked into the dining room. "What do you mean, blame it all on you? Blame *what* on you?"

"His personal problems," Carl said, baring his teeth and still looking at the knife blade as though trying to see if he had anything stuck between his teeth. "His perversions, his inability to maintain a normal sex life. You see, we—" He looked at Chris as though seeking guidance. For a moment he seemed stumped. Then he waved his hand as though he'd tell the whole story; she'd hear it soon enough anyway. "When we were little, his mother used to bring him over to our house. She worked and our mother didn't, so he spent a lot of time at our house. He was really a truly cute kid. I mean, you'd have to have seen a picture of him when he was ten to understand. The prettiest black hair with all these little curls. Kinda like ringlets. And skin as smooth as a marble statue. He was probably the cutest kid I've ever seen, and I'm including the movies and television when I say that. In fact, he was so cute and feminine-looking we used to call him Bobby Louise."

Lori was feeling nauseous. She had in fact read an inscription in Chris's high school yearbook from a Robert who had insinuated a sexual relationship with him. She couldn't remember now exactly how it had read but it had referred to Chris as a good "piece of ass." She was feeling worse and worse. A defense other than the twin-brother ruse was going to be necessary.

Chris said, "We'd get out in the backyard and get all dirty, and Mom would make us take a bath. We all three bathed together. And Carl and I used to flip a coin to see who'd get to rub baby oil on Bobby Louise when we got through. We loved shining that boy up. He had skin like you wouldn't—"

"This is a *boy* you're talking about?"

"Yes," Chris said, irritated with the interruption, "but you've got to understand how pretty he was. He hardly looked like a boy at all."

"Well," Carl said, "he looked like a boy when *you* got through with him." To Lori, Carl said, "Chris loved to get oil all over his hand and . . ." He didn't say it but made a circle with his fist and then moved it back and forth.

"It was just a hand job," Chris said. "It wasn't like we were sodomizing him or anything."

Lori sat before she fell, hand in front of her face to cover her open mouth. My God in heaven. The people of Waco were going to hear about The Grays and Bobby Louise? This would be in the newspapers? On television? Her husband and his brother giving hand-job motions to the jury?

"Something's burning," Carl said.

This couldn't be. Why hadn't she probed more deeply into that yearbook inscription, found out about Bobby Louise before they'd gotten married, and gone to visit him to see the extent of her future husband's perversions?

"There's smoke coming from the kitchen."

She couldn't begin to gauge the extent of damage this would do to them all. Or maybe in these perversion trials, the media coverage was limited. How could she find out?

"Lori," Chris said. "First: we're kidding; second: something's burning."

The words sunk in slowly, as though she were being aroused from a dream. Someone was shouting at her as she slept. "Kidding? You were kidding?"

Now the brothers were laughing, as though something were funny, hilarious, and Carl reached to backhand Chris on the shoulder. "She bought it," he said. "She bought it. I knew she would."

Chris, laughing just as loud as Carl, walked into the kitchen, pointing at Lori as he passed. "She did, she bought the whole story. I hope the encyclopedia salesmen never find out where we live. God, we'd have every one of them coming by here, every damn one." He disappeared into the kitchen and yelled, "Hey, come in here."

Carl, laughing and shaking his head, looking right at Lori as though she were the eternal butt of all good jokes, walked into the kitchen.

"I've heard of black bread, but this is the first I've ever seen," Chris said.

"Yeah, it's extra crispy."

"It'll go great with the Armstrong vinyl spaghetti."

Lori, her jaw clenched, got up and walked to the front door. She wasn't about to serve any food to these two clowns, not now, not ever. They'd almost given her a heart attack, caused her to have a nightmare in the daylight, and made her mad, mad, mad.

They were laughing so hard, trying to find the Tonka tomatoes, that they didn't even notice when she left.

She required penance of Chris for three or four days after the Bobby Louise story. His duties involved mostly washing dishes and cleaning house, and she was thinking about adding orange juice in bed, but she didn't. Still, every time he got that amused look on his face, she knew he was thinking about the big joke, and she gave serious consideration to clobbering him with a brick. He didn't help his own cause by saying, more than once, "I just wish I'd had a camera. The look on your face was classic."

"I just wish I was convinced it was a joke and you never knew a Bobby Louise. Both of you are perverts."

Their sex life wasn't what Lori had envisioned before they'd married. The boy who had told her he was oversexed and would wear her out daily had started laughing right in the middle of the act the other night.

"What's wrong?" she had asked.

"God, I'm thirsty."

"Well, do you want a drink or do you want to finish?"

"I want the coldest drink of water in the house."

It was just like a man to introduce a woman to an activity, teach her to love it, and then lose interest. Chris hadn't lost interest altogether, but he certainly wasn't wearing her out. He needed a stimulant, he said.

"Talk dirty to me. That'll help."

"Okay. I want you to jump my bones."

"Lori, that's not dirty."

He wanted her to use the F-word, which she didn't use, and then he wanted her to tell him about one other guy she'd made love to. One other guy? Did he think that she had a file of dossiers, that all she had to do was haul one out, pick one from hundreds, maybe thousands? She wouldn't have told him any such thing, and she certainly wasn't going to now.

Still, between using the F-word and going without, she found a middle ground—new and unusual places to make love. They did it in the backyard, in the car at the park and at the lake, and Chris, who always took suggestions to an extreme, discovered not a new place but a new time one night when her mother called.

She was lying on the bed after her shower, feeling clean and slippery, talking to her mother when Chris walked into the bedroom. He moved around the bed slowly, checking the view from every angle, and then he lay down beside her. He started kissing her stomach, and she would have told him to stop, but her mother was on a boring story about some great uncle Lori had never even known, so she watched Chris's mouth climb slowly to her breasts. About the time Mrs. Conner got to the part about the uncle's recent surgery, Lori was kissing the top of Chris's head to encourage him. When the uncle was closed up and out of surgery and back in his room because the doctors couldn't find anything wrong, Chris was stripping. And he entered her just as the uncle up and died for no apparent reason. Chris was on top, his face on the left side of Lori's head while she tried to hold the receiver squeezed between her right shoulder and ear.

"Ummm," Lori said.

"Yes, it's really a strange story."

"Umm hmm."

"Well, how are *you* doing?" Mrs. Conner asked.

"Umm hmm," she sang.

Mrs. Conner returned to her story about the uncle, remembering the most important part, the reason she'd brought it up. The uncle's children wanted to sue for malpractice and they were having trouble getting the records from the hospital. They suspected the records were being altered. Mrs. Conner stopped suddenly and the line went silent.

"What's that noise?" she asked. "Is that a siren?"

Lori swallowed, realizing the noise was a high-pitched whine she herself was making. She lifted her face up, bringing her mouth away from the phone, trying not to sound like an ambulance, trying to keep her mother from realizing her daughter had just topped the big hill on the roller coaster.

"Lori?"

She'd never in her life have the discipline necessary to keep her mouth shut at this particular time, and she said, "Oohhhhh."

"I know, I know, it's terrible to think a hospital would do that."

"Goddd!"

"Lori, I wish you wouldn't talk like that."

7

During the first week of his junior year, when he was loaded down with business courses, Chris discovered a depressing fact—he was becoming a *Republican*. This revelation came as he sat in a class listening to a professor tell them they were going to set up a business of their choosing, design the financing and marketing, and make it a success. Excitement was suddenly in the air; students who all their lives had waited for the chance to foist widgets onto the American public got glazed looks of ecstasy. Chris didn't have any objection to a project, any more than he objected to reading a book about the Marshall Plan in history.

But it hit him—he was supposed to be doing this for the *rest of his life*. He had embarked on the study of making money.

He had several conversations with Sandy about his desire to change his major—to what he wasn't sure, but he wanted to change.

Sandy was the sort of person with whom he could discuss any matter, whether it was menstrual cramps or the Hindus. She wasn't a person he was going to introduce Lori to, however, regardless of the demand. The two women would be natural enemies, on the opposite sides of the barricades. Sandy was coarse and uninhibited, and she had the strangest and wildest hair he'd ever seen. He wasn't even sure what color it was—blackish maroon, maybe, with lighter tints of red. And she was as brassy-acting as she was insecure. Orphaned at an early age, she told people her mother has been a Pontiac, her father an eighteen-wheeler, the two vehicles involved in the accident that had killed her parents. But she'd been "born" at the moment of impact because she'd been shot down the road to truth. Actually, she insisted, she was glad her life had followed its track because otherwise she would have grown up stupidly happy and ignorant when there was no reason to be happy.

Chris had been attracted to her because she'd speak freely about women, a subject upon which he knew he was endlessly confused, and he wanted some insight. And he could also discuss anything, including religion, with her. He could wonder aloud if religion really was the opiate of the people without being branded an intellectual atheist or the conversation being considered a slanderous assault on God.

She concurred with his opinion that he would be miserable as a Republican.

"The problem is," he said, "I don't know what else I want to do. Coach, maybe. Or teach."

"Oh, right, you'd love teaching. The first time you tried to get a kid to think, you'd be burnt at the stake."

"Well, coaching maybe."

"Sure. You want Bubba's father calling you at three in the morning to ask why *you ain't playing his son*," she said with a bumpkin drawl.

He'd had a thought, a far-fetched one. Maybe he'd be a hospital chaplain. Maybe he should transfer to S.M.U. and go to the liberal school of theology there. He'd like dealing with people when all the bullshit had been stripped from their lives, when the issues were simple and basic—life and death, survival, authentic human relationships. He'd deal daily with the gut issues and wouldn't get overcome with the mundane—utility deposits, gas for the lawn mower, oil changes on the car, wrong numbers on the telephone. He'd mentioned the thought in passing once to Lori, and she'd all but hooted him from the house.

"A chaplain? You don't even believe in God."

"What're you talking about?"

"Oh, yeah, you believe in some clockmaker God, the one who set the world ticking and then walked off."

"I don't have any problem in praying to Timex, Inc. 'Our father who's switched to quartz, hallowed be thy accuracy.'"

"You see what I mean? You can't even discuss God without getting sacrilegious."

His second favorite topic with Sandy, one which made him feel traitorous, was how to make Lori tougher. He didn't like discussing his wife with another woman, but he didn't know what else to do. If the principal at school criticized her, she came home and cried. If the kids were mean, she came home and cried. If a parent jumped on her, she came home and cried. She got terrific headaches, popped Darvon like peppermints, took two-hour naps, and then woke up so washed out she was useless.

She came home one afternoon teeth-gritting mad, and Chris thought, oh, boy, today someone else is tossing down the Darvon. She'd finally told somebody where to stick it. She threw her books and papers onto the couch and then stood in the middle of the living room breathing like a cartoon bull.

"This lady," she said, shaking her finger at him. "This *lady* came barging in just as the kids were leaving, I mean like a real steamroller. I asked her if I could help her, very nicely even though I could tell *she* wasn't going to be nice. And she said, 'I doubt it.' Can you believe that? What kind of *stupid* person starts a conversation like that? She said from the stories her son told, she doubted that I could help her.

"Well, I had to go to the bathroom because I hadn't been since lunch, and I could tell she was probably going to preach for an hour. And when I told her I'd be right back, you know what she said? She said, 'I'm in a hurry.'"

Lori, still pointing and shaking her finger at him, nodded and said, "That made me mad."

Chris stood, anxious to hear the story, wanting her to say she'd walked from the classroom and knocked the obnoxious bitch on her ass on the way out. He wanted all the details. "You did go to the bathroom, didn't you?"

"No. I couldn't because she *was in a hurry.* She had to tell me that her precious little boy, her precious little boy who *pees* on other children in the restroom, her precious little boy isn't being challenged. She said, 'Jason could read when he was three years old.'"

She was angrier than he'd ever seen her. They had met in the center of the room, and Lori had grabbed the front of his shirt and was shaking him.

She yelled, "This is the little boy who writes on his own forehead with Magic Markers!" Suddenly she released his shirt and shook her head, sighing. "I was going to be nice. I asked her how she thought I could help her little genius. And she said, 'You're the teacher, and you're asking me?' And then I got so mad I told her that her little genius had emotional problems and I'm not a psychiatrist.

"And then, and then," Lori said, throwing her arms out to indicate the enormity of the situation, "she went into this rage. It was like—well, she just went into a rage. I thought the old bag was going to have a heart attack right in my class. She started telling me about all her friends on the school board and how she knows this one and that one and if I thought I could slander her child I'd better think again. She was going to see that I was fired for incompetence. And she went flying out of the room to the principal's office before I could even apologize."

"Apologize?" Chris yelled. "Apologize? For what? What the hell are you talking about? You should've coldcocked the fat bitch."

Lori looked confused. "She's not fat. Did I say she was fat?"

"Lori, get on with the story."

"Okay, but she's not fat. Anyway, in about two minutes the principal called me on the intercom. Could I come to the office? I went down there, and, and, thank God, the lady was gone. The principal said he was sure I hadn't really meant Jason was mentally ill—I *never* said he was mentally ill—and he thought Jason would be better off in Elizabeth's class. I was a new teacher and didn't have enough experience to help a gifted child like Jason. A *gifted child*. This child is so gifted he wrote an obscenity on another little boy's lunch box, and he wrote 'fack.' The gifted little fart can't even spell."

Lori exhaled a tremendous sigh and fell backward onto the couch, sprawled there. "I got so mad."

"And?" Chris said. He walked to the couch and looked down on her, feeling the adrenaline, ready to go find this complaining woman and let Lori play tee ball with her. Give Lori a baseball bat and see how far she could knock the woman's head. "And?"

"I started crying."

They talked about dealing with people and she knew how. She handled herself with confidence. In fact, he watched one day from the hall at school and was impressed with her as a teacher. But she couldn't deal with the consequences of a confrontation.

Her adoptive mother in Waco was one of her co-teachers named Elizabeth, a wiry little lady who looked like a retired hooker. She had a wrinkled face that had seen things, but she probably made the perfect grandmother. Loving but tough. She had married and divorced (everybody seemed divorced) a wealthy man and had ended up with a large piece of property twenty miles west of town. She encouraged Chris and Lori to go out there as often as they could so Lori could relax.

They accepted the offer because it was a beautiful place with hills overlooking grassy plains. In the evenings it was so serene under a soft sky and gentle breezes that they were reluctant to return to

93

town. Occasionally they took food with them and ate supper on the bank of a small creek, watching the water flow slowly past their feet. The creek wound around the property below limestone overhangs and they talked about getting inner tubes and floating its length.

One Saturday afternoon they were standing on a rock shelf that overlooked miles and miles of deserted countryside. The sun had set, the horizon had lost its color, and the earth had fallen into a sigh.

Lori said, "I'm going to take my clothes off. Nobody can see us. Can they?"

"There's nobody to see us."

"Do you think I should?"

"Only if you want to."

She undressed, slipping out of pale yellow shorts and matching T-shirt, monitoring his face for reaction. Once she'd stripped to her underwear, she stopped, thumbs in the waistband of her panties, waiting for a sign of disapproval. Then she asked, "You won't tell anybody about this, will you? I mean, especially Carl."

"I won't tell anybody, especially Carl."

"Because this is just the kind of thing you *would* tell him."

"I promise I won't."

She finished undressing. Her tan from the summer was almost gone, the pale areas that had been covered by her bikini now blending with the rest of her. For a moment she seemed uncomfortable, unsure of what she was to do. Chris started to strip, then decided just to watch for a minute because this spontaneous streak was the part of her he liked best. It was so often buried under rigid notions of proper behavior that he couldn't always tell what was Lori and what was Lori's image. She wanted to be the perfect wife, and the perfect wife was already ready on a moment's notice to leap into bed. Which was all right, Chris thought, but how was he ever to know exactly what her attitude really was?

She stood on the ledge, her eyes closed, her legs spread slightly, arms limp at her sides, feeling the air around her. The elements had claimed her.

He watched, smiling.

The inevitable occurred. Lori and Sandy met.

Chris was eating lunch with Sandy in the Student Union Building, and they were talking about *Play It Again, Sam*, a movie that had been on TV the previous night. Chris told her that he had experienced a problem with a blowdryer similar to Woody Allen's. Lori, who didn't know that "on" switches also functioned as "off" switches, had put the dryer up without turning it off. When he had plugged it in, it had immediately whirred into full blast, blowing a canister of bath powder into the toilet bowl. He'd tried to catch it but had instead knocked from the toilet tank a bottle, uncapped, of Lori's bath oil, and then had jammed his fingers on the side of the bathroom sink. Sandy, with a bite of hamburger in her mouth, couldn't swallow because she was laughing. To prevent herself from choking, she placed one hand on Chris's to shut him up.

In walked Lori.

She was normally very composed in public regardless of the situation, but when he spotted her, twenty feet from his table, she looked as though she'd just witnessed the decapitation of Peter Pan. And he had a difficult time appearing nonchalant because he was well aware of Sandy's warm hand resting atop his. He knew exactly what Lori was thinking: well, he finally found the fleshy body he's always wanted. He stole a quick glance at Sandy, wanting to see her as Lori did, and he could only shake his head.

Sandy was wearing faded Levi's with a cropped white blouse that seemed to have been stuffed with two pumpkins, two very plump pumpkins. And Lori, her natural adversary, stood in a white dress with green borders and buttons. A revolution could start right on the spot, he thought, dwarfing any that had occurred in Russia.

He moved his hand from beneath Sandy's and stood, waving Lori

95

over, wondering why he felt guilty when he'd done nothing. But if he'd done nothing, why did Lori look fatally injured? Depriving her of a smile always made him feel guilty.

He pulled out a chair for her and explained what they had been laughing about, the movie they had watched last night. Remember? But his amusement had vanished. And Lori, her face frozen in partially repaired offense, pulled the offered chair three feet away from the table and sat. Folding her hands in her lap, she said nothing.

"It was really a funny movie," he said, unable to conjure up even half of a ha ha. "It was the funniest thing I've ever seen. That's one of my favorite movies. Of all time probably." Now he knew what a comedian felt as he delivered a monologue to a dead audience. Silence. Black silence. He may as well have been speaking English to a Chinese immigrant.

It occurred to him that he should introduce the two women, and he did, standing, trying to think of a way he could exit. He wanted to run, and the two women's reserved salutations—silent nods of acknowledgment—didn't help his nerves. He began to sweat.

Okay, he thought. I'll find witnesses to my purity. Call forth the diners of this establishment and ask what they saw. Two people talking about a movie, two people who had never been anything but simple friends, as asexual as neighboring rocks. Come forth and speak to this blonde woman who suspects what isn't.

"Why don't you sit down?" Sandy said.

Oh, great, he thought. Another woman ordering Lori's husband around. Way too familiar. And he suddenly knew Sandy was going to say something she shouldn't. He had to get Lori out of the building immediately, even though he had barely touched his hamburger or Coke.

Sandy looked Lori over as though she were an inanimate object and said, "Do you want lunch? Or just a Darvon?"

Chris groaned. Sandy looked at him as though the situation were reversed—Lori was intruding on husband and wife—and gave him a sad shake of the head. This blonde is hopeless. And Lori glared at him as well, freezing one of the co-conspirators who had been talking about her behind her back. She could glare more effectively than anyone he'd known, but this was the first time she'd ever turned her icy eyes onto him.

She made him feel like a slug because he hated to hear women talking about their husbands, and he would never have talked to Sandy about Lori if he hadn't been seriously wanting some advice. That transgression was bad enough, but while Lori was turning him into an icicle, he thought of something else.

One rainy day he had walked with Sandy to her car, and she had been carrying so many books she couldn't get her car keys out of her pocket. When they'd reached the car, she had asked him to get the keys from the pocket of her raincoat. The coat had had one of those trick pockets, through which a hand could pass to a pocket beneath the raincoat, and he'd overshot the first pocket, and his palm had ended up resting on her stomach, making him think of a line from the Song of Solomon: "Thy navel is like a round goblet . . ." The accidental nature of this fondling wasn't what now made him feel guilty; it was the enjoyment they'd both experienced, the urge to cuddle standing beside the car on a rainy day.

He had to get Lori out of the building; she could see a sinful relationship Chris hadn't even realized existed.

He left his hamburger and told Sandy good-bye, escorting Lori onto the street and trying to think of some way to explain the unexplainable.

Before he could think of any story, Lori stopped in the middle of the sidewalk and said, "Why didn't you just *fuck* her right on the table?"

He lost his breath. He had never heard Lori use that word. She got uncomfortable when she heard it used in a movie. And the fact that her mouth had suddenly turned trashy had to be his fault.

Suddenly he saw the divine record of his sins on a sheet of paper that stretched endlessly into space. God's hand added, "Makes wife say F-word."

"Well?" she said.

"Did you hear what you just said?"

She looked away but not before one lonely tear had dripped along her nose. She took a deep breath to drive away a sob, and he felt as if he'd ruined Lori Lynn from Abilene. He walked around her and stood in the street, hoping the move was suicidal, hoping a cussing truck driver with ten felony convictions would come along and flatten him. He deserved it.

"I came by here," she said, but had to stop, looking at her feet until another sob passed. "I came by here because this is an in-service day and I was going to surprise you." She added, "And I did."

He moved a few feet backward into the street, not so far that he'd have to shout to be heard but far enough to challenge a car. "Lori, we were eating and talking about a movie. I said something funny and she choked, and she put her hand on mine so I'd shut up. She was trying to save herself, trying to *keep from dying.* She wasn't holding my hand."

"You said something funny?"

My God, he thought, looking both ways down the street and wondering why there wasn't any traffic. He couldn't say anything funny outside his own house? "Lori, we were talking about a movie I watched with *you,* not her. I wouldn't do anything with her. I love you. You know that."

He waited for a response but got only a sucked-in sob and wrinkled chin. She got a Kleenex from her purse and dabbed carefully at her right eye. The tissue came away with a black stain of mascara.

"I've got to go back to school and my makeup's ruined."

Well, at least they were dealing with the practical side of her again, he thought.

She inhaled and attempted to compose herself. "I'm going back to school now and I hope if I ever do anything this stupid again, I hope God just strikes me dead."

Chris went home, cutting a class and trying to shake the feeling that he would die and go to hell before the sun set. His guilt seemed greater than the offense suggested. Why? He had to take a closer look at his statement to Lori in front of the Student Union Building: "I wouldn't do anything with her." Had he in fact been slowly unzipping his pants where Sandy was concerned? The process had been so natural and nice he had never thought about where it was leading.

And besides the guilt, he carried a feeling of doom as well, a feeling his life was over. He hadn't forgotten he was married; he knew that. But he really had never faced the fact that his love life would be forever limited to one person. He was forever required to ignore any other woman who came along, whether she was Jane Alexander or Deborah Foreman. How could he give up the one thing he had consistently liked about life? He had always loved women in general. Always. And he wasn't after another woman; he didn't want another woman. Not now. Not yet.

He was only twenty-four years old. He could live another sixty years. And a woman was the only true wonder of the world, such a varied mix of mystery and desire.

My God, he thought. This is worse than being a Republican.

When Lori came home, she dropped her books and purse on the couch and sat in pure dejection. She removed her shoes, no longer the graceful lady, more the cowboy wanting his boots off sore feet. Looking around, she obviously wanted to talk but didn't know where to start. Finally, she asked, "*What* were you doing with her?"

He told her again what they'd been doing—nothing—and he should have changed the story because Lori still didn't buy the truth. And the more he talked, the more discouraged she seemed to

99

become. And then she was crying again, this time unworried about her makeup.

"What am I supposed to do?" she asked. "I can't cook, I can't teach, I can't do anything."

The twist in the conversation threw him for a moment. What was she saying? Lunch with Sandy had arisen because Lori was a klutz? What? "Lori, this hasn't got anything to do with you."

"It has everything to do with me."

Then he understood. This was the woman with whom he shopped for groceries, not because he wanted to but because one night when he'd told her he wasn't going, she'd looked as though he'd kicked her in the stomach. She'd stood suddenly dejected with her list in her hand, and said, "I thought you *liked* going with me." This was the woman who drove him crazy in the car because every time he looked to his right to check for traffic, she smiled. She thought he was looking at her.

She now said, "You don't laugh like that with me."

"That's not so and you know it. We laugh all the time."

"You were having *fun*."

8

Teaching had ruined Lori's life, had made her sickly and wimpy and unattractive, just as if she'd caught some terrible disease and had a leg amputated. If teaching hadn't disfigured her, then she'd still be Chris's reason for being. But reasons for being didn't have to take Darvon and late afternoon naps.

Nor did they walk into the Student Union Building and see their husbands courting some other woman. The scene had shocked Lori almost out of her shoes. She'd seen the look on Chris's face before, that same look, when he had been trying to make her laugh. And

100

Lori had probably laughed and placed her hand on Chris's, right before they'd walked into the bedroom and made love.

She'd never thought men and women could relate platonically, although Chris had convinced her that Sandy was just a friend. And it had occurred to her as she'd walked into the Student Union Building and seen her husband gazing lovingly into the eyes of another woman, "relating platonically" was just a euphemism for the F-word.

Her marriage wasn't working at all. Nothing was working. She didn't even know who she was anymore. She had a new name, a new house, a new husband, a new job, a new church. For almost twenty years, she had known people who had loved and appreciated her. She couldn't walk in the door of the church without twenty people telling her she looked beautiful, she looked as pretty as the spring day outside, she looked lovely. No one told her anymore. She couldn't even fish a compliment out of Chris. If she tried, if she asked, "Do I look okay?" he said, "Yeah. Why?"

She even had a lousy name. Gray. It probably made people think of a plastic raincoat. Every Sunday morning Lori read the wedding announcements in the newspaper to see how the girls were doing on names. She felt sorry for those who didn't trade up. Congratulations to Shirley Longbotham who married Ben Darling. But Miss Montgomery who had married Mr. Snodgrass had to really be in love.

There were alternatives to her present life. Her parents could send them money so Lori didn't have to teach. She didn't dislike teaching; it would have been fine if the obnoxious parents stayed at home and if principals were prohibited from talking to their teachers, eavesdropping over the intercom, requiring ridiculous paper work. But the only solution at the moment seemed to be for her parents to support them. They'd be glad to do so since Chris was a member of the family.

But when she suggested that very thing to Chris, he gave her the strangest look, as though she'd expressed an interest in moving to Haiti.

"Your father's not paying my way through school. Nobody is but me."

"*I'm* already paying your way through school."

"You are not. A loan and the GI Bill are. Not one penny of your money's going to school."

What hairs the boy did split. What difference did it make if Lori's money went for groceries or tuition? It was all the same thing. "I don't want to teach."

Chris adopted his fatherly face and said, "Lori, I don't want to be the one to tell you this, but everybody's got to grow up sooner or later. I guess this is your time."

This was the same boy who had told her the other day she should tell off the next parent who gave her trouble, just say, "Go fuck yourself," and if she got fired for doing so, no big deal. They'd make it some way, but she didn't have to take crap off anybody. And now she wanted to avoid ever being put in that situation, and he refused to agree.

She called in sick the next day and when Chris had left the house, she called her mother to ask for money. And there was so much wrong that all of her frustration boiled right up and she couldn't even talk. Her mother told her it was expensive to cry long distance and maybe Lori could get herself together and call collect.

Wonderful. Lori was dying and her mother wanted to conserve her daughter's money. She sat on the bed for a minute, taking several deep breaths, and then called her mother collect.

"Now I know why people commit suicide."

"What?" her mother asked.

"I said I know why people commit suicide."

"What on earth are you talking about?"

"Suicide, Mother. Where you kill yourself because you're so unhappy you just want to die."

"Oh, Lori, let's please don't go through this again. Please? Okay? Do you know how unhappy it makes me to hear you talk like that?"

Lori shook her head. Her mother made it sound as though she called daily threatening to kill herself. The *only* time she'd ever done such a thing had been when they'd shipped her off to a school in Virginia. How she had ended up there, she still wasn't sure, but her parents had tricked her with some slick brochures that showed lovely young girls riding horses and playing tennis and attending formal dances. And when Lori was finally coerced and bribed and fooled, she went, only to find a bunch of snotty girls who had called her Tex. And the very first time she had stood on a fence to pet a horse, the animal had all but bitten her entire arm off above the elbow. For weeks, she'd had a horseshoe bruise of mean teeth marks. One time Lori had mentioned suicide in a phone call, and then she'd practically had to live with a counselor. They'd given her a bunch of tests as though she were warped.

"I wasn't talking about killing myself, Mother. I was just talking in general about being unhappy."

They talked for an hour. Her mother gave her a speech about life and unhappiness and said she had a lot of faith in her. When she set out to do something, she could do it. Hadn't she taken piano lessons for a whole year once? She could succeed at teaching and being a wife at the same time. She could get everything under control. And Mrs. Conner would have Lori's father call Chris and see if they needed any money.

"Just send us money, Mother. Chris won't take it from Daddy."

"Then how can I send it?"

"Just put it in our bank account and I won't tell him."

Mrs. Conner thought maybe the men ought to handle the financial affairs, but she wanted a promise from Lori that she wouldn't do anything foolish.

Lori didn't tell Chris her father was going to call, and she tried to listen to the conversation but Chris was whispering. Still, the longer they talked on the phone, the better she felt. Obviously her father was telling Chris he'd have to accept a monthly allowance. And now that she thought of it, she wished she'd filed a complaint on his language. He'd been about to go shopping for new boots the other night when she had pointed out that his toes had come through the ends of his socks. And he wouldn't change socks. F-word 'em if they don't like my socks, he'd said. Her father should also be telling him, "You clean up your language, son."

And then Chris said on the phone, "No, no, we don't need any money."

Lori's mouth flew open and she stomped across the room, pushing the button down on the phone and disconnecting them. This was *exactly* the way she'd felt in Virginia, completely unloved, ignored, and disregarded. But back then she'd been young, and now she wasn't. So she locked herself into the bathroom and plotted her future.

She was moving to New Orleans and becoming a thousand-dollar-a-night call girl with her own bordello and a waiting list a year long. She'd become famous for her bright red dresses, and people from all over the world would make their last requests before they died—to sleep with Lori Lynn just once. She'd grant interviews to her hometown newspaper: "Lady In Red to Parents: Drop Dead!"

The next morning she didn't even call in sick but Chris woke her up anyway because he wanted to talk. So she put her pillow over her face and didn't say anything. She felt too bad to say anything. She felt too bad to even cry. So Chris tried peeking under the pillow and then put his hand on her hip and made her wallow around like a side of beef. He thought he could amuse her as though she were Boxcar Sandy.

"Are you just going to quit on me?" he asked.

He sounded almost concerned, almost loving, and he gently massaged her stomach. So she looked from beneath the pillow to make sure he was being serious and not the closet beatnik she'd seen in the Student Union Building.

"If you want me to, I'll quit school and get a job," he said.

She blinked, trying to bring him into focus. She'd never had a serious conversation this early in the morning and her eyes hadn't begun to function yet. "I want you to stop being pig-headed about taking money from Daddy."

He brushed hair back from her eyes and said, "I hate to tell you this, but he didn't offer me any money."

"I don't believe that."

"It's true. He didn't offer a penny."

"That's because you told him we didn't need any."

"No, he said he wants you to grow up, and if you don't do it now, you won't ever do it."

Grow up, shit, she thought, and replaced the pillow over her head, pulling it tightly against her face and giving consideration to smothering herself. And she would have if only she could have also attended her own funeral to see the weeping of all those who now deserved to weep.

"If you don't want to teach anymore, I'll quit school and get a job."

"As what?" she asked into the pillow. "Bellhop on a boxcar?"

"What?" he asked, trying to remove her pillow. "I can't understand you."

Lori was feeling worse and worse. Everyone she loved was telling her she had only two options—continue teaching or let her husband get a minimum-wage job so they could eat red beans and rice for the rest of their lives. There were about ten zillion options but she'd been given two.

"Life sucks," she yelled.

"Live rocks? What'd you say? Move that pillow so I can talk to you."

But she didn't move the pillow and finally Chris left. She conducted an interview with a wide-eyed Abilene newspaper reporter for a while, telling him that little girls were abused and misled and letting him look up her red dress. She made him stop peeking so he could get this quote in its entirety: "My mother and father made me think they'd do anything for me but I learned they meant only real simple things, like talk. Talk's cheap. When I found out the truth, I moved to New Orleans and started making sixty thousand a day. No more cheap talk. Money talks, bullshit walks. Get that down, boy, and stop looking up my dress."

She fell asleep talking to the nerdy little reporter. And she either had a terrible nightmare or dreamed she was in *Private Benjamin*, she wasn't sure which, because she heard someone yelling at her as though she were a private in the army. A strange voice commanded, "Wake up! Wake up!" And a rough hand shook her until she got whiplash.

Waking up the first time was always difficult, but the second time was nearly impossible, which was why Chris always threatened her if she went back to bed on Saturday mornings. "If you go back to bed, I'm leaving now and won't be back until tomorrow morning. I'm not going to look at a zombie all day." But now all the drapes were being pulled open and that same rough hand sat her up in bed. She could have spit Seven-Up more easily than she could have maintained an upright position, but the hand jerked her up as she fell.

"Wake up, Lori Gray. Wake up and see the sunshine."

She recognized the voice. It was the psychologist from Virginia come to give her the test. You always had to answer questions when you said the word suicide publicly. Would you rather look at a sunset or meet your friends at the drugstore? Would you rather be the lady in red or a bimbo named Sandy?

"Come on, Lori, you've got to wake up. Open those beautiful eyes."

Lori opened her eyes, and there was, of all people, Elizabeth.

Why would Elizabeth be in her bedroom? Oh, Lord. She'd seen the interview in the paper and had come to wash her mouth out with soap. Ladies, even in red, weren't allowed to say, "Bullshit walks," or "Life sucks," or any such thing. Or maybe she'd taken Elizabeth with her to New Orleans as a lady-in-waiting.

"Come on, come on," Elizabeth said and pulled her up from the bed.

She guided her into the bathroom, where Lori kicked the base of the toilet and probably broke her toes. Just like that, Elizabeth pulled her gown over her head, then pushed her into the shower before the water was even warm. Lori stood with her mouth open, too surprised to do anything but stare at the shower head.

"Is this what you use?" Elizabeth asked, sticking her hand around the shower curtain, offering Head and Shoulders.

She didn't—it was Chris's brand—but she took it anyway, too tired and confused to argue. If Elizabeth wanted her to use it, she would.

She showered, hearing Elizabeth singing, "It's a beautiful morning" as she came and went. The older teacher said that Lori's underwear was on the sink; she should hurry up because they were already late. They both had children who were suffering through substitutes, children who were waiting on them, who depended on them.

Well, now Lori had something to teach those kids. Always view with extreme suspicion any adult who said you had to grow up. They were the same people who told you suffering leads to wisdom and hardships will make you strong. If that were so, her own mother and father would be sleeping outside on the ground and spending their days trying to catch the flu. Only other people were supposed to grow up; those who preached the sermons didn't have to do diddly shit, to borrow from Chris's vocabulary.

Somehow she ended up in Elizabeth's Toyota, and when she pulled the visor down to look in the mirror, she was surprised to see she looked as she did every morning. Somehow she had makeup on and her hair was brushed, all of which was proof, she supposed, that she could get ready with her eyes closed.

"If you'd smile, you'd look like your normal lovely self."

She thought, I may go to school, but I'm not smiling.

"What do you say we go eat breakfast?" Elizabeth asked, starting the car. "It'll be my treat. And we're two hours late anyway."

They left the house and Lori still wasn't certain she was awake; the world seemed a fuzzy place, hard to see even if your eyes were open. She wasn't sure about what was real and what wasn't. She wasn't even sure about who she was anymore. Had something changed? If so, what? Life was always the same, wasn't it? She didn't know. But she apparently was going to continue teaching, and if she was, she had an important question.

"How do you deal with these parents who're—who're so hostile?"

"Be nice," Elizabeth said. "Always be nice and blame the problem on something or someone else. The system's always good. The system gets blamed for everything. That's why people hate it. If someone comes to you mad, tell them it's all the system's fault, and then stand around and complain with them. Complain like crazy; the more the better. If they get mad, you get mad. You know, things like, 'Something's got to be done with the system. It's just killing us.' Then when they leave, they're not mad at you and your hair's not even messed up or anything. Then you go home to your family and forget about it."

"Always blame the system," Lori said.

"And if someone asks what they can do about the system, tell them to be sure and vote. Don't ever tell them the truth. Don't ever tell them changing the system is impossible. Just tell them to get all their friends registered to vote in the next election."

"So there is a system?" Lori asked.

"Maybe," Elizabeth said, smiling. "Nobody knows."

9

Since meeting Lori, Chris had not been required to deal with the Conners alone until Lori decided to withdraw from life and sleep all the time. He and Mr. Conner had occasionally watched baseball or football games on television during visits, and Chris had discovered the man had a sense of humor. They'd been watching Reggie Jackson at bat one Saturday afternoon when Mr. Conner had said, "You know Reggie leads the league in batting against left-handers that use Odoreaters, don't you?" Chris, who prided himself on his mental quickness, hadn't understood the comment until the network flashed onto the screen a graphic showing Reggie's lifetime batting average in home games played at night in August when facing right-handed pitchers coming off three days' rest.

But he had been impressed with Mr. Conner's level-headed approach to handling Lori during her withdrawal.

"Listen," Mr. Conner said, "I know what you're up against. She and her mother both think being unhappy's something terrible, like dying in your sleep. But let's draw the line, just like the Alamo. If she doesn't grow up now, hell, she won't ever grow up. We've been through this before. I tried putting her to work during the summer, we tried a boarding school one year, but this time there's a difference. This time we've got her mother on our side. I say that. We've got her as long as she's convinced Lori's not suicidal."

"Suicidal?" Chris asked quietly because Lori was sitting nearby in the living room eavesdropping. Suicidal? Did a person contemplating suicide do her nails? Well, maybe, if she was Lori. She'd be concerned about the kind of corpse she made, but he couldn't believe she was a potential victim of her own hand.

"I don't think that's a problem," Chris whispered. "She's doing her nails."

"Why're you whispering?"

"Because she's ten feet away."

"Oh. Well, if you see any problem in that regard, let us know. Otherwise, let's hold the line. You keep Lori there and I'll keep her mother here if I have to tie her up."

Chris had been uncertain how to handle the matter when Lori had decided to stay in bed on the second day. He had called Elizabeth, who hadn't seemed overly concerned but who had offered to help. And whatever she had done had worked.

Lori came home that afternoon from school acting like an adult. She seemed neither happy nor sad but somewhere in between. And Chris was so glad she'd gotten up and gone to school that he'd hugged her. She collapsed in his arms and he thought he'd brought on another fit. But he hadn't.

"Will you keep me even if I'm ugly and sickly?"

"What do you mean, keep you? I'm not planning on donating you to Goodwill. You wouldn't fit through the collection box door."

"Be serious. Please."

"I am serious. I don't have any idea what you're talking about. I want you right here. I want to be married to you forever. I love you, remember?"

She rested her face against his chest. "I'm glad you love me. I hope you always will."

He stood, holding her, thinking that a change in majors, from business to whatever, would require additional schooling, and he'd probably make as good a Republican as something else. He couldn't think of anything better anyway.

"Chris?"

"What?"

"Can we go out to eat tonight? I don't want to cook."

He could tell by her voice she was smiling, but when he put his finger under her chin, wanting to tilt her face upward to verify that she was indeed smiling, she resisted, keeping her head level.

110

"You did all this just so you wouldn't have to cook, didn't you?"

"No, I did it so I could call Mother collect."

She looked up and she was smiling. A little sadly, maybe, but she was smiling.

part two

10

The day Lori and Chris moved from Waco, after his graduation with a BBA degree, several of the neighbors thought they were having a party. Her mother and father, Chris's father, Carl, and several of Chris's friends gathered early on a Saturday morning to help them load a U-Haul truck. Until Chris arrived with the truck, everyone stood around outside on a warm June morning and talked and laughed and drank coffee. The Mr. Coffee machine, which would make only ten cups at a time, was kept in almost constant use.

Lori rather liked her mother's presence when Carl was around. She kept the two brothers from gleefully remembering every dumb thing Lori had ever done. While Mrs. Conner was in attendance, Lori didn't hear, "Remember the time she was worried about getting shocked when she reached into the refrigerator because there wasn't a light bulb in the socket? She was afraid the air was *electrified*." Carl seemed much more interested in impressing Mrs. Conner with his own presence than in making jokes at her daughter's expense.

The two fathers seemed to get along well, primarily, Lori thought, because they were both workaholics. If Mr. Gray had been born in the west part of the state rather than east, and had grown up in the oil field rather than the cotton field, he probably would have been rich. Or maybe he was anyway. Chris speculated that his father banked almost all of his money, and it should have amounted to a large sum by now.

Lori was moving to Austin because Chris was going to work for Carl's law firm. Of all the businesses he had interviewed with, he had been more interested in an investigator's job for lawyers than in anything else. Which meant, of course, that Lori would be seeing Carl more than she wanted to.

She and Chris had driven to Austin one day before he'd made his decision so Lori could see the law offices and look around the city, and she hadn't been impressed until she'd learned that the offices were on the eleventh floor of a bank building that was all gold-colored glass on the outside. When they got off the elevator, they faced a smoked-glass door front with huge gold letters over the doors: "LINDSEY, CHAPMAN. LAWYERS." The offices were rich, quiet, and smelled of money. They were almost seductive.

They had, she learned, entered a harem. Every time she turned around, she saw a beautiful girl that was built like you know what. When she mentioned to Carl, who was guiding them through the maze of offices, that the staff seemed "well-groomed," he said, "That sign over the front door didn't say we were pig farmers."

She didn't want to leave Waco or their house, but they'd had no choice about the house. The landlord's daughter was moving from Florida and was going to live there. Lori had come to love their barren little rent house, even the dust balls. In the days of "fully carpeted," they were like antiques.

They wouldn't have found a nice house in Austin had it not been for her parents, who had told Chris they wanted to make a down payment on a house. They hadn't actually decided to make such an offer, Lori didn't think, until they'd all met in Austin one weekend to look at houses. And all she and Chris could afford was one of the small tract houses in the far north or south parts of town where little houses had sprung up like mesquite trees.

They'd been in one that had a brick front with the other three walls covered with some kind of board, and Mrs. Conner, with a sick look on her face, had said, "Milton, maybe we should tell them about Chris's graduation present."

Mr. Conner, who never liked to appear that he'd been caught off-guard, had slowly nodded his head and said, "Yeah, maybe this would be a good time. You wanta tell them?"

"We decided to make a down payment on a house. Let's go find something nice."

Chris had been opposed at first to accepting a substantial amount of money from his in-laws until he discovered how substantial the amount was: $20,000. The sum put them in a completely different neighborhood. There were no broken-down cars on blocks in the areas where they began looking, no dirty children running around unsupervised in diapers. Instead there were big trees and quiet streets. After making an offer on a brick three-bedroom, two-bath house with a bay window in front, a home with personality and potential, not to mention a covered patio out back with a gas grill, she and Chris drove back to Waco in a good mood.

"I can't believe your parents would give us that much money for a down payment."

"Well, I guess Mother doesn't want me in what she considered another dump."

"We weren't in a dump."

"That's why I said what *she considered* a dump."

"I had to wrestle with taking their money. I felt like my integrity was being compromised."

"Yeah, you wrestled until you heard the amount of money."

"That's right. I figured integrity was nice, but that house was nicer."

Leaving her friends in Waco proved to be even more difficult than Lori had expected. She watched the guys move their furniture from the house to the truck, stepping on each other and colliding in the halls because so many were helping, and several of her friends stopped by to check on the progress. Lori met them all out front and felt as if she were receiving mourners at a funeral. Elizabeth brought lunch, a great stack of chicken salad sandwiches and chips.

Mrs. Conner knew Elizabeth, and they talked for a few moments, creating such a physical contrast that Lori almost laughed. Elegance and beauty in her mother's case, wrinkles and a very coarse appearance in Elizabeth's, but both as lovely and loving as any two women Lori had ever known.

Elizabeth said she didn't handle good-byes well. "So let's just decide now that we'll see each other later in the summer and we won't have to say good-bye. Okay? Oh, please don't cry, Lori. Come here. Now you've got me crying." They hugged for a minute, Lori overcome with thoughts she couldn't express. Elizabeth held her steady, hands on her shoulders, a foot away, and said, "I don't know what I'll do without you. I had two sons but no daughters until you came along."

"She does make a lovely daughter, doesn't she?" Mrs. Conner asked.

"The very loveliest. If she wasn't yours, I'd take her in a second."

Lori didn't want to stand out front and cry all morning so she kissed Elizabeth good-bye and went inside, a move which didn't make her cheery. Her house was all but empty. She wanted to sit down in a deserted spot and tell it good-bye, but there were too many people walking in and out, carrying furniture and boxes and seeking out what was left.

Mr. Gray, who always made her feel tiny, walked in the front door and saw her. "Empty houses aren't happy places, are they?"

"Not unless you're moving in, I guess."

They stood in the now empty living room and looked around. Lori considered how long Mr. Gray had lived alone, decided she could tolerate only so much sadness, and thought about something else. The scratch on the wall. Chris had been acting goofy one night, twirling around like a ballerina, and had almost stuck his finger through the sheetrock."

"Keep an eye on Chris down there," Mr. Gray said. "Carl's not the best influence in the world."

"I notice that every once in a while."

"Chris has been trying to outdo him since the day he was born. The problem is, there's some things Carl does Chris doesn't need to be trying."

"I hope he doesn't try to outdo him on wives."

Mr. Gray laughed. "If he does, he's in trouble with me."

†

The arrival in Austin was met with a bad omen. Lori stopped her car and found in front of it, in the gutter, a dying bat. She'd never seen one before, and she thought it was the most evil, poisonous looking animal she'd ever seen. Its wings looked like parchment paper and seemed to be as old as Dracula himself. She poked it with a stick, thinking it was dead, but it hissed at her, baring its fangs. Lori immediately understood a phrase she'd heard all her life —a bat out of hell—because the tiny monster looked as though it had flown in from the depths of perdition. She showed it to Chris, who said, "It's just a bat," and dropped a brick on it.

She seemed frightened by everything—loud noises, strangers, stray cats. She couldn't sleep at night because she was certain bats lived in the attic and fluttered around at night searching for fat neck veins. Chris thought she was crazy when she wanted to pull up the carpet and look underneath for scorpions.

"There aren't any scorpions under the carpet."

"There could be. I saw one in the garage."

She lacked Chris's enthusiasm for living in Austin. Driving there seemed the quickest route to destruction. Cars careened around curves and over hills on four-lane streets that were barely wide enough to carry two lanes of traffic. She put off grocery shopping until Chris came home, and even then, all the meat looked funny. It was packaged wrong. It was too red. Or too pale. It was *Austin* meat.

The move did have one unexpected benefit. Chris seemed at times just as nervous as she did, and he needed her again. Over the past year, romance had leaked out of their lives as though it were air escaping a tire with a slow leak. It had been a process with sufficient irony for a lifetime. When they'd been separated by 180 miles and unmarried, they could overcome discomfort from periods, runny noses, even the flu. Once when Chris had come to Abilene to visit,

119

Lori had awakened that morning feeling terrible, and by that night she'd had a full-fledged case of the flu. Chris had kissed her on the lips and said if she had the flu, then he wanted it too. Now if Lori was sick, Chris wore a pollen mask around the house, made sure Lori used her own towels and drinking glasses, and washed his hands continually.

They had gone from sleeping naked in each other's arms to spending the night a mile away from each other in a king-sized bed. If Lori got over the imaginary center stripe on the mattress, he got mad.

"You radiate heat, Lori. You're like a blast furnace."

"It's stored-up love. If I don't release it, I'll burn up."

"Right."

Lori had become such a common object in her husband's life, she had to beg for attention. Usually she asked him to rub her back. She'd remove her blouse and bra and lie on her stomach, and if she was lucky, Chris would say, "I love these tiny blonde hairs on your back. When you're really tan, you look like—I don't know, an animal maybe." And they'd make love. But if she tried the same trick again the next night, he'd ask, "Is your back really aching or are you just wanting attention?" She had to describe in detail the ache in her back before he'd touch her.

But after the move, he seemed uncertain, needy again. He hugged her every time they passed in the house, and she collected more kisses during the first week in the new house than she'd had in the past year.

He woke her up one Saturday morning and told her to get dressed, he had somewhere to take her. Although she would have preferred sleeping, she got up and dressed. They ate at a restaurant on the way out of town, ordering sausage and egg tacos, Chris's now-favorite breakfast, and were driving through the hills west of town before Lori ever woke up.

"I had to come out here the other day and take pictures," Chris

120

said. "Some idiots wrecked a canoe, one of them broke his arm, and he sued the company that made the canoe."

Lori wasn't real clear on Chris's job. Mostly he seemed to drink with lawyers. How that qualified as investigating, Lori didn't know, and when she asked him each afternoon what he had done, he said, "Not much." He was being paid fairly well but not enough to become an alcoholic.

Far out of Austin, they left the highway and took a road that twisted and gradually degenerated until it came to a low-water crossing on the Pedernales River.

"Come look at this," Chris said, leaving the car. "It's beautiful."

She followed him onto the concrete roadway that crossed the river, and they stood under a beautiful summer sky, in a morning that was warm but not yet hot. The river flowed from around a bend, splitting around trees and rocks, clear as tap water. It was a scenic spot, the image of wilderness. Cypress trees grew on the banks of the river, its bed full of rust-colored rocks.

Listening to the constant roar of running water, Lori said, "You like it down here, don't you?"

"You mean Austin? Yeah, I love it." He paused, then asked, "Don't you?"

"Well, I need some time to adjust."

"You want to wade?"

They walked back to the bank and sat beneath a cypress tree, removing their shoes. Lori waded in a small pool that was only a foot deep, the water gently swirling around her ankles.

"I want you to like this place as much as I do," Chris said.

"I will." She looked up through the small leaves at the sky, which was free of clouds, and felt suddenly good. The cold water gave her a pleasurable chill and she closed her eyes. Did the river ever get tired? It just ran and ran and ran. Having a house here would be ideal. She could open her bedroom window at night and listen to the sounds of the river.

121

"What're you doing?"

She opened her eyes and smiled at him. "Just enjoying this."

"That's the first smile I've seen since we moved."

"Well, bats and scorpions and traffic don't make me want to smile much."

He walked through the water to where she stood, coming up behind her and placing his hands on her breasts, his face against her neck. He kissed her.

"I like all these kisses I've been getting."

"I like giving them to you."

"How long will this last?"

"How long will what last?"

"Your loving mood."

Before he answered, he pulled the tails of her T-shirt from her shorts and ran his hands up her stomach, her ribs, stopping on her breasts. Such a move always made her stretch, hands over her head, and writhe contentedly. Chris always had warm hands and they knew just what she wanted. "My loving mood will last forever."

"Ho, ho."

"Or at least until tomorrow."

He raised her bra over her breasts, then covered them with his hands. The heat from his palms spread into her, downward, flooded her system.

"I'd like to come out here at night," she said. "We could do it right under that tree."

They heard a car coming, and Lori rearranged her clothes. The car turned out to be a pickup, and they silently watched it roll down the hill and across the low water crossing. The driver, who looked like an old farmer chewing on a cigar, waved, a gesture they returned. Lori found a smooth large rock to sit on at the edge of the pool she'd been standing in.

"How are you and Carl getting along?"

Chris sat beside her. "I don't want to talk about Carl. I want to talk about making love. Right under that tree."

122

"Right now?"

"Right now."

"In the daylight?"

He nodded. "We can hear anybody coming."

His hand was beneath her blouse again, the very persuasive hand that it was, tempting her toward the tree. And they had heard the pickup in plenty of time. She wasn't sure what they'd do if another person came by because the river wasn't deep enough to disappear into. Still, the thought of the sun warming her entire body, the thought of making love to Chris. . . .

"Let's walk farther up the river," she said.

"Let's go."

The first guest they invited to their new house was, of all people, Carl. Chris, the culprit who had extended the invitation, said he'd grill steaks outside and they could bake potatoes so Lori wouldn't have to cook at all.

While the brothers sat on the patio, apparently believing that whiskey would protect their eyes from the smoke of the grill, Lori looked at her house and thought about teaching, about the money it would provide for the improvements she wanted to make. If they could live on Chris's salary, then Lori could dedicate hers to making the house truly theirs. She'd been thinking only about new wallpaper, new painting schemes, minor things, but as she completed the small projects in her mind, big activities cried out. The kitchen needed new appliances, the patio would make a beautiful sunroom, the bath in the master bedroom could be easily expanded and a sunken tub installed. A gazebo out back, a little here, a little there.

After three years of teaching, her attitude toward omnipresent parents was less extreme; still, for her, the ideal classroom was full of orphans. Last year, she had taken fewer Darvon, experienced fewer crises. But now she would be without Elizabeth in the next room, and Elizabeth had helped her more than Darvon.

She had called the personnel office for the Austin school district and asked for an application; along with the assurance that she'd get the application in the mail, she'd also received a large dose of discouraging words. According to the lady she'd talked to, *everyone* wanted to live and teach in Austin. It was the most popular place in the *entire world*. But there were school districts all over the place.

The brothers were shouting at each other. First they argued over whether Idi Amin was still alive, then whether Tom Landry should retire. They leaped from the lawn chairs and paced the patio and waved their arms. They argued over whether Lance Alworth had played football for Arkansas or Oklahoma, and they brought their argument inside.

As Chris opened the door to the kitchen, he said loudly, "You're thinking of Lance Rentzel. You're so stupid you can't keep your Lances straight. Go get on the phone in the bedroom. You won't take my word for it, so you listen to what he says."

Carl walked through the kitchen, on his way to the bedroom, and as he went, they argued over how much to bet—a hundred bucks, a thousand? Come on, come on, put your money where your mouth is if you think you're right. They finally settled on five dollars and Chris called one of the senior partners of the law firm, a well-known expert on football trivia.

Lori got the lettuce so she could make the salads, thinking her house had been incredibly peaceful until now.

The senior partner said Chris was right—Lance Alworth had played football for Arkansas.

"Pay up, sucker," Chris shouted into the phone.

"Pay up?" Carl yelled from the bedroom. "I'm the one who said he played for Arkansas. You said Oklahoma."

Chris slammed the phone down and said, "I'm going to kill the son of a bitch. He's been sitting out there swearing he played for Oklahoma, and now he won't pay up. I'm going to kill him."

Lori thought he was speaking figuratively, but he opened a drawer and got a big knife that looked almost like a meat cleaver except it was pointed. And he went stomping off toward the bedroom. Lori dropped the lettuce and thought, My God, he has a knife. A *knife*. Her husband had a knife and had just said he was going to kill his brother.

She stood open-mouthed at the sink, listening to Carl yell, "Put that knife up, you dumb ass." And then there was the sound of shoving, furniture moving. Grunts. A loud grunt. Then she heard Carl yell, "You bastard! You cut me!" More shoving. It sounded as though a nightstand had been upended. Then, "Goddammit, get away from me." And she heard the sounds of movement, footsteps, coming toward the kitchen.

Carl, running, his white shirt and pants turning red with blood, hit the kitchen door and went flying into the backyard. And Chris, the knife still in his hands, as bloody as Carl's shirt and pants had been, was running just as hard.

"Chris!" she screamed.

He was gone, just as quickly as Carl, leaving Lori standing at the sink unable to believe what she'd seen. Chris had undoubtedly been mad, but that mad? Or was it the whiskey? She didn't know what to do. Call the police on her own husband? What was she to do? By now Chris may have already killed his brother. How could this be happening?

She walked to the back door and looked outside, praying she wouldn't see the bloody dismembered body of Carl. And she didn't. What she did see was two brothers standing twenty feet away, laughing so hard they were holding their stomachs, and pointing at her, unable to speak. Chris tried, shaking his finger as though to emphasize he wanted to say something about Lori's stupidity, but he couldn't stand up straight.

Lori, her heart pounding like a machine gun, closed her eyes. Who was more stupid—two brothers who pulled such pranks, or the wife who believed them? Very slowly she said, "Do you think giving someone a heart attack is *funny*?"

Neither brother could respond. She'd never seen such laughing. Chris was breathless, down on his knees and holding his stomach, and Carl was leaning against the house, the phony blood—she recognized it now—all over his clothes.

She walked closer to them and screamed, *"Do you think giving someone a heart attack is funny?"*

Chris, nodding, collapsed onto the ground. Carl tried to agree but coughed instead. He had tears on both cheeks.

"You're both sick!" she shouted. "Sick, sick, sick!"

After they'd been in Austin a month, they acquired a little brown short-haired dog named J. D. (Jack Daniels) that had belonged to one of the lawyers who was divorcing and who couldn't keep it in the apartment where he was presently residing. J. D. seemed terribly neurotic to Lori. Whenever he was approached, he flipped onto his back and urinated, sometimes only a few drops, sometimes an impressive stream. And it didn't matter how he was approached.

His stay in the house was brief, but in the backyard, he seemed lonely sitting on the steps waiting for someone to come visit. Lori discovered he was just fine as long as no hands reached for him, so she began letting him in during the day. They both needed company. He followed her from room to room and lay near her feet if she was stationary very long.

"I think we need to go look at wallpaper," she said to him one day.

J. D., curled into a ball, looked up at her.

"You think Chris is going to help on this project?"

The dog, thinking he had been paged in error, returned to his previous position.

"I don't think he's even going to like it."

11

Chris had hired on with the Lindsey, Chapman law firm thinking that somehow his job would be related to a noble concept, that of justice. But it wasn't a concept anyone in the office seemed intimately acquainted with. The two moving forces behind what went on were more common. One was winning, the other money. The firm specialized in representing insurance companies, and they paid the bills, but the paying clients seemed only to exist peripherally as another opponent in the fight.

Carl's favorite line was, "Hell, Vince Lombardi didn't know anything about winning."

Chris discovered exactly what Carl meant during the first two days on the job when he was directed to watch a trial so he'd "know what happens when the investigator approaches his job like it's a circle jerk." The plaintiff was an older man who had allegedly injured his back three years ago while changing the oil in a car at a gas station where he was working. He had never returned to work because he claimed to be totally and permanently disabled and wanted the maximum benefits he was entitled to under the worker's compensation law.

The previous investigator, a man Chris knew only by reputation, had discovered the man was working in the garage at his house full-time repairing cars, and the investigator had rented a house directly behind the plaintiff's in hopes a professional photographer could videotape the allegedly disabled man as he worked, bending and stooping and lifting, all recorded through the back door of the garage.

"Through the back door. Wasn't that great? We've got a movie of a bunch of ghosts picking their noses. The movie doesn't show shit," Carl said. "The one time on the entire tape the man was outside in the light, he was twirling a red rag. Otherwise, all we got were these phantoms."

All the lawyers were consistently upset when the investigator's name was mentioned, and Chris couldn't figure out why, if the man had been so soundly and thoroughly detested, he hadn't been fired a long time ago. No one seemed to know. "Oh, he was all right. He did a fair job at times." Then, one night under the influence of several drinks, Carl told the secret: the investigator had known a great deal about the personal lives of the lawyers and threatened to tell appropriate parties if he was fired. Every time the subject of his poor performance arose, the investigator had mumbled something appropriate. "Oh, hell, I just got hit with one of those worst-case scenarios. What if Lesher was going through a really ugly divorce just as *Texas Homes and Gardens* was doing that layout on his house. Talk about your worst-case scenario." Of course, Lesher, one of the partners, was not expecting to get divorced; he probably wouldn't unless his wife discovered he was flying in a girlfriend once a month from Denver.

The investigator had finally quit, somehow retiring at the age of forty-eight, and the lawyers were all glad to be rid of him, until one wondered aloud what he might have taken with him, and under what circumstances he might resurface. No matter, one would say, they could handle it. The lawyers had great faith in their abilities to talk their way into or out of anything. Which was why Carl was upset over the course of the trial involving the home garage mechanic.

Since the investigator had failed to convince any of the plaintiff's neighbors or customers to testify, they had nothing with which to prove the man a liar. Only useless videotape.

It was a point the plaintiff's attorney kept reminding the jury of. "If the insurance company really believes this man is capable of working, they'd have every one of his neighbors up here telling you how often they'd seen this man bending, stooping, and lifting. They'd have dates and times. They'd have color pictures. They'd

128

have videotape. They'd have a *parade* of witnesses in and out the door."

When Carl rose to respond, he calmly went back over the medical reports, none of which contained objective findings, all of which consisted of subjective complaints. And then he turned as indignant as an old maid whose virginity had been questioned. "And I resent that my honorable opponent would even suggest that I'd bring into this courtroom spies and skulkers, that I'd go around encouraging one neighbor to peek out the window and watch another. I would never, and I mean *never*, suggest that my client take pictures of a man without his knowledge. I simply wouldn't do it and I'd never again represent a company that wanted to."

Because of the breadth and width of that lie, Chris was glad when the jury gave the rag twirler everything he wanted. He tried to find Carl afterward to suggest that his brother repent of his sins, but the two opposing lawyers were in the hall talking.

"Oh, don't feel so bad," the plaintiff's attorney said. "You couldn't have won this dog if you'd had a tranquilizer gun. I still can't believe the insurance company wanted to try it."

"The blackest day of my life was the one I decided I'd go into insurance defense. Insurance companies have cornered the market on stupidity. I mean, they've got it all."

"No, not all. My man's got a bunch. He's making thirty thousand a year working on cars and he hasn't filed a tax return for the past three years. He thinks lying to the IRS is no different from lying to an insurance company."

As Chris left the courthouse with Carl, he still couldn't quite comprehend the fact that his brother had walked into a courtroom and told the jury an outrageous lie. A courtroom, in Chris's mind, was a more sacred place than a church.

They walked to Carl's car and Chris said, "Let me get this straight: an insurance company pays you a hundred dollars an hour to lie to a jury, is that right?"

Carl opened the door of his white Mercedes and said, "No, they pay me a hundred dollars an hour to win their cases for them, which I can't do if the investigator's playing with himself."

Once they were in the car, Chris said, "You just told that jury a bald-faced lie."

Looking over his left shoulder, Carl pulled away from the curb into the traffic. He didn't respond.

"I said, you just told that jury a bald-faced lie."

"Yeah. So?"

"It was a trial. It was in a courtroom. That was a jury."

Carl looked at him twice, wondering why Chris would even bring up such a matter. "Little brother, you're not on TV; this is life, this is the real world, this is win or lose. If you lose, you get nothing but the court costs and a goddamn insurance company that wants to know why you're not defending it properly. You'll find out that insurance companies are the true whores of the eighties. They have no loyalty to anyone, not their customers, not their stockholders, not their employees, not to anyone. They follow the dollar, wherever it leads."

"And so that's why you lied to a jury?"

Carl shot him an angry look. Normally he didn't find anything Chris did worthy of an extreme response, but he was mad already over the loss in court. "*What* is your problem? Are you the Conscience of the Western World? I just told you, this is the real world. You can't stay clean when you're fighting in the gutter, and the man you saw in court is A-one prime slime. If you think I'm going to sit there and watch him lie his ass off to a jury and just let it go, think again."

"Well, it just looks like there'd be a way without having to stoop to the same level."

"There is and that's why you're employed. I hope you can do more than the last dumb ass."

The morning's events left him in a state of shock, similar to that provoked by the death of a loved one. He just couldn't believe what he'd seen, especially since it had involved his own brother.

He kept hoping that the trial wasn't representative of what he'd see in the future. Surely all the lawyers in the firm wouldn't lie so unashamedly to a jury.

The other lawyers proved to be the biggest stumbling block to his accomplishing any work. They all gave him files with questions they wanted answered; yet they saw him as virgin ears, a new audience for their stories. Ah, they all seemed to think, he hasn't heard the one about Snuffy Smith. He was told the story by almost every attorney in the office.

The plaintiff's name hadn't been Snuffy Smith and no one now seemed to know what it had been, but Tom Lesher, the senior partner of the firm, had been the defense attorney, and he was the first one to tell the story to Chris.

"This was a worker's compensation case where old Snuffy claimed a back injury, total and permanent, just like they all do, and he lived out in the middle of nowhere in a shack. Well, our investigator happened upon him one day when he had a deer hanging in a tree, butchering him. Old Ben, our investigator, was too smart to lie, and said he'd love to have a movie of Snuffy cutting up that deer. Well, Snuffy agreed and he skinned that deer and in the process he assumed any number of toadlike and contorted positions that a man with a bad back shouldn't have been able to assume. Ben and his camera left, and old Snuffy was hit with a vision—he was going to star in his own movie right in court.

"He called his lawyer so we didn't have the advantage of surprise, and his lawyer approached me on the day of the trial and he wanted to know what the movie showed. I told him, 'I like you, you're a friend of mine, so I'm going to tell you the truth. We've got a movie of your man fucking a hog.' Well, the lawyer didn't believe me, but he didn't disbelieve me either because Snuffy was just that sorry and degenerate. And he had lied to his lawyer a bunch.

"Well, the trial proceeded and as my last witness, I brought in Ben, our investigator. I put him on the stand and established his identity and I asked him if he had a movie of Snuffy. He said he

131

did. I said, 'Are there any hogs in this movie?' 'Just one,' Ben said. Male or female? He said he couldn't tell. 'Is it a central figure in this movie?' It was one of two central figures.

"Ben showed his movie. And in the process of filming Snuffy skinning this deer, he'd swung around and caught a hog just standing, staring at the camera. And as we'd rehearsed it, Ben killed the projector and started fiddling with it like there was something wrong and he left the hog on the screen, looking at us.

"I looked over and Snuffy's lawyer had fallen out of his chair and was yelling, 'Your Honor, I think I've had a heart attack. I need a short recess.'

"We settled the claim for twelve dollars and seventy-five cents."

Chris assumed the story was true; regardless, it was widely believed, and it explained at least two notes he had found attached to files: "Get me a movie of this man fucking a hog."

Chris's secretary, Margie, represented two extremes—she looked wonderful but engaged in no work. She was long-legged, had silky black hair to her waist, a blouse that wouldn't button from midchest up, and skin that looked and smelled like bath powder. She sat right outside Chris's rather small office watching television all day, and she hated to be bothered during a game show or soap opera, which seemed to be on from nine to four. Carl had explained her this way: "She's dumber than a stump but she's Lesher's niece."

Chris asked her once where the Gallagher file was. She didn't answer because she was watching "The Price Is Right" on a small TV sitting on a typing stand. When he asked again, she pointed behind her with a thumb.

"Which file cabinet?"

"Shh. Third."

He passed her desk one day on his way to make copies and she started bouncing in her seat when she discovered where he was headed. She asked if he'd make her some copies since he was going to make some for himself. He sighed and agreed. She handed him a stack of papers that he had given her the day before. His note was still attached: "Please make one copy of each."

He tried to be a good husband, realizing now that he had more or less been inattentive toward Lori for the past year. She wanted to work on the house and yard, and he wanted to explore the countryside, so they painted and pulled weeds on Saturday, and then on Sunday after church they acquainted themselves with the Austin area.

One of their most enjoyable trips was to the Guadalupe River sixty miles south of Austin. Between Canyon Dam and New Braunfels, the river was badly overdeveloped, twenty miles of river bank that had been turned into camping spaces and picnic areas. Cars and campers and motorcycles and pickups parked on the barren banks and the river was full of canoes and rafts and tubes. Chris and Lori rented three inner tubes with circular plywood bottoms tied on to protect tender areas from scrapes on the rocks in shallow water. He used one, Lori the second, and the third was used for a cooler of beer. They put in a few miles below the dam and then floated several miles downriver.

Normally Chris preferred the wilderness, but the crowds and commercialism gave the afternoon a holiday atmosphere. They floated below several limestone bluffs and clouds that looked like huge icebergs roaming across the sky.

Chris opened the cooler in the third tube and got a beer, thankful that Lori hadn't yet complained about the beer accompanying them.

In the black bikini he'd picked out several years ago, she looked better than any other woman on the river. How was it, he wondered, that he lived with her, saw her morning and night, yet hadn't really been looking at her lately? She looked better, if that was possible, than she had when they'd married. She had the same promising face that belonged on a cereal box, but it was more mature, less self-conscious.

He said, "I do believe you're the best-looking woman I've ever seen in my entire life."

Reclined in the tube, her arms and legs dangling in the water, she looked both surprised and pleased. "Are you drunk yet?"

"No, I'm not drunk."

"Then thank you."

They hit a small rapid that split around an island in the middle of the river and he paddled to catch her, dragging the beer tube behind him. When he reached her, he tied their tubes together with some of the excess nylon rope that held the plywood seats on.

"There. I don't want us to get separated."

They stopped at a giant cypress tree that had grown partly into the river, and he climbed up through the great grooves in the exposed roots so he could swing on a rope that had been tied to one of the higher limbs. The traffic was so heavy—screaming kids packed into canoes, leisurely travelers on inner tubes—that he had to wait before swinging out over the river. When he did, letting go at the far end of his arc, he felt like a child again, flying freely through the air. He had a momentary but intense desire for a much simpler lifestyle, one where he didn't have a house to paint and heat and cool, cars to keep up—maybe something like a bait-stand owner on this very river. Or a canoe-rental business.

The desire lasted until he came up out of the water, seeing Lori through blurred eyes, languidly holding their trio of tubes to a root on the cypress tree. She wasn't bait-stand material.

"You didn't want to swim?" he asked.

She shook her head. "I like it right here."

He swam to her, then hung on the side of her tube.

"You better not turn me over," she said, tilting under the pressure from his hand. As he increased the pressure, which made her list more severe, she said in a warning manner, "Chris."

"I wouldn't turn you over," he said, and then did, pulling on her tube with both hands and sending her shrieking into the water on top of him.

She came up fighting as though she were drowning, blowing and yelling, her mouth open. He caught her under the arm and pulled her to a point directly in front of him so she could latch on to the rubber tube. She coughed, her blonde hair slicked onto her scalp, dripping water. When she had finally cleared her throat and lungs, she shot him a mean look.

"I hate you. I can't believe you did that."

"I like dealing with the real you."

Lori wiped hair from her forehead, still blinking away the water in her eyes. "The real me?"

"Yeah, the real you, the one I fell in love with, not the one who's worried about getting her hair wet."

"That *is* the real me."

Chris shook his head. "No, that's part of the image you want to project."

She shook her head as though she had water in her ear. "Then who am I?"

"You're the one I fell in love with, I just told you."

She sighed, pulling herself up so she could rest her entire arm on the tube. "Describe the real me. I'd like to know who I *really* am."

"Well, you're slightly lazy but you've got a great sense of humor when you let your guard down. And you like sex in strange places. You'd probably do it in the middle of Congress Avenue if you knew nobody could identify you and you wouldn't get run over. And you've got this spontaneous streak I used to really count on. If you hadn't had it, or if I hadn't seen it right after we met, I'd have never asked you out. Or if I had, you wouldn't have gone."

He suddenly felt serious and didn't know why. Right in the middle of the Guadalupe River, along with hundreds of others who were floating along, acting as though they were on the midway at the state fair, Chris was feeling serious.

"On the other hand, you can be level-headed and practical in ways I never am. I'd probably have made a good bum. I've had this feeling ever since my mother died that nothing I did mattered and

135

even if it did, it wouldn't be worth it. I keep having this urge to drop out and I need somebody to keep me in it. I couldn't handle being a dropout; I figured that out in the navy. I knew what I needed before I met you at Baylor. I needed a girl to love, to love me. And I still need you, whether I tell you or not, I really need you. I love you too. But you know that."

She pulled him toward her and, as she hung by one arm on the tube, kissed him. Although the river wasn't very deep in most places, they couldn't touch bottom. Two silver aluminum canoes full of teenagers floated by and the kids whistled and cheered when they saw them kissing.

"Put it on her, man," one yelled.

"Suck her brains out."

Chris waved without breaking the kiss. Lori transferred herself from the tube to Chris, holding onto his shoulders and wrapping her legs around him. The extra weight pulled his arm from the inner tube, and they sank to the bottom of the river, which was no more than two feet below them.

Surprised by the fact that Lori hadn't immediately broken the kiss and fought toward the surface, he opened his eyes. Her blonde hair floated like limp weeds in the murky water.

Then, both out of air, they surfaced, gasping but smiling as well.

"Is that the real me?" she asked.

"I hope so."

Hanging onto the tube again, not enough space between them for a minnow to swim through, Lori slipped her hand up the leg of his cutoffs, her fingers finding their target.

For someone who claimed to be naive and was often genuinely and inexplicably gullible, she was also wise in the ways of men. She knew what he liked even when he hadn't told her. She knew he liked to see, in a clandestine manner, her untanned breasts in the summer. The white skin, in contrast with her otherwise tanned body, heightened the effect when she bent over, wearing a scooped-neck blouse without a bra. She knew what affected him.

136

He'd been sitting in the backyard one night, enjoying the evening, when he'd noticed a light come on in their bedroom. For the next few minutes, he had watched Lori's silhouette undress. T-shirt over the head. Off came the bra. Stoop and remove shorts, then, after a short exhibitionist delay, her panties. Several times she had walked back and forth, obviously naked. Greatly aroused, he'd returned to the house, finding Lori nude on the bed, waiting on him.

"If the water wasn't so clear, we could do it right here," she said.

He looked down into the water, seeing wavy mirrorlike images of legs and feet. "I don't think we could hanging onto these tubes."

"Three years ago you would've found a way."

"That's old age for you."

"We could go home and practice in the bathtub."

"If we keep practicing, pretty soon we'll know what we're doing."

"And won't we have fun then."

On Saturday nights they made new friends, almost always being the ones to invite others to their house. Until Chris learned about the other couple, he invariably refused to go to visit them because all these friends came from church and, as Baptists, they had been trained to avoid controversial conversations and play board games instead. Monopoly was God's favorite; all Baptists were instructed in Monopoly right after they were baptized. It combined the spiritual activities of acquiring property and bankrupting others, activities that were not only godly but American, and therefore Baptist.

It was after one of these Saturday night visits when Chris was helping Lori wash dishes that he decided to tell her something he'd been wanting to tell her for two years. He had given her two months to settle in, to make friends, to meet everyone she wanted to know at church, and the time had come, if it was ever going to come—he was through with church. He had started going only because it had given him a chance to be with Lori when they'd been dating, and he had no interest in regular attendance.

137

So as he put a dried coffee cup into the cabinet, he said, "I'm not going to church in the morning and I'm telling you now so we don't have a big fight and you won't have to go to church with puffy eyes in the morning."

Lori, wringing out her dishrag, through washing, said, "Why would we have a fight?" She asked this question in the same manner that a psychopath, razor in hand, would say, "You didn't think I was going to cut you with this, did you?"

He watched her walk out of the room thinking, oh, no, it can't be this easy, while devoutly wishing it would be. He didn't want to discuss his attitude toward church. If he told her he had a theological difference with the Baptists then she might suggest an alternate denomination. He didn't want to go at all. He wanted Sunday mornings totally to himself. He wanted to get up late, read the paper, drink ten cups of coffee, and sit around in his underwear. He wanted one morning of the week off.

She went to bed without so much as a goodnight, leaving him sitting in the living room to consider the extent of his guilt. He hadn't yet missed a service and already felt like a traitor.

She cried just loud enough for him to hear. The next morning, while he feigned sleep, she dressed, sighing no more than once a minute. When the sighs didn't work, she came and sat on the bed and rubbed his stomach. Something was wrong, he thought. She'd been up and moving for at least an hour; yet there she sat in her sexiest bra and panties. Had she dressed, then undressed?

"Why do you want me to go to church by myself?" she asked.

"That's one question, Lori. But there's another. Why do you want me to go when I don't want to?"

"I want us to be together on Sunday morning when all families are together."

Her bra had a clasp in front, and it happened to be unhooked, causing the flesh-colored cups to strain outward against her breasts, threatening to pop open and reveal her all. He wanted to help the cups pull away; he wanted to rub both breasts. But she probably didn't know that. Probably the entire scene was accidental. It was probably accidental also when she lay across him, her torso across his thighs, and the cups slipped away from her breasts like lazy slingshots.

He did exactly as she expected he would—he pulled her up beside him and as she lay with her head propped on her hand, so she wouldn't mess up her hair, he rubbed both her breasts.

"I'm going to be a messenger," he said. "I'm going to go throughout the world spreading the gospel, and the gospel is this—boys, don't marry a woman who's beautiful and sexy and a spoiled little bitch on top of that. You know how unfair this is? Do you know? If there was anything I wanted from you, I don't have any tricks similar to this."

"Will you go with me?"

"What do you think?"

It was her happiness when he gave in that drove him crazy. Suddenly she was the happiest person in the world, and her great and wonderful smile said, "Only someone truly mean and cruel would make me unhappy."

He gave her one, then two—oh, what the heck, why not three —weeks to get used to the idea of solitary church attendance. And then he got up on the fourth Sunday morning knowing that he'd have to leave the house altogether to successfully avoid church. So he picked up the newspaper and said, "I'm going to eat breakfast. You'll have to go to church without me."

Standing in the hallway, having stepped out of the bathroom in a lime green slip as she did her hair, she looked both shocked and mystified. "You're not going? Why?"

He stopped at the front door, convinced he had never in the past years shown even a tiny bit of resistance to attending church and was now springing this horrible surprise on her at the last minute. How, *how* could she make him think he had failed to give her proper warning and if he failed now to thoroughly discuss his reasons, he was guilty of gross marital neglect? How did she do it?

He left without saying anything further but was too distracted to even read the paper while he ate at a restaurant about a mile from the house. What had he done? He kept checking his watch. If he left now, he'd be home in time to get dressed. If he didn't leave within a minute, he'd make them late. And if he didn't leave *right now*, he was going to miss church altogether. He visualized Lori driving to church alone, tears dripping down alongside her nose. He could hear her sobs over the clatter of dishes and silverware in the restaurant.

But he didn't leave.

She had nothing to say for several hours when she got home, but by evening she did. "The Nelsons go to church, the Albrittons go to church, the Waverlys go to church, the Brooks go to church, the Martins go to church, the Petersons go to church. . . ." She went on for what seemed hours to him, naming every person she could think of who went to church. Then she switched gears and he didn't even realize it until he heard Hitler's name mentioned. "Attila the Hun didn't go to church, Ho Chi Minh didn't go to church, the Boston Strangler didn't go to church, Charles Manson didn't go to church—"

"I think I know what you're saying."

"Then will you please go? Please, Chris, just for me?"

He couldn't look at her; he shook his head.

In a voice that was almost lighthearted, she said, "Then I guess you'll just die and burn in hell."

12

Lori had seen the month of July as a staircase; with each day, she had taken another step toward improvement. She had been adjusting to life in Austin, making friends, worrying less about bats and scorpions, and enjoying the attention of Chris. She had even got a job teaching third grade in a suburb, and with the knowledge that they'd have a second income, she had started working on a master plan for the house. For two weeks, she was a regular face in the Kelly-Moore store near the house, and she picked up paint charts, took home books of wallpaper samples, and dreamed up new color schemes. She had done most of this herself because Chris hadn't wanted to discuss in depth what she was doing.

"We get a house you like, a house in almost perfect shape, and you want to *change it*?"

He didn't want to come home each night and paint; he didn't want to spend all his free time working on the house. And since he didn't want to redecorate, Lori avoided using the word "remodel." He had no objection, however, if she wanted to do the work.

And so she took one step and another up toward what seemed to as perfect a life as she was capable of attaining, and then Chris blew up the staircase. He quit going to church. Of all the things that could have happened to her, his dropping out of church was one of the worst. She could have handled a double radical mastectomy more easily. She knew women who went to church alone; they were either divorced or they were married to sodomists or alcoholics or child abusers. And all the way to church alone in her car, she heard the tires running across the pavement providing music for a horrid little chorus: "There goes Lori, all by herself. There goes Lori, all by herself."

And she wasn't going to be able to use the same excuse very long to explain Chris's absence. How long did the flu last? Not indefinitely. And telling someone inquiring into her absent husband's whereabouts that he had decided to drop out of church sounded too much like, "Oh, he's decided to become a communist."

She had to do something before next Sunday to return the lost sheep to the fold. She had to think of something.

Something was going on between Chris and Carl and she was having difficulty determining what it was. Since they'd moved to Austin, Chris had asked Carl several times to come over and eat or drink or watch baseball games on TV, and he played as hard to get as an overconfident debutante. No thanks, he had other plans, all of which seemed to cast considerable insignificance on the suggestions Chris made.

But things changed. Carl called the house on Saturday looking for Chris, the first time he'd made such a call, and Lori had told him Chris had gone to buy shrubs.

"Tell him to call me when he comes in," Carl said. "I've been so busy at work I don't think I've talked to him for a week or two."

Carl as concerned brother? As interested friend? Something was up, she thought.

And it was. When Chris returned from the nursery with a trunk full of shrubs, he made a face upon hearing the request that he phone Carl.

"I've got nothing to say to him. I'm not about to call him."

Carl called back in the afternoon and suggested Lori's dedication to and interest in being a good wife were in doubt if she wouldn't even give a message to her husband. Lori told him, and not without some mean pleasure, that she had most certainly delivered the message to Chris upon his return to the house.

"He would've called me."

"I guess you'd have to talk to him about that."

"Where is he now?"

Lori looked through the kitchen window, seeing Chris planting the same shrubs he had bought earlier in the day, and said, "He's out on another gardening mission."

"And you told him I'd called."

"Yes," Lori said slowly, as though Carl had difficulty understanding. "I told him you wanted him to call."

"And what'd he say?"

"Carl, I delivered the message. If you have any other questions, ask Chris."

"Well, fuck him," Carl said. "I just won't ever call him again."

So what? Lori thought as she hung up. You've never called him before. And although she wasn't particularly interested in seeing more of Carl, she was curious about the obvious rift that had developed between the brothers. Until that time, it had seemed to her that Carl could have committed any offense against the relationship and Chris would have overlooked it. He had expressed doubts about Carl's sincerity and reliability but he had never chosen to ignore him altogether.

Lori walked into the backyard and to the fence along the street at the side of the lot and sat in the grass near Chris. He was busily digging a hole for a shrub, down on his hands and knees. Sweat dripped from his face into the hole. The grass was thick and cool, a pleasant contrast to a hot August afternoon.

"What's going on with you and Carl?"

"Carl's an asshole," he said without breaking the rhythm of his work. "I've got no use for Carl."

"What happened?"

Chris rocked back on his heels, wiping his forehead with the back of his hand and smearing dirt. "He's a liar, cheat, and a fraud, that's all. Otherwise he's a real fine guy."

The older brother had done something; that much Lori was sure of. There was too much anger boiling up very close to the surface on her husband, so much in fact that she wasn't sure she wanted it released. She didn't know whether to ask any follow-up questions. But she didn't have to.

"The first thing he did was tell a bald-faced, out-and-out lie to a jury. He told them he'd *never, under any circumstances*, suggest that one of his clients spy and skulk on someone, when he always demands that very thing. That was bad enough, but I'll tell you what's worse."

He sat back, forgetting his shrubs for the moment, and took a drink from an insulated Coke glass he'd filled with tea. The ice had melted.

"Everybody in our hometown, *everybody*, thinks he's a goddamn war hero. He was in the marines during the Vietnam War, from about sixty-eight to seventy, and everybody thought he was a war hero. He got the Silver Star during the Tet Offensive. Now it may not mean anything to you, but it meant a hell of a lot to me. Ashworth's a conservative place; there weren't any protestors there, just a lot of people who thought we should've bombed the entire country over there back to the Stone Age. Anyway, I've believed he was a hero since I was twelve years old. I mean, I saw him come home in his uniform with a Silver Star.

"You know what? He got the Silver Star from some disgruntled marine in a bar in San Diego. He had a friend in a personnel office write a phony news release, and he mailed it to the local paper at home. This great write-up about his heroism, and it was nothing but a fake and a fraud. That's all he is, a fake and a fraud.

"I've been thinking he's a hero for fifteen years, and I find out different when Randy Stevens at work makes a joke about 'our resident war hero.' Stevens knew the whole phony story, and I was sitting there *arguing* with him. God, he was making me mad talking about Carl that way, telling me he'd never got the Silver Star. I was about to beat the crap out of him, and Carl walks in and says it's all true. A damn wounded marine, a guy who'd lost his arm over there and got totally disillusioned about the war, gave Carl his Silver Star. He didn't want it.

"Now, that's about the worst thing I can possibly think of."

He went immediately back to work, digging with a vengeance, jamming his small garden shovel into the dirt as though it were Carl's heart.

"Did Carl laugh at you? In front of Randy?"

"Oh, hell yes," Chris said, hitting a rock and digging with even more vigor. "He laughed and told Randy what a naive little shit I was. Yeah, they had a real good laugh at my expense."

She would have given in to an urge to comfort him had he not been attempting to dig a hole through the earth in the next twenty seconds. But he would have resisted her efforts anyway because he didn't want to believe he was a naive child. And in some ways he was; he could be as cynical as Carl, but the difference between the

144

two brothers, as far as Lori was concerned, was this—in Chris's heart, he wanted everyone to be a nice guy, to follow the Golden Rule, and to love one another.

She was so disturbed by the image of Carl and Randy laughing at Chris that she returned to the house and dialed Carl's phone number. When he answered, she said, "You ought to be ashamed of yourself."

"Oh, I am. I've thought about trying to make myself less good-looking but I haven't tried very hard. And I am ashamed for not trying harder."

"Do you know how you've hurt your brother?"

There was a pause and Lori could almost hear Carl's mind analyzing the situation, trying to come up with an appropriate line, something with a twinge of superficial regret, just enough to put him back in a naive brother's good graces while retaining his superior position. Lori decided to cut off any such attempt.

"Carl Gray is an empty suit. There's nothing to him. Nothing. Stick a pin in his skin and he'd deflate."

"Wait a minute," he said, already angry. "You know nothing about me. *Nothing*. And I don't need to hear any judgments from a skinny little bumpkin bitch who blew in off the prairie."

Lori almost smiled, wanting to congratulate herself. They'd gone from pompous baloney to the truth in a few sentences. "My judgment isn't important. I'm telling you you've hurt your brother, first by lying to him, then by laughing at him for believing you. And we're not talking about a simple little lie; we're talking about a complicated, glorious story that's lasted for years and years. You've been letting him think you're a war hero for what—fourteen years?"

"Hell, he deserved it. The little fart used to write me letters telling me about the heroes he was seeing on TV, in the movies, reading about in books. He wanted me to jump on a grenade and kill myself so I'd get the Medal of Honor. Your dear husband isn't quite the innocent you mistakenly believe he is. He would have liked nothing better than for me to come home in a body bag decorated with

145

a blue ribbon. It would've been his claim to fame. He could've gone around the rest of his life introducing himself as the brother of Lance Corporal Carl Gray, posthumous Congressional Medal of Honor winner.

"And I'll tell you something else. I joined the goddamn marines because of him. I mentioned, just mentioned, at the end of my senior year in high school, that I was thinking of joining the marine corps—although I wasn't thinking about it very hard—and he went all over town telling people I was enlisting. And people started congratulating me for a decision I hadn't even made.

"And what's even worse was, the little bastard almost got me killed. I won't ever forgive him for that. Besides that, the son of a bitch wanted me to be a hero and he didn't know what it was like. You think he wanted to hear what it was like? Hell, no he didn't. He didn't want to hear the first time I ever actually *saw* NVA I pissed in my pants and got so weak-kneed I couldn't stand up for ten minutes. He didn't want to hear reality. He wanted to live his fantasy through me. And he didn't have any idea what the cost was. He had no idea at all."

Oh, my, Lori thought, listening to Carl grow so emotional that he could have already been crying. Oh, my. Why wasn't this simple? Why couldn't one person be completely guilty and the other completely innocent? What was wrong? She sat on a bar stool with her eyes closed, shaking her head.

"Carl, will you please do something? Will you please come talk to him? Neither one of you has any idea what you're doing to each other."

"No, I won't," he said loudly. "I'm tired of the pressure. I'm tired of his goddamn moral judgments on me. He's more interested in what I do than he is in himself. I don't want to be his hero. I don't even want to be his brother. Fuck him."

Carl slammed the phone down and Lori sat listening to an empty line. It sounded hollow, full of failure. He had called to talk to

Chris, and now, after hearing what Lori had to say, he didn't want to even be his brother.

Way to go, Lori Lynn. You handled that really well.

She pushed herself off the bar stool with an effort, feeling sluggish and suddenly depressed, thinking she wouldn't feel so bad had she not just felt so good for making Carl cut through the crap. He cut through the crap all right, and it had been Lori's.

Chris was still attacking the same hole, but now it was three times as wide and looked large enough for a child's small swimming pool. At the bottom of the shallow hole was the white surface of a big rock.

"How do you get rid of a rock that big?" she asked.

"I'm fixing to hire a blasting contractor. I hate these rocks."

Panting, he sat back and rested a moment. His gray T-shirt was thoroughly soaked with sweat and his hair was wet, matted. He looked as though he'd been farming all day long.

"Would you take a break so I can talk to you?"

"If it's about Carl, no."

Lori sat beside him, already sweating and uncertain if she was because of the heat or because Chris was so hot. "You don't know his side of it, Chris."

"He hasn't got a side worth listening to."

"Yes, he does. You've felt the pressure to do better than he has, and he's felt the pressure from you. He said he wouldn't have joined the marines except you started telling people he was before he'd ever decided."

Chris was shaking his head in a long arc. "Lori, I've heard all this crap before. It's just more lies from Carl Gray. That's all it is, more lies. I don't want to talk about Carl right now. I'd rather talk to this rock than talk about him. So just forget it."

Lori sighed and looked at the sky. She was a diplomatic failure.

Besides that, she didn't know whether Carl Gray warranted sympathy or not.

147

†

The confusing Chris-and-Carl controversy got pushed from her mind when Chris stopped going to church, and the magical answer came to her as she walked out of Kelly-Moore with a big book of wallpaper samples. The answer came when she saw a woman getting out of a bright red Corvette. A beautiful woman.

Gina. Gina would get Chris back in church.

Every time Lori had mentioned inviting someone from church to their house, Chris invariably suggested the same person—Gina. Not Sam and Gina, just Gina. If Lori could have been granted another body, she'd have chosen Gina's. A woman shouldn't be both leggy and breasty, both hippy and thin. She was pretty too, but that part didn't seem so unfair, especially since she wore big glasses that made her look like an owl. Her husband, Sam, was almost homely with red curly hair and a sad face, but he seemed nice enough and he was a prosperous architect.

If Gina came to the house Saturday night, then Lori could suggest they all eat lunch together after church on Sunday, and if Gina agreed, then what could Chris do but go to church? The lost sheep would be returned. There would be rejoicing in the kingdom.

On Saturday evening, Chris set a fan outside on the patio since the evening was warm, and he cooked steaks on the gas grill. Gina arrived, towing Sam, and she looked like an embodiment of every man's dream, her tanned skin contrasting beautifully with a loose white dress. It had a square neck and she didn't have to bend forward five degrees before her braless breasts made their appearance. They seemed even larger than Lori had remembered. Candidates for the Z Cup Award.

The meal went very well. Chris had splurged on the steaks, buying huge aged T-bones and "losing" the receipt on the way home. Lori could look at these slabs of meat and tell they were worth a week's salary. The husbands seemed to have one thing in common, two if she counted attraction to Gina. They were both

148

fond of rivers and talked about canoe trips. Lori's plan seemed well on the way to perfect execution until they'd finished eating and she got up to cut slices of a lemon meringue pie she'd bought. Gina and Chris had alternative plans for dessert.

Gina had brought a huge bottle of rum and a number of cans of a frozen strawberry daiquiri mix. In mild shock, Lori watched her pie get upstaged. She had envisioned sitting around the table with pie and coffee having civilized conversation about church and lunch tomorrow; instead they were going to sit out back and sweat and drink like rednecks.

Gina pointed a finger with a bright red fingernail at her and said, "You *are* drinking a daiquiri, aren't you?"

She looked at the beautiful but uncut and unwanted pie in the bakery box and wondered where all these drinking Baptists had come from. But what was she to do? Poop her own party-centered plans?

So here they went, the newest branch of Future Alcoholics of Austin, carrying their foamy pink drinks into the backyard. They sat on lawn chairs on the patio, and Lori thought the pink drink was tasty except for a slightly medicinal undercurrent, which she assumed was the pirate's potion. Yo, ho, ho, down the hatch and get it over with. The drink was pleasant and cold, and it helped offset the heat of the night. She was sitting next to the box fan and the steady whine of the motor helped relax her.

"Chris," she asked, "can I have another—"

Lord, the boy had jumped up and whisked the glass out of her hand and was leaping up the back steps and into the house before she even got to finish her sentence, the last part of which was going to be, "but without any rum in it." What was she going to do with two drinks? She couldn't think of an excuse to drink the second, except Chris was always telling her she should "loosen up."

Gina sat forward, crossed her legs, and rested her elbow on her knees. "You are or aren't going to teach?"

Lori nodded, thinking, what a strange way to ask a question.

149

"Does that mean yes, you are going to teach, or yes, she's right, you aren't?" Sam asked.

Lori laughed. No wonder these two dissimilar people had married; they were the only two who understood each other. "Yes, I'm going to teach. Third grade."

"Have you been teaching third grade?" Sam asked.

Why were these two so confused? They'd only met a few weeks ago and Sam and Gina both were well aware she and Chris had just moved here from Waco. How could she have been teaching third grade if she'd been moving? Oh, now she understood. Sam meant had she taught third grade in Waco. But before she could answer, Gina had started giggling and Sam was repeating his question as though she were deaf.

"Have you been teaching third grade?"

"In Waco. Yes, I did. Teach third grade."

"One more drink and she'll be reducing fractions," Gina said.

Lori started to inquire about the meaning of the last remark, but Chris placed the pink drink in her hand, and the glass was so cold against her skin, so refreshing to feel, that she took a long sip. A reason to drink it didn't seem required.

The three of them—Chris, Gina, and Sam—all traded glances, smiling as though they'd watched a monkey at the zoo commit an off-color act they couldn't discuss but could smile about. Their amusement seemed to grow until Chris started laughing and pointing at her.

"What?"

"You've got a pink mustache."

Lori wiped her lips with her fingertip. "What's this thing called?"

"A mustache," Chris said. "A pink mustache."

That comment drew an even bigger laugh, and Lori wasn't sure she should join in since they were laughing at her. So she didn't. "No, no, no. I mean this thing in my hand. What's it called?"

"A daiquiri," Gina said. "A strawberry daiquiri."

Actually, she thought, she shouldn't take offense because they were merely sharing good humor, just a good comradely laugh. She looked at the glass and had already forgotten the name. Dockory. Dickory. Hickory, dickory, what? Lord, her brain was gone. One pink drink and her memory banks were wiped clean. She couldn't remember one simple word more than a few seconds.

Then, before she realized it, she was feeling downright goofy. She brushed her cheek, thinking a mosquito was biting her, and she couldn't even feel her cheek. It was numb, as though she'd been to the dentist. And her neck was so limber that her head wanted to roll around in big circles. My goodness, she thought, I'm drunk. As a skunk. Actually, she kind of liked the feeling. She could have been a child again, just playing house with all these people. And weren't they going to be surprised when they discovered how Gina had manufactured her mature appearance by putting two little puppy dogs in her mother's bra. Lori started giggling, visualizing Gina bending over and the two playful puppies leaping for freedom.

Lori started to order another drink but discovered her glass was full. How could it be full? She'd only had one and one-fourth drinks. She looked at Chris and asked, "Did you fill up my glass when I wasn't looking?"

"How many drinks have you had?" he asked, sounding like a Department of Public Safety trooper checking her sobriety.

"One and one-fourth," she said, clearly and loudly. "And my reflexes are just like that." She snapped her fingers.

Chris pressed his lips together, as though he were watching a child who shouldn't be encouraged in her mischief. Then he said, "That's at least your fourth drink."

Everyone was laughing again, and Lori decided to tell a joke, so they'd keep laughing, keep the atmosphere of the party light and happy. This joke was one she'd heard at church and she'd intended to tell it to Chris and had forgotten. "There was this woman—no, the man woke up on his honeymoon, well, the woman would have woken up first because she was tickling the man's forehead with a feather. Anyway, when the man woke up, his wife was tickling his

151

forehead with this little feather. And he said, 'What're you doing, tickling my forehead with a feather?' And she said, 'You remember last night when you said you were going to love me to death?' And the man said, yes, he remembered. She said, 'Well, that's what I'm—' No, no, that's not what she said."

Gina stole the punch line right out from under Lori. She finished the joke. "The wife said, 'Comparatively speaking, I'm beating your brains out.'"

Well, how do you like that? Lori asked herself. A woman who'd steal your punch line would probably engage in all sorts of suspect behavior, including but not limited to overt attempts to disgrace smaller breasts. And Gina and Chris, enjoying this joke theft, got up together and entered the house, laughing like dear old friends. Those two had no regard for the proper ownership of punch lines and she didn't think they had any business in the house together, so she got up to follow them in.

Whoops, careful. She hadn't moved for some time, and when she did, she was surprised to find herself off course as though a strong wind was blowing from her left. She was a little bit tipsy. And her face was still numb.

Chris was inside at the kitchen counter making another pink drink, but Gina was nowhere to be seen, probably off stealing something else of Lori's, like her good reputation or her fondest memories. You had to watch women like that every second; they could make you feel worse than pimples could.

"She stole my joke and you laughed," Lori said, leaning on the counter beside Chris.

"It was a funny joke. Anyway, two people can tell it better than one. Especially when one's had too much to drink."

"I haven't had too much to drink." She picked up an empty glass from the counter and then slammed it down. "Set 'em up, barkeep. This round's on me."

Chris snickered—he didn't laugh loudly as he had when Gina had delivered the purloined punch line—and shook his head. Gina returned to the kitchen, looking healthy and lovely and endowed like God's favorite daughter. And what did Chris do? He gave Gina the pink drink and they walked right out of the house without even inviting Lori along. What could be any sadder than that? The last drink went to the biggest breasts.

Lori walked to the storm door and looked outside. The three people on the patio were having a good time, and they didn't even remember that a few minutes ago a fourth had been among them. This was how it felt to die, to watch life go on without you, to watch people who should have missed you going right on with their lives, laughing and drinking and playing.

Then all three stopped talking and looked at her standing there, framed by the brass border of the door. They whispered and laughed. Lori couldn't hear the words but she knew what they were saying.

"She could pass for your brother, Chris."

"Yeah, she is a skinny little bitch, but think of all the money we've saved on bras."

Lori had been omitted from her own party. She was so unremark-able, she didn't even deserve another drink. And now the future was flashing before her eyes. She would die and Chris would still live here, unbothered by any memories of her, and he would in-vite beautiful women over here to eat expensive cuts of meat. And they'd drink pink drinks and he'd take them inside and they'd kiss and go to the bedroom . . . and they'd. . . .

Standing at the door, she began to cry.

Chris, shaking his head, came inside and wiped her tears away with his finger. Lori wasn't even worth a Kleenex anymore.

"What's wrong with you?" he asked.

"You gave my drink to those big titties."

"Lori, you are *through* drinking. Forever. I didn't make that drink for you. And I can't believe you're standing here crying when you were out there telling jokes a minute ago."

"She stole my joke. I only had one joke to tell, and she stole it."

153

Still shaking his head and now laughing, he led her into the living room and sat her on the couch. The room was dark but the drapes were open over the picture window, and the moon was brilliant over the trees. It was such a beautiful, personal scene that it must have come from God. It was his way of saying, "I forgot to give you the big mammaries, so this is for you."

Chris sat beside her on the couch and asked, "Have you ever heard the phrase, 'can't hold your liquor'?"

"Maybe."

The problem was that she'd been tricked. Those little pink drinks looked as innocent as popsicles, and if she'd known how potent they were, she'd never have consumed one and one-fourth of the things. And now, she was going to be known not only as a skinny broad, but as a skinny broad who couldn't hold her liquor.

"Are you moving?" she asked.

"No. Why?"

"Then we're not falling?"

"Uh oh," Chris said, standing, watching her for a moment.

She gagged. Her stomach was announcing a real dislike of the pirate's potion and it was just about ready to evict all of it from within.

Chris ran to the kitchen for the trash can, returning with it just in time for her to vomit all over the empty daiquiri mix cans. She threw up until her stomach was empty, and then she threw up some more as if her stomach wanted to make certain all that horrible stuff was gone altogether and to impress upon her the wages of drinking.

"This is the best part of getting drunk," Chris said, sitting beside her and holding her forehead as she stared into the gaping mouth of the trash can.

He brought her a wet cloth and wiped her face. She felt weak and depleted and discouraged, and she tried to remember the purpose of having friends over for dinner. She'd had a purpose, hadn't she?

She couldn't remember.

13

Chris went about his new job with enthusiasm, secure in the knowledge that Carl couldn't fire him. He talked people into testifying when they really didn't want to get involved, and he followed the allegedly disabled to their places of employment and obtained the necessary evidence, usually payroll records, to prove them liars when they claimed to be unemployed. He researched court records in hopes of finding that a plaintiff had a criminal background, preferably one involving murder or sodomy, so they could, as one of the lawyers said, "prove the lousy son of a bitch deserves the enmity of the jury." It was all rather fun and he enjoyed it, and the lawyers, pleased with his performance, promised him the first Christmas bonus ever paid an investigator.

He enjoyed the job when he didn't think too closely about it. He kept having the recurring feeling that Christmas wasn't just around the corner; it was here. He had opened all the presents and although what he got was all right, he hadn't got what he'd really wanted, even though he didn't know exactly what that was.

Part of the problem was that he began to see Carl was right. It was a game, maybe the biggest in history, and much wilder than those that Margie, his secretary, watched on TV. It was bigger than Ed McMahon's lottery. Every citizen had the right to take his injury, real or imagined, and shoot the moon. Go for it all. Millions, billions, the sky was the limit. He heard plaintiffs' attorneys talk about their clients. One had watched a husband push his wife to the front door of his office in a wheelchair, so severely disabled she was, having slipped and fallen in a local grocery store, only to see the wife arise from her wheelchair to open the front door. That sight had been strange enough, but it became downright bizarre when the woman wheeled into his office and announced she suffered total paralysis from the waist down.

And the insurance companies were just as bad. They knew there was no point in settling a lawsuit today for $50,000 when they could settle it later for that same amount. Why pay and lose the interest? Legal obligations and moral premises were insignificant when compared with interest rates. They delayed payments in every way they could. When Chris told one claims vice-president that he had found a unique situation, a plaintiff who was actually injured, whose damages were real, and they ought to pay since the family was suffering, he said, "Hell, we can't pay that claim. We've got almost a million reserved and we can settle it for a quarter of that. We've got to keep that reserve up until after the rate hearings."

Plaintiffs squandered their settlements and lost whatever values they'd had, and insurance had destroyed the basis for personal responsibility. Nobody cared what happened. Let the insurance company take care of it.

Chris adjusted his sights somewhat, making decisions on his own. If there was no question in his mind that the plaintiff had a good claim and actual damages, he was careful not to turn up much adverse testimony. And if the claim looked phony, he dug up all the dirt he could find.

It finally occurred to him that the nagging problem, the near depression he was experiencing, wasn't really with the job. It was with life. For twenty-five years he'd been waiting for life to grab him by the throat and issue him a challenge, one that would obsess him, would carry him through the next sixty years in an exhilarated manner, and although life hadn't grabbed him by the throat, it had issued him a challenge, and it was this—just try to stand up to this drudgery for another sixty years.

He wanted to talk to Lori. He wanted to take both her hands and say, "Lori, Lori, we're not so far into this that we can't get out. We can still make Rome. You won't believe the history you can feel in one city. There's more in the Forum than in all the history books you ever read. And the Via Veneto. You'll love it. We can drink wine at a sidewalk café and talk about what it is we'd really like to do. There's too much to learn, too much to do, to sit around here thinking only about making money."

He wanted to, but she was too busy scraping the wallpaper from the middle bedroom walls. Besides, he suffered from the guilt of having changed her anyway. He was always encouraging her to live beyond the confines of Lori Lynn, and when she cooperated, he realized he was corrupting her. She'd been actually drunk, she cussed, she got depressed, she was suspicious.

He felt so bad over what she had become that he began to go to church with her again.

"Oh, this makes me so happy," she said the first Sunday they rode to church after his absence.

"I'm glad," he said. "I like to see you happy."

Chris thought of a line he'd heard spoken about George Allen after he'd been made head coach of the Washington Redskins. "He was given an unlimited budget, and on the second day, he exceeded it." If Lori bought a seventy-five-dollar sconce for the den wall, and he didn't object, she assumed he was agreeable to an eighteen-hundred-dollar dining room table. What had started out as a simple remodeling project had become an overhauling of their economic system.

Still, there was a benefit. Gina started spending more time at their house, and it was difficult for him to object to seeing the Goddesses of Pert and Plenty hanging wallpaper in the bedroom. In a way, Gina reminded him of Carl. She never seemed to talk to him as much as she seemed to conspire, face close to his, and she was impossible to ignore. Like Carl, she didn't want to be ignored.

She gave Lori troubles in dressing. Every time they were scheduled to visit in Gina's home, Lori had trouble selecting the clothes she needed to wear. She'd try on an outfit and ask, "Well?" He'd tell her to put on her tight jeans with the beige silk blouse. She'd try another dress. "Girl next door," he'd say. She'd try on four or five more outfits before she settled on the tight jeans and beige blouse.

Chris discovered two facts: he shouldn't have told Lori to go ahead with whatever remodeling project, just to do it but leave him out because he didn't see the logic in buying a house you liked only to change it, because, like George Allen, she had no regard for money. She felt free to spend whatever her salary was, but she was working on an annual salary in the first month of the project. Then too, Chris felt as though he were separating from the house. He remained physically, but spiritually, he was cruising through the West on a motorcycle. He'd stop at some little diner, a biker in need of music and drink and conversation. The waitresses would recognize him for what he was—a drifter, irresponsible but irresistible. Two would fight over him, and he'd go with the lanky, big-nosed girl who didn't get any propositions. They'd spend the night in her trailer at the lake, and the next morning, she'd beg him to stay while she fried bacon and eggs over a stove that hadn't been cleaned in months, her hair a mess. Chris would kiss her good-bye and ride off, wiping bacon grease from his mouth with the back of his hand.

He fell prone to the fantasies even at Gina's, in a house Lori lusted after. It was built in the hills west of Austin on split levels and had huge windows with a beautiful view of the city below. One night as they sat digesting dinner, looking out the windows at a sea of lights below and beyond, Chris watched moving lights, knowing that one of them was a man on a motorcycle, some guy who hadn't got a haircut or shaved in years. He wore a floppy hat and called himself by one name. Boots or Willie or just Man. In the winter, he drove along the coast, in the mountains during the summer. He flew down the highway, a throbbing machine roaring beneath him.

He'd sit in traffic in Nashville, waiting on a traffic light, absently adjusting the idle of his walloping machine with a screwdriver he carried in his hip pocket, his manner and appearance thrown to the winds. A station wagon would pull up next to him, and a ten-year-old boy would lean out the window and yell, "Hey, Boots, gimme five." Boots would give him five and roar off down the road, leaving one knowing child among a station wagon full of open-mouthed tourists.

When he got tired of riding, he'd rent a little beach house on Padre Island, the kind on stilts, and spend hours wandering up and down the beach looking at the surf and gulls and clouds. He'd find a girl in the dunes who looked exactly like Gina, wearing a pure white bikini over her incredibly tanned body.

They'd talk for hours over what one was to do with his life.

"I'm going to Rome next month. Want to come?" he'd ask.

Of course, she'd want to.

"Why're you listening to music so much?" Lori asked.

Chris opened his eyes and saw his wife's face only inches from his. He lay on the floor near the stereo in the living room, headphones over this ears, listening to Willie Nelson sing "Bloody Mary Morning." He started to answer her, to tell her his fantasies needed a soundtrack, but he didn't. She'd want to know the content of the fantasy, and he didn't want to tell her.

"I just like music."

"I like my husband, but I don't ever see him anymore."

"Turn the light out and lay down with me."

She obviously had matters on her mind, and included in them was not lying beside her husband listening to music. But she turned the light out, opened the drapes over the picture window, and lay down. Chris disconnected the headphones, and inserted a Delbert McClinton tape into the player. The room filled with the sounds of a guitar and piano and drum and Delbert singing about sandy beaches.

"Does it have to be so loud?" she asked, moving against him.

"If we're going to listen to music, yes. If we're going to talk, no. I thought we were going to listen to music."

"We can't do both?"

"Listen to this song," he said because the words of the song would come closer than he ever would to telling her what he wanted.

They listened, and McClinton served as spokesman, telling Lori about slow boats to China and disappearing to places where they couldn't be found and having nothing else to do but make love. Lori was always missing from his fantasies because she didn't want to go. Chris wanted her to go, wanted her in faded Levi's and a black T-shirt riding behind him on the motorcycle.

"Do you like his voice?" she asked.

"Lori, listen to the damn song."

"His voice bothers me. I think he smokes too much."

"But what about the song? Does it do anything for you?"

"Well, it sounds kinda like a hippie song to me. You know, a dropout song."

"Well, don't you ever feel like dropping out?"

"Sometimes at school I do. But not when I come home. I look forward to coming home and working on the house. Don't you like what I'm doing?"

"I think you're doing a good job," he said, trying to hide his disappointment over her confirmation that she hadn't changed overnight and become just like him. She'd look great on a motorcycle. She looked great anywhere.

"If I turned the light on, would you look at the wallpaper I picked out for our bathroom?"

He sighed. "There is *nothing* I'd rather do."

"And maybe we could turn the stereo down so we could talk a minute. I need to get your opinion on some other things."

"Wonderful."

"Oh, good. It'll only take a few minutes."

Chris even heard the *shik, shik, shik* of Lori removing wallpaper as he sat at his desk at work. She seemed to him obsessed with redoing the entire house. He saw sketches lying around that he avoided looking at, hoping he wouldn't come home some afternoon to find his bedroom moved to the other side of the house.

Carl provided him with a distraction one morning, sauntering into Chris's office to break a silence that had lasted several months. If Carl had wanted any work on a file, he sent it to Chris with a note attached; Chris completed the investigation, wrote up his report, and sent the file back to Carl. Otherwise, they hadn't communicated at all.

Carl sat in the only chair in Chris's small office and stretched his legs out along the front side of the desk. "Randy says you can't find Larry Sheffield, that witness in the Grimes file."

The Grimes file involved a fatality, a gross negligence lawsuit over the extremely sloppy and unsafe operations of a small oil field drilling contractor who had been drilling fast and furious during the boom, getting rich and leaving a long line of injured roughnecks behind because he wouldn't spend the time necessary to maintain his rig. Chris had in fact found Sheffield, now an unemployed oil field hand, and the man was anxious to testify for his former employer. He was not only anxious, but he was willing to say things that weren't true.

"What about him?" Chris asked.

"I know where he is because he called me a week ago or so. I got involved in something else and I forgot to tell Randy the guy had called."

"How about that."

Neither of them spoke for a minute, each looking at the other and playing a waiting game. The scene had the feel of a negotiating session in which one person wanted to hint at what he knew but wouldn't come right out and say it. Chris sat back and played with the cap off a plastic Bic pen.

"You know what I think?" Carl finally asked. "I think you knew where he was. I think you might have even talked to him."

"What makes you think that?"

Carl shrugged, straightening his suit coat. "Nothing more than the fact that Sheffield had your card and said you'd come to see him."

Leaving the card had been a mistake, no doubt about that. Chris

161

had known as soon as he'd driven away from the man's hovel of a house. He'd known he wasn't going to mention Sheffield's whereabouts or his willingness to testify because Chris thought the claim should have been settled long ago. Years ago. And bringing in a favorable witness at this point, especially one willing to lie, would only prolong the process.

He couldn't determine what Carl's purpose in this visit was, but the older brother wasn't going to hold anything over him. If Carl wanted to go to one of the partners and squeal, then he should feel free. Chris could then go buy a motorcycle and ride off into the sunset.

"I'm trying to figure something out," Carl said. "You can help. Why is it you'd locate a witness, talk to him, learn he can help our client, then come back and write a report to Randy saying you can't find the guy."

Chris sat forward at his desk and said, "It's real simple. The insurance company knows they're going to have to pay Grimes' wife. Grimes' wife is sitting in a low-income apartment with three kids waiting on the money. She's been working at a minimum wage job for five years waiting on the money. The insurance company ought to have paid her long ago, and I'm not going to admit there's a liar in Giddings willing to help the cause of an insurance company that's been fucking around this long."

He wasn't sure what sort of reaction he had been expecting from Carl, but when his brother smiled, Chris was shocked.

"You're beginning to see how this works, aren't you?"

Chris didn't answer.

Carl sat up straight, then leaned on Chris's desk and spoke in a conspiratorial manner. "If I remember, you're the same guy who gave me a long sermon on lying to a jury. You're the same guy. You didn't understand what happens then, you didn't understand how far you'd go to counterbalance all the weight on the other side of the scale. Did you?"

Chris shook his head. "No, I didn't, and I'm not saying now I'd lie to a jury, and I'm not saying I approved of what you did. Maybe I do understand a little more than I did."

He wasn't accustomed to being on the same side as Carl, to feeling like a co-conspirator with him, especially after all these months of silence and the knowledge of Carl's deceptions.

"What'd you tell Randy?"

"I told him Sheffield called and said he wanted to testify for Leon Drilling. That he said, quote, 'I really wanta help Leon out. You just tell me what to say and I'll say it.' End quote."

"And what'd Randy say?"

"He said if I repeated what I just told him, he'd not only kill me but he'd kill Sheffield too."

Chris smiled.

Carl stood and said, "I've got a surprise for you after work. Call Lori and tell her you won't be home. I've got something that's going to knock your socks off."

"What?"

"You'll see."

Chris was suspicious about Carl's surprise, but he was ready to take a night off from the dust and paint cans and rags and general mess of the house. They left the office together after work and drove to, of all places, a topless bar.

"What're we doing here?"

"Look," Carl said. "For once just relax and see what happens. You've always had this idea that everything around you has to have some sort of significance attached to it, and it doesn't. Just relax."

They walked into the rowdy, smoke-filled bar. There was a small stage at the front of the room, bordered with lights, and dancing was a stringy sort of girl wearing bright red bikini panties. Her body didn't seem to have matured; it had just gotten hard. Smiling, she gave the finger to one of the customers sitting along the edge of the

163

stage. The other waitress-dancers moved about the room with small trays, expertly dodging hands and lewd invitations to trespass on a face.

"One hell of a surprise," Chris said as they sat.

Carl shook his head as though his brother was a hopeless cause, then waved to someone.

"You know somebody in here?"

"Just a friendly sort over there."

Chris ordered a beer, not happy to be in such a place. It reminded him too much of his inane behavior in the navy. Not that he considered sitting in a topless bar inane behavior; it was the general effect such a place had on him and the general deterioration of his personality that almost always followed.

The music and dancer changed about the time a waitress delivered two beers to their table. The new dancer was much prettier, wearing a black dress and sporting frizzy blonde hair. She danced to an old ZZ Top song called "La Grange," and the music started off slow and subdued. Chris remembered the song and he was ready for the change that followed a drum transition. An overwhelming bass blasted the girl into high speed. She removed her black dress with one quick movement and threw it against the mirror at the rear of the stage. She had a finely tuned body, wore silver panties, and she moved with the music, which was now revving like a dragster. Another drum transition and more speed. The dancer was a blur of skin and blonde hair.

The lights in the bar went off and a strobe ignited. The music whistled, screeched, and pounded. The dancer fell onto her back, bowing her body upward from toes to shoulders, a bridge for the blinking strobe to cross. The rapidly flashing light accentuated her movements, translating them into a stop-action sequence, a series of negatives, illuminating a fine gloss of hair on her body, a coat of glistening sweat. Chris watched as if stoned, the bass and strobe pounding into his head. Carl, his face in profile, seemed to disappear and reappear in the same instant.

164

Was this the surprise? he wondered. If it was, it wasn't bad, but there had to be something more.

And there was.

When the blonde dancer finished her frantic routine and the lights came back on, the previous dancer, the one whose body had never seemed to mature before petrification had set in, appeared at their table with her small tray.

"You said you'd bring him," the dancer said, smiling at Chris.

"I said it, and here he is," Carl said proudly.

In an instant, Chris comprehended terrible reality—he knew the dancer. Ruth Hill, or Little Ruthie, from high school. The cadaverous face had inspired a thousand juvenile jokes. He had tried hard to repress her memory, but she was the best example in the world of his inane behavior that resulted from too much drinking. Too much drinking had led him to commit the most personal act, the most personal act the first time ever, with the girl. It had been the most closely guarded secret of his life, but of course Carl had found out.

"Hi, Ruth. I didn't even recognize you. How're you doing?"

Wearing a man's plaid shirt, unbuttoned down the front, she pulled a chair from a nearby table and sat facing Chris. He wanted to suddenly disappear and reappear in someone else's body, preferably in Siberia without women or alcohol, and there he would live, happily or unhappily—it didn't matter which—for the rest of his life.

She sat forward, resting her hand on Chris's leg. "I'm doing fine. I've been dancing here about a year. I can't believe we haven't run into each other." When he didn't respond, she added, "This is a pretty good job. I get lots of tips. Guys just stick dollar bills right down there." She opened her shirt so he could see her depository, bright red panties. And her walnut-sized breasts. "So, what're you doing?"

"Working with him on that game show. What's the name of it?"

Carl said, "The Great State Crap Shoot."

"I thought you were a lawyer," she said to Carl, leaving her hand on Chris's leg, her fingertips playing the piano on his inseam.

"I am. I guide people through the crap shoot. There're thousands of people each day wanting to become an instant winner."

"Yeah? I fell off the stage the other night and sprained my ankle. Can I get anything?"

"Hey, can you roll the dice? If we can prove you're not an employee, you'll get a free roll. There's no warning around the stage, no guard rail, no bright paint to mark the edge. *Come on down!*"

Ruth smiled, nodding. "Yeah, there oughta be something. Besides, I need some money to pay my other lawyer."

Carl looked at Chris and said, "She was arrested the other night. By the vice squad." Winking, he added, "It *had* to be a mistake."

Ruth turned and looked at Chris as though trying to gauge the effect of this news, gazing hopefully into his eyes. She rubbed his leg as if to soothe any pain Carl's revelation might have created, and her hand was too ambitious, climbing too high. He stood and excused himself, looking for the restroom.

He wanted to stay in the restroom longer than he did but the floor was wet and drunks were coming and going, stumbling over each other. He wanted to sit and think, to determine why he was depressed. Seeing Little Ruthie shouldn't have had a depressing effect, nor should the thought that Carl had arranged the meeting. Carl was an expert at setting up reunions with people you never wanted to see again.

In the bar, Chris saw not only Ruth and Carl but the blonde tornado standing there, all chatting as though long-lost friends.

After Chris had wound his way through the smoky interior of the bar and arrived at the small group, Ruth said, "We're all going to get something to eat when we get off. We's us, me and Barbi, and you and Carl. Okay?"

"I can't. I've got to get home."

"Oh, you don't have to get home," Carl said. "Tell him he doesn't have to get home, Barbi."

The blonde smiled an implicit promise. It was a practiced smile, almost automatic, but coming upon the heels of her impressive performance, it meant much more. And Chris, not at all intrigued, decided he must be getting old. A few years ago, faced with returning to a house covered with the powder of sanded sheetrock and sitting to drink a few beers until an acrobat got off work, he would have been happy to sit and drink.

But he shook his head. "No, I'm going home. Good to see you again, Ruth."

"Girls," Carl said, "I'm going to take him back to his car, but I'll be back."

"Don't bother. I want to walk."

"Hell, it's five miles back to the office."

"I don't care. I want to walk."

He was out of the bar before Carl could say anything else.

Walking along a busy street in his suit and tie, he cut across the front of used car lots and parking lots for stores, trying to figure out why he was depressed, why he felt so gloomy. And when he couldn't think of any reason, he began telling himself to snap out of it, think about all he had going for him. He had a good job, the exact wife he wanted and needed, and a house that he would like when Lori got through with it. The mess was temporary.

And then it hit him: he was depressed because he wasn't ever going to ride off on a motorcycle, he wasn't ever going to make Rome, he wasn't ever going to do anything but get up and go to work at a job that made no sense if it was closely analyzed. At the end of every fantasy stood a Little Ruthie, like a goblin, reminding you of reality, making you remember exactly what you were.

14

Lori thought the middle bedroom was a work of art, as beautiful as anything she'd ever seen. It had contrasting wallpaper on the top and bottom of the walls, separated by bright blue molding. She'd bought a bed for the room so her parents wouldn't have to sleep in the living room on the sleeper sofa when they visited, and she'd had to search high and low for exactly the right bedspread.

When the entire room was finished, she asked Chris to come look at it. He walked down the hall and tripped over an empty paint can, then kicked it the length of the hall and scarred the closet door at the other end.

"Lori, why're we living in a mess? Why did we buy a house we both liked and then start tearing it apart, room by room? Why do I trip over a goddamn paint can every time I walk down this hall?"

Lori, flipping on the light switch in the bedroom asked, "Do you want me to stop?"

"No. I don't know."

Lori watched him step into the room, feeling the effect she'd wanted—the flip of the switch and the illumination of a bright new room—fade away. He was still upset over the stray paint can. Looking around the room as though it might have been a torture chamber, he nodded.

"It's nice. You did a good job." Then, realizing the complete lack of enthusiasm he was showing, he said, "Really. You have a good eye for all this. The guy who owned the place ought to come back and see what you've done."

"Do you want to see what I got for the other bedroom?"

"Not right now. All right? Maybe later."

He wasn't home many nights, so why should he complain? He was off drinking with lawyers, apparently preparing himself for the AA meetings he would be attending the rest of his life. He went to bed before she did most nights, as soon as he got in from his latest round of drinking, and when Lori climbed into bed, he was almost always snoring. A drunken snore loud enough to make her chest vibrate.

When she started working on the third bedroom, she kept the door closed and confined all her equipment to the room. When she began stripping the wallpaper, she chinked the door with towels to keep the dust from infiltrating the rest of the house. Doing all that chinking was a real pain, and every time she had to go to the bathroom or get a drink and pull all the towels out of the space around the door, and every time she had to stuff the towels back in with a putty knife, she had to tell herself she was doing this because she loved her husband. She loved him even if he was spending far too much time drinking in the afternoons.

But she also loved remodeling the house. She would often sit in the middle bedroom looking at her handiwork, her color schemes, and think about what the room had looked like before she had started. Seeing that bedroom was a completely satisfying feeling, more than worth all the work.

She was chinked into the third bedroom, which was on the corner of the house, when one afternoon she saw a white MG turn into the driveway, followed by Chris's car, a blue and white Buick Skylark. Chris got out of the MG, Carl from the Skylark. The two brothers stood around on the driveway looking at the MG.

Lori, hoping beyond hope that she was wrong in her assumption, jerked all the towels from the crack around the door, and walked hurriedly down the hall and out of the house.

Carl smiled and said, "Now you get to tell her."

"How do you like it?" Chris asked, pointing at the little white convertible in their driveway.

"It looks like a rollerskate."

"Yeah, that's the beauty of it. It corners and handles like a rollerskate, not like an oversized American car."

He wasn't going to volunteer the information, so Lori asked: "You're not going to buy it, are you?"

"Already have."

She'd been fearing this very thing. Chris was due to get a Christmas bonus of $2,000, just enough to finish their bathroom. Her plan was to take out Chris's closet, enlarge the bathroom, and install a large tub with a Jacuzzi. She could get the whole job done for $2,000.

"Your Christmas bonus?" she asked.

"It was just enough."

She turned and walked back into the house, not about to discuss the matter in front of Carl. He was waiting for the big fight, she could tell, and would encourage them both once they got started, trying to prolong it.

"Let's take a ride," Chris yelled.

She didn't respond, returning to the bedroom. She was through chinking, she knew that. She'd chinked her last and now couldn't believe she'd wasted so much time doing it before. Picking up her putty knife, she returned to the job of stripping the old wallpaper but found she was using the broad-bladed scraper so viciously that she was gouging the wall.

She stepped back, needing to do something. Break a window, call down bats from the attic and direct them at the two men out front. She stretched out her arms, made fists, and started to scream as loud as she could, but she didn't.

How could her husband be so stupid, so childish, so silly, and buy a third car? The more she thought about it, the angrier she got. She stood near the window and watched the brothers drive off in the little car, music blaring from its radio, and watching them, she got axe-swinging mad. Mad-dog mad.

She threw down her putty knife and walked to the phone and called Gina.

"I need a drink," she said when Gina answered. "I need one of those pink things. In a bar. I want to smoke a cigarette and—" She'd almost said "pick up a man." She didn't want to pick up a man, but she did want a pink drink in a bar. "And I don't want to be here when Chris comes back, so I'm bringing clothes to your house and I'll change over there."

"What happened?" Gina asked, amusement in her voice.

"My stupid husband just drove off in my big bathtub."

"I could've predicted that would happen sooner or later. Maybe not buying a car, but something. He went too long without protesting."

"Well, he just protested. He drove home his Christmas bonus, and he never even discussed it with me. The least he could have done, the *very least*, was tell me what he was doing."

"You would've talked him out of it and he knew it."

Lori closed her eyes, trying to remember if she'd ever been so mad. If she had been, she couldn't remember it. So now she was going to wear Chris's favorite outfit, the tight jeans and beige blouse, and she was going out with Gina. Chris had been begging her to do that very thing with him for years, and she'd always refused. But now she'd go all right, just not with him.

They went to the bar on top of the Holiday Inn near the river, and Lori was surprised by what a cozy, friendly place it was. She hadn't been in many bars, but she'd always visualized them as dirty places full of roughnecks with drilling mud all over their boots breaking pool cues over one another's heads. But this bar not only had a wall of windows but had a good view of the freeway below and Town Lake.

Gina suggested a number of other bars—she seemed to know every nightspot in town—but the names were far too provocative. Places where you could probably get in trouble. She hadn't changed clothes at Gina's before she'd begun to regret the decision to go out for a drink, but every time Gina had asked a question about Chris's newest acquisition, she'd gotten mad all over again.

Besides, there was hardly anyone in this bar; they'd have one drink and Lori could go home.

"Has Sam ever done anything that dumb?" Lori asked.

"Sam's never done anything dumb. I wish he would. At least once. Personally, I'd love it if he came home in an MG."

Lori spied a waitress headed their way and said, "Order for me. If I remember the name, I'll mispronounce it."

The waitress took their order for a daiquiri and a margarita and suggested they help themselves to hors d'oeuvres. There was a fondue tray of sausage across the room, the blue flames bright in the nearly darkened bar, but Lori wasn't hungry. Gina, who seemed to eat all the time but never gain a pound except in the places she wanted it, ate enough sausage pieces with a toothpick for both of them.

"Why don't you just go ahead with your plans and put it all on Visa?" Gina asked.

"Because Visa's already overloaded. I have next month's salary on Visa. And Mother gave me February's salary."

"It sounds to me like Chris deserved the MG."

"Don't say that."

"Listen, girl, you've got the best husband I've ever seen. My God, he worships the ground you walk on, he's sexy, he's good-looking, he does whatever you want. Up to a point. Be grateful you haven't got a deadhead like Sam. All Sam does is make money, which is all right, I'm glad he does, but he's so boring. His idea of a big night is to take a shower at eight and then get in bed and read. How's your sex life? I bet it's better than mine, or better than mine with Sam."

What did she mean? That she had affairs? The pink drink had loosened Lori's tongue, made her neck feel so relaxed that she could turn her head without any effort at all, so she asked, "Do you have, you know, affairs?"

"Sure, don't you?"

"No. No, I've never done anything like that."

Lori wasn't sure what to make of Gina's revelation, coming as it did upon the back of her comment on Chris, who was, in Gina's opinion, good-looking, sexy, and correct to have bought an MG with Lori's remodeling money. Was Gina the sort to go looking for Chris so she could sympathize, soothe, and then F-word him?

Right in the middle of Lori's meditation, she heard a male voice ask from her left, "And how are the ladies tonight?"

She looked up to see two men standing at their table, drinks in hand, ready to sit with them. Lori froze; she couldn't swallow for a moment. First she wondered why on earth these men thought she and Gina were available, then remembered they were in a bar. This must be like hunting season; fix some game in your sights, and bang, Lori would be tagged and hanging from a tree like a deer.

"The ladies are fine," Gina said. "How're the men?"

To Lori's horror, the two men sat down at their table. The older one, a man in a corduroy jacket with an open-necked shirt, the one doing the talking, had apparently chosen Gina. The man sitting down beside Lori was younger, maybe thirty, wearing a pink knit shirt. He was nice-looking, tall and broad-shouldered, and she pegged him immediately for a salesman simply because of his automatic smile.

The waitress arrived with fresh drinks for all of them. "On us," the corduroy jacket by Gina said. Lord, Lord, Lori thought. Even the waitress was in on the hunt; they were being circled and run into a trap.

Lewis in the jacket, sitting beside Gina, facing her, his hand already on the back of her chair, introduced himself and his friend, Jim, whose smile compounded as he nodded politely toward Lori. Gina responded, giving first names only, and Lori had the feeling she was suddenly and without warning cast into the role of a one-named harlot. She was headed for an orgy, ready or not. Never in her life had she introduced herself by her first name only.

"We've been watching you from across the room," Lewis said, getting comfortable, almost hugging Gina's chair. "We were trying to figure out what you do. We finally decided, you're in public relations," he said to Gina. Then, pointing directly at Lori and making her sweat, he said, "And you're one of her clients. You just bought a string of massage parlors and you're trying to upgrade their image."

Gina found this speculation hilarious and threw her head back

173

to laugh. Lori tried hard not to blush but did anyway as the men looked at her and smiled.

"Must've gotten close," Lewis said. "Look at her face."

Lori mentally tried several responses but couldn't think of one that wouldn't make the situation worse. Instead she tried to think of a graceful exit, devoutly wishing she'd brought her car, wishing even more devoutly the man to her left wasn't staring at her as though she were already naked. She could tell he was waiting on encouragement, no matter how minor, and if she offered it, he'd probably have his pants unzipped before she could clear her throat.

Gina gave the two men a serious look, glancing from one to the other, and said, "Okay, let's see. If I'm in PR and she gives massages, then you're probably her best customer and he wants to be."

The two men laughed in appreciation and Lewis said they were both from Corpus Christi, both electronics parts salesmen up for a meeting. "You ladies from Austin?"

"No," Gina said. "We're from Houston. And we work for Blue Haven Pools. You've probably seen her in the ads, you know, coming out of the pool on a chrome ladder, smiling at a man with a drink in his hand."

Lewis looked at Jim. "You said you'd seen her somewhere. TV, I bet. Is the ad on TV?"

"It is," Gina said. "You're exactly right. I'm glad someone is seeing our ads. I put too much time in on those things for them to go unnoticed, and I know Lori here is happy you remember. Aren't you?"

Lori said nothing, sending instead an evil look, the same look she'd sent Carl Gray's way on more than one occasion. It said silently that she recognized scum in both plant and animal forms.

"Well, I do remember," Jim said, the first words he'd spoken, "and the reason I remember is because I kept thinking the name of the company was Blue Heaven, not Haven. I figured it had to be Heaven." He smiled at this slight witticism.

"Excuse me," Lori said, rising.

Jim was out of his chair, pulling hers away from the table before she was upright, and she walked toward the restroom. The bar had grown suddenly crowded without her notice, and she made her way through the tables, spying the exit before she saw the restroom.

In the hall outside the bar, she stood for a moment fanning herself, close to hyperventilating, and experiencing hot flashes in her ears. She walked the circular hall, looking for a phone because the only solution to her problem was husbandly intervention. Chris needed to come get her.

She found a phone and called, hoping he'd find more to laugh about than to get mad about in her predicament, but the choice was moot. The phone rang and rang. Wonderful, she thought. He was probably out with Carl, acting as Lewis's and Jim's counterpart in some other bar, mouthing inanities such as, "I figured it had to be Heaven."

Well, her only other option was to call a taxi, and she'd never even seen the interior of one. Probably, unless matters grew worse, she was as safe in the bar as she was alone in a taxi, driven by some psychopath who'd drop her off, then sneak back to her house and look in her window. He'd wait for her to take out the trash, and then he'd rape her and dismember her body. At least Jim didn't appear to be a murderer.

She returned to the bar and the table. Jim was up and on his feet, pulling her chair out, ready to tell her once he'd assisted a lady with her chair two times, he was ready to get down to some serious sex. She avoided looking at him, concentrating instead on the pink drink before her. She couldn't drink it. She'd never touch one of those things again.

Gina and Lewis were entertaining each other with Aggie jokes, shooting them back and forth and hardly giving the other time enough to laugh.

"You heard about the skeleton they found at A&M, didn't you? Found it in the back of a broom closet."

"No, who was it?"

"Hide and Seek Champion of 1947."

While the two slapped each other's arms and bent forward as though huddling, Lori watched, turning her glass on the table, waiting for Gina to look at her so she could signal *let's go home*. But Gina was a walking Aggie joke collection; she knew thousands, maybe millions, more than any other living person.

Jim scooted his chair closer to Lori's and leaned forward. "Do you believe in fate?"

"No," she said, lifting her drink and looking at it as though she might take a sip. "I'm a Baptist." Then she added, "A drinking Baptist, but a Baptist." The wrong thing to say, absolutely wrong. Jim wasn't discouraged and she'd given him the opportunity to think he could fill in the blank prior to Baptist with whatever moral exception he chose. Was she a swinging Baptist? Or better yet, a f—— Baptist? What was wrong with her?

"Well," Jim said. "I'm a strong believer in fate. I can see certain lines intersecting—"

"I'm not an intersecting Baptist."

"I was driving up here with Lewis and I had this feeling something really terrific was going to happen. It was just a feeling, but it was really strong. Really very strong. And when I walked in the door over there, I looked right at you. The first thing I saw in here was you."

She gave him a sweet smile and said, "I'm not a thing either."

"Well, you know what I meant," he said, moving his chair even closer, his knee now touching her thigh, his hand on the table creeping toward hers, moving the last obstacle, Lori's drink.

The touch of his knee may as well have been a syringe injecting anger into her leg, an emotion which displaced all of her nervousness. She might be sitting in a bar right in the middle of hunting season, but a rutting male who thought she could be made in a matter of minutes should forever remember her.

"You know, you remind me of a boy I knew in high school."

"Really?" he said, attempting to cover her hand with his, missing when she picked up her purse and set it in her lap.

"Um hmm," she said pleasantly. "His name was Elmer, and his ears stuck out kinda like yours and his nose had that same kind of twist, where it didn't sit quite level on his face. And his ambition was to work on a farm because of all the things he did best, the thing he did best of all was shovel horseshit."

Without waiting for a reaction, she got up and started toward the door, disappointed to see that Jim was close behind, following her through the tables. She had to slow to open the door that led to the hall, and when she did, he caught her.

"I don't think I deserved all that," he said. "I was just trying to be nice."

She made her way toward the elevator, punching the button before she answered him. "I don't know what you deserve and don't care. Go crowd some other woman. I'm leaving."

"Okay, I'll back off. No problem," he said, waving his hands as though he were backing off although he hadn't moved an inch.

Where was the elevator? she wondered, and why was this happening? Of all the men running around Austin wanting to pick up a woman, she'd found one determined to charm her, a persistent omnipresent salesman who believed he would still succeed. He now leaned against the wall and gave her his innocent, boyish look, one in which he obviously had great faith. And with good reason, she thought. He was cute, and he probably could be charming, and his success rate with women was probably high. But if the elevator didn't come very quickly, she was going to smack him right between the legs with her purse and take the stairs.

"You might as well come back to the table. Otherwise, I'll just go walk around outside and come back in an hour and then tell your friend we went to my room."

How could he say this so innocently? With a smile? "I just want you to understand one thing—I'm leaving here, *by myself*, and there's no chance *whatsoever* that I'm going anywhere with you.

177

When the elevator gets here, I'm getting on it, and you *aren't* getting on it, because if you do, I'll pick up the phone and call security and tell them to call your wife so she can come mop up your overactive hormones." She was out of breath after delivering this long threat and tried hard to breathe normally as she stared at the salesman. She tried to put every bit of hostility she could muster into her stare, and she must have succeeded because after a long while, Jim sighed.

"You're basically a bitch, aren't you?"

"Basically."

"Your basic ball-busting bitch."

The elevator finally arrived and Lori stepped into it with, as the Supreme Court would say, all deliberate speed. She watched the doors begin to close, but of course, Jim didn't allow her to go without a parting word. He caught the doors and pushed them open.

"Should I tell them you went down on me first, or the other way around?"

"Just tell them I basically busted your balls. Now get your hands off the doors."

He made a kissing gesture and released the doors. Lori watched them close, grateful to be alone, grateful also that Gina had introduced them by first names only. But then, Gina was much more experienced at evading, or purposely stepping into, snares. Sitting up there like a professional barfly, the girl didn't realize how lucky she was to have a husband who wanted to read in bed. If she was smart, she'd take up reading too.

She had to take a taxi all the way across town to Gina's house, a trip that cost her ten dollars, and then she still had to drive back to the south side of the city in her car.

And there in the driveway, under a floodlight on the eave of the house, in a white MG convertible with the top down, reclined her husband. He lay across both seats, his head propped on the passenger's door, his feet sticking out the other side. He was reading what appeared to be an owner's manual.

"Where've you been?" he asked without moving.

She couldn't decide whether to answer him since he had his stereo up too loud, listening to that Delbert McClinton dropout tape, serenading the neighborhood. Finally she said, "With Gina."

He closed the owner's manual, his thumb holding his place, and he seemed about to say something but he didn't. She assumed he was wanting to comment on her clothes, and she took satisfaction in knowing she'd worn his favorite outfit. This was the third such blouse she'd had just like the prototype, and they were getting harder and harder to find.

I've been beating the men away, she said silently. One tried to hold my hand. Another thought I owned massage parlors. They wanted my body and I started to make a partial donation but I couldn't find anybody my type.

"Where'd you go?" he asked.

"To get a drink."

She walked into the dark garage, smiling, headed for the back door.

"It took you four hours to get *a* drink?"

"I nursed it," she said, walking into her partly remodeled house and slamming the door behind her.

She went about her remodeling efforts silently for the next two days, ignoring Chris. When they passed, they were extremely careful not to touch each other and always left a wide corridor between them. Their eyes didn't meet. Chris tried to turn their bed into a trampoline at night, turning in a way that would bounce her onto the floor. She had to sleep with her hands stuck under the mattress for security. Lori sighed loudly every time she thought he might be falling asleep.

The part that puzzled her was this—Chris had no reason to be mad at her, none whatsoever, but he was. He was supposed to apologize for buying the MG and wouldn't. Basically, he was as stupid as the two men at the Holiday Inn.

The Holiday Inn wasn't a subject she wanted to think about. She wasn't sure why since she hadn't done anything, but she felt as guilty as if she had.

Then too, Christmas was only a week away and she wasn't only wasting her Christmas vacation but she wasn't even in the Christmas spirit. While everyone else was singing "Silent Night," she wanted to belt out some country song about husbands locked in dog houses.

To put Chris in a proper mood for expressing his sorrow, she fried fish one night, one of his favorite meals but one she disliked cooking. That got her nothing but, "Um, good meal." He was too busy reading his MG owner's manual, some greasy book that ten thousand hands had handled, to even think about apologizing.

And since she couldn't speak on the matter before he did—because the entire matter was his fault—she got up early the next morning, on one of her Christmas vacation days when she could otherwise be sleeping until noon, to make him breakfast.

She was at the stove making a Spanish omelet when he walked in and sat at the table as though waiting to be served, as though he lived in a restaurant, as though Lori made him breakfast every morning. She was tempted to let him stew in his guilt indefinitely, but since she was a loving wife, she decided to go ahead and open the discussion.

"How long are you going to be a horse's ass?"

"Me?"

"Yes, you. Who else would I be talking to?"

"Hey, I'm not the one giving you the silent treatment. I'm not the one spending thousands of dollars on a perfectly good house and then getting hysterical when my spouse drops a measly two grand on a sports car. And I'm not the one out tooling all over town at night without even leaving a note on where I went."

Lori, watching the omelet, smiled. So he had been punished.

She offered no comment on the Holiday Inn excursion, preferring to let him wonder about what she'd been doing in his favorite outfit. She wasn't going to feel guilty over one night out on the town. If she felt a little guilt creeping her way, she just walked to the window and looked outside at the MG, its glassy eyes full of stupid male laughter.

Some of us are just born to boogie, she thought.

"Lori, have you got any idea, any idea at all, how much money you've spent on this house?"

"It's covered, no problem," she said, thinking she could sound like a man without any effort. "Don't worry about it."

"I've seen people on a roll before, but I've never watched anybody spending money as hard and as fast as you are."

She popped the omelet onto the plate and delivered it to the table, letting the plate clatter somewhat. She started to point out he had no silverware and wouldn't until he got off his butt and got it himself, but she didn't.

"We've got a new bed, dining room table, two recliners, end tables, coffee table, and I don't know how many rolls of wall paper and gallons of paint and I don't even know what other kind of shit."

He sat there like the customer he thought he was, waiting on Lori to get his coffee and silverware, and so he would know that her mealtime efforts were complete, she sat down and stared at him.

"Mother bought the end tables, and I don't think you're out any money. When we started this, I said I'd pay for it all with my salary, and I am."

"Yeah, and what'd you plan to do with my bonus?"

Lori felt suddenly caught, exposed, trapped in spotlights. "I was going to work on the bathroom."

They looked at each other until they both started laughing. He got up, shaking his head, and walked around the table. Pulling her up from the chair, he drew her into his arms and hugged her. In a different tone of voice, one more conciliatory, he asked, "How much money have you spent?"

181

"Why do you have to worry about money all the time? It's not blood; it's not something important. It's just money. You make money, you spend money, that's all."

"How much?"

She kissed his neck, smelling his shirt, the shampoo he had used on his hair, his skin, the omelet, the coffee, all at the same time, all homey smells that she loved. And she let her face rest against his neck so the words didn't come out very clearly. "Hardly eight thousand dollars."

He pulled away. "How much?"

She knew because she couldn't believe she'd already spent February's salary and had done so little. She added everything up twice. "Chris, I'm paying for all this."

"How much?"

"Less than thirty thousand."

"Lori. How much?"

"Hardly eight thousand."

He sat as though weakened by the figure and then pulled her into his lap, waiting to speak until he had worked one hand through the folds of her robe and gown and onto her breast. She pressed his warm hand tightly to her.

"For twenty-five percent of that, I got punished."

"But you'll love the bathroom. You'll love it. We can play in the bathtub, we can work in the yard and then relax in the tub. Why do you make me unhappy when it would be so easy to make me happy?"

"It isn't my job to make you either; that's your job."

"Is it too late to take the car back?"

"It was too late when I came in one afternoon and saw the business card from a remodeling contractor and that booklet on bathroom fixtures."

"You mean you knew what I wanted to do? You knew, and you went out and bought the car?"

He nodded.

"Do you know how that makes me feel?"

He gently pushed her from his lap so he could stand. She took the empty chair as he walked to the counter.

"Lori, how much am I supposed to do for you? I ruin every Sunday for you because I go to church with you when I really want to stay home. Sunday morning could be my favorite part of the week, but instead I'm in church. The first semester of my junior year, I was going to change my major because I had this strange idea. Since I was in college, I wanted to study something other than the science of making money. Instead, I stayed a business major because I didn't think you could take any more teaching. I figured I needed to graduate as soon as possible so you could quit. And now here we are, I'm working in a stupid job with the Great State Crap Shoot, and you're *still* teaching, just so you can spend every penny you make on this house. What kind of sense does that make?"

Lori sat in shock and looked away from him, at her feet first, then her hands, as stunned as if he'd slapped her. Her own husband resented her, walked around not with love in his heart but with a boatload of bitterness. And she hadn't even known it. Maybe no one had. Hadn't Gina told her that Chris worshipped the ground she walked on?

He must have read the shock on her face because he walked to the chair and leaned to kiss her on the top of the head. She didn't offer her lips.

"Lori, I don't mean to hurt your feelings because I love you. I just—I don't know. I'm sorry if I hurt your feelings. I really do love you."

She nodded, thinking, yeah, you love me. You just don't love me as much as I thought.

They spent Christmas Eve and night with Mr. Gray in Ashworth. For the first time since Lori had begun making the annual visit, her father-in-law put up a Christmas tree, just for her, he said, because she deserved something in return for spending every Christmas with

Chris. The tree looked as though it had been removed from a store display window. It was artificial, decorated with small red apple ornaments and tinsel. Lori thought it was very pretty.

When Carl arrived that evening, the brothers were determined to force an admission from their father, to make him confess that he hadn't spent a single minute in tree-trimming. They eventually succeeded. A neighbor, a widow, had bought it, set it up, and then completely decorated it.

"What'd you expect?" Mr. Gray asked. "I never decorated one of the things in my life. I haven't even seen one in fifteen years."

The brothers then speculated on the extent of their father's relationship with this widow, a lady they both knew extremely well, and wondered how life would be when their father married her. Had she changed since she had chased Carl around the church with a fly swatter because he had pinched a little girl on the butt? Or tracked Chris to the baseball field, locating him on second base after hitting a double, and making him recite his memory verse, the one he was supposed to have memorized by the coming Sunday?

"I still remember it," Chris said. "First John four-eleven: 'Beloved, if God so loved us, we ought also to love one another.' She stopped the entire game, stood right by second base, and made me recite it until I got it right. Once I did, she yelled, 'Play ball!' and left."

Lori thought the family communicated in a strange way. Neither son seemed comfortable with his father alone. In tandem, however, they acted like the loving sons they could occasionally be. They teased, they touched, they laughed. Of course, they also argued and attacked, all three of them, usually two against one, the sides shifting with the subject.

Chris and Carl seemed to be working out a new sort of relationship, one in which Carl was no longer the automatic superior, one in which he wasn't completely comfortable. He uttered opinions about his younger brother's deeds and manners, opinions that had carried the weight of law in the past but that now seemed no more significant to Chris than eighteenth-century religious tracts.

For years Chris had avoided wearing any kind of hat in any circumstance because Carl thought hats revealed you to be a bumpkin of the worst sort. Now Chris wore a green gimme cap with a winged ear of corn on it just to irritate him.

Chris was also threatening, on Christmas Eve after Mr. Gray had gone to bed, to expose Carl's status as a phony war hero. As the three of them sat in the living room near the Christmas tree wishing their father drank, both sons expressing a need for Christmas cheer, Chris suddenly interjected, "I guess it's a good thing we're not drinking. I might tell the old man about your Silver Star."

Carl said nothing, caught between requesting that he go unexposed, and admitting his younger brother was no longer the consistent inferior, and wanting to remain the aloof, untouchable brother he had always been.

Lori just wanted a nice quiet Christmas. She said, "Why don't you two just observe Christmas. Try to remember that you went to church once upon a time and heard about peace on earth and goodwill toward men."

"Why don't you go put on red leotards," Carl said, "and come sit in my lap. Better yet, don't put anything on and dance around like the sugar plum fairy."

"What kind of peace on earth are you talking about?" Chris asked.

"You know, now that she mentions it, I did find peace on earth, right out behind the church. Sunday nights, Linda Jo and I did all our foreplay on the back row during the sermon and then walked out back behind the church in that cotton field. We kept the blanket in one of the top cabinets in the kitchen. We'd get it after church, walk out the back door into the cotton field, spread that blanket between the two rows of cotton, and I'd plant her on the spot."

"Yeah," Chris said, "and you almost got caught once, didn't you?"

Carl gave him a look of remembered disgust. "Only because some little twerp turned on all the floodlights out back and yelled, 'Hey, I think I see a body out in the field.'"

Chris smiled proudly, nodding.

"I'm sorry I ever mentioned it," Lori said. "You two are so warped you don't understand the simplest Christmas message."

"I do," Carl said. "I understand the messages behind all those Christmas carols, like 'Oh, Come All Ye Faithful' and 'Here Comes Santa Claus.' "

" 'Here Comes Santa Claus' isn't a Christmas carol," Lori said.

"No, it's porno," Chris said.

"I think it's comforting to know that Santa Claus takes his pants off, one leg at a time, just like everybody else."

They exchanged gifts the next morning, Christmas Day, before Chris and Lori left for Abilene. Mr. Gray always gave them a hundred-dollar bill in one of those little wallet cards, the kind with the oval hole that Ben Franklin peeked through. Lori always fretted for weeks over what to buy her father-in-law, and this year, before she'd made a decision, Chris bought him a welding helmet. Lori at first refused to let her name be placed on the tag, then relented when she couldn't think of anything suitable. She had suggested softening the harshness of this gift of hardware with a sweater, but Chris said his father wouldn't wear a sweater.

"He might if it was real pretty," she'd said.

"He *dang* sure wouldn't if it was pretty."

Chris and Carl never exchanged any more than parting shots.

As the four of them stood in the driveway before Chris and Lori left for Abilene, Chris slapped Carl's white Mercedes and said, "See you in the Marine Hall of Fame. In that room way at the back where they honor winners of the Tarnished Star."

"Yeah, well, I won't have any trouble finding you. If I do, I'll just give Little Ruthie a call. She can check her social disease register."

"She told me she asked you once if you knew how to satisfy a woman, and you said, no, but you could fake it."

Mr. Gray, in the process of kissing Lori on the cheek, shook his head and said, "I don't know either of them."

Lori returned the kiss and thanked him for the gift. "Merry Christmas. And I loved the tree."

"Thanks for coming. You're what this house needs."

She and Chris arrived in Abilene in time for a late dinner of turkey and dressing. Her mother had decorated as lavishly as ever, stringing tiny white lights through the live oaks in the front yard and around the eaves of the house. Her tree in the living room was as large as ever, and she always bought a new ornament for Lori each year. This year's was a green ceramic Christmas tree with "Lori" written over the branches in script.

The house was much quieter than the one in Ashworth and there was less bickering. Chris and her father sat in the den and watched a football game and yelled unChristmasy things like "Bad Call!" and "That's interference if I ever saw it!"

After the game they opened gifts around the tree. Lori had bought Chris a leather jacket, and she watched him open it, waiting for a great and wonderful smile, which she never got. He tried it on and said, "Boy, it sure is stiff." Then he looked at all the tags, obviously hoping one of them showed the price. Tightwads, Lori decided, were incapable of happiness.

Then she immediately regretting calling him a tightwad. She opened his gift to her, a thin box that was about a foot square, and discovered it was full of wadded up newspaper and pecans. In the bottom was an envelope that contained a one-thousand-dollar gift certificate to the store where she'd looked at bathroom fixtures.

"Where'd you get a thousand dollars?" she asked.

"Don't ask."

"You sold the MG."

He snorted. "No, I didn't sell the MG. And I said don't ask."

He wouldn't tell her until that night when they were in Lori's brass bed and the house was dark.

"I borrowed the money from Carl because I wanted to make you happy."

"That's the very sweetest thing you've ever done."

"How're we ever going to pay all this back?"

"I don't know but you don't talk about it on Christmas."

She lay partly on him under the covers, propped up on her arm, and she dropped her face onto his, kissing him rhythmically. She had to enjoy being close to him, his bare leg between hers, while she could because within two minutes he'd start complaining about the heat she radiated. Unless they were going to make love.

"You ever think about having a baby?" he asked.

The question shocked her. Why was he always springing things on her at strange times? "Well, I haven't lately."

"I had a dream last night. We had a little boy and I took him to Six Flags. He wanted to ride the Judge Roy Scream over and over."

"What'd he look like?"

"He was cute as everything. And I woke up and missed him. He was the neatest little kid, and he wasn't even real."

"Dreams are good places for things like that. Then if you have problems, you just wake up and, poof, it's all over."

"I want a little boy."

"I don't think you can order one."

"No, but think how much fun it'd be trying."

He rolled her over on her back and made her toes curl under.

Lori wasn't ready to become a mother but she couldn't resist Chris as a would-be father. He was so loving and kind and gentle, seeing her as the beautiful source of a child, that she found the thought of pregnancy more attractive than she'd expected. Then too, she began seeing pregnant women everywhere, and although they often looked clumsy and uncomfortable, they always seemed to be accompanied by a person who wanted to tend them. Pampered was what they were. And Lori hadn't been pampered in a long time. *Pampered.* What a nice word.

She threw away her birth control pills.

188

part three

15

Chris watched Lori's stomach grow and continued to dream about a son. He was always five years old, cute, and loved roller coasters. He could sail a frisbee over a twenty-five-year-old pecan tree and he had the vocabulary of a college student. Father and son romped, hand in hand, over the city of Austin and the surrounding countryside. They ate hot dogs and walked along the river and talked. The only tiny baby he ever dreamed about was a boy who popped from the womb, looked around, and said, "Okay, here's my first word—mobility." These boys were never discipline problems and never asked stupid questions, such as, "Daddy, is all that whiskey good for your liver?" And they were always, *always*, normal healthy kids.

And then there was reality. He had friends whose children weren't normal. One little girl was born with a heart defect, another was severely retarded. And the thoughts that visited him during the middle of the night when he wanted to be dreaming about Six Flags weren't pleasant ones. He was reminded of the religious concepts of his youth and the Old Testament—the sins of one generation were visited on the next. He didn't intellectually adhere to that principle, but in the middle of the night, intellect was like a lamp that had been turned off for the night.

He'd look across the bed at Lori sleeping soundly, the mound of her stomach bulging beneath the sheet, and he'd think about the trip to Mexico he'd taken at the age of sixteen, the trip when he'd come home convinced he'd contracted syphilis, even though three blood tests had shown nothing. He visualized a baby in a hospital incubator born without arms. Or a brain.

Finally, he decided he was a manic-depressive. One minute he

191

was joyous over the thought of this child, the next he was terribly depressed over what the birth was going to mean. Lori was going to quit teaching at the end of the school year, and they'd be left with his salary for support. And although he was glad to have a job that would financially support them, he wasn't happy with the thought that now he was locked in with Lindsey, Chapman. No one else would pay an untrained, unskilled college graduate anything. He'd been first enslaved to a woman, then to a house, now a job, soon a child. Not only was he not going to make Rome, he wasn't even going to make the Guadalupe River on a weekend anymore.

None of this bothered Lori. She was happy with her new shape, and her mother bought her the nicest wardrobe a pregnant woman had ever owned. She briefly experienced morning sickness, then bloomed. Chris would find her standing before a mirror, checking her profile, patting her gourd-hard stomach. Mrs. Conner wanted to stay with her daughter the entire nine months, but Mr. Conner talked her out of it. She came for a week on several occasions, and on more than one of them, she bought Chris's son a dress.

"You're wasting your money, Mother-in-law."

She refused to accept the facts.

He wasn't good at waiting. Toward the end of Lori's pregnancy, the obstetrician committed the unpardonable sin of telling her the baby would probably be early, and three weeks before the due date, Chris was ready. He was tired of worrying about the sex and health and vocabulary of the child. He wanted to know. And when nothing happened, when Lori went for her weekly appointment and the doctor said, "Well, it won't be this week," and when he repeated the hateful words three weeks in a row, Chris was ready to call the Travis County Medical Mafia and order a horse's head for the doctor's bed. He started running, not jogging, to consume the nervous energy that was keeping him in a state of agitation. He ran until he couldn't, until he had to stand in the road, hands on knees, bent over gasping for breath. And the more he watched Lori lumber around with her basketball stomach, complaining, the worse he got.

His condition led to a serious exchange with Margie at work.

"Do you remember that affidavit I gave you last week? I needed it yesterday. Here it is today and I still don't have it."

Margie couldn't respond until she popped the big pink bubble she was blowing, and then she pointed at the TV. "This guy can win a *Gucci* Cadillac if he solves this puzzle."

"Margie, the last time I looked, this was a law office, not your living room. Affidavits have to be filed timely."

"Shh. It doesn't have to be filed before he solves this puzzle."

He turned off her television just as the contestant shouted his answer, and demanded that she type the affidavit. He stood protecting the on-off switch, and the size of her eyes indicated the extent of his intrusion. She jumped up and said she was going to tell on him.

When her uncle told her she probably ought to go ahead and type up the affidavit, she sulked for two weeks.

When Scott Gray did finally appear late one afternoon, and Chris saw him lying in his glass bassinet in the hospital nursery, just one little red-faced baby among others, he was somehow disappointed. He didn't feel what he wanted to feel. He wanted to drop to his knees in awe of the miracle of life; he wanted to feel like a father. Instead he was merely curious. A kid. Hmm.

He stood watching the child through the glass window and noticed that every few minutes, Scott's arms flew heavenward in shaking spasms as though he were being forced to embrace a great fright. Then he'd lie very still in his green blanket, until his arms flew up again, waving nervously in space.

My God, Chris thought. It's a nervous disorder. The result of paternal syphilis. He had always known those blood tests had been wrong. All these years he had known.

193

He asked a passing nurse to watch.

"Oh, that's normal," the nurse said. "I think." She added as she walked off, "It's probably nothing."

Chris whispered a prayer to anyone who might be listening. "Please, please, let it be nothing."

He held him in Lori's room and felt the first stirrings of parental pride and love for the child with the fine blond hair, the mashed head and flattened nose. He wasn't the kid who'd been riding roller coasters, and he didn't know what "mobility" meant, but he was something, that baby.

When they took him home, they took him to his grandmother, who apparently had moved in for the duration, or at least until she was sure Scott didn't need any help with algebra. Every time he cried, four female hands reached for him, and usually Lori, who expressed total ignorance in the art of motherhood, deferred to Mrs. Conner. What amazed Chris was the helplessness of the child. If he lost his pacifier, he cried but didn't know what was wrong. If he had known, he was still incapable of locating the piece of rubber, and if he'd located it, he couldn't possibly have retrieved it, and had he picked it up, he couldn't have popped it back into his mouth. He was capable of three activities—crying, sucking, and relieving himself, all of which he did with unbelievable regularity.

Chris was ready for Granny to vacate the premises because after a week, he was intrigued. He thought the sight of Lori breastfeeding Scott was one of the most loving and naturally right sights he'd ever witnessed. And for the first time in her life, she had substantial breasts. She pulled the flap down on her maternity bra and, lo, there was a breast. And Chris was the home guard, there to protect Scott from too many prying eyes and lifting hands. Visitors seemed to think he should wake up and entertain them.

Finally Mrs. Conner left one weekend when her husband came to get her, and the three left behind got acquainted. And although Lori was nervous about being on her own, Chris felt as though he belonged in that house at that time for the first time ever. The birth of Scott was the best thing that had ever happened to him. He took pictures, roll after roll of film, loitering around Scott's crib waiting for his expression to change. He fed him, changed his diaper, told him that he loved him and was glad he was there.

Later, he would see himself as a proud parent barely attempting to conceal his pride, accompanying a smiling wife eager to exhibit her product. He would also understand that they had spent far too much time entertaining him and suggesting he entertain others. Their main objective in those days was to prevent him from crying even though it seemed to Chris that once they had learned the difference between a cry of boredom and a cry for food, they should let him experience boredom, let him understand that occasionally he would be on his own.

Scott liked the routine just fine. In fact, he loved it. He fought against going to sleep at all at any time. If his eyes closed for more than three seconds, he came out from under the curse of sleep as though he were fighting his way from the bottom of a swimming pool. He couldn't express an opinion, but Chris was sure if he could, it would have been, "Sleeping is for bears, and *only* in the winter."

Then too, Scott loved his parents. They had offered their attentions, and he had accepted. He liked the feeling of arms and hands, particularly if they were lifting him, holding him, swinging him, entertaining him. Nothing on the floor held his interest unless someone was sitting beside him. His company couldn't stand, couldn't sit across the room, couldn't get up and leave; his company had a spot and it was *right beside* him.

Chris didn't know how much Scott's inability to entertain himself was attributable to his parents' inability to leave him alone, but even after he and Lori agreed they were part of the problem, Lori couldn't stop. If she heard Scott cry through the night, she froze. Chris would suggest they let him cry himself back to sleep, but Lori couldn't go more than thirty seconds before she was rushing to his bedroom.

Chris suggested several times they get a babysitter so they could go out, but she wouldn't seriously discuss the matter. If he pointed out that someone not physically and emotionally exhausted could do a better job, she cried, believing he thought she was a lousy mother. The only breaks she took were week-long visits to Abilene, and she took one a month.

It was an evolution that Chris didn't see until later. One day he was married, the next his wife had been kidnapped by a tiny tyrant.

16

Lori would never have believed it was possible to feel as overwhelmed as she did when Scott was born. This little baby had a mother who was as helpless as he was. She felt sorry for poor Scott, getting Lori Lynn as a mother. Surely she was the least prepared woman in history to undergo childbirth. She'd entertained wonderful visions during her pregnancy of a beautiful child sitting on her floor, sucking on a rattle, merrily playing alone and gurgling when she walked by. "Ma-ma, Ma-ma." Friends would comment on the beauty of Scott and on Lori's extraordinary confidence in caring for him.

Nothing had ever been further from the truth. Nothing. Ever.

For the first three weeks, Scott had slept and barely whimpered, and Lori had been amazed at the ease with which he fit into their home. With her mother's help, she'd regained her strength and thought she had enough confidence to mother Scott by herself. Lori hadn't realized that at three weeks, Scott the Terrible was about to wake up.

Breastfeeding gave her some trouble at first. At times she gave no milk; at others her nipples were as sore as boils. The doctor told her she was trying too hard and she needed a shield, which she got.

Feeding Scott reminded her of the child's complete dependency on her. Holding him when he was nursing, his entire being focused on that one task, Lori's entire personality focused on her desire to nourish him, she felt closer to and more loving toward him than she had ever felt toward anyone or even thought possible.

Chris didn't understand how totally involved she was. The sound of Scott's cry was the call of her name. If he was crying, he wasn't feeling loved. Her only function was to care for this child, and his cry meant Lori's failure. And there was no way she could just drop him in a babysitter's lap as though he were a bundle of laundry. She couldn't take an evening off as though she were an employee.

"Lori, will you *please* find a babysitter? I want to take you out Friday night. And if you won't do it for yourself, then will you do it for me?"

"I don't know who to ask."

"Call Ellen. She's got two kids and she's got to know of at least *one* that's trustworthy."

She didn't know what to tell him because she had no intention of using a babysitter.

"You're on this course and I'm on this course," he said, his hands departing in different directions. "We're getting farther and farther apart."

She didn't want to grow any farther apart and she knew she wasn't being the kind of wife he wanted her to be, but what it all boiled down to was this—she loved him but she didn't love him as much as he thought she did. He was making the same discovery she'd made the day he drove home in an MG. And she didn't give him the advice she wanted him to hear, the same advice he'd been giving her for years—grow up.

On the other hand, she felt sorry for her husband because she had some clue on how he felt. Just as she'd figured out who she was as Lori Gray, about the time she felt like an adult, all her relationships started changing. Her friends were suddenly those with children;

197

the childless ones drifted away, including Gina. She now issued invitations in this way: "Why don't you get a babysitter and we can meet for lunch."

Gina really seemed a stranger that Lori had met on a long trip, and once they'd arrived at their destination, they didn't have much desire to be friends. One day as Gina watched Lori change a dirty diaper, she gagged and said, "I knew there was a good reason I didn't want kids."

Lori needed friends with children, needed someone to talk to when Scott cried for three hours for no obvious reason. She called Ellen, who lived three houses down. She was a veteran with two kids; she understood. Mrs. Conner asked once if Lori wanted some hired help, and Lori said yes, she wanted a full-time pediatrician. But since she could not get a pediatrician full-time, she settled for Ellen.

She could put herself to sleep easier than she could rock Scott asleep at night. After his last feeding, he wanted to coo and play in the rocking chair beside his crib. He didn't want to go to sleep. Lori usually managed to wait him out, often while she napped.

On this night she had carefully arisen from the rocker, tiptoed in slow motion to the crib, and laid Scott down. The process was as nerve-wracking as handling unstable explosives. One wrong move and bang, he was awake and crying.

As quietly as possible, she left his room and pulled the door closed, headed for the big pillow on the den floor. She wanted to watch something lighthearted on TV after being cooped up with her son for three days because of rain. Even as tired as she was, she still hated going to bed simultaneously with Scott because then she had no time free of his demands.

Stretched out on the floor, her head on the big pillow, she read the TV listings, the remote control at her side.

Chris appeared over her head, holding a beer as though he were going to release it like a bomb, right on her forehead.

"You remember the day I bought the MG?" he asked.

"How could I forget?"

"You remember that you got mad and left the house?"

She sighed. "Yes, I remember."

"Where'd you go?"

She didn't like the tone of his voice, could in fact tell that he wasn't making conversation; he was interrogating her. She suddenly felt peculiar, as though an old sin had just flown in the window and roosted right on her shoulder. "Chris, I have about thirty minutes before I pass out, and I don't want to spend it talking about a night I'd rather forget anyway."

"It won't take you long to tell me where you went."

"I went with Gina to get a drink. Now, I don't want to talk about it anymore. I want to watch TV and rest." She flipped on the TV even though nothing was on but reruns.

"Who was the guy you left with?"

Oh, Lord, she thought. He'd been talking to Gina, and she could imagine the conversation. Both of them were mad at her because she didn't have forty-eight-hour days, didn't have the ability to control and order her life as they wanted her to. If one more demand was made on her by one more person, she was going to check her and Scott into a sanitarium.

"I didn't *leave* with anybody. I left to get away from a guy who had sat down with us. Uninvited."

"You didn't leave *with* him?"

"Good God, no, Chris. I left and I came home. And I really don't want to talk about it."

She was very close to crying, to losing control altogether. How could God allow that night to arise as a topic of conversation? Why wouldn't God protect Scott's mother, whether he personally liked her or not, whether he approved of her or not, just as a favor to a tiny baby? And then the tears came, out of frustration more than anything else, because Lori couldn't balance all the acts required of her.

199

She got up, the exertion requiring such an effort that she groaned, and went to bed, closing the door behind her because she didn't want Chris following her into the bedroom. Falling onto the bed with her clothes on, she had only one small request to make of God, and that was to let Scott sleep all night. She could hear him through the vent if he cried, and she begged for silence from the vent.

Chris woke her up in the middle of the night, shaking her in the darkness, because she was crying in her sleep. At first she thought the sobs were part of a dream, but they were real. She had a headache and a stopped-up nose, and she took some comfort in knowing that nothing could be so wrong as it seemed. In a minute she'd remember everything was all right, and Chris would put his arms around her and she'd be able to sleep. But then she realized that things were even worse than they seemed. Chris hated her and was going to pin a scarlet letter on her chest; he was determined to. And they'd have to finish the conversation he'd started before bedtime. She'd rather die right now than finish that conversation.

"Are you all right?" he asked.

"I don't know."

Suddenly concerned, hearing her lack of confidence, he sat up and turned toward her. "Are you awake?"

"I am now."

"You were crying in your sleep."

"I know. I know."

"What's wrong?"

"I want to sleep, that's all, just sleep. That's all and it's so little to ask."

"How about if I take you to Abilene in the morning? I think you need a break. Your mother can help you and you can rest."

"Maybe that'll help. I don't know. I don't know anything anymore except I just want to sleep."

"Well, I'll take you home and you can sleep."

"I'd *pay* somebody for sleep. I'd *buy* it."

"Okay. Okay. I'll take you home and you can sleep."

Chris wasn't especially nice on the way to Abilene, a drive of about four hours. He talked to Scott, who rode in a car seat in the front seat between them, pointing out every cow and horse and truck they saw, all those things they saw in the books they read every night. Lori didn't want the subject of the Holiday Inn coming up before she'd had some rest, so she didn't speak except to tell him once she wanted a drink.

Once in Abilene, especially after Chris had returned to Austin, she felt as though a great burden had been lifted from her stooped shoulders and she could stand up again. Her first item of business was to hand Scott to her mother, who gave him a greeting in baby talk, and go to bed.

Her second item of business she took care of after she got up, just before suppertime. She found her mother feeding Scott on the kitchen table. Scott, in a plastic carrier reclining at a forty-five-degree angle, accepted each spoonful of Gerber's peas and then wiggled all his limbs in utter joy and contentment.

Lori made a glass of iced tea and sat, no longer feeling emotionally and physically exhausted. Now she was merely tired.

"Mother, how is it a billion women a year have a child and I feel like I'm incompetent, like it's a miracle that anyone at all can do this?"

Better yet, how did Lori's own mother look like both a model and a grandmother simultaneously? She could go from one role to another without blinking, and Lori couldn't handle one.

"You're expecting too much out of yourself, Lori. It won't hurt this precious baby boy to cry every once in a while, will it, you little dictator?"

Scott gave a joyous shout in answer.

"See? He said it was okay."

201

"Sure, it's okay until he wants something and he doesn't get it in about two seconds."

She watched Scott and smiled. At the moment, he was the happiest child in the world, getting fed by a doting grandmother who grabbed his foot and squealed every time Scott did anything at all.

"Was I that demanding?" Lori asked.

"Not until you were about six. Then you wanted everything you saw."

"Did I get everything I wanted?"

"Sure," Mrs. Conner said, guiding another spoonful toward the open and waiting mouth of her grandson. "Unless I thought it was something I didn't think you needed, and then I made your father tell you no."

"You were brave."

"Mothers aren't brave; they're loving."

Lori sipped her tea and said, "My problem is I don't know what's loving and what's not."

"All you can do is the best you can."

Mothers weren't philosophers, Lori thought. They worked more on instinct than knowledge, and instinct didn't always seem completely reliable.

She told her mother she had to make a call and went into her father's study, ready to start putting the Holiday Inn matter in order. Marital problems took on a new slant when a child was involved. They were no longer marital problems; they were family problems.

Sitting at her father's big wooden desk, she called Gina at work before she went home, or wherever it was she went after work, and for a few minutes they chatted as though Lori were in Austin and they were still friends. Gina never asked about Scott; she ignored him as though he didn't exist, a fact which excluded her as a friend of Lori's.

"Did you tell Chris anything about that night we went to the Holiday Inn?"

"The night you left with that guy in the pink shirt?"

"I didn't *leave* with him."

"Hmm. It certainly looked that way."

"Well, whatever way it looked, why'd you tell Chris?"

"Oh, you know me and my mouth. I can't keep a secret."

Lori knew one thing for certain; she'd made her last call to Gina, unless it was to detonate a bomb in her telephone. Lori had known some snakes in her life, but Gina's belly was scraped and bleeding from slithering on the ground. She and Gina had obviously never been close, and she didn't understand why the appearance of a baby and a change in her life would make Gina vicious.

Lori felt like a different person when Chris came to get her a week later. Rested and ready. He was distant upon arrival, and as she suspected, he wanted to explore her alleged infidelity as soon as they hit the city limits sign on the way back to Austin.

"Will you please tell me this story about you and Gina at the Holiday Inn."

She explained the night, from her anger over his purchase of the car and the fact that she wanted to remodel the bathroom, to the fact that she decided to punish him by doing what he had been badgering her to do for years—go out and have a drink—without him. "I'd just about changed my mind when I got to Gina's, but every time she asked me anything about that car—whether it had a stereo or whatever—I got mad all over again. Anyway, we went to the bar on top of the Holiday Inn and these two guys came over and sat down, and we didn't even say they could.

"I kept trying to get Gina's attention so we could get out of there because we were in her car, but she and this older guy were telling Aggie jokes and just generally having a high old time. And then the older guy's friend decided I must be as easy as Gina and we had this conversation—a short conversation—on fate. I kept telling him I wasn't interested, and he kept pressing, and I finally just left by myself.

"I might also add right here that in the middle of all this, before

Romeo started talking about fate, I tried calling you to come and get me. And where were you? Nowhere to be found. So I took a taxi to Gina's house and got my car, and then I came home."

She hadn't thought to any extent about the pink-shirted salesman, but as she told the story, she grew angry all over again. She hoped by now that he had acquired a number of different social diseases, none of which could be transmitted to unsuspecting females. And if there was any justice in the world, his organ by now would look like a dried-up chicken bone.

"If that's the sin of the century," she said, "I'm sorry as I can be."

Feeling better, as though normal relations were just ahead at the upcoming intersection, she reached over and pulled on Scott's foot. His carseat was strapped down between his parents, and he jumped forward, pulling against his belts, to show Lori his approval of her attention.

"Why didn't you just tell me that the other night?"

"Because I was so tired I didn't want to discuss it."

"Lori, I hate to sound like your Sunday school teacher, but do you remember the day you were supposed to deposit your paycheck, but you wanted to go to Kelly-Moore? And you didn't have time to do both? So you went to Kelly-Moore. And when you got home, I asked if you'd deposited your check. And you said, yes. And you didn't. And then you forgot about it altogether and four checks bounced, including the one you wrote at Kelly-Moore."

As usual, Lori was wrong. Normal relations weren't just ahead; she'd seen a mirage, an image of a wife with a husband who didn't resurrect her every oversight. "Are you saying you don't believe what I just told you?"

"I'm saying that when you don't want to tell me something for one reason or another, you just lie. That's all, you just lie because it's so easy. And I don't ever know whether you're telling me the truth or not."

"You didn't answer my question. I said, do you believe what I just told you?"

"I don't know. I really don't know."

She sighed loudly and slumped in the seat, resting her head and looking up. "That is wonderful. That is just truly wonderful. We have such a tremendous amount of trust here." She sat up because she couldn't believe how stupid he was acting. She'd just told him the whole truth, and he'd rejected it. "Chris, we aren't talking about Kelly-Moore and the bank. We're talking about trust. And you're sitting over there thinking I've been fooling around. That's what you're saying."

"No, what I'm saying is that I don't ever feel all that confident that I'm getting the truth. The other night you told me you left the bar and you just went right home. Now it sounds almost like you're adding to it to make it agree with what Gina told me. My point is, I don't ever know when you're telling me the truth and when you're not."

"Okay, fine," she shouted. "You believe Gina because she's *really* trustworthy."

Lori smiled at Scott to counteract her shout and tickled him, making him giggle, even though she wasn't feeling at all sociable. When was she going to learn? The fabric of life was dirty. And torn. A person who had always considered herself sweet and loving could end up miserable. She could marry a man who loved her, a man with the ability to make her heart hurt, and pretty soon he'd be squeezing the very devil out of her most important organ just because he could.

"I'm not saying I believe Gina," Chris said, sounding tired. "I'm saying I want somebody I can *always* believe. I've got a brother who's been lying to me all my life, and I want a wife I can believe without having to worry about it. That's all."

"You can believe me on this one. You can believe me or you can believe you're married to a whore."

He didn't answer. Lori spent the rest of the trip shaking her head. She kept getting slapped in the face with the same fact—depending on anybody but herself was a real mistake.

17

Chris couldn't say Lori hadn't warned him. On more than a few occasions, when he'd seemed to read her mind or anticipate her answer to a question before she gave it, he'd made her mad by saying, "I can read you like a book. I know more about you than you know about yourself." And with fiery eyes, she'd say, "You don't know *anything* about me." Ever since they'd married, he'd been readjusting his view of her. Either she was interrupting her tantrums to say something surprisingly mature or she was intermingling with her self-centered view of life some shocking objectivity about herself, her parents, or him.

He had feared, before the birth of Scott, that she'd want to enlist an indiscriminate army of babysitters and flee the ties of motherhood; instead, she'd remained steadfastly at the other extreme, refusing to leave him anywhere for any reason.

The Kelly-Moore, unbanked check incident had involved one of an untold number of lies he'd discovered in their marriage, and she had exhibited less fidelity to the truth than any politician; yet she often proclaimed she was the ultimate in trustworthiness. These lies had ranged from the slight—little white lies, which didn't bother him—to those more intricate, primarily relating to her sexual history prior to their marriage.

He had discovered, while snooping through a box of high school mementoes in the Conner house in Abilene, a letter from some guy named Randy, who had written effusively about a family vacation to Padre Island. Lori had accompanied them and had obviously performed a valuable service for Randy because the last sentence of his letter was, "I'll never forget the night you made me a man."

Chris had nonchalantly asked who Randy was. Lori first professed complete ignorance of any male named Randy; then admitted she might have known someone in high school by that name, but only vaguely; then seemed to recall, well, yes maybe she had dated a Randy; then, okay, yes, she'd taken a vacation with him and his family. But she had not, ever, certainly not on a family vacation, "made him a man, whatever that means. And anyway, what're you doing snooping in things that aren't even yours?"

He wasn't at all sure who Lori was, and he was so confused over her credibility that he wouldn't have been surprised to see her picture on the news at six o'clock and learn that she was a Russian spy who had just returned to the motherland. She had reportedly been living in Texas as a housewife and her husband was being sought for questioning.

The details concerning the Holiday Inn foray had come from another source whose credibility was questionable. He had seen Gina downtown during lunch one day and invited her to eat with him. She worked in one of the state office buildings near downtown and he saw her periodically if he got close to the capitol. On this day, they went to an old-fashioned hamburger stand.

Gina was perhaps his favorite sight and he could sit for an hour and simply look at her. She was almost bony in places but fleshed out generously in the right spots. He stood behind her in line, waiting to order, and couldn't get over how full of breasts her green sweater was.

She asked, "Why don't we ever see you anymore? We used to have such fun together. I think the night Lori got drunk on daiquiris was the most laughing I've ever done."

He shook his head. "Lori can't find a babysitter that suits her."

Gina shook her head. "I've never seen anybody just change overnight like she did. One day we're the best of friends, the next she doesn't have time to say hello. Or the next or the next."

She sounded disgusted, as if Lori was obligated to please her and had failed. Chris understood her attitude but didn't think she worked hard enough at the friendship to deserve such an attitude.

He did, but she didn't. She was an outsider, rightfully displaced by Scott. "Oh, I think she's trying too hard right now. All this is new to her."

"She's trying to be Mrs. All-American Mother-of-the Year. She acts like she's up for the award and wants everyone to know it."

He didn't respond, preferring instead to drop the matter because Gina's sentiments offended him. But Gina wasn't ready to drop Lori as a matter for conversation.

"She reminds me of this friend I had once that got hooked up with some holy rollers. She started carrying a Bible everywhere she went and acting holier-than-thou. Lori reminds me of her. Now she's little Mrs. Responsibility with her diaper bag and nursing bra and stroller. I mean, she acts like she's been waiting for this all her life and wants everybody to vote for her for mother of the year."

Chris shook his head. "No, no. You're not reading her right on that. She's so damn nervous about being a mother she doesn't know what she's doing half the time. She's trying to do too much, but not because she's been waiting all her life to do it."

"Oh, get serious, Chris. She's never had an ambition other than to be a mother and a wife. The feminist movement shot over her head like a Roman candle."

That matter taken care of, in Gina's opinion, she turned her attention to him. Or so he thought. Her dark eyes seemed to be sending him a message that almost caused him to quiver. How much resistance, how much discipline, did he have? Before he could decide, they reached the front of the line and placed their orders for hamburgers and Cokes.

On their way to a booth, Gina took his arm, pulled it into her large and comfortable breast, and said, "Anyway, *we* can still have fun. Can't we?"

Thank God Lori couldn't see him because she would have noticed his pupils enlarging, the galloping pulse in his neck, the rigidity of his body. He had known, somewhere in the back of his mind, that this moment was coming, when Gina would make an obvious invitation to play. He had dreaded its coming while willing it to occur. She tried guiding him into the same side of the booth with her so they could continue their public cuddling, and he was saved only by Gina herself. She'd made it difficult for him to consort with a woman so openly hostile toward Lori.

"Let's take the afternoon off," she said, leaning toward him.

He sat back, attempting to elude her sexual aura, and pushed his knees into hers. Hers caught his left and squeezed, then opened, inviting him in. She slid forward in the seat, her thighs a fleshy sheath about to capture him.

I'm not responsible for this erection, he said mentally, in case Lori was somewhere reading his thoughts.

Gina, like a contortionist, had stretched her legs far enough forward so that her right knee was close to his groin, and she was managing to massage his left leg with both of hers. Her heels alternated in rising from the floor, her thighs twisting his.

She seemed to typify the atmosphere of Austin, one in which a person could find or do anything. He had been propositioned by conservatively dressed women. Streetcorner flower vendors sold cocaine. Prostitutes on Sixth Street flashed drivers. It was all more than one person could handle, and Gina was more than he wanted to handle.

He sat straight up, breaking away from her homing knee, and said, "I've got too much to do this afternoon to be taking off."

"Don't you want to get even?"

They embarked on an hour-long guessing game. For every bit of information about the Holiday Inn she revealed, he had to ask forty questions and wade through puns, smiles that seemed to contradict her words, and oblique allusions. But he finally got the story of Lori and her salesman. He also got a nauseous feeling.

He spent the afternoon in a daze. Every time he started to work on something, he was distracted by Gina's story, the images of Lori and a salesman sitting across the table from her, whispering. Then leaving together.

Quizzing Lori didn't help at all. Like Nixon's tapes, there were too many minutes missing. Regardless of whose version he accepted, Lori had disappeared into a void of several hours, last seen being accompanied by a salesman.

After taking her to Abilene, he returned home and searched the place. The evidence was right at his fingertips, if only he could find it, letters from men throughout the country, thanking her for their newfound masculinity. Pretty soon she'd have her own magazine ads, the female Charles Atlas.

He looked through the pockets of every coat and robe, in every shoebox, in every drawer and under the paper lining of those drawers, in jewelry boxes and crates of school junk. Everywhere.

And the only letters he found were from him or Mrs. Conner.

It was difficult to maintain the belief that Lori was the most active slut alive in the face of no evidence. On the other hand, neither did he find any proof that she'd told the truth about the salesman.

The conversation over her truthfulness on the way back from Abilene didn't fill him with confidence. She was convincing, but so was Carl. Chris had believed his brother was a war hero for years. He'd believed Lori was faithful for years. What he wanted to do was forget all about the loyalty/faith/trust issue. He wished he'd been born two hundred years ago and was a real sailor.

He would have had a house high on a cliff overlooking the gulf, where he'd lived with his maid, a lively wench who'd scrub floors in a burlap dress, naked underneath. She'd stand at the open window during the day feeling the sea breezes, watching for the return of his ship. When the sails appeared, she'd run barefooted to the pier. At night, Chris would walk down the hill to town and drink whiskey and trade sea stories with his cronies. Women in long dresses with laced bodices would flirt and dangle their wares.

That was it. He should have been born two hundred years ago.

The best part of the day was coming home and seeing Scott. With light in his eyes, he'd shout and go into his arm-and-leg wiggling routine. Chris would pick him up and they'd tour the living room, checking out all the items on the wall. They'd look over a sconce, Scott would point at it and attempt to speak, then signal them forward to the next item he wanted to examine.

Before Lori put him to bed, she breastfed him in a rocking chair in his room. Once through, she'd sit lovely and exposed, making Chris hurt with desire as he lay on the living room floor, supposedly watching TV, instead looking at the mother in the rocking chair. They'd often make love on the living room floor in the moonlight, and when they finished, they lay without speaking. There was an obstacle he just couldn't overcome, and it prevented him from saying, "I love you," or, "You feel so good," or "I liked that."

One night as they lay on the floor, Lori asked, "Don't you think you've paid me back?"

"I'm not paying you back."

"Then what're you doing?"

He didn't answer her immediately because he wasn't sure. He rolled onto his side, looking out the big window at the shadowy branches through which the moon glinted. He could forgive her an indiscretion with a salesman, if it had actually occurred, easier than he could adjust to her lack of dedication to the truth. He wanted to know absolutely if she was telling the truth. And he could ask, and she'd say, yes, she was telling the truth, and he still wouldn't know if he could believe her or not. There simply didn't seem to be an answer to the problem.

"I'm trying to figure out who you are," he said.

"Lord, Chris," she said as though fatigued. "Surely you've got that figured out by now."

"I don't."

"Well, when do you think you will?"

"I'm working on it."

"Soon?"

"Sooner or later."

He'd never figure out who she was; it wasn't in her nature to let that information out. He had asked her once how an apparently religious person such as she was could lie without feeling guilt, and she'd said, with a naive look on her face, "What's lying got to do with religion?"

All he could do was decide how he was going to treat her. He simply didn't know if he could wholeheartedly give himself to a person he didn't wholeheartedly trust.

"Do you know how much it hurts me when you walk in the front door, look at Scott and smile, and then look at me and get this completely blank look on your face, like you're not even sure you want to talk to me?"

"I'm sorry. I'll do better."

"Maybe you can skip the trying part and just do better."

"Okay, I'll do better."

Part of him succeeded. That part came home in the afternoon and inquired about her day, tried to be kind and considerate and helped with meals and dirty dishes, told her that he loved her. But another part sailed off on a flight of fantasy, engaged in thoughts about a girl from his past, a long-lost love named Caroline. He lay in bed on Saturday morning, pretending to sleep when he was really talking to Caroline.

"I told you I'd always love you," she said. "I told you eight years ago, and you can still believe it. I could be married, I could be sick, I could even be dying, but I'd still love you."

He believed her; she was that convincing. She had expressed that very thought in a letter eight years ago, the last time he'd heard from her. And now she lay facing him in bed. They touched beneath the sheet, not sexually but intimately.

He began to see her when he went to the store. She stood two checkout counters down, paying just before he did, not seeing him. He got his change and stuffed it into his pocket on the run, catching her just as she got to the door.

"Hey! Where are you going?" he asked.

"Chris. You scared me."

"So where are you going?"

"Wherever you are."

On a rainy day, they drove slowly to the low-water crossing on the Pedernales River, sitting in the car beside the road, watching raindrops trickle down the windshield. Leaning comfortably against one another in the middle of the seat, they held hands. She played with his fingers as he tried to explain that although he loved her as much as she loved him, he couldn't leave his wife because he couldn't stand the thought of leaving Scott.

"You don't have to leave anybody," she said. "I'm here. I'll always be here when you need me."

And she always was, just as she had been when he was in the navy. She'd come halfway across the Atlantic, met him on the deck of a ship in the middle of the ocean. She'd appeared his first year at Baylor, before he'd met Lori. They'd slept together in his dumpy apartment. Every time he needed her, she always appeared smiling, often before he even felt the need to invoke her spiritual presence.

She was uncanny, her timing perfect. She was perfect, and he .could trust her completely.

Scott, as one and only grandchild on either side of the family, drew intense attention from all three grandparents. But what surprised Chris the most was the manner in which the grandfathers related to the child. Here were two very serious hard-working men, neither prone to displays of affection, but both turned rubbery-kneed in the presence of their grandson.

Chris's father, when holding Scott, once came as close to openly communicating about his desires for Chris as he ever had in his son's presence. The comments were directed to Scott, but since Chris was present, he obviously heard.

"Scott," Mr. Gray said, holding the child in one arm and in-specting the tiny hands of his grandson. "You look to me like you're going to be a farmer. These hands right here like the dirt, I can tell, because you got ten fingernails and all ten of them's got dirt underneath."

"His mother'll die if you point that out."

"Shoot, she ought to be proud of this boy, already taking to the land like that. These two hands right here are spaced just right to fit on the steering wheel of a tractor. Just right."

"What if those hands would rather do something else?"

"Well, there's four hundred acres of farm land that need somebody looking after it. There's one thing on this planet there'll never be any more of, and that's land. And good farm land's a gift from God, that's all there is to it. You hear that, Scott? We got four hundred acres you're going to have to farm like your grandfather and great-grandfather. Looks like we'll have to skip a generation, so you better get to growing up, boy. I just hope you can look at that farm and think there's something good and right about working it."

"As much as the kid likes being entertained, I just don't see him as a farmer."

"I don't know, maybe I complained too much about the weather or something. I won't complain around you, Scott."

"I never heard you complain about anything but Republicans," Chris said, wondering why his father was taking the blame for two children who hadn't liked anything connected with farming except the finished cotton shirts they bought in a store.

When they went to Ashworth, Mr. Gray took Scott out to the farm and drove him around on the tractor, a treat Scott loved. But Chris had also liked riding on tractors. Until he'd discovered the actual use of the implements.

If the child grew up with the blood of both families coursing through his veins, he was going to be under constant tension, with the staunch democratic blood of the land mixing with the risky high-rolling republicanism of Lori's father.

He wanted Scott to be a geologist and prayed he had a nose for oil. They one day strapped his carseat in Mr. Conner's Lincoln and took him out on a location. Unfortunately, to get there Mr. Conner

214

took a shortcut, right across a field overgrown with Johnson grass. The car bounced, bumped, and whipped through weeds so high they obstructed Chris's vision.

"Can you see where you're going?" he asked.

Mr. Conner looked at him as though he had expressed doubt in capitalism. "Yeah, it's just right over here."

As he drove blindly through the field, Mr. Conner patted Scott's leg. "Yeah, this boy's a natural-born salesman, you can tell by his personality. He'd going to put packages together so easy nobody'll believe it. He'll have investors begging to get in on one of his deals, and the words, "dry hole" will never pass his lips. This boy'll be famous with his nose for oil. He'll go into the history books. You will use our rigs, won't you, Scott?"

They suddenly drove out of the weeds, without incident, without accidents, and somehow had ended up pointing directly at a drilling rig operating in the middle of a well-built location.

"Prettiest sight in the world, Scott, a working rig. But don't worry about that part of it. Hell, there'll always be drilling contractors around. What we need is somebody who can find the oil, somebody who can say, 'Poke a hole right here, boys, 'cause I can smell it.' You got that kind of nose?"

Scott giggled when Mr. Conner checked his nose, then pointed at the rig painted characteristically blue and white, the colors of Conner Drilling Company.

"See, he knows what that is. He knows what they're doing too."

Even Carl seemed taken in by his nephew although on the first few visits he was reluctant to hold the child. But Scott, one of the most naturally social creatures Chris had ever seen, seemed aware of the lawyer's reluctance and made a bigger-than-normal show of wanting to be held when Carl was around. He grunted and kicked his legs vigorously.

"He only does that when he sees Carl," Lori said.

"Yeah, it's probably gas," Chris said.

"Gasoline," Carl said. "He's ready to go. When he sees me, he knows he's got to be ready to rip. He's on the fast track. Right, Scott?"

If Lori appeared at the office, Carl carried Scott around and let him visit with anyone having the time and inclination. They were usually followed by one or two ladies who couldn't get over how cute he was. And the more new faces Scott saw, the better he liked it. He cried only when Lori left with him. As they stood waiting on the elevator, Scott reached for the front door of the Lindsey, Chapman law firm, crying as though he was being deprived.

Carl and Chris stood watching one day as Lori held the crying child.

Carl said, "Look at that. The kid already knows where the money is."

"Just like his mother."

"You know, seeing him almost makes me wish I'd stayed married more than a year."

Chris watched until the elevator swallowed up his wife and child, and then he returned to his office, unable to get interested in work. He tried reading a file but ended up thinking about Caroline.

For several years, she'd just been a girl in church, two years younger than Chris. She reminded him of a little puppy, small and soft and cute, something you wanted to hold. Then one day he did a double take—had Caroline grown breasts overnight? Had she always smiled that way at him? By the time he decided she could graduate to the status of girlfriend, her family moved to Corpus Christi.

That development set a precedent for the rest of their relationship. They missed more connections than an unlucky commuter. They corresponded while Chris was in the navy, but the name Lee started appearing far too often in her letters. She expected him to come rescue her; he thought the matter was so serious and settled that any attempt would be futile. She made wedding plans and asked a mutual friend to let him know he had one more chance. But when he appeared at her doorstep, her mother looked disturbed and told him he was interfering with wedding plans that were etched in concrete. Feeling guilty, he left, and Caroline didn't know he had even made an attempt to see her until her mother let the news slip several months after the wedding, at which time Caroline looked at the disappointing state of her marriage and sent a signal to Chris via their mutual friend. She was unhappy.

When he got the message, he took a week's leave and drove nonstop from Virginia to Corpus Christi, staying in a cheap motel along the bay and living off junk food. While Caroline's husband worked, she and Chris either went to the motel or sat in his car along the bay, kissing, expressing intense regrets, and holding each other.

One minute she was kissing his face and begging him to take her away, the next she couldn't believe he was demanding that she leave with him.

"Why can't things be different?" she asked.

"I wish I knew."

"Things could have been different."

"Let's make them different. Come with me. We'll go somewhere. New Mexico. Anywhere. We'll go live somewhere and love each other the rest of our lives."

"Take me away."

"I can't leave without you. You've got to go with me."

Then the change.

"I haven't tried to make my marriage work. I have to try. Why didn't you come see me before?" she asked.

"I did. You know I did. But that doesn't have anything to do with now. Let's go."

"I can't."

His heart was wrecked. He couldn't understand how he could want Caroline more than he had ever wanted anything, could sit with her in his car or lie with her in the motel room, but find that she was beyond his reach. He would have to live his life without her.

Eight years ago he had driven back to Virginia in a depressed stupor, and the last letter he'd received from her had said, "Please don't think I don't love you because I wouldn't leave. I love you and always will, no matter what. Nothing will change that, not marriage or sickness or anything."

And there the affair had dangled, unresolved, for those eight years, stirred occasionally by the mutual friend who passed news of each on to the other. Periodically, he had thought about calling her. Now he thought seriously about it. He could call her. She was as close as his phone.

And the phone was only inches from his hand.

18

Lori had never been a soap opera fan, but now she watched them every afternoon, flipping channels until she found the right music, the facial closeups, the nibbling lips. She didn't know any of the characters; she just wanted to see people in love.

Or she sat in the backyard with Scott and watched a jogger pass her house every afternoon about four. He was tall, blond, wiry, and he never wore anything but shoes and shorts. The curly hair on his neck was always wet with sweat, matted on his skin, and she wished he'd stop for a drink of something cold. They could talk over the fence.

Every day they'd follow the same routine; he'd drink, then touch her hand and thank her for the iced tea.

Then one day he glanced at her, overly long and obvious, and she knew all he wanted was sex. He was thinking about jumping the fence and running across the yard to attack her. He'd jump right on her as she sat in the lawn chair, knocking her over backwards, and there Lori would be, in a sitting position on her back, legs straight up in the air, a sex maniac raping her.

218

But the man never stopped, and Lori spent her days followed by a crawling Scott. When she was in the kitchen, he sat on the floor, opened a cabinet, and took out his pots and pans. He stirred a potful of air with a wooden spoon. When Lori dusted, he brought up the rear dragging his own rag. He'd pull himself up, do a little dusting, and then they'd move on to the next piece of furniture.

Chris's "improvement" continued. He came home and asked her about her day as though he were a neighbor from the other end of the block. He told her he loved her, but outside sex, he never touched her, never teased her. The improvement was really the opposite. He acted like a father who didn't want to lose his son, so he sprinkled some crumbs of kindness for her to munch on, hoping she'd stick around for the next snack. Lori felt like hired help, a nanny, and she didn't like it.

The only time she'd left Scott had been at the nursery at church for an hour, and she was so encouraged by the fact that he always seemed just as happy there as at home, in the reliable hands of the nursery workers, that she decided to be brave and try Mothers' Day Out. She'd take her husband to lunch.

Dropping Scott off went so well—he hit the indoor-outdoor carpet in the nursery crawling, headed toward the blocks without a glance back over his shoulder—that she left the church full of hope, an emotion that seemed to carry over to every thought. She was capable. She was rearing a healthy, well-adjusted child. And she could put her marriage back together. She was, after all, doing what Chris had wanted her to do for months—go out on a date.

The receptionist at the office looked up as Lori pushed the smoked glass door open and looked surprised. "Where's the littlest lawyer?"

"Mothers' Day Out. This is our first time."

The receptionist, who was single, gave her a tolerant smile, and said, "I think Chris is in his office."

On the way down the hall, she passed one of the legal assistants, a grandmotherly type who asked, "Where's Scott?" Lori repeated her answer, thinking she had gone from spending twenty-one years as the daughter of Milton Conner to becoming the mother of Scott Gray. And in between, she'd sped through a number of other roles, and she wasn't sure yet that she'd ever simply been herself.

She expected to see Margie sitting at her post watching "Scrabble" on TV, but she wasn't there at all. Chris's door was open and he sat with his back to her, looking out the window as though he were either in deep thought or a sound sleep.

"Wake up," she said.

He spun around in his chair, surprised to see her. "Where's Scott?"

"Mothers' Day Out," she repeated for the third time in a minute, thinking she ought to have a sign made up so people wouldn't have to ask. "Buy your lunch?"

He nodded. She saw him every day when he left, dressed in suit and tie, but here he always looked different, more professional somehow. She sat in the chair in front of the desk and looked at him for a moment, thinking that when Gina had said he was good-looking, sexy, and worshipped the ground she walked on, she'd been right on two out of three.

He reached for his phone. "I'll see if Carl wants to go."

"I wanted to take you, not you and Carl."

"Oh," he said without enthusiasm. "Okay then, let's go."

They left the office and neither of them could decide what sounded good. Chris suggested a Vietnamese restaurant nearby, but Lori always felt uncomfortable with any product originating from a Southeast Asian's hands. So they walked farther uptown to an Italian restaurant. Lori took his hand as they went, but he held it only briefly before finding an excuse to release it. In the lunchtime crowds on the sidewalk, he moved behind her to let a group of women pass, and he never took her hand back into his.

He told her about a wetback named Lupe Villa, the scourge of the insurance industry, who was filing claims on a bad back with every business in town. Lupe was a cute little illegal alien with a

Buster Brown haircut and a cowboy hat, and he could aggravate his back condition by sneezing. He'd gone from working a week or two before making a worker's compensation claim to alleging an injury when he'd stuck his time card in the clock slot the very first time ever at a garden center.

Lori thought at first he was telling her about his work, then decided he was talking about Lupe so he could avoid talking about them. Chris Gray as your typical husband. She'd never thought she would see the day when the man with such a capacity for intimacy and love would turn into the normal avoiding husband. He was in fact the same man who refused to visit another couple if they insisted in breaking up the group by sexes because, he'd once told her, most men didn't want to talk about anything but their jobs. They were afraid of meaningful conversation.

They ate in the dungeonlike basement of the restaurant, between stone columns that seemed historically old. Chris sat across the table from her, his back to the wall, munching breadsticks and looking around the restaurant as though everyone in sight was more interesting than she was.

"This isn't exactly how I thought it'd be," Lori said. "I thought the first time we had a 'date' without Scott, we'd just talk and laugh. And tell dirty jokes maybe."

"Well, tell me a joke. Maybe I'll laugh."

"There was this man who woke up on his honeymoon, and his wife was tickling his forehead with a feather—"

"I've already heard it."

He cut her off with a smile, but he cut her off all the same, and the smile didn't remain on his face long. Within a matter of seconds, he was looking around the dungeon again.

"When are you going to forgive me?" she asked.

He looked at her as though the words hadn't registered and she wondered almost immediately: is he having an affair? Because forgiveness didn't seem to be the issue. If it was, he had relegated it to the bottom drawer. The man across the table wasn't someone who felt any closeness to her at all. She had known all along, when he was asking her to find a babysitter, that the consequences of insisting he be the father much more than the husband would not be easily repaired. But she had visualized leading him back lovingly, as though he were a hurt child needing special attention. She hadn't visualized this much difficulty in breaking the wall down.

"I love you," she said.

"Thanks," he said, breaking a breadstick in half, his eyes roaming the room again.

Her mistake had been in marrying for love. She should have found someone like Randy, one of her boyfriends in high school. He had been in awe of her, would have performed any deed she suggested. If she'd had friends over for a slumber party, she'd called him at midnight to get, buy, and deliver a pizza. He'd happily comply. In payment, she'd give him a giggling peck at the front door and send him away smiling.

He'd gone off to Texas Tech and impregnated some poor girl up there, married her, and now had a daughter. Mrs. Conner said he still asked about her, referred to her in those glowing terms Lori hadn't properly appreciated back then.

How was it, she wondered, that you learned too late?

"You want to make this a regular date?" she asked.

"If you want to."

She shook her head, suddenly feeling forty years old, just another old married bag.

She was on her own by 1:00, still with two hours of freedom and nothing with which to fill her time. Next week, she'd plan better. She'd get Ellen or someone to go out for lunch and a little shopping. As it was, she picked up Scott early and they rode the train in Zilker Park.

While Scott was down for a nap in the middle of the afternoon, the phone rang, a sound which always sent Lori flying through the house at such times, stubbing toes and twisting ankles and banging her hips against furniture, trying to answer it before the noise woke up Scott. It was one of those otherwise mundane occurrences that acquired a new significance when a baby—a demanding baby— had taken up residence. Six months ago, Lori would never have believed her life could be so thoroughly changed by one normal, everyday event.

Sam was on the phone, looking for Gina.

"She's not here," Lori said, wondering why he would be calling when she hadn't even spoken to Gina in well over three months. Did he really pay that little attention to the movements of his wife?

"Oh, well," he said. "She took the day off and I need her to run an errand."

"Well, I'm sorry I can't help you."

"That's okay." He paused, then asked, "How're *you* doing? I never see you anymore to ask."

She told him she was fine, and for a few minutes they chatted about recent developments. She thought as they talked that Sam was one of those Randy types who made good husbands, but women like Lori weren't aware of that fact until they'd already mistakenly married someone for love. Was Gina more perceptive than Lori had been?

The longer they stayed on the phone, the more personal Sam became.

"I really wish Gina wasn't so set on never having a baby. I really enjoyed watching you and Chris when you were pregnant. And hearing about those dreams, you know, those trips to Six Flags and all that."

"Well, keep in mind, we haven't been to Six Flags yet. It's not that simple. Everything, and I mean everything, changes. Name something, and it changes. Just like the phone. You called and I ran as fast as I could to get it so it wouldn't wake Scott up. I've almost broken every toe on both feet doing that."

"You say *everything* like you're not completely happy with all the changes."

She was saying too much, she thought, probably because she'd held it all back. Now all her frustrations came pouring forth to drench the first innocent caller who asked. Shut up, Lori Lynn, she told herself. She hated women who constantly complained about their lives. "Well, who's ever completely satisfied? Nobody. You know, if everything changes, there's bound to be some things you didn't want changed."

"Like between you and Chris?"

She'd never known Sam to be so direct, and she wasn't at all certain of where he was headed or why. If Gina was satisfying herself in the Holiday Inns of the city, then maybe Sam was in a state of sexual neglect. Maybe he saw Lori as the remedy. No, not Sam. Not possible. She laughed and said, "Well, not long after Scott was born, Chris said he'd never slept with someone else's mother. So, yeah, that changes too."

"You know what I really don't like about Gina's attitude about children? I won't ever get to see her pregnant. The most beautiful women in the world are pregnant. I love pregnant women. I love watching them. And you were the most beautiful pregnant woman I've ever seen. You didn't put on much weight except where you were supposed to, and you looked, well, I don't even know how to say it. You looked great."

"Thank you."

"I'd like to come by and see Scott sometime, if that's all right. I won't bring Gina and then we won't have to listen to complaints about dirty diapers."

"Sure, you can come visit," she said, wondering now if he'd misinterpreted her quote of Chris. Maybe he thought she'd sleep with anybody who didn't mind the fact that she was a mother.

"Maybe I'll just pop by there some afternoon when things get slow around here. Say after lunch or the middle of the afternoon, something like that."

She suddenly remembered—this was the man who had expressed a real interest in "feeling the baby" when she'd been pregnant, a man whose hand had usually been too high or too low to ever have felt much of anything other than a breast or a pubic bone. She said, "Sure, come on by. Scott usually takes a nap between two and three."

"Okay, great. First time things slow down, I'll do that."

She said good-bye and hung up, suddenly hearing what she'd said about Scott's nap time. Lord, why didn't she just nail up a sign that said, "Undisturbed sex between two and three every afternoon"? What was wrong with her?

Nothing, of course. She was only giving Sam the schedule so he'd know when *not* to come if he wanted to see Scott. Or when he should come if. . . . She shook her head. She didn't have to suspect her own motives where Sam was concerned. She was nice to him because he was one of the authentically nice people Lori knew. He didn't make jokes at the expense of others, as did the champion Gina or the runner-up Chris. And when Gina and Chris got started, Sam always gave the victim a sympathetic smile. And if she was pregnant, a subtle fondling.

She shook her head as if to cleanse it of impure thoughts. Suddenly she seemed obsessed with sex. Wanton. Spread-eagle on her back.

Well, if Sam liked her, that was fine. Someone needed to like her. Besides, there was no telling what Gina and Chris had done. Gina showed more when she was "dressed" than most women did naked. And Chris was the one who had given names to Gina's breasts. After Lori had told him about the vision she'd had the night she had drunk too many pink drinks, about visualizing two playful puppies leaping from Gina's bra, he had begun calling them Maxie and Bobo after two dogs he'd known as a child. Maxie, according to Chris, was the biggest, always crowding Bobo. So what was worse —a man who spontaneously grabbed a feel when a woman had allowed him to feel the baby moving, or a man who lusted after another woman's breasts and named them after his favorite dogs?

She returned to the job that the phone call had interrupted— making a grocery list—and heard Scott "talking."

The time after his nap, after he woke up, was becoming much

calmer. Instead of screaming as soon as his eyes opened, demanding immediate release from his wooden prison of a crib, he now played and jabbered. And when he tired of those activities, he'd pull himself up and shout for Lori. The sound wasn't an intelligible word, but it was distinctive; it meant he wanted his mother to come visit. And as soon as she appeared in the doorway, he began to jump, making the mattress and springs squeak, and a great smile appeared on his face.

She went to check on him, wondering why Chris had never told her she'd been the most beautiful pregnant woman he'd ever seen.

19

Caroline's telephone number was written on a yellow legal pad, and Chris sat at his desk at work staring at it. He had easily obtained it from information, and he could just as easily call her. Pick up the receiver, hit eleven buttons, and he had leaped eight years backward. So far, he hadn't been able to bring himself to make the call, even though he couldn't think about anything else.

He sat listening to Margie offer assistance to the contestants on "Sale of the Century," most of which was erroneous. (When the host started talking about the president who had ended slavery, she shouted "Kennedy!") He kept thinking, I need to call now before someone walks in here and ties me up the rest of the morning.

He wasn't, after all, making any commitment by calling her. And who said that news had to pass through a mutual friend, that they couldn't talk to each other directly? Didn't old friends call each other?

He saw Carl walk down the hall, a sight which moved him to action. After closing his door, he took a deep breath and then without giving the matter any more thought, dialed the number. He sat listening to the electronic beeping and blinking, trying to visualize the phone as a time machine hurtling him backward, but mostly he felt as though he was making a phone call from his office.

A feminine voice answered and he asked for Caroline.

"This is Caroline."

There was something wrong with the voice other than the tone, the fact that it didn't sound like the voice he'd been hearing in his head for eight years. He asked again, "Is Caroline there?"

"This is Caroline, dear."

With the completion of that reassuring remark, he heard an off-line conversation ("I *told* you not to do that anymore") and the receiver was obviously rescued from a child. Then he heard an adult voice but it still wasn't familiar. He was about to identify himself when he heard, "Do you want to play with Jennifer? Then you put the lipstick up." Pause. "Hello?"

"Caroline?"

"No, I'm not taking you to Jennifer's right now but you do have to put the lipstick up *right now*." Another pause. "Hello?"

He waited this time for further admonitions aimed at Jennifer's friend, and when he didn't hear any, he said, "This is Chris Gray."

Silence. Then, "Good God Almighty."

The next minute was burlesque. They both attempted to talk, neither of them hearing the other but waiting for an answer nonetheless, then both making the same unheard attempt. Finally, he shut up.

"Where are you?"

"I'm in Austin. Who answered the phone?"

"Sherry. Who won't live past her sixth birthday if—you put that up. No, you *may not* wear that necklace. Put it up. Mama's talking to a friend and she doesn't want to be bothered. Take it off and put it up." She sighed and apologized. "This is the most unbelievable thing that's happened to me. In at least eight years."

She'd been counting too, Chris thought. She knew it had been eight years without having to stop and compute: "Let's see, the last time I saw you was right after I got married and I got married in . . ."

He sat at his desk smiling, getting closer to the phone as though it put him closer to her.

"Tell me how you are," he said.

"Oh, I guess it depends on how you look at it," she said. "Some days I'm fine and other days I'm not."

He sat back, hearing this noncommittal statement, and they lapsed into an old-friends conversation, trading items of interest and news capsules on children and other family members. Sherry was her only child, and she hadn't yet heard that Chris had become a father. The conversation wasn't especially the one Chris had hoped for but neither was it cold and formal.

He decided, what the heck, no guts, no glory. He'd ask her what she thought about a visit, and he needed to ask quickly because he could hear Carl's voice in the outer office. He had stopped to talk to Margie and would be in Chris's office any minute. He had no regard for closed doors or personal phone calls.

"I was thinking about coming to see you sometime."

"Great. Y'all come whenever you can."

"I'm not talking y'all. I'm talking me."

"Fine," she said as if he'd suggested a wiener roast. "Do you know when?"

"Oh, what about tomorrow?"

She laughed and gave him directions to her house, and he assumed if she was inviting him to her house, she would work out any husbandly complications.

"Is noon okay?" he asked.

"Yeah, that's great. I'm really looking forward to seeing you."

He hung up on that positive-sounding note, just as Carl opened the door and walked in. And as Chris could have predicted, he sat as well.

"You have a member of the local constabulary waiting to serve you," Carl said.

"For what?"

"Lupe Villa has sued you individually *and* the law firm, for, I think the petition says, 'tortiously inducing him to drunkenness' and intentionally deceiving him about his worker's compensation claim with Pipe Pottery Company.' "

"Oh, bullshit. He signed the statement."

The insurance company had asked Chris to determine whether Lupe was bending, stooping, or lifting, and if he was, to take pictures. Chris went to visit Lupe, who was becoming an old friend, but didn't take his camera because he knew Lupe wasn't straining himself. He didn't have to. But the wetback was growing more and more bold and had filed claims against two businesses where he hadn't been known to show up for a job.

Chris had visited him in his east Austin home, furnished by Sears indirectly since they owned Allstate. Lupe had offered Chris a drink from a gallon of Canadian Club, holding the bottle up and kissing it. "Aetna, I'm glad I met ya," he said with a trace of a Spanish accent. They sat and talked for a while. The house on the outside (the "outerior" as Lupe put it) was plain and fit in well with his impoverished east-side neighbors, but inside it had the best furniture on that side of town.

Lupe had filed a claim with Pipe Pottery Company and as of then hadn't retained a lawyer to represent him, so Chris explained that Pipe Pottery was the biggest employer of illegal aliens in Austin, and Lupe was about to put them out of business. Their insurance rates would go so high with Lupe's claim, they wouldn't be able to afford the expense, and what would all those wetbacks do then?

"No shit, man?" Lupe said, concerned over his river-wading brethren. "They really go out of business?"

"Really," Chris said, crossing himself.

Lupe couldn't tolerate the thought of wetbacks without paychecks so he agreed to drop his claim. Chris wrote out a statement for his signature that said, "My name is Lupe Villa. I live at 1403 East Allegro in Austin, Texas. I am living illegally in the United States and do not have a social security number but I use several different ones when I apply for jobs. I do not have any dependents but always list my family in Mexico on my job applications. I did not injure my back or any part of my body while working for Pipe Pottery Company. I do not want to make a claim for worker's compensation benefits because I was not injured in any way at Pipe Pottery Company."

Lupe read it and said, "Now this don't do nothing to something else, does it?"

Chris assured him it covered only the claim at Pipe Pottery, and then Lupe signed it. Chris asked everyone walking in and out of the house, a steady stream of traffic, to witness Lupe's signature, and he came away with Macho Camacho's name although Chris didn't remember seeing him.

"Well," Chris said, standing to go sign for his papers in the reception area, "who's going to defend me?"

"The insurance company damn sure better pay for it," Carl said. "They're the ones you were working for."

They walked down the hall and Chris told his brother that he had leads on four good witnesses on Lupe in Corpus Christi and he was going tomorrow to locate them. All four were supposedly working at a grain elevator. This lie rolled out as easily as all of Carl's had over the years, and had the same effect. Carl wished him luck.

His lie to Lori was more elaborate than he wanted to tell, primarily because she suggested a family outing when he told her he was going to Corpus Christi tomorrow. It seemed to compound itself as he talked.

Sitting at the dining room table, which was set as though company were coming, with china, silver, and candles, he began to feel like the worthless liar he was. First, he had planned to take the MG because it hadn't been on the road for a while and needed the soot blown out; there were only two seats. Then he would probably be parked along the harbor for several hours while he interviewed the four phantoms at the grain elevator; he'd already obtained clearance from the superintendent. And the superintendent knew of another

230

possible witness who lived in the slums, and Chris would probably have to drive down there.

"Well," Lori said, sitting across from him and moving one of the burning candles so she could see him directly. "I guess it doesn't sound like much of a family outing then, does it?"

"No. But this dinner looks great. Normandy pork chops. We haven't had them in months."

"I seem to have more time than I used to. Scott doesn't have to be held all the time."

Scott, in fact, wasn't even in the room. He was playing by himself in his bedroom with a plastic box out of which popped heads of various sorts when he got the correct combination—turning a dial, pulling a lever.

"I had a strange call today," Lori said. "Sam. He said he might come over to see Scott during the day so he wouldn't have to bring Gina."

Chris, ladling sauce over the pork chop and apple slice, shrugged. "I don't blame him. I wouldn't want to bring Gina over here either."

Scott yelled and Lori said, "Listen."

"What?"

"That means, come here, Mama. You listen. He'll do it again."

Chris listened, aware Scott had shouted but thinking he had only given an order to a head to pop up and shortcut the process of manually bringing it up. And sure enough, Scott yelled again, a short burst of throaty energy.

"I bet you he wants to show me something," she said, leaving the table.

Chris watched her go, wishing she and Sam had met before he'd met Lori. They were suited to each other and both deserved better spouses. Sam was a low-keyed guy with low expectations, and he'd have treated Lori better than anyone Chris knew, would have indulged her remodeling, her haphazard ways with money, her desire to lead a boring life. He didn't deserve Gina, who took advantage of him and gave nothing in return.

Lori returned, smiling. "You heard his first word. Or sentence, or whatever it is. He wanted to show me how the heads came up." She sat. "We have such a smart child."

"How could we have missed?"

They ate in silence, and suddenly Chris was overly aware of the table setting. It had to mean something. They rarely ever ate on the dining room table alone; it was usually set only for company. But Lori ate and didn't offer any hints, which was unlike her. She was an expert at hinting, at communicating obliquely. He started to ask, then decided he'd rather avoid any argument, which would surely result from a conversation on their relationship.

He finished the meal without having to talk about anything other than Scott.

He got up early the next morning and watched the sun rise as he drove into Sequin, wondering why he felt no more excited than if he was actually going to interview witnesses. He'd expected the same crazed, gut-curling emotions he'd experienced eight years ago. He wanted to be insanely in love, but he wasn't and couldn't figure out why. Maybe he was worried about Caroline's appearance, the possibility she'd turned half hippo, one of those ladies whose legs and butt weighed two tons but whose upper bodies were normal. Or maybe he was worried that he'd arrive to find her husband ready to show him the sights. "We got a real nice beach downchere. You just gotta see it. And if the messicans bother you, just don't look."

He descended slowly toward the gulf, his fall bottoming out near Beeville, where the earth flattened and opened up to farmland. The trees thinned and coastal plains appeared. And then before he was ready, he was on a divided highway lined with palm trees and could see the superstructure of the harbor bridge rising upward in the haze.

Once in town, he stopped at a motel along the bay and called Caroline to tell her he was early. She told him to come on.

Within a few minutes, he had ended his journey into the past at the curb in front of her house, a white brick with a carefully manicured lawn and poodle-shaped ligustrums out front. In the front yard stood two women talking.

Caroline—it had to be her—stood laughing with a blonde, looking at Chris and the MG. He switched off the ignition and panicked because he didn't recognize her. She was unbelievably pretty. Television pretty. But she'd changed. He couldn't believe that in eight years a person could become unrecognizable. But what luck, he thought, what fantastic luck. He was here for the woman who would always love him, and this wondrous woman was about to ignite his emotions. He was ready for a full-scale assault.

But then she turned and walked across the yard, away from him. Leaving. And the blonde—the *blonde*—was walking toward his car. She walked into the street, coming around to open his door.

"Chris. How are you?"

He recognized the nose, that was all. And since it was too late to make a break, he got out of the car.

"Howdy, stranger," she said.

They hugged, side to side as if avoiding intimate contact, and he followed her into the house.

"You've got a nice house," he said.

"Thank you."

After eight years, his opening line was, "You've got a nice house." How could that be? How could Caroline have blonde hair?

The interior of the house reeked of yellow. Everything—the dinette suite, the wicker end tables, the bamboo-frame couch—was yellow. And the house smelled hauntingly familiar. It reminded him of an aunt's in Freeport from years ago.

She stopped halfway across the room and looked at him closely, which was more that he was willing to do because she may as well have been wearing the head of a mop, as foreign as the blonde hair seemed.

"Well, how've you been?" she asked. "You look good."

"Oh, getting old's all."

She offered him coffee, an offer he accepted gratefully because all he could think of to say was, "What in God's name have you done to your hair?" He walked to the far end of the living room and examined a picture of Sherry, her eyes and smile readily admitting she'd answer a phone and say, "This is Caroline, dear."

He stood by a sentry palm, listening for noises from the other part of the house, especially the emission of any husbandly grunts. He expected to see a greasy husband, gut hanging over his belt, entering the bathroom and making a guttural sound which meant he'd take care of Chris as soon as he took a leak. First things first, know what I mean?

"Where's Lee?" he asked.

"San Antonio. All week. And Sherry's at a friend's."

Just his luck, he thought. At this point, he would have preferred a visit that was strictly defined and nonsexual. He wanted to be there for beer and dominoes, just a couple of friends getting together. Maybe if he acted appropriately austere, he could get away with such a visit.

"Shit," she said from the kitchen.

He walked into the kitchen hoping she'd injured herself. Then he could drop her off at the emergency room on his way out of town. But she was standing at the counter, on top of which were two cups of coffee, both looking like they'd leaked, sitting in the middle of a small brown sea.

She offered the sight of both her shaking hands. "Do I look nervous? I can't even pour coffee."

He smiled and she did too, and when she did, he suddenly watched a veil being lifted from her face. He knew her. He knew that smile. For the first time, he was certain of her identity. The gaudy hair faded from view and his eyes focused on her truly pretty smile. He remembered trying to reproduce it in his mind, but he'd never succeeded, never been able to see the lines of her lips and the look of her teeth. The smile.

He reached for her shoulder, expecting at the last instant she'd avert her face. But she didn't. He kissed her. Slowly, lightly. When

234

he moved away, her eyes were level, staring into his neck, hiding a reaction.

What worried him was his reaction. He'd just kissed Caroline after eight years of wanting, and he felt nothing. He wouldn't have felt anything had a pep squad marched in and led a cheer. And for the first time in his life, he felt old. If not old, then aging. He had come to Corpus Christi looking for the cute little girl who'd hung around his house when he'd been seventeen. She'd had the look of pure innocence in her wide smile and blue eyes, but she'd also exhibited an interest in growing up. He could look at her then and see a girl who'd be content if he'd simply held her. And now he looked at her and wanted to cry because she'd become a woman who said shit and had cynical blonde hair.

"Listen," he said. "You're nervous, I'm nervous, so why don't we take a ride?"

She thought it was a good suggestion. "Eight years," she kept saying as they left.

They drove in the MG to Padre Island, and he had to keep blinking his eyes to clear away a film. The sun baked them as they drove with the top down, and he grew dizzy and disoriented. Maybe it was the drop in elevation; maybe it was the equivalent of jet lag, this attempt to span eight years in a day. He didn't know. Before they reached the causeway, he stopped at a convenience store and bought two six-packs.

They drove toward the island and then turned toward Aransas Pass.

Finding a sparsely populated beach, they turned into an opening in the dunes. They drove down the beach and he watched the endless water roll onto the shore, and he parked facing the gulf. The monotonous ever-present sound of the surf made him think that he had lived long enough to have loved this woman eight years ago. Eight years had passed since he'd first fallen in love. He had gone through the navy, through college, had married and fathered a child since he'd last seen Caroline.

They sat quietly for a long time, watching the gulls dip and screech in the wind. From the corner of his eye, he watched Caroline. She swallowed, her chin bobbing. She blinked once as if in pain. She tilted her head and looked sad.

A guy and girl walked in front of them at the water's edge. Chris saw two lovers before him, and he tried to remember all he had felt eight years ago, trying to remember exactly what it had felt like to want something as much and as terribly as he had wanted Caroline. And he couldn't remember any of it.

The couple played near the water. The girl, foam washing over her feet, spied something in the sand and bent to inspect it. Her boyfriend kneed her from behind and then pushed her forward onto her hands and knees. She jumped up and chased him into the surf, wrestling him down.

Chris slid down in the seat and tilted his face upward, closing his eyes and seeing himself splashing in the gulf with a bikini-clad girl. She jumped on his back and they fell into the sea. Salty water flooded his ears and nose. And when he realized the joyous girl on his back was Lori, he sat up and gasped.

Lori. My God, he was fantasizing about his own wife.

"What is it?" Caroline asked.

"Nothing. I thought I recognized that woman for a minute."

As though she were glad the silence had been broken, Caroline said, "When I think about eight years ago, I remember how unrealistic I thought you were. Wanting me to run off to New Mexico." She looked at him and smiled. "You'd never even been to New Mexico."

"It was a place. A distant place."

She slumped, matching his posture, and took a beer can in both hands. "But you know what's unreal? This relationship. I've never had one like this and I don't think many people have. It's like a soul come down and split into two parts; one was you and one was me. Why have I always felt so close to you?"

"Well," he said, surprised that her thoughts were so different from his. What accounted for it? The hair? Would the situation have been reversed if he'd shown up with a platinum mohawk? He watched a ship moving across the horizon and he wished he were on it, standing on the fantail watching the widening wake and the swooping gulls. Bye, bye, Caroline.

"We had so many missed connections," she said.

For the first time, he began to see those missed connections in a different light. Maybe they hadn't been so unfortunate after all. What would he do with a wife whose natural hair color never suited her?

"What's wrong with us?" she asked. "We haven't even talked in eight years."

"That's a long time, all right."

"We should have gone. Eight years ago, we should have gone to New Mexico."

My God, he thought. Eight years ago he had been willing to leave the navy altogether. UA, they had called it. Unauthorized absence. And for eight years he would now have been living with the despicable tag "absentee wanted by the armed forces." What would he be doing? Working on a ranch and trying to hide among the illegal aliens? Had he ever been that stupid? Had he ever thought love was worth that price? He wanted to thank her for refusing to go back then; he wanted to grovel in the sand he was so grateful.

He started the car and turned around, heading back toward the city. He wanted a graceful way of leaving once they were back at her house, but he knew she expected more of him than that. He did feel comfortable with her, and he could envision a relationship continuing into the future if she wouldn't talk about soul-splitting or running off to New Mexico. And as long as they both kept their clothes on.

As they drove along the bay in town, getting closer to her house, he said, "Caroline, I'm going to drop you off and get back to Austin. I think we both need some time to decide what it is we want. We need to think. If I go back home with you, I know what I'll want to do, and maybe it'd be all right and maybe it wouldn't. I just think we ought to give it some thought."

"I've thought about it. I've always known what I'd do if I saw you again. I don't have to give it any thought." She reached over and patted his leg, letting her hand remain halfway up his thigh. "It's up to you."

He had thought he'd always known. But he hadn't. He hadn't at all.

He hadn't known anything.

By the time he turned the corner and saw his house sitting in the hot shadows of afternoon, he was overly tired. He'd driven four hundred plus miles in a sports car with the top down, the equivalent of being locked into a steambox and bounced down a hillside. He was sunburned and stiff and hungry and had a headache from the beer earlier in the afternoon.

Pulling into his driveway, he saw a sight that made him groan— Carl's white Mercedes.

Then it hit him, like a phone ringing in the middle of the night. Trouble. Emergency. Sickness. Carl never visited when he wasn't there.

He parked beside the Mercedes, closing his eyes and uttering a prayer: please, God, please, it can't be Scott. It can't be. He was relatively certain he could handle any of life's disastrous surprises except one, and that was any problem involving Scott.

He walked into the house and found two somber faces in the cool kitchen—Carl's and Lori's. They sat drinking iced tea at the table, and the scene was much too calm for Scott to have been hurt.

"We've got a problem," Carl said without preliminaries. He got up to refill his glass from a pitcher of tea on the counter.

Waiting for Carl to explain, Chris looked at Lori and was unnerved by the concerned but observant eyes of his wife. She was waiting to see how he accepted the unrevealed news.

"The old man had a heart attack," Carl said.

"You're kidding."

"Nope." He leaned against the counter and sighed. "Mattie called the office just about the time I was leaving. He'd been out at the farm trying to start a generator and pulled on it for maybe ten minutes. And he had a heart attack. Somehow, he drove himself back to town. Mattie was at the house and called Griffin's. I can't believe he didn't die when they got a hold of him. But they took him to that new medical center in Halton."

Chris listened to this short narrative and looked twice at Lori to make sure she was appropriately serious; if she wasn't, Carl was engaging in a practical joke, a bizarre one, but bizarre jokes were nothing new to Carl. Griffin's, the funeral home in Ashworth, used a white hearse as an ambulance, the only one available locally, and the reference to the funeral home had to be significant somehow. No, this was a joke and Lori didn't know it.

"Well, good," Chris said. "What's for supper?"

"Chris," Lori said, standing, disturbed over his attitude.

"It's a joke, Lori. He's fixing to give us the punch line. The hearse arrived and the old man thought he'd died and said, 'Whoa, I'm all right now,' or something like that. It's a joke."

Lori shook her head. "He just called the hospital."

"Right. He picks up the phone, calls time and temperature, and says, 'Hey there, Doc. How's my old man?' Right?"

Reality set in. There was no joke, not unless Carl had exceeded his acting abilities. And now that Chris looked at his brother more closely, he believed Carl had been crying. His eyes were red, slightly swollen.

"He's alive?" Chris asked.

"He was the last time I checked. Which was about ten minutes ago," Carl said. "He's in the cardiac care unit."

"Son of a bitch," Chris said because he didn't know what else to say. "When'd it happen?"

"Probably about four. He had time to drive back to town before Mattie left, and I think she leaves about four-thirty."

Chris nodded, suddenly concerned about the timing. Maybe God had decided to punish him by sending a heart attack the old man's way. What had Chris been doing at four? Nothing really, probably just passing through Karnes City. Still, he felt caught, divinely exposed. For the rest of his life he'd think, my father had a heart attack the day I went to see Caroline.

"I've already packed some clothes," Lori said, "and Scott's at Ellen's. She's going to keep him tonight and tomorrow. I'll go with you and come back if you need to stay."

He nodded, wondering if it was his fate to feel continually disoriented and confused. Maybe it *was* jet lag. Little souls were shot from heaven to find a place on earth and never recovered from their first voyage, made at the speed of light. There had to be some rational explanation for the fact that he could never get a handle on the events occurring around him.

"Let's go," Carl said.

20

Lori felt like the third person who made the crowd as they drove in Carl's car to Halton. She'd started out sitting in the front seat between the brothers, but when Chris had failed to acknowledge she was there, had failed to express any need for comfort from or communion with her, she'd moved to the back seat when they had stopped at Denney's for coffee. Neither brother asked why she had moved. She understood their concern for their father, but she didn't understand why she felt she'd become a stranger.

The two in the front talked about their father the entire way.

"He couldn't be all that happy with his life," Carl said. "He does nothing but work all day and then come home to an empty house at night. He goes to bed, gets back up, and does the same thing the next day."

"He's not like us," Chris said. "He doesn't think about choices, all the things he could do. Didn't he ever give you one of those sermons on rights versus obligations? I got it at least once a week. You don't worry about your rights; you fulfill your obligations.

That's all you worry about. His obligation is to farm that land. Farm that land. That's all he's ever thought about. The man has a divine mission. God outfitted him with overalls and a hoe, and, by God, that's what he's going to do."

Carl nodded, sipping coffee as they drove up an interstate that always seemed crowded to Lori. She looked at Chris's arm lying across the top of the seat. Occasionally his hand moved down the back of the seat, aimlessly, feeling the upholstery, and she moved, placing her knees directly below his hand, giving it a warm and loving place to land.

"I've always thought he must be bored out of his mind," Carl said. "You can fulfill your obligations to God and mankind or whoever without staying bored out of your mind. Hell, he could've retired when you left home. He probably hasn't spent more than a dime at a time since then. He could be traveling, building houses, pursuing some mindless hobby like bird-watching, but he's still there *farming that land*," he said with a bumpkin twang.

Chris's hand finally found Lori's knees. It stayed only long enough to give her a friendly squeeze and then was gone. What was wrong with him? She wanted to cuddle and comfort him. If her father had just suffered a heart attack, she'd want someone to hold her. Tightly. Here she was, desiring to be a warm and loving wife, and he didn't want her attention.

"If I didn't have to work," Chris said, "I sure as hell wouldn't. I'd go back to Rome and Athens. I'd get in my car and drive around the state to all the places I haven't been. I've never seen the valley or Big Bend; hell, I've never even been to the Panhandle. I'd like to get in my car and just go find out what the hell's going on, talk to everybody I meet. Then after I figure out what's going on over here, I'd go to Russia and China and see what those people are thinking about. Have you ever thought about how working ruins your life, I mean, just completely ruins it?"

Carl shook his head. "You're completely screwed up, you know that? Completely. You're from some other planet."

✝

The medical center was being put to bed by the time they arrived at nine. The east Texas sky provided a white backdrop for the building, which Lori had seen a number of times as they'd driven by. It looked out of place in the crumbling little town of Halton. It was built of deep red brick and smoked glass, and the awning out front over the main entrance resembled the upswept wings of a bird that was about to take flight.

The cardiac care unit was on the ground floor, and the waiting room seemed so clean and unused that she was afraid Mr. Gray had died while they'd been en route. There were two couches and a number of chairs, all in a yellow and orange color scheme that gave the room a warm appearance. The magazines were neatly stacked on a table.

A nurse advised them that the normal rules allowed only two visitors with a patient at a time, and only for fifteen minutes, but Mr. Gray was the only occupant of the unit and he had already demanded that all three be admitted simultaneously and indefinitely. Since he was in stable condition, she'd agreed to allowing all three in. Any sign of a flare-up though and they'd all have to vacate. She quietly opened the door and pointed at the only one of six beds that was curtained off.

Lori followed the brothers into the unit and thought Mr. Gray looked like a character in a science fiction movie, here to get his components checked by the bank of electronic monitors and scopes with green lights. The hard-working farmer and welder looked out of place in a hospital bed, but even though the lights were dim, he appeared to Lori almost as healthy as he had the last time she'd seen him.

Awake, he smiled upon seeing them. "Hey, just like Christmas. All three of you. Only one missing is Scott."

The sons offered their hands, shaking, and Lori kissed his forehead.

"How're you feeling?" she asked.

"Like I've been knocked down with a fire hose and washed down the street. Otherwise, just fine." He patted the side of the bed. "Here. Sit down."

She sat and he pointed to the other side of the bed, directing Chris to balance his wife. Carl took a chair near the head of the bed.

They listened to an almost impersonal recap of the afternoon's events. He'd been at the farm trying to start a generator that didn't want to crank. He gave it tug after tug, determined it would start whether it wanted to or not. It won the battle. He began noticing a pain in his chest, no worse than indigestion at first, but it grew in intensity until he felt as though he were being crushed, as though a tractor was backing over him. He hadn't been totally confident he'd make it back to town.

"I drove with one eye on the ditch, just hoping I'd head that way if I passed on and not across the center stripe. I didn't want to surprise some little old lady headed to town to buy groceries."

Lori had known her father-in-law to be a faithful member of the church, but he wasn't an outspoken one. She heard him speak the first religious words since she'd known him: "If I didn't learn anything else, I learned you can go pretty quick, whether you want to or not, whether you're ready or not, and you oughta be right with God *all* the time."

"Your life flash before your eyes?" Carl asked.

"It must've been yours," Mr. Gray said. "I didn't see a thing."

"Ha," Chris said. "If it'd been his, you would've been arrested for being in possession of prurient material."

"No, if it'd been Carl's, I would have had a second heart attack. A fatal one."

"On the other hand," Carl said, "watching Chris's wouldn't have been bad. You could've died laughing."

"Be nice," Lori said, looking at Carl but intending all three to heed her order. She couldn't believe this family. The father had

243

been brought to the doorstep of death, laid there, and they were all trading gibes still.

For a few minutes they talked about the new hospital, the quality of medical care, and the number of things which needed to be done on the farm, all of which Mr. Gray would tend to as soon as he got out of the hospital or was moved to a room with a phone. There was too much to be done for him to lie around very long.

Carl, antsiest of the three visitors, stood and asked, "I'm going after coffee. Anybody else want some?"

No one did. They were quiet for a moment after the older son's departure and then Mr. Gray looked at Lori.

"I feel cut off from the world without a way to look at the sky. I need a room with a window. I can't watch the weather in here."

"You watch the weather a lot, don't you?"

"Every farmer does. I've been watching it all my life, just like a stockbroker watches economic indicators. It was in my blood from the beginning. What I can't figure out is how the bloodline ended before the Gray family did."

Chris reached and tapped his father's arm to get his attention and said in a voice so loud it shocked him as well as his father and wife. "Hey, Pop. Why don't you say that to me?" Mr. Gray turned in surprise. "We've been beating around the bush for years. You'll tell Scott you couldn't interest me in farming and you'll tell Lori and you'll tell everybody you see but me. Why don't you just tell me?"

Mr. Gray turned away, acting for a moment as though he hadn't heard. Or as though he were thinking of a new, less controversial subject.

Chris continued. "I kept expecting you to bring it up for the last two years I was at home. Every time you said something to me, I thought, 'Well, this is where he asks me if I'm staying. This is it.' And it wasn't. You never mentioned it even though I knew it was on your mind. Then the next time you said something, I'd think, 'Well, *this* must be it.' And it wasn't. We haven't talked about it yet and I've been gone almost ten years. But I know it's still on your mind because you keep talking about it to other people."

Mr. Gray cleared his throat and stared at his sheet, pulled up chest-high. He felt the white material with his fingers. "I can't talk to you."

"You can't talk to me?"

Mr. Gray seemed to deliberate on whether to continue the conversation. Lori, watching with great interest, would have bet that two days ago, he wouldn't have. But now he looked at the ceiling and said, his voice suddenly catching, "You remind me of your mother."

Lori wanted to cheer. She was witnessing actual communication between two Grays, normal communication most humans were capable of but which this family seemed to skirt most often. She wanted to shout encouragement, to congratulate them, but she sat quietly and didn't intrude.

"How do I remind you of my mother? I don't look like her. Do I?"

Mr. Gray made a face that Lori understood. He was reining in his emotions. "Right after your mother died, I didn't think Carl'd ever say her name again. You know him—too tough to cry. He wouldn't talk about her at all. But this one," he said to Lori, pointing his thumb at Chris, "this one didn't want to do anything else. He'd get up every morning and pick out a shirt and he'd bring it to me. He wanted to know if his mother would have wanted him to wear it to school." Mr. Gray stopped, wiping a tear from his eye with a thick finger. He waited a moment before continuing. "Then he'd sit on the bed, the side she slept on—" He stopped again, shaking his head and looking directly at Chris. "And he'd start crying. And he'd want to talk about her. So we'd sit and we'd talk and we'd cry. He wanted to start every morning that way. I didn't. But I didn't know how to tell him that. Don't shake your head because I'm not making this up. After a while, I started leaving before you woke up so I wouldn't have to talk about it. I didn't want to cry forever.

"You knew what I was doing and it made you mad. As far as you were concerned, she'd never been anything but your mother. She'd never even known me. Or been my wife. And you went for the longest time without saying much of anything to me. You were like a kid who had a secret and you wouldn't share it with me."

Chris shook his head. "I don't remember *any* of that."

Mr. Gray was about to respond when Carl appeared at the foot of the bed, coming around the curtain, and said, "Okay! Let's get the music and the dancing girls in here. Get this man back on his feet."

Lori shook her head. Another example of the older brother blowing up the road to improved relations. Mr. Gray and Chris said nothing else, as though they'd been discussing confidential matters, and Lori was disappointed but still, father and son had made a start. They'd talked to each other.

Then Chris surprised her by saying, "I'm not sure I understood what you're telling me."

Mr. Gray slapped Chris lightly on the arm. "I don't even remember the question."

With the father in stable condition and no further threats to his health imminent, the three left the next afternoon to return to Austin. Lori was both literally and figuratively in the back seat. Carl and Chris talked almost the entire way back about Lupe Villa, the Mexican plague on American insurance. He was scheduled to give his deposition tomorrow night and Chris wanted to be there to record his new lies.

Lori didn't know what to do about her marriage. Had they settled into the rut most marriages ran in, having gone from true love to the blahs? Maybe nothing was wrong with Chris anymore except that he'd become the Great American Husband—taciturn, numb, and unwilling to change. Maybe nothing could be done for their marriage. Maybe she'd call Elizabeth and see what she thought. He didn't seem either mad or hurt anymore, just distant.

Lori loved summer mornings, loved sitting in the shade of the patio before the heat of the day set in, watching Scott crawl after

J. D. The dog either thought the crawling child was a funny-looking dog or was smart enough to recognize him as a child who wanted to play. J. D. ran around and barked and made Scott laugh, then lay down on his back to wait for his playmate to catch up.

The day after she had returned to Austin with the brothers, she was sitting on the patio with a cup of coffee, wondering how the morning could be so cool but the afternoon so hot, when the phone rang.

"I'll be right back," she said to Scott.

She walked inside and reached for the phone on the kitchen wall, and when her hand was a foot away from the receiver, she stopped, knowing suddenly who it was as though she'd walked into an aura of knowledge, one that made her psychic.

She answered it. And it was indeed Sam.

"Can Scott eat pizza?" he asked. "I thought I'd bring lunch with me."

Lori laughed, almost lighthearted with happiness over the fact that he had scheduled a lunchtime visit, not one starting precisely at naptime. "No, he's not quite that advanced. We're still on the mushy stuff. A French fry's about all the fast food he can handle."

"Oh. Well, he'll catch up, no doubt."

"Just come over and I'll make lunch. You don't have to bring anything."

"No, no, we can't visit if you're worrying with lunch. I'll bring you something. Tell me what you want."

They decided on sandwiches from a deli nearby; she liked a good sandwich but rarely ate one because Chris was never home for lunch.

After hanging up, she thought briefly about calling Chris to tell him Sam was coming over, but she'd already told him about Sam's plan to visit. Why did she feel guilty doing something she had already discussed with her husband? Especially when that same husband was probably taking Margie to lunch and staring at her pampered and powdered bosom while she ate something more expensive than he'd buy his own wife.

Sam arrived with two sandwiches, pickles, a pint of potato salad, and two canned Cokes, a ready-made picnic for the kitchen table. He set everything on the table and told her all she had to do was find paper plates and plastic forks. "Let's just drink from the can. That way you won't have to clean anything up. I know all about this because Gina hates cleaning up."

He also brought a small present for Scott, wrapped in paper covered with colorful balloons. Scott, who hadn't yet met a stranger, had enough experience with visitors to know what he saw in Sam's hand. He sat in the middle of the kitchen, reaching and bouncing, anxious for the gift to be delivered.

It was a small xylophone. Sam squatted beside him and tapped out a tune for him, then placed the hammer in Scott's hand and attempted to direct him in repeating the tune. Scott, however, had other sounds on his mind—noise, lots of it, manufactured as quickly as possible.

Rebuffed, Sam stood. "Independent sort, isn't he?"

"He's getting that way."

Lori got the paper plates and plastic forks, thinking Sam didn't look as homely as he had, but she couldn't figure out why. Maybe he had a new hairstyle. He wore light blue pants and a matching knit shirt, and he seemed somehow more contemporary. Or was her mind, knowing she felt deprived, compensating for him, trying to serve up crawfish as lobster? Whatever, he was always comfortable with himself. He wasn't a lady's man, like Carl, and didn't try to sneak up and ambush you, like Chris.

Sam opened his wrapped sandwich and said, "I'm not sure what all they put on these. Maybe everything. I hope you like everything."

She assured him whatever was on the sandwiches was what she wanted, having to speak loudly because Scott was pounding vigorously on the new xylophone. He was creating an atmosphere in which his mother could easily develop a headache, so she lifted him under the arms and carried him as he hammered to his room. She set him down near his crib and he carried on without missing a beat, his face radiating determination.

She returned to the kitchen to find Sam seated and patiently waiting for her. Sighing, she sat, suddenly feeling strange across the table from him, a virtual stranger, even more so with his new appearance. Besides, she could smell aftershave now with the distraction—Scott and his musical instrument—gone.

"You look nice," he said.

"Thank you."

She wore the pale green sundress she'd put on that morning. After his call, she'd considered changing, then decided she didn't want to go through the process of selecting other clothes. Or thinking about the reasons behind any particular selection.

"It must be amazing to watch him grow."

"It is, it really is. Chris notices it more than I do when we go to Abilene for a week. He says he can see the change over just that week. I can see it, but sometimes I don't notice until later."

She wasn't a bit hungry and didn't want to pick up the sandwich, feeling that by eating Sam's offering she was committing an act of intimacy she wasn't prepared to commit, such as combing his hair for him or brushing a crumb from his leg. Besides, he hadn't yet taken his eyes off her. They shifted occasionally, from her face to —where? Her breasts?

"I guess Chris is anxious for him to get big enough to go to Six Flags. Ride that roller coaster."

Lori, growing uncomfortable with Sam's eyes, was relieved to hear Scott utter his one-syllable demand that she appear. She got up, explaining this method of communication.

Sam got up to follow, and there was something about the way he moved, all but leaping upward as though he'd been waiting for a chance for much too long, that bothered her. They stopped in the doorway of Scott's room, looking at the child in the middle of the floor who had suspended all efforts until his mother arrived. He mouthed gibberish, which Lori interpreted as, "Watch me beat the devil out of this," and he began pounding the xylophone again, making a metallic racket that caused Lori to close her eyes part-way. But she was more aware of Sam's proximity than she was of her son, and it was only a moment before she felt his hand on her shoulder, right over the strap of the dress.

"Think he's musically inclined?" he asked.

Lori shook her head, not knowing what she should say about anything. Every sensation in her body had traveled to and gathered at her shoulder, leaving the rest of her body numb.

She stopped breathing.

Sam moved his hand to her neck, an overtly intimate touch, an accelerating signal, that made her close her eyes. She tried to stand so still that her neck quivered, and she was about to leave the room, thinking that such behavior was ill-advised, particularly in front of her son, when Sam moved into the bedroom.

He sat in front of Scott and reached beneath the crib to get a discarded plastic drum. "Let's make music, Scott."

Lori silently exhaled a great breath, the one she'd been holding, and returned to the kitchen alone, thinking she could still feel Sam's hand on her neck, the warmth of his slightly caressing fingers.

She couldn't possibly eat now, probably couldn't even swallow, so she cut her sandwich in half and threw one section away. Then she tore a few bite-looking pieces from the remaining half and set it back on the paper plate, giving the appearance of having made actual progress in eating. She sat at the table, listening to the racket from the two-man band in the bedroom.

The image of Sam sitting on the floor, facing Scott, led her into thoughts she'd never considered. Sam as husband. The house would be happier, calmer, with a father who wasn't constantly disgruntled, hating the status quo. Sam didn't court change, didn't despise routine as Chris seemed to do. Then too, Sam would listen. Chris wanted to hear only the extraordinary. When Lori had been teaching, telling him about her day, he'd tuned out anything mundane and ordinary. He wanted to hear she'd told someone off, wanted to hear she'd coldcocked someone.

Somehow, she and Sam had found the wrong mates. Gina would have made a much better wife for Chris; she could have gone to the Holiday Inn, displayed Maxie and Bobo, then come home and titillated Chris with the details. And meanwhile, Lori could be telling an attentive Sam about the accident she'd nearly had coming home from the grocery store. Then instead of hearing, "Lori, you *almost* have an accident every time you leave the house," she'd hear something much more understanding and sympathetic, such as, "I bet you were frightened by that, weren't you?"

Scott would be a calmer child too, she was sure of it. As it was, Lori was always nervous because she worried about Chris's criticism and observations, and she in turn made Scott jittery. How many times had she heard, "I know just how your father must have felt?" It was Chris's favorite line because he was daily accusing her of spoiling Scott, just as her mother had spoiled her. As if a baby could be spoiled. "You and your mother were determined you'd have your way, and you just waited until your father was gone so you could go ahead and do whatever it was you wanted. Just like you're doing with Scott now." Lori could look at Sam and know he'd never say such a thing.

The "music" from the bedroom lost its plastic drumbeat, and she busied herself with the appearances of eating, knowing Sam was about to reappear.

When he did, trying to hide with a slightly ridiculous smile his sexual intent, headed directly toward her, she had a startling realization, startling because for a moment she'd thought his hand on her neck had indicated an accomplished smoothness on his part. As he walked around behind her, stopping here, she thought, he's one of those missionary-position guys. Flip him over and he loses his erection.

Still behind her, he lifted her face with his hand as he bent to

251

kiss her. The kiss was almost brotherly, a dry-lipped, closed-mouth one that just seemed to hang on her face without any particular purpose, and it was so uninspiring, she took the time to consider a thought.

Chris could light a fire so deep within her that it almost couldn't be extinguished. His problem was that she had difficulty interesting him in sex at times, a variation of the ordinary/extraordinary conflict. Kiss, kiss, place his hand on her breast, take him to the bedroom, didn't work very often. He wanted to push her to an extreme, make her admit she was stimulated by sights or thoughts when she didn't want to make such an admission. Still, her sex life with him was infinitely more satisfying that it would ever be with the suckerfish hanging on her mouth at the moment.

The same hand he had used to lift her face now dropped into her dress, coming to rest on her breast.

He broke the kiss and whispered into her cheek, "I dream about watching you breastfeed. I want to see the bra Gina told me about." He pulled the top of her dress away from her chest and looked down, then rubbed his nose across her cheek. He gave her another asexual kiss, so dry their lips stuck together. And his hand had burrowed into her dress like a Boy Scout sliding into his sleeping bag, already too comfortable to move.

Lori twisted out of the partial embrace and stood. "Sam, you can see a nursing bra in any Sears catalog. There's nothing unusual about it except a flap. And I don't think we can finish eating if you're standing over here." When he was slow to move, she took his arm and escorted him around the table, pulling his chair out.

He sat reluctantly and Lori returned to her place, picking up her plate and dumping it in the trash. She wasn't going to sit across the table and have the suckerfish stare at her.

"I'd do anything to see your bra," he said.

"Try this, Sam. Stop at Sears on your way home and buy one for Gina. She's got much more than I do anyway."

"She wouldn't wear it. She thinks it's gross."

No, Lori thought, Gina wasn't the type to put Maxie and Bobo to their intended use. They'd always be playful little puppies.

He pushed his plate away and said dejectedly, "I'm not her type. I don't know why we ever got married."

How many times had Lori heard that phrase: "I don't know why we ever got married"? A thousand? Forty million? How many married people lived in the entire world? Lori had always thought she'd known the answer to that question and wouldn't have to ask it, but she was no longer certain.

She decided to call Elizabeth when she got rid of the whining Sam. She'd never figured Sam for a whiner, but he was, and he almost pushed her to accomplish a feat Chris was always suggesting: coldcocking him. Before he left, he begged in a nasal voice that she nurse Scott so he could watch. The red-haired clown didn't possess a bit of sense.

After calming down, she called Elizabeth and asked what her old friend was doing with her summer. She usually taught summer school, but this year she was taking her three-month vacation to paint her house. And she visualized taking even more time than was allotted because she truly hated scraping. For a while they talked about houses. Lori told her what all she'd done to their house before Scott put an end to all remodeling.

Then Lori said, "You remember when I had a battle-axe of a parent coming in and I'd come ask you what to do? And you'd tell me, and everything always worked out? Well, I need you to tell me what to do. Chris is acting like, well, I don't know what he's acting like. Maybe just a typical husband. But I don't want a typical marriage."

The more she talked, the more like a cliché her life sounded. Two who had promised to love and to cherish had apparently stood in the middle of the church and told big fat lies. Well, Chris had. Lori wanted to love and to cherish. Didn't she? So why had Sam been in her kitchen not twenty minutes ago with his hand down the front of her dress? They had become a joke, two characters living out a soap opera—the glum silent husband, the frustrated wife who let a red-haired clown kiss and fondle her. She was making herself sick.

"Oh, Lori, you know my record on marriage. Ask somebody's who's been successful, not me. I don't know anything. But I do know this: it breaks my heart to hear what you're telling me."

"It breaks mine to hear me saying this aloud. The more I talk, the more ridiculous it sounds. You know how it feels to hear your voice on a tape recorder? You say, 'Oh, Lord, that can't be me.' That's what this conversation is like. I'm telling you this story and I keep thinking, 'Oh, no, that can't be me.' And it is. It's pathetic but it is."

"Don't be too hard on yourself."

Lori watched Scott come crawling down the hall, obviously looking for trouble, and she felt sorry for him too, this poor child with such inadequate role models. He'd grow up to be Chris, Jr., convincing some girl he'd love her forever without telling her his definition of forever. Three hundred sixty-four days. On his first anniversary, he'd forget what day it was and go get bombed with the guys.

"I don't know what to do," she said, suddenly tired.

"That's what happens, I think. Marriage is too much work, so we just end up watching TV because it's so much easier."

Lori laughed without amusement, suddenly realizing what she was going to do. For Chris, there would be no harder work than going to see a marriage counselor. She didn't think he'd ever agree to go, and she wasn't completely sure she wanted some stranger listening to the rerun of their soap, but she was going to ask him. Maybe she could at least get his attention, make him understand she was disturbed.

"I just figured out what it is," Lori said, smiling, seeing a glimmer of hope. "You told me a long time ago and I forgot. It's the system. It's the system's fault."

"It's always the system's fault. How stupid of me. I can't believe I forgot."

21

Chris woke up the morning after his return trip from the hospital depressed. He should have been pleased that his father had survived the heart attack, but all he could think about was that his father could have as easily died. Anyone could. You could have a heart attack at any time, while mowing the grass, while eating supper and getting ready to tell your wife a joke. Anytime. You could be engaged in a major life-changing deal and simply die before you saw the deal consummated. And once you died, that was it, whether you'd accomplished anything at all. You were through. The final chapter was written whether it followed the second or the fifty-second. Life reached down and wrote, "The End," regardless of what you did or didn't want.

Then too, his fantasy was dead, one he'd had for eight years, and it had meant more that he had known. Caroline had visited him whenever he'd needed her, whether he'd been sitting on a steel deck on a ship in the middle of the Atlantic seven years ago or whether he'd been sitting in his car at the low-water crossing at the Pedernales River a week ago. She had never failed him.

And how he looked at her picture in his wallet, the one of her holding a single red rose, her eyes fixed on nothing, and for the first time, the picture had been mute. It hadn't spoken a word. It was just another photograph, just another picture of a girl.

He stopped at Arby's to eat breakfast, wishing he'd meet some dewy-eyed girl who'd take him home and play Stevie Ray Vaughn for him, just because she wanted to. He sat in the restaurant, which was apparently a morning coffee spot for pest-control workers, the lot full of their trucks, and he looked the waitresses over in their brown shirts and didn't see one who even looked like she might know who Stevie Ray Vaughn was.

Maybe he'd just live out of his MG, sleeping in it and stumbling every morning into some fast food place until he found the right waitress, one who'd throw her girlfriend out of her apartment so he could live there. She'd fret over his wild and animalistic appearance, fearing he was a drug dealer wanted by the law, but her loyalty to his mental health would prevent her from ever lifting the phone to call the cops. She'd make sweet love to him in the bathtub.

He looked out the window and saw a four-foot roach riding on top of a pest-control truck, and he thought, my God, even my fantasies are neurotic, completely irrelevant.

Well, if he couldn't have a fantasy, he'd like to at least have a wife who was tolerant, one who could hear his thoughts on religion without labeling him "a stupid atheist who thinks he's smarter than God." Or one who understood that he wasn't being facetious when he said that if he had to play a game—in this case, the Great State Crap Shoot—he'd at least like to be involved in one that made sense to him; maybe he'd like to coach football. And she had yet to respond to his desire to return to Europe, and not as a package tourist with an itinerary.

Lori. She wanted her future on a well-defined track so she could hear the stops called off. "Doubled Salary, Doubled Salary, next stop Five-bedroom House." Chris wanted off the track. He didn't want to see the future. He wanted to believe that he still had options, that he might make Europe yet. He wanted to tell her that as a friend, but Lori didn't keep such friends, and she certainly didn't want such a husband.

He sat in Arby's wishing things could have been different, wishing their marriage could have worked. As it was, the farm boy had never had any business marrying Miss Photogenic to begin with.

He moved through the day emotionally paralyzed, unable to accomplish anything. He even turned down an invitation from Carl for lunch, a free meal on his brother.

He tried calling Lori in the afternoon to remind her he was attending the deposition of Lupe Villa and wouldn't be home for supper, but the line was busy every time he dialed. On the last attempt, he decided the hell with it if she didn't answer, but she did.

"Who've you been talking to all afternoon?" he asked.

"Elizabeth. And it's only been for about thirty minutes."

"You can't call her at night when it's cheaper?"

"I needed to talk to her."

He nodded, looking at a page of rather depressing doodles before him, a yellow sheet covered with the faces of witches, lightning bolts, storm clouds, and barren trees. He needed something cheery to look at, so he tried drawing a picture of Scott.

"I want us to go to a marriage counselor," she said.

He laughed, but not so Lori could hear. A marriage counselor. Right. A conference in which he could be jointly assassinated, two very level-headed people placing their practical hands on the handle of one large knife, bringing it down into his maladjusted heart.

"You don't have any response to that?" she asked.

"What's a marriage counselor going to tell us?"

"I don't know if he'll tell us anything. Maybe you just need to talk to one since you won't talk to me. I've tried everything I know, from asking right out to hinting and trying to put you in a talkative mood. Nothing's worked, and I don't know what else to do."

"We're talking right now."

"We are?"

"Sure. I'm saying things and you're saying things. That's talking, isn't it?"

"Then why don't you tell me what's been going on with you lately?"

Okay, he wanted to say. Try this. I'm depressed because the most important fantasy I ever had got steamrolled by peroxided reality. I'm depressed because I live in a world where anything can happen and I can't take advantage of the good things so I get stuck trying to tolerate only the bad—heart attacks and fantasy funerals.

"Chris."

"What?"

"You're proving my point. I hear nothing but silence."

He sighed, sitting back in his chair and propping his feet on the desk. He couldn't draw a picture of Scott anyway. What he needed was someone to eliminate all his choices, someone to make him straighten up, someone to threaten him. You put your heart in being a damn good middle-class citizen or I'll sneak in your bedroom and emasculate you. And I don't mean your balls.

"We need to know whether this marriage is going to work, Chris."

"Someone else is going to tell us?"

"That's not what I mean."

"I know what you mean. You mean we're going to a counselor and I'm going to talk to him and then we'll all get together and decide how I'll change. How I can do a better job of pleasing Lori Lynn."

"That's not what I meant at all."

He was mad and wasn't sure why. Except since the day he was born, he'd been trying to please first one person and then another. Everyone else was granted the right to act as he desired; Chris had adapted, had never been himself. Well, the hell with it. He was tired of trying to please people.

"We'll talk about it later," he said. "I called to let you know I wouldn't be home for supper." Or any other time possibly. He might just go get in his car right now and set out for Big Bend.

He did nothing for the rest of the afternoon but sit at his desk and watch people walk up and down the hall, hoping one would stop and ask why he was merely sitting, passing time. He wanted to tell somebody he was through with the crap shoot. Fuck the crap shoot and all the players involved.

The idea that the game was approaching absolutely ridiculous limits was reinforced that evening when a number of them gathered in the library to take one more deposition from Lupe Villa. This claim had been filed with a business at which no one could remember hiring Lupe or ever even seeing him before. He claimed however that he had injured his back while helping push a truck, one that wouldn't start, during his first hour of employment. His lawyer, a slight man with a curly perm whose nature had been transplanted from a pit bull, never even bothered preparing Lupe. He knew that insurance companies preferred settling claims to spending money on defense costs.

The lawyer insisted Lupe be deposed through an interpreter, even after his client had shaken hands with Chris and said, "Hey, buddy! How's it hanging?" Chris, who had no official function at the proceeding, pointed out that anyone who could pronounce Employers of Wausau probably didn't need an interpreter.

Standing across the room, the lawyer pointed a ballpoint pen at Chris and said, "You, you need to learn to multiply by three. Look up the meaning of treble, as in treble damages."

"I'll do that if you'll look up parasitosis, as in parasite, you fucking hookworm."

"Both of you shut up," Carl said, "and let's get this wetback deposed."

Chris sat in a corner monitoring falsehoods, amazed by how sloppy Lupe was getting. He was now testifying that he'd had numerous surgical procedures on his back even though he'd never been touched with a scalpel. And he only remembered one or two previous claims.

After a while, Chris decided there wasn't any challenge in trying to catch Lupe lying and quit listening. Parasite, he decided, wasn't the right word. Symbiosis was, because the insurance industry and the plaintiff attorneys thrived in conjunction even though they both swore they hated each other. After all, big lawsuits and huge verdicts sold more insurance than any salesman. Who in his right mind wanted to go without liability insurance nowadays? And on the other hand, who derived more profits from insurance than the plaintiff attorneys? No one, not even the executives of the insurance companies.

Disgusting. Worse than politics, he thought.

When the assembled parties finished, Chris was getting ready to leave when the court reporter, a woman named Gwen East, asked him if he'd carry her stenograph machine to her car.

"Show me your macho side," she said, smiling.

He readily agreed. She was wearing a simple yellow dress with strings for straps at the shoulder. She had light brown hair and eyes that were set either too low or too high, he'd never been able to decide, but the feature made her face very expressive. She could look right into your heart. And her skin was the stuff of dreams; she was lightly and thoroughly freckled, almost silky.

They took the elevator down into the parking garage, which was below the building, and as he looked at her, riding the gold cube down, he thought, this could happen only in Austin, the city of dreams. She looked at him twice, smiling.

In the garage, his footsteps down the ramp were light; he was happy merely to be in her company. They came to her car first, an orange Audi, and he loaded the machine into the back seat, then stood beside her door, waiting for her to get in. She didn't. An invitation? he wondered. He hoped. He didn't want her to go yet. He wanted to suck on the strings that held her dress up until they were wet, while he smelled her perfume, which had the scent and sensation of flowers and light.

"Let's go look at the moon," he said.

"I've seen it before," she said, crossing her arms and leaning against the car.

What was expected of him? He didn't remember anything about how to pick up a woman, hadn't even tried in years. "I've seen it before too. In fact, I looked at it earlier and it was flashing a message across the side kind of like the Goodyear blimp does. It said, 'Personal message to Gwen at ten. Can be seen only at the lake. Be there.'"

"Really?"

"I'm telling you the truth, man," he said, mimicking Lupe Villa. "You know I wouldn't shit you."

She laughed and said, "I don't have long."

"Thirty seconds is better than nothing."

He suggested they go in his car, the MG, since the top was down, and it was made for the winding, hilly road to the lake. As they drove through the night and artificial light of downtown, Gwen turned in her seat with her knees near the gearshift, holding her sandy-colored hair back with one hand in an informal ponytail. They drove west from town, occasionally following the river, and the air turned cooler. Gwen's yellow dress caught air currents and ballooned upward in the dim illumination of the dash lights.

"I know a good spot to look at the lake," she said. "Our lakehouse. Take a right up here."

Chris slowed the car.

"Besides I need to call Kevin."

Kevin, a little cartoon squirrel of a guy. Chris has seen him at a party once and had been appalled that Gwen would have married such a person. She deserved a movie star at the very least. She deserved someone whose existence Chris couldn't verify.

Following her directions, he turned several times, and found a gravel road that dropped toward the lake. He could see the reflection of the moon on the water below, a romantic but almost gaudy sight that could have been painted on black velvet.

He waited for her in front of a dark A-frame while she called her husband. Such moments were the very best of life, the beginning, the start. They could end up in Mexico before the night was over, living in some primitive hut in the foothills of a mountain range. The villagers would know he and Gwen were in love, would see them passing hand in hand looking into each other's eyes. "Look, the gringo and his woman," the men would say, shaking their hands as if they'd been burned, and the women would smile sweetly as they made tortillas.

When Gwen came out of the house, she took off running, her sandals in her hand. "Race you to the lake," she yelled and was gone, rounding the corner of the house. He chased after her, deliriously happy, wanting to freeze her and place her in a woodcut that illustrated enchantment. He ran without knowing his feet were moving, without getting tired.

By the time he got to the lake, she was already sitting on a small wooden pier near the end. He watched her scoot forward so she could dip both feet into the water, and her yellow dress slid in folds into her lap. Smiling, he thought she looked like a farm girl, not at all self-conscious. Or even sexually aware.

He sat beside her. "Is it cold?"

"It's just right. You could say perfect."

She looked at him twice as he removed his shoes and socks, a task he was undertaking while staring at her.

"You're not looking at the moon," she said. "You might miss the message."

"I already know what it says. I'll tell you if you want me to, but I have to whisper it in your ear."

She gave him a knowing nod. "Right."

He caught her arm, his fingers beneath and touching her breast, and moved his face into her hair. He whispered, "It says, 'Your best side is revealed in the moonlight. Indulge yourself tonight. Go skinnydipping.'"

"Um hmm."

He kissed her. It was a short and light kiss that caught her off guard. And it was a moment Chris wanted to prolong, stretch out indefinitely. He pushed her gently back onto the pier and looked at her face, propped up by his elbow. With his fingertip, he traced the lines of her lips, then kissed her again.

"You're not much like Carl," she said.

"God, I hope not. Why'd you say that?"

She shrugged. "He'd be zipping up and leaving by now."

Chris started to inquire into any firsthand knowledge that she might possess on Carl's speed with the zipper, but such a question would have introduced a disastrous element into the evening, much as a jumbo jet crashing into a house in which two lovers sat before a fire might mar a romantic moment. Besides, he knew, absolutely knew, that Gwen was relying solely on rumor and gossip.

She tried to get comfortable on the boards of the pier, and she shifted her eyes to the sky. Chris lay beside her and they tried to locate constellations, but he couldn't remember any other than the Big Dipper. Every time she wondered about one, pointing upward, he pulled her arm over him and buried his nose in her shoulder, following the length of her arm with his eyes. He got as close as he could and stared into the sky. Away from the lights of town, they could see millions of stars. The sky was heavy with them.

"You get an *F* in astronomy but an *A* in romance," she said. "You really aren't like Carl."

"Would you do me a favor?"

"What?"

"Don't mention Carl anymore."

She didn't answer, and Chris had to fight off a feeling of irritation. Even here the spectre of Carl hung over him. His mind wanted to review all the girls Carl had stolen from him, all those fingerprints that he'd planted on every girl who had shown any interest in the younger brother. The problem hadn't been acute until Chris was in high school, and by then Carl was too old for any of the girls, according to their mothers. The girls however were entranced by the attention of a *man*, a fact both brothers fully understood.

"It'd be a shame not to go skinnydipping," he said. He wanted to see her standing naked on the pier, a goddess arising from the water. He could look at her and tell she was structurally perfect.

She wasn't enthusiastic but finally agreed on the condition that he go first. He stood behind her and undressed slowly, thinking maybe she'd been lying. After all, she'd invoked the name of Carl twice already and probably planned to steal his clothes. He was down to his underwear and she hadn't said anything. Then he was nude. He jogged lightly across the bank to the water, feeling like a plucked chicken running from a thickly feathered friend.

"Come on," he said, now in knee-deep water, mud oozing between his toes.

She turned and looked at him, smiling, and he closed his eyes, certain he was going to hear, "Boy, you *really* aren't anything like

263

Carl. That must be why they call you Lilliput." But she calmly stood and walked to the bank where he'd left his pants. She picked them up and withdrew his wallet, then returned to the end of the pier, sitting again.

"Come on, come on. You promised if I went first, you'd come too."

But she seemed only interested in the pictures in his wallet, all of which she looked at using the light of the moon. "Did you know you can tell a lot about a person just by looking at his wallet? Hmm. Not one picture of yourself. Carl has thousands."

Chris, like a devout Baptist whose ears had been raped by constant profanity, said, much more loudly than he intended, "Why do you keep bringing Carl up? If you don't mind, let's leave him wherever he is right now. We don't need him out here."

Gwen either ignored him or failed to hear his demand and continued her examination of the photos.

"Is this your wife?" she asked.

He walked to the pier, sloshing water as he went, feeling peculiar talking to a fully dressed woman while he was naked. He was a nudist being interviewed by a reporter, so he used his hand as a fig leaf. Looking at Lori's Baylor graduation picture, he told Gwen that the picture was indeed one of his wife.

"She's really cute. I wish I had her hair."

He couldn't disagree. Almost everyone he knew complained about their pictures, but Lori's always looked just as good as she did. And now, from the wallet, she sent a message to his sexual apparatus: "Lilli lilli lilliput, don't stick out, just shrink up." The message was received. He no longer needed a fig leaf; a dime would have done the trick.

"Your son looks like your wife," she said. "I know it's your son because you have ten pictures of him."

Visualizing a tongue being drawn back into a mouth, he became sexless, neutered. He walked away from Gwen, returning to the bank, wondering now if she had ever planned on fulfilling her

264

promise to strip if he did. Maybe she was giving him some kind of test. If so, he couldn't figure out what it was. Standing behind her he dressed. When she turned to ask him a question, he was again wearing pants.

"I would've gotten you a towel," she said.

He shrugged.

She held up the wallet, still seated on the end of the pier. "Who's this?" she asked, showing him Caroline's picture.

"The only woman in the world who ever died of blonde hair."

Gwen gave him a second, longer look but didn't ask what he meant.

After he'd dressed, they drove back to town. The strands of her hair whirled up and around in the dash lights, giving her an eerie, almost mystical appearance. He slowed the car because he didn't want to return to town. He could see the lights of the city shining behind the hills, an aura in the sky, and he simply didn't want to go back.

He wanted to go live in the Smoky Mountains with Gwen. She could make quilts and bullwhips to sell to tourists, and he'd fish in the clear mountain stream behind their cabin. He'd talk to the brown bears that came to beg a fish. Gwen would wear her hair in braids and dress in a deerskin vest and skirt, showing lots of skin. They'd sleep on a mattress on the floor under a heavy blanket and he'd rise in the morning mists to cook breakfast over a fire outside.

They'd become famous because they were insanely happy, and they'd write books and appear on television talk shows to impart their secrets.

"I have a friend who analyzes handwriting," Gwen said, pulling her hair back and holding it as they swept around a curve, high above the Colorado River. "I'd like to see what she said about yours."

"Why? Am I acting strange?"

"No, not strange. You just seem real frustrated."

He laughed, not with humor but with the hysteria of recognition,

recognition of a problem he'd lived with too long and hated. Still, he hadn't known it was that obvious to another person, especially one who didn't seen him often.

"What do you want?" she asked. "In general?"

"Beats the hell out of me."

She shook her head. "You really aren't anything like Carl, are you?" She softened the breach of his demand that she not mention Carl by touching his leg.

She looked at him and shook her head. "Take me back to my car. I don't want you on my conscience."

Great, he thought. This is going to be one hell of a long life.

22

Lori woke up the next morning and listened to Chris dress for work, but she didn't get up, didn't even let him know she was awake. She didn't seem to have but one choice, and although she didn't want to exercise her right to act on that single choice, she supposed she could. The fact was that she had a husband who couldn't get out of whatever rut he'd fallen into on his own. A crisis might bring him out, just as it had with his father. She didn't want to threaten leaving him because he'd temporarily resurrect his ability to behave, only to lapse in a day or so, and he'd end up resenting her for making the threat.

The secondary problem was that if a crisis didn't turn him around, she was going to be on her own with a baby, and the only plan she could conceive was to move to Waco and teach with Elizabeth. She had trouble visualizing such a future. She tried picturing herself leaving an elementary school in the afternoon, telling Elizabeth she'd see her tomorrow, and then driving to a day care center to pick up Scott. The part that really gave her trouble was the apartment they went home to, some ratty four-room roach-infested hovel in which they'd eat potted meat and crackers for supper.

It wasn't a scenario she dwelled on; otherwise she'd lose her resolve and simply lie in bed until she heard Scott making a demand for her appearance. And she had decided this was the day of decision. She was going to Abilene and see what happened even though she hated the uncertainty.

She waited until Chris was gone before she got up, thinking if she just got up and left, she wasn't required to warn him, whereas if she was up with him before he left for work and failed to tell him, he'd accuse her of lying again.

She wanted to cry but didn't, and she had to put her mind in neutral to guard against a myriad of miserable thoughts—leaving the house she'd worked on so lovingly, leaving the husband she had loved with all her heart, removing the son from the loving father. Chris had a problem of some sort, but one he didn't have was being a good father.

She finally threw the covers down and said with a big sigh, "You have to do it now."

"Did you ever leave Daddy?" Lori asked her mother.

They sat in the kitchen in Abilene eating lunch. Lori knew from the look on her mother's face—a mysterious sort of half-smile—that she wasn't going to get the uncut version of the story.

"I did once but he never knew it. I packed my car one morning and drove to Dallas. The next day I decided I'd made a mistake so I came home. I walked in that door over there and found my note still on the counter by the phone. He hadn't been here and hadn't even seen it. He was out on location where they'd had a blowout and hadn't been home at all. In fact, he didn't come home until the next day. So, he never even knew."

"You didn't tell him?"

Mrs. Conner shook her head and offered Scott a Vienna sausage. He'd already thrown two across the room with a shout of misdirected goodwill. One had hit the dishwasher, the other a curtain, leaving a small glob of gelatin on the fringe. Now, his tongue sticking out, grunting, he reached for the Vienna sausage in Mrs.

Conner's hand as though it were the last on earth and he was required to have it or prematurely expire.

Mrs. Conner said, "If you throw this, you're a bad boy. And you aren't a bad boy, are you?"

She gave him the third projectile and he sat momentarily, holding it in his fist, giving his grandmother a look of pure smiling devilment. With a shout of gusto, he threw the sausage across the kitchen, hitting the window over the sink and leaving a streak of grease on the pane. He sat back proudly, awaiting congratulations.

"Mother, you knew he'd throw it."

"I wanted him to have a chance to show me he wasn't a bad boy."

"All boys are bad. It's their nature. Now, why'd you leave Daddy?"

"Oh, something so important I don't remember what it was anymore. Probably just a lot of little problems that seemed to build up."

"Thank you, Mother. You're always such a help."

"Well, I try." Mrs. Conner turned her attention to Scott. "If I give you one of these, do you promise not to throw it?"

Lori, shaking her head, got up and left the room.

She had arrived in Abilene while her mother was gone and therefore unable to object to her daughter's moving into the garage apartment rather than the house. She'd looked around the dusty apartment and decided that she could occupy her time and mind with cleaning the place up, but after lunch and the sausage fusillade, she didn't want to be in either the house or the apartment. So she got Scott and took him to the country club. Along with Ellen's children in Austin, he had developed a fondness for swimming pools.

They sat at the shallow end of the pool and attracted a steady stream of visitors, some of them friends from high school who apparently had never left the lounge chairs they'd used to soak up the sun back then. Lori could comfortably play the part of visitor for a few days. Scott, ignorant of any troubles or charades, sat beside her playing with a plastic bucket and water gun.

She saw her old boyfriend, Randy, as he came to play golf, and he was much better-looking than Lori remembered. Had she tried to make him seem less than he was? He was tall and blond and looked as though he'd stepped from an ad for sports clothes. He was perfectly designed, a physical beauty, and always had been. Unfortunately, he was living proof that looks weren't everything. The boy had the most disorganized mind of anyone she'd ever known outside a nursing home. He could start out talking about a restaurant in Dallas and end up on the subject of the coming Ice Age.

Still, from what Lori now knew of marriage, he probably would have been the perfect candidate because he would have given her a prosperous and uncomplicated life. She'd be getting up at noon each day, eating a breakfast of fruits out by the pool—cantaloupe, grapes, slices of watermelon—and then stepping from her gown, still chewing fruit, and making a graceful naked dive into the pool. She'd swim its length a few times before she got out for her coffee, served by a maid. If she got bored in the afternoon, she'd call him and order a yacht for a week in Cabo San Lucas. She'd lie on the rolling deck until she was golden brown.

It would certainly be helpful, she thought, to know in youth what was possible and what wasn't. The knowledge could help you avoid a large number of faulty decisions and wrong turns.

"Hey," a familiar voice said. "Somebody said you were over here and I didn't believe them. But, sure enough, here you are."

Sitting beside Scott, she looked up, seeing Randy himself. He towered over her, wearing burgundy pants and a white pullover shirt, and the first thing she noticed was the golden hair on his arm, all that curly fleece. She told him hi.

He sat down next to her, fully clothed, and crossed his legs. Wearing her matronly one-piece multicolored swimsuit, she made the first constructive decision of the past months—somewhere she was going to find an aerobics class and tone her body up. She was tired of feeling flabby, tired of having a new mother's body.

"So what're you doing?" he asked, reaching over to pat her shoulder in an innocent manner.

She knew better than to believe the touch was innocent. Nothing physical he did with her had ever been innocent. He had introduced her to the wonder of physical relationships, and they had pushed the limits on a vacation with his family in Corpus Christi one summer, right before she'd left for Baylor and he'd driven off to Texas Tech. In the dunes on Padre Island just after sunset, listening to the gulls screech and feeling the wind on her body, all over her body, she'd taken wing with the birds, released for the first time by another person.

"Gosh, I'm glad to see you," he said without waiting for an answer to his inquiry on the state of her being. "You just look so good I can hardly stand it. Is this your son?"

Lori introduced the two and neither seemed interested in becoming acquainted. Scott was too busy dipping water from the pool and pouring it on Lori's feet, and Randy was too busy staring at her breasts.

In a voice tinged with wonder, he said quietly, "You don't have little bitty titties anymore."

She shook her head, disturbed first by his assumption that he could make such a comment without offending her and second by his stupidity, his failure to make the connection between a baby and larger breasts. "It's amazing, isn't it? There's an actual use for them. They're God's gifts to babies."

Rather than being put in his place, he smiled. "So how're you doing? Still in Austin? You really oughta move back here, you know, back where all your old friends are. You'd be surprised at how much fun we still have. The other night . . ."

He started off on a story about a group leasing a plane to go to Las Vegas, and Lori tuned him out, looking through the crowd around the pool for his wife. Lori had seen her several times but wasn't always certain of her identity upon meeting her again. Randy had wanted to go to Baylor with Lori, but his father, a graduate of Texas Tech, had sent his son to Lubbock, where he had met and impregnated some lonely girl, then married her after his father had ordered him to do so. No blights on the family name were allowed. The wife had an amorphous sort of face and body, and Lori always visualized her as someone sickly, sitting around in a terrycloth robe, holding a Kleenex to her nose.

In the middle of Randy's story, during the description of the salad bar at Circus Circus, she simply interrupted him, knowing the story would go on all night. "How's the real estate business?"

"Kinda slow," he said, making an immediate transition from salad to sales. "Too many apartments and offices built during the boom. Now they're empty. We've gone from forty-dollar oil to nine-dollar oil and nobody's doing anything, including me, which is why I'm playing golf. Although I'm glad the Yankees are gone. I don't know where they went, but they aren't out here anymore, and that suits me fine. We had one guy come out here looking for ten-thousand square feet . . ."

She tuned him out again, wondering what Chris would do when he came home from work. If he did. She wasn't sure where he had been the previous night, but he'd somehow got mud on his socks, on the inside of his socks. He'd been somewhere walking barefooted in the mud. She wasn't sure what to make of that discovery, other than to theorize that he was either going crazy, wandering around naked in the woods, or that he'd been in the company of another person who'd also walked out of her clothes.

"It's been so long since I've talked to you," Randy said. "You want to take a ride?"

"A ride where?" she asked, wondering if that's how you got mud in your socks, "taking a ride," getting in a car with another person and heading for an unspoken destination.

"I don't know, just take a ride. Have you been out south of town? You wouldn't believe how it's grown up since you left. Get past the loop and half of Abilene lives out there, you just wouldn't believe it."

"Randy, I haven't been gone ten years. I come back from time to time. In fact, I've been here probably one week out of every month since Scott was born."

"You have? Why don't I ever see you?" He suddenly decided he was sitting too far away and he moved so close their hips touched. Still sitting cross-legged, he leaned forward on his elbows, looking back and up at her, his eyes alternating between her face and breasts, spending more time lower than higher. In this twisted position, he asked her right breast out to dinner. "Maybe tonight or tomorrow night."

"Your wife may not enjoy that," she said.

"My wife?" He was surprised to hear she'd been interjected into the meal. "Well, I really wasn't thinking of a family deal, not with wives and everything. You know."

"I'm a wife, Randy. That's where Scott came from."

"Oh, I've got one of those too."

She moved away from him, telling Scott it was time to go home, an announcement he received with a frown. She picked up him and then his toys, and when Randy moved to stand, obviously ready to escort her out, she said, "Good-bye, Randy," in a tone that made him understand she was leaving not only the pool but him as well.

Walking away with Scott in one arm, his toys in the other, she still couldn't believe he'd made the comment about her "little bitty titties." What a fool. A stupid man was the sorriest waste of humanity; on the other hand, a smart one who wanted to be stupid, like Chris, was just about as bad.

What was wrong with men? she wondered. She knew one woman whose husband allocated her a specified amount of money each month on which to run the household, and if she needed more, she had to provide cash register tapes that proved she was saving at least ten percent of her total bill by using coupons, all while he lost a wad of money every Tuesday and Thursday nights playing poker.

Who else but a man would name a woman's breast? That's probably what Randy had been doing a minute ago, dubbing one of hers Juanita and the other Annie Oakley. Who else but a man would say, thinking it was funny, "Women control one hundred percent of the pussy in the world?"

She shook her head and looked at Scott. "If you grow up to be a man, I'll spank your little bottom."

Her son, who was already sunburned under his eyes, said, "Unh!"

That evening, she and Scott accompanied Mrs. Conner to a local restaurant since Mr. Conner had gone to Ozona earlier in the morning and wouldn't return until tomorrow. Mrs. Conner, ironically enough, wanted to eat at the Royal Inn, which had an excellent steakhouse, which had also served as the termination point of the Midnight Express back when Chris had been making his weekend trips to Abilene.

Scott was too impatient and demanding to be a good restaurant patron, and the waitress seemed to read "Devil's Workshop" across his idle hands. She took their order and gave him three packages of crackers, all of which he smashed to powder on the tray of his highchair.

"He's the most destructive thing I've ever seen," Lori said.

Mrs. Conner, who could find no trace of error in her grandson, lifted him from the high chair and held him, cheek to cheek. He immediately became the loving, cooing grandson Mrs. Conner wanted him to be.

"That's repulsive," Lori said. "How can he go from being so destructive to being so sickly sweet. I wish you could see his face right now."

Mrs. Conner pulled back from Scott and looked at his face, rewarding him with a kiss on the cheek. "That's the way God made little boys, darling."

"Yeah, one minute they're playing with their little things, the next they want to play with yours."

"Lori Lynn, I can't believe you said that. And right in front of this precious little boy." She rubbed her nose against his cheek, making Scott giggle. "Don't you listen to that. And don't you ever play with your little thing, much less someone else's."

"You know he will."

"Well, you don't have to *talk* about it."

The conversation was interrupted by the waitress, bringing tossed salads. She looked at Scott's powdered crackers and gave him three more packages, smiling.

When she'd gone, Lori, not even hungry, asked, "Do I look old?"

"Darling, you look like the most beautiful young lady I've ever seen. What do you mean, do you look old? You won't look old when you *are* old."

"Then why do I feel old?"

"Because things aren't going like they're supposed to. And that will change. Does Chris know you're gone?"

Lori had already done that calculation, starting at 4:45, should he have come home early. If he'd appeared at the "regular" time, about 5:30, and immediately set off for Abilene, he'd be arriving in three hours. "He should by now."

Mrs. Conner moved Scott back to his highchair, on the tray of which rested three objects of intense interest—unsmashed crackers. Mrs. Conner, now free of her grandson, became suddenly serious and gave Lori a penetrating look. Lori wasn't certain for a moment whether her mother was staring into the center of her, seeing something that she disliked and wanted to exorcise, or whether she was deep in thought and seeing nothing at all.

"Chris doesn't like his job, does he?" she asked. "I don't mean he dislikes certain parts of it, or his office, or his secretary. I mean, he doesn't like his job."

Lori started to answer but didn't know what to say, and she sat for a moment feeling foolish, her mouth prepared to speak words that hadn't formed. The fact was, she didn't know what Chris thought of his job overall. He didn't like lawyers and he didn't like insurance companies, but he seemed to get excited at times when he was battling either. Or when he was proving someone like Lupe Villa to be the liar he was. "To tell you the truth, I don't know whether he does or not. We haven't talked about it."

"Lori, there have been times when I've noticed you have this little habit of ignoring anything you hear unless it comes in an official conversation, unless you're 'talking' about it. And even then you can ignore something you don't want to hear. Or think about." Suddenly Mrs. Conner smiled, looking at the ceiling, at the image of an apparent memory. "When you were four or five and wanting to act grown up, you'd come to me and say, 'Mother, let's play like we're talking.'" She laughed. "But by the time you were ten, you figured out there was a lot you didn't want to hear and you'd say, 'Must we be serious?' With your hand right here on your cheek. 'Must we be serious?' Lori, you need to listen to Chris because he'll tell you more when he doesn't mean to than when you suggest you sit down and have a *real* conversation. If you want him to *talk*, you're probably going to get his version of 'Must we be serious?' And maybe that's what you want."

Lori resented the invocation of these childish images, resented her mother superimposing them on her as though she were still a child. Not as hard as she'd worked lately trying to determine Chris's problem. "Okay, if you're so smart, you tell me how he feels about his job."

"I can tell you a few things. He doesn't like lawyers; he doesn't approve of what they do. I've heard him call them whores, prostitutes, parasites . . . what else? And he hates insurance companies even more than lawyers. Unless you're deaf, you've heard him and your father talking about insurance. They both hate it; they both think insurance has destroyed the whole idea of individual responsibility, right along with lawyers. And they both think we'd all be better off if insurance companies disappeared overnight."

Mrs. Conner shook her head finally and looked at her salad as though she might eat. After spreading her napkin on her lap, she

275

picked up her fork. But again she looked at her daughter. "What I'm really telling you is this—I'm afraid you think there's some easy answer to Chris's job problem, and there isn't. And I'm not so *smart* that I know what he needs to do. The difference between you and me isn't intelligence, it's experience. I learned some things the hard way.

"Right after I married your father, I decided to make him clean and respectable and get him a job in my uncle's hardware store. I didn't want a husband whose hands were always greasy and felt like sandpaper. So I got him on at the hardware store, just sure as we're sitting here that he'd be the manager in two months. Instead he got fired before two *weeks* were up. I don't mean he quit, and I don't mean he left on good terms. I mean my uncle thought he was a no-good lout who'd never amount to anything. They never spoke a word to each other after that, not a single word. This was the same man who'd been working sixty or seventy hours a week when things were *slow*. And my uncle thought he was the laziest person ever."

Lori shook her head, remembering something Mr. Gray had told her about Chris being selectively lazy. (See? she thought triumphantly. I do listen.) But all these unconnected thoughts about Chris and her father and marriage didn't seem to add up to anything comprehensible, certainly not an intelligent vocational plan for Chris, if that was indeed his problem.

Mrs. Conner continued. "Lori, men don't get up and go to work every morning just because they want to make their wives happy. They want to accomplish something. They want to do something useful. They want to *know* they're accomplishing something. And if they find the right thing, they'll work their fool heads off until you wish they'd find something they hated so they'd be home once in a while."

Mrs. Conner now shook her fork at Lori as if her daughter might be prepared to suggest they not be serious. "When Chris decides he can't take his job anymore, or when they decide he's the laziest man alive and fire him, then it's your job to help him. If you plan on staying married to him, and I hope, hope, hope you do. But if you don't want to help him, then you should at least get out of his way. I don't know about you, but I'd hate to think I was responsible for making another person miserable for the rest of his life."

Lori's mouth was open. Her mother was *chewing her out*. She couldn't believe what she was hearing, wouldn't be surprised if her mother withdrew from her purse a coiled belt, shook it out, and decided to spank her.

"Oh, don't look so surprised. I am your mother, remember, and I've been watching you all your life. And I know that you've managed to get your way when people, including me, were good and determined to resist your charms. Why do you think Chris is still working at that job? Not because *he* wants to."

Lori was suddenly tired, overloaded with facts and changes and her mother's perceptions. Besides, Chris hadn't been very receptive to her charms. In fact, if he was asked what charms she possessed, he'd say, "Charms? What do you mean? Like rabbits' feet or something?" He hadn't paid much attention to anything about her.

But Lori knew more than her mother gave her credit for. And more importantly, she knew why she'd married Chris. He was, in his heart, very simply a good person, and that had been what she'd wanted. What he had been planning for an occupation hadn't mattered to her at the time. She'd had friends who had intended to marry professions, not people, but that hadn't been Lori's interest.

And to prove again that her mother lacked knowledge of her own daughter, Lori thought of something else Chris had told her. Back when she'd first met him, he'd said he wanted to attend college to learn how to live and not to learn how to make a living. At the time, she'd thought he was impractical, but he'd been no more impractical about school than she'd been in deciding to marry him and not a profession.

"Okay, my smart mother, what do you think he's suited for?"

"I don't know, but he's the kind of person who'd join the police force because he really does want to protect society. Whatever he does, he'll have a reason. You may not understand it, but he'll have a reason."

Lori sighed, watching Scott all but turn blue, straining with a package of powdered crackers in his fist as he squeezed them. "Well, let's play like we're eating."

"As long as we can also play like we're not gaining weight."

Lori had just put Scott to sleep on the floor in the bedroom of the apartment over the garage when she heard a knock on the door. Her heart leapt and she quickly checked the time. If Chris was outside, he'd have left Austin well before five because it was just barely past nine now. She was wearing nothing but panties and a robe, and she made sure the robe was buttoned as she walked to the door.

Looking through the curtain over the window in the door, she saw, of all people, Randy on the landing of the stairs outside. She thought, he thinks he smells something. Fun and games with Annie Oakley and Juanita.

She opened the door, leaving the screen door latched.

"Hi," he said as though arriving to pick her up for a date. "I just had this idea when I was driving by. I had this idea that you're not here visiting because I saw the lights on up here, which is why I didn't think you were visiting. You're not, are you? Just visiting?"

Lori said nothing, watching him lean against the wooden railing and wondering if it would hold him. She didn't want to be bothered, but neither did she want Randy falling off the landing, twenty feet onto his hard head. She started to invite him in so she wouldn't have to worry about the railing, but if she did, she'd never get rid of him.

"I know this is a terrible thing to say, but I was kinda hoping you weren't here just visiting. I was hoping, well, I've always been hoping, you and me could get back together one of these days. When you get divorced."

"Randy! Why do you assume I'll get divorced?"

278

"Everybody gets divorced sooner or later. Except me because my father won't let me. But I bet he would if you got divorced first."

Lori shook her head. To think she was standing in the kitchen of her parents' apartment, her playhouse as a child, and hearing this line from a boy who apparently hadn't changed a bit. He suggested they play a variation of I'll-show-you-mine-if-you'll-show-me-yours. Now the invitation was, you get divorced first and then I will too.

"You were just, well, I don't know how to say it. I just felt so good when I was with you and so bad when I wasn't." He paused, looking briefly at the street as if to give himself sufficient time to judge his resolve. Finding it strong, he said, "Would you answer just one question for me? Just one little bitty question. If I asked if you still loved me, would you answer?"

Lori's mouth fell open.

"Do you still love me?" he asked.

"No."

"Well, I wouldn't ask that question anyway."

"Randy, go home to your wife. Maybe she misses you."

He shook his head, now sitting on the railing and making it pop, a noise he ignored. "She doesn't even love me. And I'll tell you something I've never told anybody else. She didn't even want to get married, which is what we had to do when she got pregnant. I mean, I was up there in Lubbock and all lonely and everything, and she got pregnant, but she didn't want to get married. My father talked to her father, and they made us. Get married. I didn't want to either because I was still in love with you." Then, changing the subject without taking a breath, he asked, "Do you think about that vacation we took to Corpus Christi, when you went with us? Do you think about that?"

He smiled at her and she knew she was going to have to run him off, suddenly remembering the endless cycle of their relationship and seeing Randy intuitively headed that way. She'd abuse and humiliate him, then work up enough sympathy to let him do the physical things she wanted him doing anyway, telling herself she was only doing penance for the abuse and humiliation. The cycle was endless because she hadn't known how to handle a physical relationship in a straightforward manner.

"I remember things you used to say to me."

"Randy, I'm closing the door so you can go home to your wife," she said. "Goodnight."

She closed the door because she wasn't immune after all, watching him sit on the railing, hunched over to balance himself, his hands clasped and stuck through his legs. The memories of Corpus Christi had obviously affected him, as had his stroking hands, and she didn't want to stir up any sexually nostalgic emotions. She felt deprived enough as it was without further teasing herself.

Returning to the living room, she turned on the portable TV there but had difficulty in concentrating, wanting instead to go see if Randy was still sitting on the railing, playing with himself.

She closed her eyes and thought, hurry up, Chris. Come save me from myself.

If he didn't show up soon, she'd be checking on yacht rentals in Cabo San Lucas.

23

One of these days, Chris thought, he was going to make a sensible decision. He was sure of it; the law of averages was with him.

Driving the MG to work wasn't a sensible decision. He realized that every afternoon as he sat in traffic, waiting to get on the interstate, breathing the exhaust of some big Buick and soaking his clothes with sweat. And this afternoon wasn't just hot—the entire city was mildewing under a dome of stagnant humidity.

He'd spent most of the afternoon mapping routes out of the Crap Shoot, trying to determine if he was eligible for any other jobs, and deciding he wasn't. The answer seemed to be a return to school, to finish what he'd started before he'd learned to sing, to the tune of "The Mickey Mouse Club" theme, M-a-k-i-n-g M-o-n-e-y. Like a wrongly convicted innocent man languishing behind bars, he didn't think he could tolerate any more justice. Maybe he'd been naive to expect the legal system to work any other way when it was concerned with two corrupting influences—money and men—but he didn't want to live the rest of his life as a cynic.

Visions of an air-conditioned house pulled him home, and he walked through the garage, expecting to see a blond-haired child crawling across the living room floor, reaching for him with one hand, but the house was strangely silent at 5:30 in the afternoon. Cool, but silent. All he heard was the fan on the air-conditioning unit in the hall closet. A search revealed both the house and the backyard were empty, and half the toys in Scott's bedroom were gone.

On the kitchen table he found a note, written on the back of a grocery list. "Chris," it said. "It's been pretty obvious to me that you don't have any real interest in being part of this family. I'm not going to live with someone who treats me like I'm an obstacle to his happiness. So I'm leaving. I'm going to Abilene and make plans. Lori."

He sat, the note in his hand, feeling instantly nauseous, afraid he'd throw up. His life had come apart and he hadn't even known it was happening. He had walked in the back door expecting to see Scott coming to greet him, and Scott didn't even live here anymore. How could this have happened? How could any of it have happened? How could he have gone from falling flat on his face in love with Lori Lynn Conner, senior elementary education major from Abilene, to making her think he saw her as a barricade, a detour sign on the highway to happiness?

Jesus Christ, he thought, help me throw up. The enlarging knot of fear and misery and disgust in the pit of his stomach was theaten-ing to rise up and choke him. He was having difficulty in breathing.

He read the note over several times trying to determine Lori's state of mind, her unwillingness to talk to him. She hadn't said she hated him, hadn't said she wouldn't forgive him his many and varied trespasses, hadn't said she'd irrevocably written him out of her life. But reality kept screaming in his ear—"She's gone! She's gone!" And there was no "Dear Chris" at the top of the note, no "Love, Lori" at the bottom.

No love at the bottom.

Hell, there'd never been any love at the bottom. He'd verified that fact over and over, most emphatically one morning in the mud on the Amphibious Base at Little Creek when he'd awakened himself by pissing in his pants, creating a warm contrast to the cold mud he was lying in, having wandered off course on his way back to the barracks and ended up, drunk and unconscious, in an empty field near the chow hall.

"Son of a bitch!" he yelled to the empty house.

Why did he insist on being stupid? Why did he constantly put himself into positions where he didn't want to be? Why was he sleepwalking through life, periodically waking up to check on his aimless wanderings? He didn't want to be stupid; he swore he didn't want to be stupid. But even if he was, he still wasn't to the blithering idiot stage yet, and he still had a chance to show himself, not to mention Lori, that he possessed and could use a brain.

He looked at his watch. The four-hour drive to Abilene would put him there by ten if he left now. He didn't even pack a bag; he merely grabbed clothes and swept items at random from the bathroom counter and medicine cabinet into a paper sack. And he didn't take the time to put up the MG, forsaking it for a family car, hoping in fact some thief who'd never breathed the exhaust vapor of a Buick would steal the little sports car.

Tired but certain, he drove faster than he should have. He was going to take a big chance; he was going to tell Lori his problems.

My God, he thought. What if she listened and understood? A Lori who wouldn't judge him too harshly would be a truly wondrous woman, more so than the one he'd married. Lori as friend as well as wife. Could he handle such a development?

When darkness fell, he saw proof he was headed in the right direction. Driving through the hills, he followed the center stripe, a glowing snake of orange reflectors rising magically into the air and twisting around curves, leading him onward, guiding him.

At the Conners', he saw lights in the front windows of the garage apartment, and Lori's car was parked near the foot of the outside stairs. She'd chosen to stay in the apartment rather than the house? What did that choice mean? That she was growing up? That he could talk to her and she wouldn't act on the urge to alert the intake unit at the state hospital that she had a good prospect for them?

He climbed the wooden stairs to the second-floor door, now nervous and uncertain, and found her waiting on him, standing just inside the door into the kitchen, dressed in an old green robe she wore when comfort was foremost in her mind.

"Hi," she said.

He started to say something humorous but he couldn't tell from the look on her face exactly what her attitude was. Noncommittal. She was a housewife waiting to see if he was a salesman.

He returned her greeting but didn't kiss her, even though he wanted to, and he entered the kitchen feeling as much, maybe more, a stranger than he had when he'd been making the weekend trips before they'd married. And now that he was here, he didn't know what to do or say. Finally he asked, "Where's Scott?"

"On the floor in the bedroom," she said, turning to face him but giving no clue for him to act on. "I folded a quilt and put him on the floor. I was afraid he'd roll off the bed."

"That was a good idea," he said, feeling comforted and warm over this exchange of parental sentiments. Maybe he could just burrow into that warmth and stay there, forget about talking to her.

"You want some coffee?" she asked.

He said he did and sat at the end of the kitchen table, facing the living room, the only source of light at the moment. The kitchen was half dark. She set a cup of coffee before him and then took a seat at the opposite end. Backlighted, she looked like one of those people on the evening news who would appear on camera only if they were unidentified and unidentifiable. She was a black featureless figure.

"Let's change places," he said, wanting the anonymity of the kitchen confessional.

Once they'd swapped chairs, Chris felt better. He could see her but she couldn't see him. He was nothing but a backlighted ghost drinking coffee. "Lori, I was sure all the way up here I knew what I was going to say, and now I don't know if I can. I love you, I really do, but if I tell you the truth, you'll probably end up hating me and you'll just start living here by yourself. Or maybe you won't hate me. You'll decide the hell with it, I'm better off without him."

He paused, giving her time to confirm this theory if she wanted to. He wanted to know what her attitude was at the moment, whether she loved or hated him, wanted really for her to advise him that talking wasn't at all necessary and that they could just make love if he was in the mood.

But she said, "We've got to talk; we don't have any choice."

He took a deep breath, then exhaled. "I keep having this feeling that everything's closing in on me and I can't figure out why. Or maybe I do know why. I wanted to go to Europe for a year and just look around, and I know I never will. I'm not ever going to do anything but work and get old. I'm going to get up and go to work and come home and go to bed. And then the next day I'm going to do it all over again. I'm going to do it all over again until I'm dead and that's the end of that. I don't know how to handle it. I mean, saying it sounds trivial, but it damn sure hasn't felt trivial.

"And besides that, I keep *accumulating* things. I have an MG, and I really don't even want it. I love you and I love Scott and I even like our house, but I keep getting things. End tables, couches, new bedrooms, refrigerators, dogs. I've got all this *stuff*. I don't know what I'd do with it if somebody came up and said, 'Hey, Chris, you want to go to Europe for a year? You can go but you're leaving in an hour.' What would I do? I never wanted anything you couldn't fit in the trunk of a car.

"Oh, hell, Lori, you and I both know I'm not ever going to Europe for a year, and I don't know why the feeling that I *might* is so important, but it is."

Lori had been staring into her coffee cup and without looking up she asked, "What would happen if you did go? I mean tomorrow, if you just set sail and went."

"I probably wouldn't enjoy it because I'd know I had to come back to that job. I hate that fucking job."

"That's what mother said."

"Your mother said that?"

Lori nodded, now looking up. Could she see him? Could she see the face of this lousy crack dealer who'd ruined the lives of kids but was now appearing on television to confess and make everything all right? Why didn't people just do what they were supposed to? Then they wouldn't have to confess while their features were blacked out.

"I think she remembers more of what you say than I do. She must be taking notes or something. I can't believe how much she remembers."

He was partly impressed that Mrs. Conner was interested enough to have listened, but he was also distressed. He wondered what she'd remembered, what her composite looked like. If she'd pieced him together over the years, it probably resembled a Picasso, some guy with one eye and three legs. Or one enormous overly active sexual organ.

"Has that been part of your problem?" Lori asked. "Your job."

"Yeah, it's driving me crazy. How would you like to go to work in a casino, where people were throwing all kinds of money around and behaving in ridiculous ways, lying, cheating, stealing?

285

You'd hate it. And that's the way I see the job. Hell, if this is justice, Tammy Faye Bakker is the Virgin Mary. I just can't do it anymore."

"What're you going to do?"

He frowned over the tone of her voice, the way in which she asked the question. She sounded as if her decision—whether to remain married to him or not—would be based on his answer. "That sounds like a test question. Answer it correctly or fail the course."

It was a moment before she answered. "Well, in a way it is. I don't mean about the job. You don't have to tell me you're going to find one of two acceptable jobs or anything like that. What I mean is, I've been thinking that weddings don't involve any real commitment because most of the time the people involved don't even know each other and don't know what marriage is like. The commitment has to come later, somewhere down the line, when they figure out what they've gotten into. Then they decide whether they're getting divorced or whether they're staying married. I mean, by then, the husband's figured out the wife's got bad breath and doesn't shave under her arms every day in the winter. And she doesn't always change the sheets as often as she ought to and sometimes she says she's sent her father-in-law a birthday card when she didn't. And the wife has seen her husband trying to look up some young girl's dress and knows he dreams about women prettier than she is. And he passes gas as a joke and takes his secretary to lunch at The Magic Time Machine. And his wife gets a Big Mac on her anniversary. That's when they ought to be deciding whether they're getting married, not when they don't know each other."

"You really have been thinking about this, haven't you?"

"Yes, I have."

Marriage, according to Lori, sounded like a pretty crass proposal, flatulent husbands and hairy wives and dirty sheets and unhappy in-laws. But as if to disprove what she'd just said, she stood and asked without words, without any concrete gesture, if he wanted more coffee. He shook his head, touched that they could communicate in that way. They had scratched through so many layers of superficial emotion, got beyond so much preliminary sparring, that he couldn't imagine calling it quits. She was right about one thing —a wedding vow implied no real commitment. People couldn't commit to something they didn't understand. That's why people as irresponsible as felons weren't allowed to vote and idiots couldn't enter into contracts.

And she may have aptly described many marriages, but theirs had also occasionally moved onto a plane far above the one where Ronald McDonald resided and Listerine was gargled. What better way was there to live than to make your family along with someone who had grabbed your heart and imagination and wouldn't let go? He had lived with a randomly collected group of people in the navy, and he hadn't liked it a bit. If Lori wanted to talk about hair and gas, he could give her some prime examples. No, he simply couldn't think of a better arrangement than to live and love with someone who could take him out of himself and lift him to a realm where he could look down on the physical world in wonder.

"We have to decide what we're going to do," she said.

Well, he thought, this may do it for sure. He'd open the gate for her and if she wanted to walk out, he'd understand why. "Here's what I want to do—go back to school. I feel like I wasted two years in the business school learning the art of making money. I don't care how money's made. I just don't care. Not that I'm a hippie. Personally, I like money and I'll take all I can get. But I feel like I got misdirected after two years of school, and I want to go back. And I can't answer your question right now on what I'm going to do. Coach, maybe. You know how much influence Coach Mallory's had in the town of Ashworth? I don't mean in winning football games, I mean in making kids understand what it is you have to do to succeed. So maybe I want to coach. I just don't know. I feel like I was on the right track and then I shot myself in the foot and limped off in the wrong direction."

Lori sat back in her chair as though to relax, working her head in a circle, then stretching her shoulders. "Well, I was hoping you'd say you wanted to go to work for Daddy. Or something easy. That just shows you how stupid I am."

"That's not stupid. I probably should go to work for your father."

She got up and walked to the sink, slowly as though one of her feet was asleep, and poured out her coffee. "This is driving me crazy. I can't even see your face. Can we go into the living room?"

They moved into the living room, taking opposite ends of the couch, a rather hideous piece of furniture with huge blue flowers on it. Lori lifted her feet up and placed them in his lap, the first sign of the visit that she was willing to engage in some form of intimacy. He rubbed the sole of her left foot; the heel of her right rested in his lap and made suggestive movements.

"Maybe you need to go to one of those vocational counselors," she said.

"I think if I get my life back on a track I understand, I'll get it all figured out."

"Then why don't we get married again, this time without Carl, and we can have new vows. I'll promise to help you find out what it is you want to do, and you promise to not exclude me. You have to tell me what's going on with you. I don't think you wanting to go to Europe is so strange. I don't think it's so different from what I've been feeling."

Her foot had achieved its purpose, and he pulled her by the leg across the couch. She came, scooting, her green robe hiked up over baby blue panties. He looked at her and had a thought that couldn't have been as profound as it seemed. She loves me. She really does love me. Here was a woman with a cereal-box face and short blonde hair, one so cute she made him catch his breath. And she thought he was worth her time and effort, worth living with the rest of her life.

She climbed onto her knees and then sat facing him, straddling his legs. "I haven't been very attentive, have I? I mean, to your needs. I promise I'll do better."

Her generosity moved him, and he suddenly wanted to withdraw his plan to return to school, take her home, and shape up. He'd be the kind of husband she deserved, just because she was being tolerant and kind and he owed her proper behavior and care. But within a week he'd be miserable, wanting out of the Crap Shoot.

She leaned forward to kiss him, rather shyly at first, but then she seemed to change her mind and give him a kiss he'd remember. With all the passion and pressure she could muster, she kissed him, rising up and pressing him into the back of the couch. There was, he thought, a certain amount of relief and release in her kiss. He ran his hands beneath her robe and verified what he thought, that she was wearing nothing but panties. Mashed against her, he couldn't fully massage her breasts as he wanted; he could only feel the bases where they bulged outward from the pressure of chest against chest.

"Take your robe off," he said when she broke the kiss.

She sat back, resting on his legs, and unbuttoned the robe. She looked much more like a woman than she had the first time he'd seen her. This nursing mother of their child, her abdomen marred by stretch marks, would never be a centerfold, but she was so much more desirable. A nonsexual and somewhat crude analogy came to mind, making him smile: she was like old Levi's, the fit and feel and cut of which were exactly right.

"What're you smiling about?" she asked.

"You. I love you."

The phone rang. It was an ancient wall phone in the kitchen, and it had a nerve-jangling ring.

"Don't answer it," he said.

"I've got to or it'll wake Scott up."

She ran to the kitchen and he followed, fearful she'd come to her senses and renege on her new wedding vow once she'd had some contact with the outside world if he wasn't there to remind her of his existence. He stood behind her as she answered the phone, which made every caller sound as though he had a mouthful of metal teeth.

"Mrs. Lori Gray?" a man's voice asked, loud enough for Chris to hear.

"Yes," she said, her tone impatient, restrained only by politeness.

"This is Dwight Truax with Southwestern Bell Telephone. I just want to let you know we're about to clean out the phone lines, so you might want to put your receiver in a trash can. Then that way if we use too much compressed air, it won't blow dirt all over your curtains and everything."

"You're what?" she asked.

"Give me that damn phone." He removed the receiver from her hand. "What do you want and how'd you get this number?"

"My, my," Carl said. "You must be under some kind of stress, as irritable as you sound. Of course, it couldn't be work-related because you haven't been working."

"What do you want?" he asked, carefully enunciating each word.

"I went by your house earlier to see if you wanted to go get a drink and nobody was home. So I got to chatting with one of your neighbors, a real pleasant elderly gentleman by the name of Chapman, lives just to the south of you. He was watering his flowers. Very pretty flowers, I might add, those kind with the—"

"Tell me what you want or I'm hanging up," Chris said, looking at his wife, who had taken a seat at the end of the kitchen table and was working on a cuticle with her thumbnail. The last thing in the world he wanted to do was talk to his brother, but since their father's heart attack, he expected bad news every time the phone rang.

Lori grabbed his belt loop and winched him to the chair, pulling him onto her knees.

"Mr. Chapman said he thought Lori had left on a trip this morning, so I called your mother-in-law just to inquire as to whether you might be at her house. Strictly speaking, she said, you weren't at her house—"

"Hey, dumb ass," Chris yelled into the phone. "What is it you want?"

"Nothing, really. I just put two and two together, figured Lori left you, you'd gone after her, and I was hoping to interrupt any attempt at reconciliation, especially any sexual making up you were involved in. Did I?"

Chris hung up without further words and then located a dish towel. He wrapped it around the receiver on the phone, then hooked the receiver on the back of a chair, muffled now so they wouldn't have to listen to the drone of a dial phone or some recorded message advising them they left a phone off the hook.

Lori stood, offering open arms to her husband, and said, "He ought to be shot."

"I may do it myself."

They met beside the table, bare chest against bare chest. There was something to the joys of making up, Chris thought. The feeling of loss, the sensation of nausea he'd experienced upon reading Lori's good-bye note, the threat of spiraling into a void of inane behavior —all those emotions, and salvation from them, made the physical contact that much more satisfying, that much more erotic. He wanted to swallow her as they kissed. In fact, he was so stimulated that she could have climbed onto his erection as though it were a pole on a swing set, and her feet wouldn't have touched the ground.

Somewhere in the back of his mind he heard a door slam, the door of a house, and it sounded close, as though it had come from the Conners'. But he was too engrossed with the sexual transaction at hand and the excitement of Lori. Hers fed his. With one hand she had grasped the back of his neck, and she was giving him the most thorough kissing he'd experienced in some time; her other hand had unbuttoned his Levi's and disappeared down the front of his pants.

Footsteps on the stairs outside.

He drew away from Lori and asked, "Who's that?"

"Nobody." She kissed him again.

But it was. A knock on the door. An insistent knock on the door that rattled the glass in the window. Then Mrs. Conner's voice. "Lori? Lori?"

Lori broke the kiss but before going to the door gave him a squeeze. "I can feel how hard he is and that's how hard I want him."

She got her robe from the living room and, holding it in front of her, walked to the door in the kitchen.

"Lori? Carl just called and said he was talking to Chris. And you're locked inside? Is that right? You're locked *in*?"

"Mother, Carl Gray is a lying fraud," she said through the door without opening it. "If you ever believe *anything* he says, there's something wrong with you."

"Well," Mrs. Conner said in an uncertain voice. "I wondered. He wanted me to come let you out and I couldn't figure out how you could be locked *in*."

Chris sat down at the kitchen table, thinking they may as well be trying to make out in an airport. The only things they were lacking were a public address system and Hare Krishna weirdos. Lori turned from the door to give Chris a look of disgust, then started shaking her head and laughing as though she'd experienced the vision that would push her over the border into hysteria. When he gave her a questioning glance, she pointed at the living room doorway.

Chris turned to see Scott, clad only in a diaper, crawling toward the door. He couldn't help but smile, as happy to see his son as he had been to see his wife, and he stood to meet the blond-haired kid coming on all fours. But Scott stopped and uttered a command, a definite grunt that reminded Chris of a dog's owner telling the pet to "stay." Scott got his feet under him and, in the doorway, stood up, holding his hands above him to give him balance. Uncertainly he wavered but he remained upright, his face radiating his concentration.

"Oh, my God," Lori said, her hands at her face. "He's standing all by himself. Look, he's not holding on or anything."

"No, that's not what he's doing," Chris said, mimicking his son's pose, holding both arms up, stretched toward the ceiling.

"Then what's he doing?"

"He's signaling. Can't you see it? He's saying, 'Touchdown!'"